THE
LAST
EXILES

THE
LAST
EXILES

ANN SHIN

PARK
ROW
BOOKS

PARK
ROW
BOOKS™

Recycling programs
for this product may
not exist in your area.

ISBN-13: 978-0-7783-8941-5
ISBN-13: 978-0-7783-1140-9 (International Trade Paperback Edition)

The Last Exiles

This edition published by arrangement with Harlequin Books S.A.

Park Row Books
22 Adelaide St. West, 40th Floor
Toronto, Ontario M5H 4E3, Canada
ParkRowBooks.com
BookClubbish.com

Printed in U.S.A.

For my family

THE
LAST
EXILES

PROLOGUE

A sheaf of photos slipped from a folder, fluttering over the stairs of the Rodong newspaper headquarters. Suja whirled around, her feet tap-tapping as she chased the scattering black-and-white glossies. She scooped up the photos and stuffed them back into the folder, her fingers trembling, adrenaline coursing through her body, for it was late and she was going to miss tonight's print run. She turned to run toward the lobby, the wan winter sun winking out as it slipped behind the building. She pushed through the doors, slowing her steps just enough to tap her name badge as she passed the security officer. It was the fellow with the pockmarked face sitting by the X-ray booth with his arms crossed, hat pulled low over his eyes. He grunted and let her pass; they both knew the X-ray didn't work.

Reshuffling the photos in their folder, Suja pushed through the door to the newsroom and came up short, catching her breath. The chief editor, Mr. Moon, was up at the flats, red-faced and spluttering, yelling at the editors who stood around him, desultory, penitent; cigarette smoke coiled over their heads in a cloud of discontent. The junior researchers and writers—anonymous underlings—were hunched at their desks focused on their computer screens, all busy looking busy. Suja's father had his back against the flats, a waxed column of text stuck to his finger as he nervously eyed the clock that hung between the portraits of the Dear Leader and the Heavenly Leader. There was a blank space on the front-page flats where the text had been lifted out. Someone must have made a significant mistake for that article to have been pulled last minute. The news editor, Mr. Lim, and photo editor, Mr. Roh, argued with Mr. Moon, who shouted over them, saying that the story, whatever it was, needed to go on the front page.

Suja sidled over to Mr. Roh's desk and dropped her folder of photos. She glanced at her father, who raised his brows and mouthed, 'What are you doing here?'

She pointed to her folder of photos and crossed her arms, glancing pointedly at the unfinished flats. A series of emotions played across her father's face as he regarded his child who had fought him to take on this position as the newspaper's only intern during the school year. There was such a thing as being too clever.

Leaving the editors to squabble among themselves, Mr. Kim walked over to Roh's desk and stuck the waxed column on the surface of the desk and dropped into Roh's chair.

'What happened?' Suja asked.

'Late-breaking story.'

'What's the story?' Suja asked, a lock of her hair falling into her eyes. She tucked it behind her ear absentmindedly. Apba was a tactical thinker and hated last-minute changes to layout. She had been coming to his office since she was four years old and had spent many an afternoon hanging about the flats as he waxed the backs of photos and text blocks, positioned them on the flats and pressed them down, just so. He wanted the word lengths for all articles ahead of time so he could assemble text blocks in his mind before he even started dealing with type. He taught Suja to think of photographs as moments on a page. The photo was only part of the greater whole of the newspaper, just as every journalist was an anonymous segment of the greater body of the Korean Central News Agency. So Suja's earliest understanding of photography was related to the negative space that photographs were meant to occupy—they were a small part of a greater message, filling in a gap of meaning in a story already constructed.

'Huh,' her father sighed. 'The Cornmeal Culprit escaped from prison, that boy, Jin Lee Park.'

Suja felt the blood drain from her head, and she leaned against the desk to steady herself. 'What?' she whispered.

'The bastard *escaped* from Yodok prison camp. How the hell he did that...' Apba shook his head. 'After the shame he brought to his family, that *saekee* runs from prison, saving his own skin, sending his family to damnation.' Yodok prison camp was one of the most secure facilities in the northernmost region of Hamgyong, an arid province known for its anthracite mines, and where the worst of the criminals and political outcasts were sent. No one ever came back from Yodok.

'He escaped...' she repeated softly, her face pale, eyes dialed to someplace far away.

'Did you know him?' her father asked.

She snapped to attention. 'No.'

His gaze sharpened and he watched her closely. 'He was from your university.'

'I don't know *everyone* at the university, Apba,' she retorted, pulling herself together.

Mr. Kim pressed his fingers into the text column lying

on the desk, making an impression in the wax. 'How did the saekee even get into your school, a bastard like him? A real *gangpae* criminal gets a scholarship to Kim Il-Sung U?! Bullshit. You know they're doing a purification of the entire student roster.'

'Good,' Suja managed to say in a thin voice, the blood thumping at her temples as she focused on one thing only: Jin Lee Park had escaped, he was free. Tears pricked her eyes and she blinked them back quickly as she tried to calm herself. Taking a deep breath, she started counting silently: one Heavenly Leader, two Heavenly Leader, three Heavenly Leader, four…

ONE

Jin Lee Park stood in the lobby of the Kim Il-Sung University lecture halls in a zip-up farmer's coat and state-issued boots that were so old the toes were worn through. Other students sauntered past in brand-new jackets, freshly ironed pants, sporting the latest haircut—a brush cut with the hair swept to one side. Next to them, Jin was a country *chonnom* with a bright gaze and clean-faced farm look that tagged him as fresh meat for the city boys. *Country rat-eater*, they called him. *Dung-eater, gaesakee*, they guffawed as they bumped into him in the halls, knocking his shoulder or landing an elbow in his ribs. But even in those ridiculous boots, Jin walked with a fluid and confident gait that spoke of athleticism and strength, and he could dish out as good as he got. He slung curses back at them, calling them *Idiot baptong, son of a mother's brother, son of a mother's goat.* They were strange country curses Suja hadn't heard before, and their banter in the hallway had everyone laughing along with Jin. He was good at getting people on his side, especially as they began to realize he was one of the smartest in the class. When a class was stumped, the professors inevitably turned to him for the answer. It wasn't simply that he had memorized the texts; he came up with surprising ways to see things and had razor-sharp acuity. He was *premium rice*, as they say.

But Jin was intimidated by Suja and the other Pyongyang students. While he joked with them during class, he'd duck away later, feeling like an impostor blundering through their revered university halls. He headed out alone into the city streets and found himself gaping and spluttering at the splendor around him. Oh, Pyongyang, with its wide gray avenues and traffic conductors, whose white gloves flagged lonely cars that nosed along empty streets like private jets on empty runways; Pyongyang, where women in skirt suits all wore the same shade of crimson on their lips and the sidewalks bristled with marching pedestrians, whose stern faces and square haircuts blended into one another—these city hustlers, these citizens of the real world. Even the students who walked the halls of Kim Il-Sung University were of a different breed, with their worldliness, their foreign clothes, owning things that Jin never dreamed of having, such as knapsacks with the Kim Il-Sung crest, watches from Poland, jackets from Russia. Jin's embarrassment ran so deep it wasn't emotional, it was existential.

In his hometown of Kanggye, people had all the time in the world to sit on their unemployed haunches and gibe one another, for there was no more industry there. It had suffered under the blight of famine since the Dear Leader announced the Arduous March in 1994, when state food rations and electricity were cut. His father followed the directive to *Suffer for the Greater Good, Eat One Meal Instead of Three* and began policing his family like a commissariat officer. While other men started side hustles to earn money by foraging, trading and smuggling items from China, his father refused to stoop to 'shady work,' choosing instead to continue as a superintendent at the tooling factory even when all pay was cut, even when the power was cut.

While his father ground himself down with penurious aims, Jin rebelled against that closefisted impulse and spun the energy outward, attacking everything with a fierce ambition. Most North Koreans believed one's future was writ by family pedigree, which determined the door to your destiny, but Jin was determined to rise above his family's lot. In his mind the Dear Leader was the true father figure to aspire to, and he worked to prove himself worthy, pushing stubs of pencil lead into newsprint as he studied into the wee hours every morning.

When he won a scholarship to attend Kim Il-Sung University, Jin knew he had finally broken free. His fate was no longer tied to his father and the life of a stingy superintendent. The future didn't have to be parsed out in rationed cupfuls, for Jin had surpassed his father's social rank and would be able to extend the rewards of his new life to his whole family. Having broken through the sealed doors of Pyongyang, he had secured a seat for all of them at the grand table, and he was determined to make the most of it.

Suja was the prettiest, highest-born girl Jin had ever met. She was quick-tongued and carefree, even careless as a high-born girl could be. With a pointed chin, delicate lips and a short bob that showed off her slender neck, she cut an unorthodox silhouette compared to the rest of the long-haired girls. When she and her friends sashayed arm in arm down the hall, all heads turned in their wake. Jin didn't know whether to be more impressed that she was the top-ranking student or that she was a female photographer. He had never heard of women photojournalists, for all the cameramen and newspaper staff he had ever met were men—that's why they were called newspapermen. Suja's iconoclasm and her ingenuity terrified him and enamored her to him. There would be nothing straightforward about getting to know this girl.

She started to bait and tease Jin in class, joining in on the jokes, called him everything from baptong to country bumpkin, shit-shoveler. Arms crossed and shoulders squared, Jin took it up in sport and joked back, calling her Miss Twenty-First Century Busybody, Miss Britches (as in 'too big'), and he upped the ante every day as he invented new names for her—Mrs. Chairman of the Know-It-All Department, subcommittee of the southern campus; *Mr.* Esteemed Cameraman, he once teased when she showed up with her camera. Everyone laughed, and Suja's face flushed red as she sat at her desk. She tossed over her shoulder haughtily, 'Go back to your sheep, country boy. City girls aren't for you.'

Jin shrugged. 'I could teach you a thing or two about nature.' Several guys chuckled.

'All that time with the farm animals, I bet you learned a lot,' she retorted.

'Like I said, I could teach you.'

The class broke into peals of laughter. Suja glared at her friends but didn't deign to turn around and give Jin the satisfaction. But the banter between them had begun.

When Suja joined the debate club, Jin joined it too, if only to be on the opposite team. They started walking to classes together with their books in hand, never touching, but also never far from each other either. They both joined the film club and started sitting together in the cafeteria, and as the year progressed, the phrase *Suja and Jin* was born, with Suja's name coming first of course. Jin knew that despite Suja liking him, and his academic success notwithstanding, he was still technically a nobody. He was a lowborn country hick whose family had no value or standing, and it was implausible that a girl like Suja would spend any time with him.

Suja was keenly aware of this too and intuited that her privilege could upset their delicate courtship. She downplayed her family connections, even trying to minimize her accomplishments. When she was offered a second-year internship at the Rodong newspaper, she didn't tell Jin for two weeks, worried that it would be seen as yet another sign of her privilege and her family connections in Pyongyang society. She finally mentioned it to him one day as they left class together.

They headed to the library as the late-afternoon sun slanted in through the hall, the way that winter afternoons take on the melancholy of evening. As they approached the library doors, Suja brought it up.

'You know that photography internship I do at the newspaper?' she said.

'Yeah.'

'I might continue doing it into next year.'

'I thought the internship was just for a year?'

'They said I could—' she paused '—that they could extend it.'

'Really?' Jin exclaimed.

'Yes,' Suja said in a small voice, worried that he might be upset or disappointed. Her own father had been furious about the offer and had threatened to throw out her camera. Apba wanted her to focus on her coursework rather than continue to 'gallivant' around town to shoot photos at all hours. She wondered how Jin would feel about it.

'They're extending your internship for a year? That's an honor, isn't it?' Jin stopped in his tracks. 'No one ever gets a two-year internship.'

Suja gave a small shrug, her eyes trained on her feet.

'Congratulations!' Jin whooped. 'They're keeping you on for a second year! Why are you looking so down? You should be so happy!'

'You're happy about it?'

'Of course. It's a privilege. I'm proud of you!'

'But…' She hesitated, suddenly feeling shy about what she was going to say. 'Some say I shouldn't work as a journalist, that it's not "becoming."'

'*Becoming?!* Says who? Rodong would lose a star if they didn't have you.'

'It's not the newspaper,' she said softly.

Jin searched her face. 'Your parents,' he said finally, imagining how upper-class parents might react to the idea of their daughter working as a photographer.

She nodded. 'They don't want me running around town taking photographs. They want me to be a teacher. You know, something "respectable."'

'Hmm,' said Jin as they continued down the hall, walking close to each other but not daring to hold hands in case they might be seen. 'Give it some time,' he said calmly, 'and we'll convince them.' They fell into step with each other, and Suja could feel the rhythm of their bodies naturally align, like the hands of a swimmer cutting into the velvety water of a lake. She looked at Jin and felt a sense of calm come over her. With him at her side she felt everything would go smoothly. Everything would turn out fine.

Suja started bringing Jin to the darkroom, where under the cloak of invisibility they felt the world and all its machinations fall away—the scrutiny of teachers, peers, friends and even family were parked outside the door. They stood in the fusty red gloom, acutely aware of the glow of their skin and the warmth of each other's breath as they spent hours together dipping photos in the developing baths, counting the seconds to each other, a task that was monotonous yet also comforting in its simplicity.

One time Jin dipped his finger in the stop solution and painted something on one of her undeveloped prints. He slipped the paper back into the developing vat and watched as Suja plucked the wet print out of the vat and shook it, spattering drops of developing solution on the counter. She stopped suddenly and peered closely at the print, her eyes widening.

'Opba, you wrote this?!'

Jin chortled.

'You know it's an offense to alter a photo?' she cried. 'You're tampering with property of the Rodong national newspaper and it's a criminal offense!'

The color drained from Jin's face. Shit, what had he done? 'I didn't mean… I…I'm so sorry,' he stammered. Goddammit! He reached over for the print but Suja held it away from him.

She tried to keep a stern face, but her scowl melted into a cascade of giggles. 'I'm not going to report you, Opba.' She pushed him playfully.

'Give it to me,' he said. 'We have to rip it up.'

'No.' She held the print aloft. 'It's mine. I'm keeping it.'

'But it's an offense! I didn't know, I didn't know!'

She rolled her eyes. 'It's okay. Really. No one's ever going to know.'

'But I should confess it,' he insisted.

'Oh, Opba, you're such a ninny. It's okay, I was just kidding.' She cocked an eyebrow, looking at him mischievously before finally saying, 'Maybe.'

Jin let out a slow nervous whistle and placed his hands on her shoulders. He had half a mind to shake her but instead let his arms fall around her in an embrace. She was a difficult one, this Suja, and he wasn't 100 percent sure whether she was joking or not, but he wasn't worried anymore. Something about her irreverent ways undid a latch in his chest. He could breathe much more easily around her, which was strange, for he didn't realize he had felt constrained before. He felt whole and safe in a way that allowed him to relax and inhabit his skin more freely—inhabit all the skins of his identity: the country bumpkin, the small-town runaway, the maker of his own destiny, the brilliant student, the hesitant boyfriend. It was the first time he felt at ease with himself and the world. He was terrified he would screw it up.

Suja in turn realized she had met someone who matched her in all ways in terms of intellect, temperament and ambition. It was like finally stretching to stand at full height for the first time, and she reveled in the fullness of it. With Jin, she felt she could be herself unequivocally, and like him, she was driven to do more, to do better in all pursuits, including their relationship. She continually looked for ways to surprise him and for one date she decided to test his trust. She asked him to meet her at the train station.

'Okay, and do what? Are we going someplace?' Jin asked, wondering whether he needed to bring his ID.

'You'll see,' she said cryptically.

Jin arrived ten minutes early and waited for her near the platforms, which were seething with gusts of dust, the smell of mechanical grease and the sweet smoke of burnt sugar *duk*. He stood in the lobby, looking for her as people pushed off the trains, jostling past hawkers who stood in the center of the platforms with their steaming hotcakes, yelling, *Duk, sweet, hot duk!* Jin waited for thirty minutes, scanning the bobbing heads hoping to spot her among the crowd, and was about to leave when he felt someone reach around him and drop a blindfold around his head, binding it tight. His hands shot up and tugged at the blindfold, but it was already cinched tight. He struggled against the assailant.

'Relax, Opba, it's me,' she said.

'Suja?' he exclaimed.

'Yes. We're going to go for a walk.' She placed her hand on his back, warm and reassuring. 'For the next hour or so, I'll be your eyes. Trust me.' She slipped her hand into his and took off like a shot, pulling him through the crowds.

'Wait a second!' he said, but she pressed forward, tugging him as she swerved and bumped past people. They got to the entrance, where she guided him through turnstiles and then out onto the street. Jin held on to Suja's hand, enjoying her unruly energy and the feeling of being blindly guided by her. He started playing with her, tugging her hand back this way and that, trying to pull her off course.

'Stop that,' she laughed, and pushed forward along the sidewalk.

They walked for another twenty minutes or so until she pushed open a heavy metal door and led him inside a building. She guided him to a staircase and proceeded to ascend. He followed her, listening to the sound of their footsteps echoing up the stairwell. Jin surmised that they were in an apartment building, and he wondered whether she might be bringing him to her home. He was thrilled and terrified at the thought she might be introducing him to her family. He thought no, it couldn't be. It was unthinkable for him to be meeting her family at this point, as he knew he could never bring Suja to his own impoverished hometown; she'd probably never been in a city north of Pyongsong, let alone a backwoods town near the Chinese border. So where could they be, then? His heart was pounding as she pulled him up the stairs, but as they mounted the stairwell and he relaxed into the steady rhythm of their steps, a quiet feeling of trust bloomed between them.

Finally Suja opened a door and guided him through, and they stepped out into the open air. Jin felt the wind against his body and could hear the distant sound of traffic below. He took stock of the situation and surmised they were on a rooftop somewhere. That's when Suja let go of his hand.

Jin froze, his hands dangling at his sides. 'What do I do now?'

'Walk forward until I say stop.'

'Really?'

'Really.'

He hesitated, all his senses alive to the feel of the breeze and the sounds from below that were carried up by the wind: the faint voices and footsteps of pedestrians on the street, a truck accelerating along a road, twittering sparrows. Jin took a deep breath and advanced a couple of tentative steps, then stopped.

'Keep going,' she said.

Jin took a few more steps, growing more confident with each step as he continued until Suja yelled, 'Stop!'

She ran up to him and stood at his side. 'You ready?' she said breathlessly.

'Yes.'

She untied the bandanna.

Jin was standing a hundred yards above street level, looking down at Pyongyang's main promenade. To his right were the immense presidential buildings and the stately Kumsusan Avenue, which was the route for all the national parades. To his left he could see the statue of Chollima, the flying horse with wings arched into the sky, its nose pointing toward the heavens. Chollima was the famous messenger horse that flew to military outposts during the Manchurian War, helping Chosun fight off attacking forces and to eventually rise victorious. The flying horse was the symbol of the nation's fighting spirit and of its fast economic development, and here he was standing at eye level with it. All the famous landmarks of Pyongyang were laid out in front of him.

'*Omona.*' He exhaled, his heart skipping a beat.

'It's gorgeous, isn't it?' Suja said softly.

'I had no idea.'

Suja beamed, her eyes shining as she looked out onto Kumsusan Avenue.

'This is it, Jin Lee Park. This is our future.'

He took a deep breath as he surveyed the view and then looked at her. For the first time in his life he felt he understood what the word *magnanimity* must mean. He reached for her hand and looked out at the skyline with her. With Suja, he could finally feel how relaxed, how full, how bounteous life could be. His life in Pyongyang was taking root, and he was molting like a dragonfly from its chrysalis.

'You know, Suja, this is how you make me feel.' He held his arms out in front of him, as if to embrace the landscape. 'You've opened my horizons, I mean, not just by bringing me up here,' he laughed, 'but in other ways too. You've opened something inside me…'

She waited for him to continue, almost throwing in a joke, but something in his eyes made her bite her tongue and wait.

'I don't know.' He finally shook his head and pulled her into a hug. But he did know exactly what he was feeling.

TWO

Along the foothills that surrounded Pyongyang, the trees were yellowing, dropping leaves that littered the sidewalks and skittered along the streets. It was term break again, and for Suja, whose family lived in Pyongyang, it was time for the student work term. She and hundreds of other students were to be bused to the country along with the other Pyongyang students in order to sling bushels of rice alongside the farmers. But with the floods, the fields were blighted with disease, and many of the rice plants rotted in the fields. Work crews who were carted in the backs of trucks to the farms had nothing to do, so they stood with their hands in their pockets, kicking at the earth.

Most of the students, including Suja, were staying in the city this work term. She planned to audit lectures with her friends, while Jin prepared to leave to visit his family in Kanggye. Jin didn't tell Suja how his family was hit by the crop failures and could barely put together one meal a day.

Nor had he told her about the student rations he had set aside to take back to his family. It was more than a year since Jin's family had received state-rationed food, and his mother had to go out to forage for food. Like most of the *ajoomas* in their neighborhood, she scraped pine trees for their soft inner bark and mixed the shavings into a porridge with whatever else she could find. She did this every day, and this was the enduring image of her that Jin held in his mind, a woman who kept going by sheer dint of will, her survival instinct ground to its primal essence.

They walked to the train station together and stopped by a street vendor where Suja bought a sweet duk rice cake to share between the two of them. They stood together, clouds of steam rising from their lips as they bit into the hot sweetness.

'Does your family ever visit you here in Pyongyang?' she asked.

'They might,' Jin lied, knowing full well that they couldn't afford the trip. 'But they like to have me come back home. That way everyone gets to see me.' He winked.

'I'm sure they miss you back home. I'm going to miss you and it's only for a week.'

'It'll be great to introduce you to my mom and sister. They'll love you.'

'And your father.'

'Of course, him too,' said Jin offhandedly. He looked down at the last bit of duk in Suja's hand. 'You take the last piece.'

'No, it's yours.'

He held it up to her lips. She took a little bite and handed it back to him.

He took it, saying, 'When I come back, you meet me here, and I'll buy you the next one.'

★ ★ ★

Jin could smell Kanggye even before the train pulled in to the station, the familiar reek of burnt plastic and garbage, the acrid sting of it in his lungs making him cough. Coming from Pyongyang back to Kanggye was like closing the door on heaven and stepping back into purgatory. Kanggye had changed since he was young and was getting worse by the year. He felt guilty about the privileged life he led in Pyongyang.

The streets of Kanggye used to smell sweet with hawkers on every street corner selling burnt sugar *yut* candies—oh, the delicious steamy smell of the caramelized sugar. But now there were hardly any candy makers; instead people burned wood, paper, plastic, anything they could lay their hands on to keep warm. The so-called 'sparrow' orphans flitted in and out among people on the streets and huddled together like so many piles of dirty rags along the train platforms. In the evenings they bedded down with the homeless against the station pillars. In the mornings sanitation workers would come by with their carts and their sticks, prodding and poking to see which bodies had stiffened overnight.

Jin left the station with his satchel over his shoulder and walked toward his family's apartment building. The sun was setting as he approached the building, and noticing the people standing outside, he wondered if a market had been set up outside their building. But as he got closer, he could see there were no cooking pots, no blankets or sheets of cardboard with wares spread out. Something was wrong. People were standing in their slippers with sweaters hastily pulled over their shoulders. He picked up his step and pushed through the crowd, searching for his family. He found his parents and his sister, Young-na, squatted on their haunches in the dirt, with their arms tucked between their knees, hands folded to conserve heat.

'Jin!' his mother exclaimed when she saw him. She and Young-na ran to hug him, and he embraced them tightly.

'Umma, it's so good to see you. Young-na, how are you?' he said, rubbing their arms as if to warm them up. He could see that they had both lost weight and felt a pang of guilt. He looked up toward his father and nodded. *'Anyung hasae yo.'*

'Anyung.' Mr. Park gazed at his son stiffly. Ever since Jin won the scholarship, it was hard for him to know how to speak to the boy. He was proud of his accomplishment but he could see that Jin was changing, moving away from their way of life, and as the patriarch of the family, Mr. Park couldn't help but take it as an affront.

'So you made it. How was your trip?' He tried not to sound defensive.

'It was fine,' Jin replied, looking away. 'What's going on here anyway?'

'It's a raid,' Young-na whispered, and went on to explain how the state police stormed their building, telling everyone to get out. They treated it like sport, shouting to one another like players on a soccer field as they ran from door to door. *You guys still on the second floor? What's holding you up?* they yelled, their flat-topped caps bobbing in and out of view through the apartment windows.

Jin looked up at the building, watching anxiously as the police reached the fifth floor and his parents' apartment. Every family kept something hidden in their homes, an emergency stash of food or a gold heirloom to be hawked, and he was sure his mom had a stash somewhere; she was the kind of woman who put things aside for later.

By the name of the Dear Leader, Jin prayed, *let them pass quickly, don't let them find a single thing.*

The police slowly ascended to the sixth floor and the next, then the next. By 7:00 p.m., they had finished on the tenth floor and they left, lifting their batons from where they had jammed the main door handles, allowing the residents back in. Jin and his family climbed the stairs in the dark and found their apartment door ajar, pots and cutlery scattered across the concrete floor. In the main room the wardrobe's cupboard doors were slanted open, with blankets and clothes spilled onto the floor.

Umma fell to the ground and rummaged through the cupboard, scrabbling through the blankets with feral ferocity. 'It's gone, it's all gone.' She collapsed into the pile, sobbing aloud, her arms flailing as she tossed up a buckwheat husk pillow.

'What's wrong?' Jin asked and crouched down next to her, gingerly touching her hair, which had thinned so much the white of her scalp gleamed through the carefully combed strands of permed hair. She was only fifty years old.

Young-na came up to him and whispered, 'They took our cornmeal.'

Jin's eyes widened.

'Apba,' Jin called out.

Mr. Park was standing motionless with his back against the wall, thumbs wrapped in his fists as he silently watched his wife. Young-na knelt next to her mother, tears spilling down her cheeks. Jin looked at his father again, willing him to step into the breach and say something. He wanted to shake him, somehow wake him into action. *Tell Mom you'll find more food. Tell her our home is safe, tell her our lives aren't lost, tell her anything. Lie. You are the leader of this family, do something.*

But his father was paralyzed as he watched his wife and daughter collapse in despair. Finally Jin leaned over and whispered to his sister, 'I've got to do something about this.'

'What can you do? You don't even live here anymore.'

She looked at him. From this angle Jin could see how gaunt her cheeks had gotten; her arms were as thin as a child's. He turned away in shame. While the family had been starving in Kanggye, Jin had been getting daily rations at the university cafeteria—they were simple meals of barley or cornmeal or cabbage, but at least he was eating. But for his mother and sister, life had gotten worse.

Jin pulled out two small bags of barley and corn flour from his knapsack and dropped them by his mother. 'Umma, here's some food for the family.'

'Oh, Jin,' she sobbed, 'you shouldn't have.'

He bent down to hug her, leaning over the bony curve of her back. He remembered how she used to hold him and sing the Dear Leader's song to him, 'No Motherland without You.' How solid and safe the world seemed to him then, held within her arms. She was a small woman now, much shorter than she used to be, and so very frail.

She placed her hand over his and held it tightly for a long time. When she pulled away, she had left a little velvet sack in his palm. She closed his fingers around it. Jin looked at the sack, opening it to find a jade necklace carved into the circular shape of a dragon swallowing its own tail. Embedded in its mouth was a sparkling diamond. His mother had shown it to him years ago, explaining that it was her mother's necklace that they managed to keep in the family throughout the Japanese occupation and the Korean War. The hoop snake design signified balance in the universe, the harmony between yin and yang.

He looked at his mother. 'What should I do with this?' he asked.

'Take it, it's of no use here. Sell it in Pyongyang to buy textbooks before they find it in the next raid.'

Jin shook his head. 'No, I'm not taking this. Keep it here.'

'Take it,' she insisted. 'I'm telling you, they'll find it. You take it and keep it safe.'

Jin didn't know what to say. He looked around the disheveled room, his gaze landing on a pile of snail shells that had tumbled out of a bowl, and he remembered how snails were easy to find, once upon a time, but since the famine, they too had become scarce.

'We have to do something about this,' Jin said to Apba.

His father sighed heavily. 'What can we do? They are the police.'

'But that can't have been authorized!'

'This is what they do.'

'Are you telling me they've done this before?' He glared at his father, then at Young-na. Both remained silent.

In a fit of anger Jin leaped toward the door and ran out into the unlit hall, the heavy hand of darkness closing around him as he heard the sound of sobbing coming from other apartment units. They were not the only ones who had been robbed. Jin kept running, trailing his fingers lightly along the wall until his hand pushed out into open air. He had reached the stairwell, which was pitch-black like the hall, but his body knew the steps, having run up and down them thousands of times since he was a kid. He turned down the stairs and his long legs took two at a time as he spiraled down five flights and spilled out into the night, gasping.

Zipping up his jacket, Jin ran toward the main road, fists pumping, his feet attacking the road in that long-legged, loose-hipped gait of his that his friends used to mock him about. But funny walk or no, damn, he could run.

He ran hard, unsure of where he was going, but he felt the fingers of his mind expanding, gripping onto familiar landmarks. As a kid, he and his friends used to run in bare feet, coursing through the streets like rats seeking the best gutters.

If a city were the map of a soul, then Kanggye—with its rain-dampened concrete, pale gray-blue buildings and broad boulevards; its straggly stands of trees that had been stripped bare by the bark collectors; its growing legions of beggars and street orphans; the acrid air that was once smoky with the fumes of the steel-coking industry and was now gray with barrel-fire smoke; its rusty green Russian C-31 trucks rerigged to run on burning wood instead of gasoline—the whole smoking, decaying, decrepit mess of it, was the heart muscle that fueled Jin's ambition.

He turned onto the main boulevard, which used to be lined with tall pine trees with branches that spread their dark glistening needles over the sidewalks; but the trees had been illegally scavenged, first stripped of bark, then one by one hacked down for firewood. Only the tree stumps remained. Jin stuck close to the dark buildings as he jogged north toward the Gullae Dong police station. Like a carrier pigeon returning home, his eyes locked in on the portraits of the Dear Leader and the Supreme Leader that were posted at the top of the squat white building. The sight of their beneficent smiles calmed him, and he felt his chest broaden, his shoulders relax as he ran toward his Leaders. The portraits galvanized him like a compass needle finding north again, and his whole body vibrated, propelling him forward, bolstering him with an increasing sense of righteousness. If the Party kept track of everyone, then even the police would be held accountable, wouldn't they? The Party had always been staunchly opposed to Party officials abusing power, so not only would it be right to report police misconduct, but it could be considered downright heroic that an individual stood up against the tyranny of corruption among the police. Jin was sure it was the honorable course of action.

He would meet with the commissioner and tell him about

the theft, which happened not just this once but many times.
If the Dear Leader had known what these police officers were
doing, surely they would have been punished long ago. The
portraits of the Dear Leader and Eternal Father loomed large
as Jin turned down Police Commissioner's Avenue. He slowed
his step as he drew close to the police compound, approaching the crumbling concrete wall that surrounded the grounds.

He thought about what he would say to the police
commissioner—how does one report on the police? He realized he didn't have the name of a single officer, nor a shred
of evidence. Jin crouched next to the wall, the dry, powdery
smell of the limestone mortar filling his nostrils. The station
yard was empty, the side entrance door closed shut, but in
one window shone dimly a flickering yellow candle. Like
the rest of Kanggye, the police station had no electricity.

Just then there was a flash of movement in the bike shed.
Jin ducked down and peered through a hole in the concrete
wall. A police officer was pushing a hefty pale-colored sack
about the size of a kimchi jar into the corner of the shed. His
uniform, cinched tightly at the waist, hung loosely from his
short, scrawny frame as he kicked at the sack. He was trying
to push it under a pile of bicycles, but the sack was too large
to fit under their crankshafts. Deciding on a different tack,
the officer reached down, yanked the sack back out again,
and stretching himself across the top of the bikes, he dropped
the sack behind the bikes. He then reached up into the raf-
ters above his head and tugged at big black inner tubes, laced
his arm through a handful and tossed them over the bikes.
The saekee was trying to hide the sack! The officer shoved
the bikes with his foot one last time and then, finally satisfied, turned into the police station and opened the door to a
round of laughter.

That bastard was up to no good.

Jin stared at the bike shed. The sack that the officer had been struggling with had the heft and weight of cornmeal... It could very well be the stolen cornmeal. If he could lead the commissioner to the bike shed and present the sack as evidence, there would be no questioning Jin's story. But first he had to confirm that it was indeed cornmeal.

Jin crouched forward, catlike, watching the back door of the police station as he shifted his weight from side to side. He took a quick breath and pulled himself over the wall, landing inside the compound in front of an electric fence. He parted the wires and climbed through it without so much as a spark—as he'd guessed, the electric fence was dead.

He shimmied to the right, putting the bike shed directly between him and the police station. The evening gloom deepened into pockets of darkness between the buildings. The officers couldn't see him, but Jin was close enough to the closed door to hear their voices and to catch a whiff of cigarette smoke that tinted the air. Jin inhaled the scent deeply. Goddamn, it had been months since Jin had had a real cigarette. He squatted there for a few seconds, every muscle in his body tensed and alert.

Uncoiling from his crouched position, Jin sprinted to the bike shed and maneuvered toward the bikes, his eye on the pale sack nestled in the corner. He was so sure he could taste it, smell it—it had to be cornmeal. Hunkered down, Jin reached his hand along the ground beneath the bicycle chain sprockets, but his fingers couldn't reach the sack. He stood up, sucked in his gut and stretched over the bikes, hanging his arm down as far as it would go. The bikes gave way, clattering as they collapsed under his weight.

He froze. *Shit.*

He scrabbled for the sack of grain, and just as his hand grabbed hold of the burlap, he heard a shout. Jin turned around to feel a shattering blow to his face, and his body went into flight.

Jin ran blind as a foal, his hand clenching the burlap bag as he ran flat out, the sack banging against his thigh. He could have dropped the sack and run free, but his fingers had held tight as he ran blindly, hands pushing through air until he collided into concrete and his head snapped back; the dark sky above him reeled. Spluttering blood, Jin reached up and felt along the crumbling lintel until his fingers found purchase, and he pulled himself up over the edge, and then, legs unfurling, his feet hit the ground with the rhythm of a runner. He was out of there, almost. He could barely see into the dark rabbit warren of streets that lay before him, his mind tunneled through to a dozen dead ends until he quit trying to map out the place. Just go, dammit, go.

Jin ran past row after row of Kanggye's infamous harmonica housing—long stodgy buildings that were built in the seventies with square windows cut into the sides like musical frets. But there was no music to this architecture, not a light in the windows, or flower box or children's toy in the front yards. The streets were as black as the eyes of these tenements' inhabitants, and as unwelcoming. People had left their thatch-roofed houses in the fields to move here in the 1970s to work in the factory. They moved in before the building was complete, and then it never got completed. Half the units were without glass panes in the window frames; instead sheets of cardboard were taped across the windows. There were lamp poles at every intersection, but no light bulbs in the electric sockets.

It was surrendering time, when natural light gave in to darkness and one by one people had turned in to sleep. Those that had candles were blowing them out, but most of the units had no light in their windows. There was no hanging out on front stoops, no backyard conversations. There was no meat to grill over a coal firepit, no rice wine to share, not even a streetlamp to brighten one's doorstep. They huddled in their dark rooms and pulled out their sleeping mats, closing their eyes as they awaited the release of sleep. For the next seven hours they could escape the sensation of hunger.

Young-na and his parents would be going to sleep now too. They must be wondering what had happened to him. Jin headed down an alley between two units, feet splashing in water as he ducked into a storage alcove. He hunched his tall frame to fit in and leaned against the wall, ribs heaving with each breath. He ran his hands over his feet. Shit, his feet were freezing. The newsprint lining the toe of his boots was soaked through now and his toes were numb. He massaged his feet.

Shouts and the staccato of running footsteps reverberated from several streets over. Police were running helter-skelter through the housing project, their shouts ricocheting off the concrete walls. Jin reached inside his jacket and felt the weight of the sack of cornmeal: it was heavier than a newborn baby. People would kill for half that amount of food, easy. He pinched the gritty grain through the sackcloth and felt heat flush up the side of his neck.

What was he doing with this bag in his hands? Why hadn't he dropped it, leaving it where he had found it? He closed his eyes as a wave of vertigo passed through him, and he let out a ragged breath. He hadn't intended to run off with it, but he couldn't very well turn back and hand it to the police now. They would accuse him of stealing it.

So here he was, stealing it.

He stared at his hands. They were too big, not simply big-boned like the rest of him, but overly large, overly capable; they took on too much. Some people had big eyes; they wanted too much or aspired for more than they were destined. Then

there were those who were plagued with envy of wealthy
Party members who had access to hidden villas and estates.
But Jin's failing was his hands. They committed him to things
he didn't want to take on.

He edged along the wall toward the next unit, his lean body
stretching along the face of the building, his legs poised to
run. He opened his mouth slightly, breathing carefully, every
muscle taut, every sense alive.

The officers' shouts grew faint, the spattering of footsteps
fainter still as they fanned out in different directions away
from him. At some point they would return. He had to get
out of here somehow to survive this and bury this story. He
would bury it with his grandma's kimchi pots in the old courtyard, where it would sleep the cold sleep of winter. Please,
Heavenly Leader, let it be so.

There was a scuffling noise from the other side of the wall
inside the unit, and the high-pitched cry of a woman. 'They
just raided us last week.'

'It's not a raid,' said a gravelly voice.

'What do they expect to find?'

'It's not a raid, I said.'

'Take the dead bodies, why don't they? Take away the
corpses.'

'*Sang-nyun*, shut up before you get us into trouble, bitch.'

Jin scowled as he listened to the argument and shifted his
weight away.

'They should reap what they sow. A bounty crop of dead
this year and no one wants the bodies,' the woman whined.

'Shut up!'

'Except the meat sellers on the black market.' She was interrupted by a loud slap followed by another. The woman
started to weep.

Jin cocked his head to one side to crack his neck. He had

half a mind to smack his hand against the wall and stop the man, but he had his own mess to think about. He pushed himself up against the wall and peered into the dark, puddled street, listening for sounds of the police. Taking a deep breath, Jin bolted down the lane and ran past door after closed door, each painted with the same faded limestone whitewash.

It was past curfew by the time Jin saw his family's apartment, a concrete shell with empty windows that gaped open like dark, ghostly maws. Home. He ran to the side entrance, pushed against the heavy door and grabbed the handrail to run up the stairs, but his legs were shaking so badly that he sank to the floor and sat there for a moment, limbs trembling. The stairwell was dank with the smell of iron, like water in a rusty bucket or blood smeared on metal. Jin wiped a string of spittle from his mouth and realized the entire left side of his face was numb. He touched it gingerly: his left jaw and cheek were swollen, his left eye half-shut. *Oh, God.* Jin hunched over his knees as he realized the extent of his injury. You can't hide a black eye from your family, let alone your classmates. People were going to ask.

He stared at the grimy concrete beneath his feet. Only twenty-four hours ago he was in Pyongyang with Suja, sharing a piece of sweet duk, and now he was running through the streets of Kanggye with the police chasing after him. God, how he hated this town and what it did to him. He wished he were back in Pyongyang right now. He never should have come.

He reached down into the sack and squished grains of cornmeal between his fingers. Food, the firm gritty feel of real food. With this sack his mother and sister could eat again.

Jin knotted the top of the bundle again, pulled himself to standing and trudged up the stairs, but with each step after heavy step, the urge to run and go into hiding grew stronger. At the fifth flight of stairs, Jin stopped on the landing, wavering in the dark, debating whether to run or to face his family. His mind retraced his steps. Could he take it back to the police station and stash it away again? Or could he throw it away somewhere to get rid of the evidence? But he couldn't possibly let this precious food go to waste.

Jin finally pushed through the door and turned into the hallway, running his fingers along the wall, counting until he got to the sixth door on the right, then feeling along the door until he found the familiar gouge along the door handle—from when his father had brought an adze home and accidentally dropped it against the door handle. He put his hand on it but couldn't bring himself to go in.

'Who's there?' Apba called from within.

Jin held his breath.

'Who is it?!'

Shit. Jin pushed the door open and walked through, his hands cold and clammy. His mom and dad and Young-na were huddled around a small candle. Apba was sitting cross-legged on the floor with his hands thrust in his lap. When he saw Jin, he leaned forward over the candle, and flickering shadows danced across his deeply lined face.

'Where were you?'

Jin unbuttoned his jacket, grabbed the sack by the knot and pulled it free from his belt. The sack landed on the floor with a raspy thud.

'What is that?'

'It's for the family.'

His mother reached over, tugged the sack to her and untied the knot. 'Omona, look at this.'

'Unh?' his father grunted. 'Where is it from?'

Jin leaned back against the wall and slowly slid to the floor as an immense tiredness overcame him, bearing down on his limbs; it was too heavy to sit up anymore, too heavy to breathe. Jin's mother and Young-na were both bent over the sack, eagerly pulsing their fingers through the cornmeal.

'Idiot, where did you get this?' his father rasped, careful not to raise his voice in case the neighbors might overhear him.

No words. No thought. Jin was silent.

'This is…' His father stopped abruptly. 'You're bringing home the dogs of damnation.'

Umma, still bent over the bag of cornmeal, licked three fingers, dipped them into the sack, then raised her powder-covered fingers to her mouth.

'It's fresh!' she exclaimed, her jaw rotating as she chewed. The powder mixed with saliva in her mouth, becoming a sticky paste.

Jin stared at the candle, his eyes swallowed by the hot yellow center of the flame.

His father stood up and smacked Jin on the side of his head. 'Who taught you to steal? Throw it out, you bastard. I can't have it in my house.'

'*Janyu*, please.' Jin's mother tried to pull her husband back.

'I can't sit and watch you all die,' said Jin.

'What have you brought into the house? Where is that from?' Mr. Park shouted and smacked Jin's head once, twice. Jin's neck jerked to the side, exposing his swollen, disfigured left cheek.

'Opba!' Young-na gasped. 'What happened?' She crawled over to him; her cold fingertips fluttered across his face.

'Oh no, who did that to you?' His mother let go of her husband's arm and rushed to Jin.

Mr. Park watched his wife fuss over their son, his lip curling as she wrapped her arms around him to cradle him.

'Get away, woman,' he grunted.

'What did you do, Jin?' his mother cried.

'Nothing happened.'

'The bastard stole the corn,' his father growled. 'What kind of idiot brings this into my house? Unh? Get rid of it.'

'I could take out a little for us and you can return it, okay?' Jin's mother whispered. 'Young-na, get me a bowl from the kitchen.'

'There's no place to return it, Umma. This corn is ours.'

'But—this is more than what we had.'

'It's ours,' Jin said emphatically.

'But…' Umma fell silent and pulled her hand out of the sack.

Without another word, Jin dragged himself up and walked out the door, tripping down the echoing corridor, until he found himself at the stairwell again. Clumping down the stairs, he sat down on the lower landing, the chill of concrete seeping through his pants, making his pelvis ache. Jin slapped his legs and arms to warm himself. These were his university-issued vinalon pants, made of the fabric emblematic of the Eternal Leader's philosophy of Juche, which called for patriotic self-sufficiency. If North Korea couldn't raise sheep or cultivate crops of cotton or linen, they would synthesize fabric from what they had—so they rendered anthracite coal ore into a durable synthetic fiber: vinalon. Like water from wine, they had made fabric out of coal. Jin, like his peers who were expected to become leaders of the next generation, was proud to be wearing this glorious fabric, for it was emblematic of Juche.

A wave of light-headedness came over him as the events of the past several hours shifted randomly in his mind: the police raid, the officer in the bike shed, the blow to his face, the sack of cornmeal. The scenes flashed in his mind like moments from a movie, or like pieces of a puzzle that were slowly rearranging and cohering into one terrifying thought. Because the cornmeal had been in state hands, technically it was the Dear Leader's. He had stolen from the Dear Leader.

Jin doubled over and heaved violently, once, twice. His empty stomach retched up strings of saliva. He had to get out of there as soon as possible to escape detection.

THREE

Suja smoothed the front of her A-line skirt and reached up to adjust her shirt collar: crisp, white, ironed down at the points like wings neatly tucked in, wings tightly bound with metal bands. Suja knew how to keep herself close like a winning hand of cards, and she knew when to put them down on the table. She twirled on her toes, making her heavy skirt flare out, and felt the thrill of cold air on her bare legs. It was early October, and the cool breeze brought with it an end-of-season unease, a scattered sense of urgency pulling her body in different directions.

'What are you doing?' her mother called from the door as she arranged her mink stole over her winter coat, positioning the caramel-colored tail carefully over a coin-sized patch of missing fur. It wasn't that cold outside, but she wore the stole on all official occasions. It had been gifted to her years ago from Aunt Juwon, who had married the deputy minister of public works. She had been a beauty, a real *mugunghwa*

flower in her youth, with cherry lips and hair curled deli-
cately to frame her face. By the age of fifteen she was selected
to perform in the Joy Division entertainment troupe, where
she was sequestered for the next decade to dance and en-
tertain the Eternal Leader Kim Il-Sung and the Party; who
knows what else she had to do for the Party. On the brink
of being unmarriageable at the age of twenty-five, she was
finally matched with Deputy Minister Cho Kee-yuk, a man
who was eighteen years her senior but who brought much
value to the family, including access to foreign luxury goods.

Mrs. Kim stepped into her black pumps and checked her
face in a small square mirror hanging from a wire on the wall.
She ran a finger along her lower lip to correct a smudge of
crimson lipstick, then turned toward the main room of the
three-room apartment and waited for her daughter. Like most
households, the main room was empty of furniture except
for three beautifully lacquered wardrobes with tall cupboard
doors inlaid with carved mother-of-pearl depicting scenes
with ladies in flowing traditional *hambok* gowns sitting by a
river. In front of the wardrobes was a round fold-up eating
table, also made of pearl-inlaid black lacquer. On the other
side of the room were two neat stacks of bright red and green
seat cushions.

Suja stepped lightly from the bathroom, her cheeks flushed,
shiny black hair swinging neatly about her face. She grabbed
her purse off the hook and shrugged her arms into her jacket.
With a high collar and a single row of buttons down the front,
the coat was styled in a fashion popular with high-school girls.
She had gotten it several years ago and now it was a touch
tight around the shoulders and bosom. They had held off on
buying Suja a new coat because of short supply at the government depots; and when it came to school uniforms, coats and

shoes, Umma always took Suja to the government depot to make sure she was wearing official Chosun clothing.

They were invited to the grand opening of a brand-new government depot, store number twelve, where they intended to get her new coat and perhaps a pair of shoes. What better way to enter her senior year at university than to buy a new coat from a brand-new government depot. It would be an auspicious omen for the year ahead, for this would be the coat that would see her into her adult life, as she followed in her father's footsteps into a career in journalism.

'Do you need books today too?'

'I've got them.' Suja checked her face in the mirror as her mother looked her up and down.

'We might as well get you a pair of dress pumps while we're there,' she said.

'Dress pumps,' Suja repeated softly, her eyes widening. Dress pumps were part of a career woman's attire, not something university students usually wore. Suja felt a quiet surge of pride as she imagined trying on the dress pumps. It was a vote of confidence and rare approbation from her mother. Still, Suja hadn't thought about jumping into the work force yet, and this suggestion from her mother made her realize how swiftly her student days would be over. Suja loved being at the university, and now that she was entering her senior year, she felt she had just started tasting life. There was so much more to explore; surely it was too soon to be buying dress pumps.

Umma examined Suja's face. 'Too much lipstick,' she said.

Suja checked the mirror again. 'It's fine.'

'Wipe it.' Mrs. Kim opened her purse and tore a corner off the newsprint she kept folded.

'It's *fine*.' She pushed past her mother.

'How dare you speak to me like that? Where did you learn to speak to your parents like that?' Mrs. Kim followed her daughter. *The things that girl got away with*. She tucked the newsprint back into her purse next to a small white invitation card, and snapped the clasp shut.

'I'm an adult, and this is the *modern style*.' Suja flipped her hair back impatiently as she waited for her mother by the stairwell. 'You always say that about my lipstick, and I don't even use as much as you.'

Mrs. Kim marched after her daughter. 'You don't want to be singled out for your beauty. You want to be noticed for your mind,' she snapped, but even as she spoke, the words fell flat, and she found herself faltering. Why didn't she simply tell Suja the real reason why she kept after her about her appearance? She hadn't wanted to name her concerns for fear it might give them more weight, more legitimacy. Instead, she had chosen to downplay Suja's beauty as a child, buying her plain clothes and never adorning her hair with pretty barrettes. As Suja approached puberty, she quietly pulled her out of the gymnastics and dance troupes, even though Suja had been a team leader in both. Her daughter was talented and pretty, liable to be spotted by the Dear Leader's recruiters. Once a girl was selected, there was no way to say no; it was much better, then, for Suja not to be noticed at all.

Now that Suja was entering her senior year, Mrs. Kim was breathing more easily, and she allowed herself a certain degree of pride and satisfaction. Her daughter had arrived at the doorstep of adulthood safely, so of course Suja should have dress pumps, and the nicest ones, just as long as she kept her face plain and her head down.

Mrs. Kim followed Suja through the lobby doors and fell into step as they headed out to Kim Hyun-jik Avenue, mother and daughter cut from the same cloth, of the same height and slender build. Mrs. Kim walked with a careful dignity, each movement weighted and refined, her face drawn into a slight frown of concentration. Next to her Suja was fresh faced, moving briskly with the barely repressed energy of a gymnast. Walking with her mother on this important shopping expedition, she felt she was stepping into the next stage of her life, and she could envision the rest of her life falling naturally into place: she would have a career as a photographer; she had met the man she loved, Jin, whom she would marry; they would live together in Pyongyang in an apartment building close to her own parents'. It was all beautifully laid out.

Turning onto Kumgang Avenue, they approached the Grand Jangmadang black market alley hand in hand. It was formerly the largest market in Pyongyang, with rows and rows of wooden stalls manned by vendors selling purloined riches from afar, everything from pure white rice to cotton socks, rain jackets, rat poison, brightly colored Chinese housewares and quilted jackets—even pirated DVDs of South Korean soap operas. You could shop for hours among stalls that displayed a bewildering array of goods, but you never dared touch anything, for once you touched, you had to buy. People made good money in the black markets, until the Dear Leader cracked down on them, shutting down what had grown into a booming industry. Now Grand Jangmadang was a ghost town.

Suja let go of her mother's hand and dawdled by the alley underneath a crisscrossing of black power lines. Most of the wooden stalls were empty and had fallen into disrepair, strips of plywood torn off their fronts. Tails of gray smoke rose from cooking fires tended by ajoomas sitting on their haunches stirring pots of noodle soup. A few other women sat with blankets spread across their laps with small piles of foraged shoots set out on sheets of cardboard. One woman had piles of yellow powder neatly shaped into conical mounds on her piece of cardboard. Suja squinted at the sandy pyramids, trying to identify what the powder could be, then recognized it as cornmeal, which was puzzling. Cornmeal was a staple ration given out by the state. Why would anyone choose to spend won and purchase it? It didn't make sense.

'Suja,' her mother called, 'there's no time!' Suja started and hurried to catch up to her mother.

They saw the queue long before they could see the signage on the government depot building, a line of people snaked around the building and down the block. Suja and her mom joined the end of the line, and they strained their heads to see how quickly people were moving up at the front. People emerged from the front doors of the depot with a bounce and swagger to their step, swinging new white plastic bags with Depot 12 emblazoned in red letters. Suja hooked her arm into her mother's, leaning into her for warmth. The sun had started its afternoon trajectory downward, and as it sank lower into the horizon, the cold seeped in through Suja's coat.

'Would you like some tea to keep warm?' her mother asked.

'No, I'm okay.' She tensed her shoulders, clenching her arms against her sides.

The queue advanced several feet, and Suja and her mother stepped forward with the crowd of people, who were beginning to grumble. At the front of the line, a man knocked on the depot door. When there was no response, he continued to rap against the glass, his knocking turning into banging until finally the door opened. He was pushed aside by a small man in a navy blue jacket with the Depot 12 logo emblazoned on the lapel who came out, cupped his hands around his mouth and shouted: 'Attention, comrades—the turnout for this grand opening has been so overwhelming that we have run out of stock. We are out of shoes and coats, and other things...' His

voice trailed off. 'It seems we have no pants either, or clothing…or housewares.'

A ripple ran through the crowd as people reared back.
'What do you mean you've run out—*already*?!'

'But how could that be?' a man shouted. 'It's your first day!'

The clerk turned to retreat back into the depot, and he
stood at the threshold with his foot propped in the door.

'Boots, are there boots left?'

The man shook his head.

'None?'

'What is this—we lined up for two hours and you're telling me you have nothing to sell?' someone yelled.

'Not nothing. We have some things, but some things are
out of supply.'

'Out of supply' was the standard hue and cry at government
depots, but for it to happen on the opening day of the brand-
new Depot 12 was a mockery. The depot was supposed to be
emblematic of the 'new economic revival plan'! Suja stared at
the clerk; her excitement at the prospect of getting new dress
shoes evaporating into confusion and indignation. Forget the
pumps, she needed a coat, at least a coat.

People muttered under their breaths and started to turn
away.

'Should we stay in line?' Suja asked her mother hesitantly.

'Wait a minute. We came all this way—we're not leaving.'
Mrs. Kim took hold of her daughter's hand and pulled her
forward, walking all the way up the queue, which was already disintegrating. She rushed up to the entrance and held
up a little white invitation card. 'Excuse me, excuse me. We
received an invitation from Minister Seo. Can we come in?'

The clerk had his hands held up in front of him, as if to
push her away, but his eyes landed on the invitation card. He

glanced at Mrs. Kim's mink stole, at Suja and back at the invitation card. He shrugged, then stepped aside to let them in.

Suja followed her mother in, feeling a little thrill run
through her body. The store was a good ten degrees warmer
than the outside, and she was able to relax immediately and
breathe more fully. Suja took a look around at the brand-
new chrome and white fixtures arranged in aisles across the
floor. The store was eerily silent with aisles of empty shelving,
glass cases with nothing on display. A red banner across the
back wall proclaimed Glory to the Economic Revitalization
of Chosun. A number of people milled about in the aisles,
touching a dish here, picking up a rice paddle there, as if they
were delicate museum pieces. A few pots and other household
items were laid out on the tables where several women had
gathered, murmuring among themselves. Suja looked at the
empty racks with dismay. There were no coats in the clothing section. No women's shoes.

This was supposed to be the flagship store heralding the
'return to plenty' that Economic Minister Seo had proclaimed
on last week's KCNA newscast. 'The fire is lit,' he proclaimed
with a broad smile. 'The Chosun economic engine has been
sparked, and it is burning hotter than ever!'

The news item cut to a crowd that had gathered for an appreciation rally on Kumsusan Avenue. '*Mansei* to the new economic plan,' the people cheered. 'Long live the Dear Leader.
Glory, glory!'

Those cheers echoed in Suja's mind as she looked down
from the red banner to the empty shelves around her. She fingered the lapel of her coat as she tried to reconcile the contra-
dictions. Where was the economic rejuvenation Minister Seo
had spoken of? How could he have made that announcement
knowing full well that there was no stock to fill the depots?
And where was the KCNA now? Shouldn't they be here to

report on this store opening? Should they be informing people that the depots were actually empty?

Suja watched her mother walk down the empty aisles, her purse tucked under her arm, toward the back of the store, where several men in suits stood beneath the banners, presumably the management team. Suja ambled around the store, pausing to admire a silver-leaf pattern on a solitary platter that sat in the middle of a shelf. She wandered into the clothing area where a few scarves and men's gloves were laid out on a table. There were no women's clothes to be seen. She picked up a pair of men's black leather gloves and ran her fingers along them, turning the cuff inside out to see that it was lined with knitting. She slipped her hand in it and found it was roomy, the fingers a half inch too long. They would fit Jin perfectly. She looked up at her mother, who had her back to her and was deep in conversation with a manager. Suja glanced across at the rows of empty racks around her and on impulse picked up the gloves. She walked to the cashier, glancing now and then at her mother, who was still deep in conversation with the manager.

The cashier rang up the purchase and Suja reached into her purse to unroll the few won bills she had brought with her. She slipped the gloves into her purse and looked up to see Umma had finished with the manager and was walking back. Suja stepped away from the cashier's desk and hurried toward the main aisle to meet Umma, whose cheeks were flushed, lips pressed together in a thin line.

'What were you doing?' she asked sternly as Suja joined her.

'I was just asking when they were getting more stock.'

'We're leaving.' Umma held her arm out for Suja as she continued swiftly toward the entrance.

'What did the manager say?' Suja asked.

Umma flashed her eyes and said nothing.

As they approached the exit, they could see there were still some people queued, clamoring to get in. Expectant faces followed them only to look bewildered, crestfallen as they looked down at their empty hands.

'Is there anything left?' a woman asked.

'Do they have sweaters?' said another.

Umma pushed her way past the people, and when they were a block away, Suja finally asked again. 'What happened, what did the manager say?'

'Nothing.' Umma adjusted her hat more firmly on her head. 'Nothing happened.'

'You were talking for a long time, Umma.'

'A long time for nothing. I told them I had ordered your coat and it should have been there on reserve, but they said there was no reserve stock this time.'

'Really?' Suja looked puzzled. 'Why not?'

'No answer,' said Umma. 'The manager didn't say, but you know all senior officials get their dibs on stock before the depot opens.'

'Was there even any stock to begin with?'

'Who knows,' her mother sighed. 'Oh, Suja, what will we do about your coat?'

'It's okay.'

'Use my other coat until we find you a new one.'

'I'm fine, Umma.'

'I'm not arguing with you.'

'It's okay.' Suja reached for her hand, and Umma tucked it in the crook of her arm, cradling it against her body. Suja leaned into her mother as they walked home together in the chill of evening.

FOUR

Suja craned her neck peering down the hall as she and Kyung-bok walked into journalism class.

'Looking for him?'

'No!' Suja said, but her neck and cheeks flushed red.

'You are.' Kyung-bok put an arm on Suja's shoulder, as she liked to do, being half a head taller than Suja. Tilting her head back, she batted her lashes at the ceiling. *'Oh, Jin, you're so brilliant,'* she sighed.

'That's right, he is.' Suja pinched Kyung-bok's midriff.

'Ow!' Kyung-bok rubbed her side as she sat down at her desk. 'Where's he been anyway?'

'Visiting family. He's supposed to be back today.'

'Where does his family live?'

'Up north,' Suja said vaguely.

'North where?'

'Kanggye.'

'Oh.' Kyung-bok raised a brow. '*That* north. Wow. I've never met anyone from there before.'

Suja was silent.

Professor Ahn tapped his desk with the tip of his pen, drawing everyone's attention.

'If your mind is at the highest state, also your work will be of the highest state—even if your brain has been damaged,' he added dryly. 'Today we'll take a look at the flood of last year.'

'Yes!' the class responded.

He pulled out his book and took a deep breath.

'Do you remember the reports? How many people died?' Professor Ahn asked.

'Hundreds,' said Kyung-bok.

'Several hundred,' Suja added, the figures springing to her mind automatically. She remembered the flood had affected the entire central west of North Korea, the richest crop-bearing land in the country. It was the worst flood of its kind, with all crops lost and entire villages drowned out, while diseases ravaged through the makeshift camps for the survivors.

'Yes, more than three hundred. I will read the official report. This is from the Korea Central News Agency, November nineteen, 1997, Juche year eighty-six, quoting a villager.

'"It was like a dream. It has been said that flood is a source of wails and cries. However, we got more than we lost. In addition, newborn babies enlarged the village population. Indeed, Marshal Kim Jong-il is the tenderhearted father of all people." This is what all the people in flood-afflicted areas want to say.'

There was a sound of running footsteps in the hall, which slowed by the door, then came to a stop. The door opened and Suja looked up. Jin shuffled in with his head down. 'I'm sorry I'm late, Professor Ahn,' he said, bowing to him before slinking toward the back of the classroom with his face averted.

The professor paused his lecture midsentence when he saw the left side of Jin's face. His cheek was swollen with a dark violet bruise that spread right up to his brow, forcing his eye half-shut. Shocked by the sight of his injury, Suja let her pencil slip from her fingers, and it clattered to the floor.

'Jin Lee Park, what happened to your face?' asked the professor.

'I had an accident, *sunsaengnim*,' Jin whispered.

'Accident?'

'I was helping my father at the tooling factory,' Jin mumbled, 'and we dropped a piece of heavy equipment.'

Professor Ahn tucked a piece of chalk behind his ear and, leaning back against his desk, folded his arms across his chest.

'Dropped it on your face?' he asked dryly.

'I was trying to save it from falling on the floor.'

'Most people use their hands to catch things.' The class tittered.

'My hands were full.'

'Humph,' said Ahn.

Jin looked down, directing his words. 'Everything's okay, sunsaengnim.'

'And the equipment?'

'Not a mark.'

'This piece of equipment—it didn't happen to be a human fist?'

The class broke out into loud guffaws, and Suja's face turned red with mortification. What had happened to him, and why hadn't he tried to contact her about it? She shifted around in her seat and shot a glance back at him. He studiously kept his eyes on the floor.

'You weren't talking back to your pa, were you?' Gon-il tossed from the back of the room. More laughter.

'It was an engine part,' said Jin, smiling, thankful for the jokes.

'Take your seat.' Professor Ahn dismissed Jin.

Kyung-bok shot Suja a glance, her eyebrows raised. 'What happened?' she mouthed silently. Suja shook her head, not letting on that she didn't have a clue. Out of the corner of her eye she could see Jin walking to the back of the classroom. He didn't dare look in her direction as he walked past his usual seat, which was filled, and slunk into a seat at the back of the group. The sunsaengnim pushed ahead with the lesson.

Suja sat rigidly with the pencil poised over her notebook, but she wasn't taking notes; in fact, she didn't hear a single word the professor was saying or read the words he was writing on the board. She glanced at Kyung-bok, who darted her eyes back at Jin and raised an eyebrow quizzically. Suja looked away, feeling ashamed and upset. What trouble could he have gotten into in the country? There were only a few reasons why Jin would get beaten up like that, and they were all no good, for only gangpae gangsters got beaten up like that. What in the world could have happened to him?

'So this flood, this natural catastrophe,' Professor Ahn continued, 'was it a tragedy or triumph?' Professor Ahn looked out across the classroom, his gaze landing on Jin first, then Suja. Neither ventured a hand.

'Gon-il, tragedy or triumph?'

'A triumph,' Gon-il answered.

'Jin.' Professor Ahn turned his head. 'Tragedy or triumph?'

'It is a tragedy for the people, but a triumph in the end,' Jin said quickly, keeping his left hand cradled against his face, 'for they received many reparations from our Dear Leader.'

It was the right answer, Suja thought. At least there was that.

'Anyone else?' Ahn asked. Everyone was silent, twenty-one pairs of black eyes on him.

'Yes.' Ahn nodded. 'It was a people's tragedy, but what an opportunity for our Dear Leader to triumph.'

This was strange phrasing, and Suja wondered why Professor Ahn would use the term *opportunity*—as if the flood were a fortuitous event to be taken advantage of.

'Every tragedy is an opportunity for our Dear Leader Kim Jong-il to triumph, do you understand?'

'*Yae.*' A unanimous reply.

'I'll say it again, you empty baptong idiots. Our Dear Leader Kim Jong-il has the celestial power to transform every tragedy into a triumph. But how can the people find out about this? How can the Dear Leader talk into every citizen's ear? If there is no electricity, no TV, no radio? How can people hear the good news of the Dear Leader?

'*We* are his eyes and his ears, but most important—' Professor Ahn's hands cupped his mouth '—we are his *mouth*. The Korean Central News Agency tells the people, *all* the people in the nation, about the Dear Leader. *We are his mouth.* And if you're lucky,' Professor Ahn said, thrusting his chin forward, 'you will be part of the KCNA too.'

Suja nodded crisply, as she usually did, to signify her commitment. But she found herself questioning the professor. If KCNA was the Dear Leader's mouthpiece, why didn't they report on things like the depot supply shortage? Was it not the responsibility of the KCNA to inform people of important things like supply shortages?

As the lesson went on, Suja's irritation and distraction deepened, and she glanced briefly at Jin. 'I'm sorry,' he mouthed sorrowfully. She turned around again, her face stony. She sat on the edge of the seat, waiting for the class to end, and when the professor finally dismissed everyone, Suja cast a cold glance at Jin and got up from her desk and hurried out of the room without waiting for either Kyung-bok or Jin.

'Suja,' Jin called, following after her. He kept to the left side of the hallway, keeping his face averted, as she hurried ahead, trying to put distance between them and the students from their class who had seen Jin's face. She ran upstairs toward the darkroom, knowing Jin would follow. She pulled the set of keys out of her pocket and let herself in, purposely letting the door swing shut on Jin. He caught it with the flat of his hand.

'I'm sorry, Suja,' he repeated, stepping into the twilight of the darkroom. He breathed in the vinegary sharpness of ammonia, a smell he now associated with Suja after spending hours with her here developing photos, coaxing shadows and lines to appear on the white paper like ghosts conjured into the world.

'I'm late with the photo assignment today,' she said stiffly, grabbing a roll of negatives hanging on a line. 'And how dare you show up like this to school? What happened to you?' Her voice slid sharply in distress.

'It was an accident at my dad's factory. I wanted to tell you before classes but I just got back,' he said, stepping toward her to hug her. 'Oh, Suja, it's good to see you. I missed you.'

'It looks like a tractor hit your face.'

He lifted a hand self-consciously to cover his cheek. 'The engine part did.'

'You expect anyone to believe that? I can't believe how late I'm going to be,' she said brusquely. It was 3:05 p.m., and she had to rush to make the newspaper's 4:00 p.m. deadline. This happened every Wednesday; Jin knew her anxiety would mount to a feverish pitch as Suja raced to print and select her photos, discarding dozens before settling on a handful that she deemed passable. She would run to the newspaper building down the block with the prints dangling from her fingers, still wet.

'You've got time.' Jin attempted a calm tone of voice.

Suja stepped over to him and brought her face close to his to inspect his injury. He kept his head stiffly canted to one side, trying to keep the extent of his injuries hidden from her view. It was all along the left side of his face, the purple-black bruise that stretched across his cheek, even his eyelid puffed and nearly closed, with the crease of his eyelid bruised black. Suja pulled back, blinking rapidly. The wound was not the result of one single blow; clearly it had been a beating, or— Suja sucked in her breath. Could it have been some kind of torture? What had Jin done?

Sensing her fear, Jin turned his head and slowly lifted his arms and ghoulishly clawed the air, wrenching his misshapen features into a ghastly scowl. Suja shrieked, then erupted into laughter despite herself and fell back against the counter. Jin smiled at this, relieved to see her laughing. Most women covered their mouths with their hand when they laughed, as if their glee and mirth were shameful, but Suja's laugh was open and broad and infectious.

'Monster.' She pushed him. 'Shouldn't you be in the infirmary?'

'You're worse than my mother.'

Suja shook her head, frowning. She turned away from him and fiddled with the prints in the developing vats again.

'Why would you come to school looking like that?'

He put his hand over his face.

'You look like a gangster. I can't be seen with you.'

'No one can see us anyway.' He pushed himself off the wall and walked over to her side, the full length of his body leaned next to hers. She was a full head shorter than him, but she was fine-boned and slender, making her seem just as tall. Her sweater, which hung loosely over her midriff, touched Jin's shirt, and he sensed the electricity of her skin. He stood next to her, his heart in his throat as he silently watched the dark lines coalesce and fix into focus on the print paper. You get a moment with your girl, you stand this close to her and all your brokenness feels whole again.

Suja transferred a photo into the stop bath and examined the print closely, pleased to see the image was fixed, crisp and perfectly exposed. At least there was this. There were some things in life you could control.

'What do you think?' Suja held up the print, her slim white arms held akimbo as she lifted the photo to her heart-shaped face. Jin's eyes were consumed by her.

'Nice,' he managed to say.

'Only nice?' she chided.

'Beautiful.'

'The photo, Opba!'

'I've seen it already.'

'No, this is new. I was taking pictures at the dance academy yesterday.'

The shadows on the print paper had coalesced into rows of women wearing traditional gowns, their heads bowed to the ground, striped sashes spilled out over the fabric of their gowns.

'Look at the composition,' she said.

'The composition is good.'

'You're not looking.'

'Sorry.'

'Oh, forget it.' Suja reached past him, her arm brushing against his ribs as she grabbed the tongs. 'Blow on this to help it dry. If I'm late again, Apba will find out.' She turned toward another vat, then paused midstep. 'And what really happened to your face? Who would do that to you?'

'You won't be late.' Jin's voice faltered.

Suja dropped another print into the stop bath and waited

for him to continue. She was expecting him to tell her what
had happened in Kanggye, but in the extended pause the
mood in the room shifted.

'Suja…if anything should happen to me… Nothing will,
but if one day something should happen…'

She turned slowly to look at him. 'Something happened,
didn't it?'

'You should know that the most important person in my
life is in this room with me right now.' He put his hand on
hers and interlaced their fingers. Suja's face glowed in the
red luminescent light. He wanted to take her in his arms and
wrap himself around her, lose himself in the depths of her
dark eyes and tell her everything.

'What happened?' she whispered.

Jin weighed the moment; they were alone in this dark, safe
place. If there was a time he could tell her, it would be now,
here. But then he thought about the possible consequences if
he told her, the chain of events that could unfold if she were to
one day be interrogated, and the different outcomes that could
transpire between them, between each of them and the state.

'Nothing,' he said, 'nothing happened.'

'Don't lie.'

He shook his head.

Suja was quiet. There were things you didn't speak about
among friends, or even within your own family. You learned
to devote them to the darkness and carry them within you silently, pushing them down, making them smaller and darker
still. The fabric of life in North Korea was riddled with dark
holes, and yet somehow it held together. Just as with their
uncle Koo, who vanished from their lives and became one
of the 'disappeared.' Everyone had their losses; they knew to
close up these losses and to go on with life, never speak of it
again.

Sometimes humans are too resilient for their own good.

'You didn't do anything stupid, did you?' she asked carefully, looking away.

'No,' he whispered. In fact, he had done something colossally stupid and treasonous, and he hoped that the Dear Heavenly Leader would never find out. His father was right to be angry with him; it put the whole family in jeopardy. He prayed the crime would be buried and forgotten in the coming weeks and months and that his life would go on as planned.

Their eyes met again, and there was a subtle shift between them.

'It's dangerous for you to come to school like this,' she said, looking at him full in the face. 'It doesn't look like a normal accident.'

'I had to see you.'

'We can meet outside school. I can meet you after I go to the newspaper office again.'

'I've done nothing wrong. I don't need to hide.'

Suja's face relaxed at this. 'It's good you have nothing to hide. But they might question you anyway, so you have to be careful.'

'I know.'

'Okay,' she said uncertainly, leaning in to hug him again. 'I have to go now, but I'll see you later tonight?'

'Yes.'

Tucking the folder of developed photos under her arm, she pushed through the door. Jin was about to follow her out but heard her say hello loudly to someone in the hall. He stopped with his hand on the knob and leaned his head against the door. Beads of sweat glistened on his brow as he waited for the sounds of their chatter to fade. He listened to Suja's footsteps retreat down the hall, her voice growing fainter and fainter until Jin couldn't hear her at all.

Pushing the door open, he squared his shoulders and stepped into the empty hall. He tried to look calm and collected. He would walk down the hall like the upstanding citizen and student he had always been and continue resolutely as if nothing had happened; and he hoped no one would discover anything different.

FIVE

Winter hung its head and the sky grew heavy with that pe-culiarly not-quite-day, not-quite-evening dark pall of No-vember. Nine hundred miles north of Pyongyang in the small town of Kanggye, stubbly trees on the main avenue leaned leafless into an unseen wind. It was already late, too late to begin foraging for roots or pine bark, but Jin's mother had to search, for there was nothing in the house to cook with. She hurried past the derelict munitions factory toward the brush lot in the back with a white plastic bucket banging against her side.

For days Mrs. Park had been making porridge out of inner pine bark and foraged grasses without touching the cornmeal Jin had found. Terrified of being discovered, she didn't cook the stolen food but kept it hidden in their apartment, unused. Her husband had flown into a rage looking for it, furious at the thought that they could be caught with the ill-gotten grain. But Mrs. Park refused to tell her husband where she put it. She had divided it into three satchels and stashed them in separate places: one small package was wedged behind a loose board in the cupboard, another was under the floor by the door, the last one was sewn inside a pillow that she hid at the bottom of the cherrywood wardrobe. Mr. Park had checked there, pulling everything out and scattering the blankets, as he shook each quilt and felt along the seams. Finding nothing, he turned to the kitchen cupboards, swiping his arm across each shelf and emptying the drawers. Grabbing a wooden spoon, he cracked it against the counter so hard that it split in half, sending the bowl of the spoon spinning up to smack against the ceiling.

'You're lying for your stupid gaesakee son!'

He lunged at her, and she ducked, curling herself into a ball, folding her arms tightly against her ribs to protect herself as he slapped her, cussing away. She remained silent, not a moan, not a cry, not a word. She was determined not to tell him where the cornmeal was—for his sake and for the sake of the family. Why let him throw out the precious food when they were starving to death? The way of secrecy was the way of survival, a lesson Mrs. Park had learned as a teen during the Korean War, when her family had been forced to leave their home during the war, as forces from the South pushed northward. They packed the farm wagon with their belongings, piling it high with treasured pieces of lacquered furniture, blankets, food. Jewelry and money were sewn directly into the clothing and covered with patches. There was no more jewelry to hide now, not a stone or link of gold left to sell, and anyway, food was more valuable than gold. There was no way she could let that cornmeal get thrown out.

Mrs. Park swung the bucket to her left hand and picked her feet through the brush as she headed deep into the back lot of the munitions factory. Her eyes scanned the brush, searching for the familiar leaves of *san namul* plants. She often foraged for san namul plants, which were tasty when marinated with sesame oil and salt, but it was harder and harder to find them these days, and it was getting too dark to be able to see. Pine bark it would have to be tonight. She approached a stand of stunted pine trees at the back of the lot, noticing by the line of their dark silhouettes that their bark had been untapped. She pulled out her kitchen cleaver and, setting the blade against the tree bark, ran it down the tree trunk, scraping off the outer layer and digging into the pale spongy layer that lay beneath it. The inner bark curled like ribbons of blond crepe paper into her basket. She worked her way around the tree, first stripping off the outer bark, then harvesting the soft inner bark, pausing now and then to push down the shavings in a bucket. She went at it for twenty minutes until her hand cramped into a fist and she couldn't feel the knife. Unclenching her fist, she shook out her hand, then wound a strip of cloth around it and set to scraping again.

She moved quickly to a second and third tree, and after she had scraped the pine saplings clean, she looked around for anything else she might forage. She tugged on a small handful of grasses and brought it to her lips, finding the grass to be tender, but without flavor. She stuck her toe beneath a long piece of rusted metal that lay among the dried grasses and lifted: no pale mushrooms underneath, only a thin smattering of albino grass shoots flattened down like matted hair. She stood up again, pressed both her hands against the small of her back and stretched for a moment, steamy curls of her breath dissipating in the blue dusk. It would be night by the time she made it back home. She turned toward the road, feeling the crunch of the frozen soil beneath her boots.

Arriving home with her harvest, Mrs. Park pulled out the

mortar and pestle from beneath the kitchen sink and dropped
some pine shavings into the stone bowl. She leaned forward,
her whole body keening as she hunched over the mortar,
pounding the pestle and grinding the pine bark into powder.
She turned the mortar now and then, adding more pine as
the crumbly shavings pushed up the side of the mortar bowl.
She ran her fingers through the sorry lump of coarse blond
fibers and heaved a sigh. There were no san namul shoots to
mix in, no fungi foraged from the underside of damp buildings, no radishes; nothing but pine bark today. Dipping a ladle
into the water bucket, she watched the water bead and scat-
ter among the yellow flakes, then soak in. The smell of pine
resin rose to her nostrils. It made her retch.

She looked up at the kitchen cupboards, her eyes settling
on the last cupboard door at the far end. The Shims in the
next-door apartment were silent. From the Bak apartment
on the other side she could hear the dull thud of their pestle
and the mumble of conversation between Mrs. Bak and her
daughter, who were making dinner as usual for this time of
day. She reached up, pushing her hand past a stack of steel
bowls to the back wall, where there was a gap in the paper-
board, and wedged her hand behind the board and pulled
out a small tightly wrapped bundle. She brought it down,
hugging it against her as she listened with her mouth slightly
open to the sounds and movements coming from next door.
Satisfied that all was calm, she set it down next to the pestle
and untied the cloth, to reveal another cloth underneath. She
untied the second handkerchief carefully, opening the corners to reveal a mound of yellow-white cornmeal. She held
the bundle over the pot and let some of the pale powder spill
out of the bundle to sift through her fingers into the pot. Her
lips spread into a quavering smile and tears sprang to her eyes.

Her boy, her Jin, had brought this to the family. How did he know where to find cornmeal?

Pine bark had to be heated and boiled for at least twenty minutes in order for it to soften enough to be digestible. Cornmeal cooked in half that time, but she boiled them together, hoping the flavor of the cornmeal would suffuse the pine. She stirred the cornmeal-pine mixture, her mouth watering with anticipation. The spuming steam smelled heavenly.

When Young-na and her father came home, Mrs. Park wordlessly put the bowls of porridge in front of them.

'That's it today?' Mr. Park asked.

'That's everything.'

Young-na dipped her spoon into the porridge and took a mouthful, pausing as the flavor of the cornmeal suffused her senses. Her eyes darted fearfully to her mom, who kept her eyes on her bowl. Young-na glanced at her father, expecting him to burst into a tirade, but he silently gulped down the porridge, barely pausing for breath as he shoveled it in. When a body knows famine, the taste of real food eclipses all thought; you do anything to get as much food in you as possible.

In the apartment next door, the Shims were lying on their floor mats drifting in and out of a dim haze, dreaming the North Korean dream: food. Mrs. Shim lay on a bright red quilt imagining the smell of white rice, of biting down into the rich texture of beef, the crunch and spicy tang of kimchi. Acidic saliva stung the back of her mouth.

A warm humid smell came wafting into their apartment through the bottom of their door. It was dinnertime and the households around them were cooking their pine porridges, their foraged root soups. Today, however, there was something slightly different in the smells. Mr. Shim and their three children didn't recognize it, but as the cook of the household, Mrs. Shim immediately recognized the smooth, slightly sweet, unmistakable scent of corn and was startled. No one in that apartment building should have had corn flour after the police raid. How could their neighbors have food and yet she have none for her own family? As the Party secretary for her block, she would have thought that she'd be the one with the last remaining stash of food. She had half a mind to go and knock on the Parks' door and inquire about that meal of theirs tonight. She didn't need a reason; she could barge in on her comrades whenever she pleased. But better to try to sleep tonight. She turned over on her side, pinched her nose between her fingers and closed her eyes tight, trying to ignore the smell of food coming from her next door.

Her envy and suspicion were quickly rekindled later that week when she picked up a copy of the newspaper by the train station, opening the flimsy weekly paper to page three. The headline read: 'An Audacious and Unforgivable Crime: Theft of the People's Food.' The article went on to describe, 'Nearly a kilogram of cornmeal was stolen from one of the Dear Leader's storage centers on Saturday, November 13, in Kanggye Area 14…' That was just last week on the night the police raided their apartment building.

Mrs. Shim looked up from the paper as an announcement truck rolled past the train station with a young woman officer standing astride the back of the GAZ-51 with a megaphone held to her mouth. The rusty green truck had been converted to run on wood-fire smoke instead of gasoline and had a wood-burning barrel on the back of the truck bed. Embers sputtered from the chimney pipe as the truck coughed and jolted, knocking the officer toward the hot barrel, but she hung on to the rail bar and quickly righted herself again. Her high-pitched voice screeched through the megaphone:

'Enemy of the state on the loose—beware! Award for information about the notorious *baegup* thief. Become a national hero—help find the Cornmeal Culprit. See him whipped and thrashed for his despicable crime...' Her shrill voice bounced through the alleys of the housing complex as the truck rumbled down the street toward the main avenue. Three barefoot kids ran out and clamored at the truck windows, ducking out of its way as it backfired, then accelerated down the street. Mrs. Shim's bright eyes followed the truck as it turned onto the avenue.

Tucking the newspaper firmly under her arm, Mrs. Shim turned toward her home, her mind roiling with thoughts and theories. She hurried up to their apartment, where she stepped out of her cracked vinyl loafers, exchanging them for her husband's black rubber boots (the best boots in the house). She licked her palms and patted down her frizzy rust-colored hair, then pulled on her daughter's favorite aubergine woolen hat. She smoothed the ends of her hair again, and thus transformed, Mrs. Shim grabbed the newspaper again and marched to the police station.

At the police station she announced herself as the Party secretary of apartment block 213 and insisted she needed to speak to the police commissioner. The officer at the front desk signaled for her to take a chair and told her she would have to wait. She could see the police commissioner at the back of the office sitting at a desk with a mess of papers scattered across it. There was another officer sitting at a desk perpendicular to his, and aside from these three men, the office was empty. Humph. Mrs. Shim went to the chair as directed and sat with her feet dangling, her rheumy eyes fixed on the commissioner. The front-desk officer went to speak to the commissioner, bending to whisper at his ear. He came back to his front post without a word.

'Can I see the commissioner now?' Mrs. Shim edged forward in her chair.

'Not yet.'

She sat back again, crossed her hands and waited. The officer returned to his desk and bent over his papers, scribbling. After some time Mrs. Shim asked again if she could see the commissioner. The officer shook his head. Forty minutes passed. Finally the officer stood up and walked over to the commissioner and whispered. He beckoned at Mrs. Shim.

The commissioner was a balding man with a large mole on his forehead and spectacles with wire frames that pressed into his temples. Having settled herself down in the chair in front of him, Mrs. Shim's chin barely came level to his wooden desktop, and looking up at the commissioner from this vantage point, she had a sudden attack of nerves. One of her boots slipped off and fell to the floor. She stretched to hook her foot back into it again, then slid back into the chair to meet the commissioner's gaze.

'I am Shim Aeja, Party secretary from the third division of housing block two hundred thirteen,' she said. 'I trust His Excellency is in good health?'

'Call me Commissioner, Comrade Shim,' he said, running a gloved finger around his neckline, the skin of his neck bulged over his buttoned-up shirt collar. He fidgeted with a pen, and Mrs. Shim noticed that the sleeve ends of his vinalon uniform jacket were greased shiny with wear and use.

'Yes, Your Commissionership. As you know, I am but a lowly woman in your precinct, but I have eyes and I am watchful—' Mrs. Shim pointed to her forehead '—and read the report in the newspaper.' She snapped the paper. 'And by the blessed hairs on my mother's head, I swear to you—I've discovered the lowly bastard who stole this cornmeal. The traitors who have been living in our midst, hiding right under

our noses, I discovered them cooking with the cornmeal that
they stole. You can't mistake the smell of cornmeal, I know
what it smells like, and I swear by our Heavenly Leader that
I can take your men to these culprits and deliver them to the
punishment they so abundantly deserve.'

Mrs. Shim went on describing the smell—the so-called
evidence—her theory about the sequence of events and of
who and how the theft could have been perpetrated. By the
time she was finished, she was yelling, and the commissioner's
liverish yellow eyes revealed neither interest nor animosity,
but he clenched and unclenched the muscles in his jaw. The
Cornmeal Culprit of Kanggye had made national news and
made this precinct look bad, very bad indeed. He had dis-
patched his entire staff on the case, for the office had received
countless tips from citizens, all of which had led to naught.
So now his career had come to this, listening to handicapped
old ladies. This was the forty-third citizen to come in claim-
ing they had found the Cornmeal Culprit, and it was hard
to keep himself from shouting at these idiotic peasants who
spouted their stupid stories, these country chonnom, these
domestic animals who walked upright on two legs.

The commissioner stood up, forcing an end to the meeting. Mrs. Shim leaned forward, getting up from her chair to
stand there, her eyes at breast-ribbon level, wondering what
was going to happen next.

'Officer Baek will take your report,' the commissioner said.

She wavered unsteadily, looking back at the front desk.

'Over here,' called Officer Baek, who sat with a shoulder
leaned against the wall, his legs splayed wide underneath his
desk. He scratched his head with a pen and pointed with it
to the chair in front of his desk. 'Have a seat.'

Bowing to the commissioner, Mrs. Shim excused herself
and walked over to Officer Baek's desk and pulled herself into

a chair, which was lower than the commissioner's chairs, so she was able to settle into it easily. Baek tapped the point of the pen on his desk and pulled over a piece of paper that was already two-thirds inked in with tightly drawn characters. He circled the pen above the paper and looked at Mrs. Shim.

'Okay, so,' he said.

Mrs. Shim cleared her throat and began her tale, her voice tentative at first, but within moments she was ranting again, her righteous exhortations as loud and vigorous as the first time she told the story.

Sitting at his own desk not six feet away, the commissioner listened half-heartedly as he sifted through the sheaf of reports on his desk, his eyelids dropped a fraction of an inch as the woman repeated verbatim the same phrases she had said to him moments ago. Four walls—what he would do for four walls. He was a commissioner and he didn't have his own office. The woman bleated on about why she believed the Cornmeal Culprit lived in her building—the fact that the family had a son visiting them from Pyongyang around the time of the theft, that he had vanished unexpectedly the very day after the theft, the fact that this family possessed any cornmeal at all when no other families had cornmeal since the police inspection (she had avoided using the term *raid*). She finished her story with a proclamation: 'I can lead your men right to the apartment if you come with me now. Catch the Cornmeal Culprit before they eat up all the evidence!'

The commissioner stopped fiddling with the reports on his desk and focused on the woman. There was something to what the ajooma was saying, and to be frank, time was of the essence in this investigation, for aside from the issue of his besmirched name and reputation, there was the problem of the edible evidence; who knows how long it would be around before it got all eaten up. The visiting son from

Pyongyang was intriguing. The fact that he was from Pyong-yang could be fortuitous if the source of evil, the perpetrator of the crime, could be traced back to Pyongyang. That would clear the precinct, and clear his name. The investigation would have to involve the National Security Force, and it would be a glorious national case, one that could advance his career and perhaps rocket him out of this godforsaken region and jockey him into a position in Pyongyang.

The commissioner shot his cuffs and tugged at the wrists of his gloves. 'Baek,' he called out.

Officer Baek, who was still taking notes, looked up from Mrs. Shim's oral report.

'Have officers Cha and Rhee investigate her claim,' said the commissioner. 'Tell them to take two constables with them.'

'Yes, sir… Er, I am still taking down her report.'

'She can finish telling her story on the way. Accompany them. *Now.*'

'Of course, Your Commissionership.' Officer Baek looked down at his sheet of paper, and snapping to attention, he squared his shoulders. 'We will continue this at your apartment.' Grabbing his hat and coat, he ushered Mrs. Shim out the door and was halfway out the door himself when he slammed his hand against the doorjamb and turned around to run back to his desk. Grabbing his pen and the unfinished report, he folded it in half along the crease and stuffed it into his pouch. He had a feeling he knew how the story was going to end.

SIX

Professor Ku stepped back from the board, dropping a piece of chalk onto his desk as he read out loud the quote he had written on the board. The chalk rolled along the desktop and fell to the floor, shattering into several pieces, startling the professor, who turned around midsentence and bent down to pick it up. He was still on the floor when the door flung open. A military police officer walked in with four other officers behind him all dressed in khakis with gleaming pistols, black bats hooked into their belts.

'Professor Ku,' the officer said, the other officers marching in behind him, their black boots scuffing the pale green linoleum. They stopped by the professor's desk, opening their stance to a V, with their hands on holsters, eyes like gun sights. Suja darted a fearful glance at Jin, then quickly looked away.

'Professor *Ku*,' the officer repeated.

The professor was still crouched on the floor, unsure of whether he should stand or remain frozen where he was.

Jin was sitting to the left of the professor's desk, in his usual seat, in plain view of the officers. He tilted his face down as they surveyed the room, grateful they were standing to his right; they would not be able to see his bruise. Their eyes scanned the class, and it was all Jin could do to remain seated in his chair. Jin wanted to tear off his face, change his identity, run and hide, be anywhere other than here, and indeed his legs were tensed and ready to run. But he remained frozen in his seat. He didn't dare turn around and look at Suja. It was too late, too late to do anything.

'Jin Lee Park?' the officer called out. 'Answer, Jin Lee Park!'

Jin's heart was pounding, blood singing in his ears as he heard his own voice, as if from a distance. 'Yes, sir.'

He didn't believe this was happening.

The officer cocked his head toward him. 'Jin Lee Park? Come with us.'

Time slowed and the classroom wavered and darkened before Jin's eyes. He rose from his seat as if his body were levitating and reached down to grab his things. The books slid in slow motion, one over the other, and thudded against his hip. *What a stupid thing to do*, he thought. *I won't need books where they're taking me.* He couldn't feel his legs, but he saw his feet move, first his left foot kicking out, then the right heel, then toe hitting the floor in slow motion, each step taking forever to land. The officer jumped and yanked him by the arm.

'Saekee, you thought you'd never get caught?' He cuffed Jin's bruised cheek and pushed him down until he was face-down on the floor. He dropped his knee onto his back, grinding him down. He let up as two other officers grabbed Jin's arms and dragged him to the door, the toes of his boots scraping along the linoleum.

Suja's heart was at her throat, her hands balled into fists in her lap. She trembled with the urge to run after them, to

scream, to do anything, but she pressed her lips tight even as
her heart thumped against her chest. What was happening?
Why had the officers come for Jin, what had he done? A terrifying thought clarified in the midst of a jumble of questions:
those arrested by the state police never returned.

Suja looked up at Professor Ku, who had collapsed in his
chair, his shirt splotched with perspiration. There must have
been some huge mistake. Why wasn't Professor Ku saying
anything? Whatever Jin was being accosted for, he was innocent! They had to point this out before Jin was taken away,
before Jin would become one of the *disappeared*.

But they were out the door before Suja could even move a
muscle. The officers had been in the classroom for no more
than a couple of minutes, and they had left as abruptly as they
had entered, leaving the class paralyzed with fear. Professor
Ku lifted a shaking hand and wiped his brow, looking out at
the class with a pained expression. No one said a word. Professor Ku struggled for his breath, casting a despairing glance
at the students.

'We will...' He paused, searching for his next words. 'We
will continue our lesson on reporting styles,' he said, his unfocused gaze falling randomly on student after student, until
it finally landed on Kyung-bok.

'Kyung-bok, do you...do you remember where we were?'

Kyung-bok glanced nervously at Suja. 'We were studying
reporting styles of the KCNA.'

'Yes,' said Professor Ku, nodding. 'That's what we were
studying. And do you remember which style we were discussing, Mee-ran?' He directed his question to Kyung-bok's
friend, who sat next to her. Mee-ran was speechless, her eyes
still wide with shock.

Professor Ku passed over her to address the students in
the front row. 'Joon-ok?' he asked.

'Catastrophe,' said Joon-ok.

'Yes,' the professor said, collapsing back in his chair again. 'Catastrophe.' He fumbled for a broken piece of chalk from his desk and turned to write on the chalkboard.

Suja sat rigid with disbelief. Was nobody going to do anything? Was no one going to acknowledge what happened? Surely the professor could say something to the officers to vouch for Jin and they could retrieve him back. They had to get him back before he was taken away. But as each moment passed and the class obediently followed along with the lesson that the professor had resumed, it became clear that no one would do anything to save Jin.

He was gone.

Suja's breath quickened, her ribs jerking with every shuddering inhalation. She knew it would be as if the arrest never occurred; worse, it would be as if Jin had never existed. No one would ever mention this incident again. She wondered frantically where she could go to find Jin, whether she could ask her father or any of his colleagues about where Jin might have been taken. But of course, she couldn't bring it up with them, she realized, and tears rolled silently down her cheeks. She herself could be reported.

SEVEN

Three hundred miles away on a windless, frigid morning, throngs of people gathered at the Kanggye train station under the sheath of a gray-white frozen sky. A crowd of men and women had gathered, stamping their feet, breaths billowing in front of them. It had been announced that the Cornmeal Culprit had been found and they were all summoned to witness the public flogging, and so they came with their babies strapped to their backs, their quilted jackets stuffed with newspapers for warmth, handkerchiefs tied around their faces to keep their cheeks and noses from getting frostbite. They came pushing carts full of sticks they had been foraging; they came with wan, empty faces, hunger cleaving to their bodies. Slowly they filled the old train station, pushing one another against walls peeling layers of paint, pillars grimy from years of use. Sparrow orphans darted among the crowd, furtive and desperate, searching for scraps of food.

Across from the main landing on platform two, a group of

military police milled about, flicking their cigarettes, their flat-topped khaki hats catching the light as they turned to glance at the growing audience. They looked ready to ship out, but instead of watching for the next train, their attention was focused inward toward the center of their group. Several of them stepped aside, opening the phalanx so that the crowd on the other platform could see a young man kneeling before an older man. A murmur arose from the crowd. It was Jin Lee Park, that scholarship student, and his father. Were they the cornmeal thieves?

A sergeant shouted to the throngs of people in a clear voice that ricocheted off the concrete platforms and pillars.

'The Cornmeal Culprit was apprehended yesterday in Pyong-yang. The coward stole the cornmeal and fled town hoping to hide himself, but we found him, still bearing telltale injuries, proof that he is indeed the thief. Look at him!' The sergeant pulled Jin up to standing and pushed him around on the plat-form, holding him out to the crowds for all to see. The swelling on the left side of Jin's face had gone down, but his cheek was still bruised and discolored. 'Jin Lee Park, the shining scholar-ship boy from Kanggye, *he* is the Cornmeal Culprit!' He shook Jin by the arm. 'This boy, this traitor, who had been given so much by the Dear Leader, turns around and steals from the very hand that gave to him. He bit the nipple that suckled him. Jin Lee Park, you are hereby banished for life to Yodok labor camp.' The sergeant threw him to the ground. 'But first, your father has something to say to you.' The sergeant stepped aside and, crossing his arms behind his back, glanced point-edly at Mr. Park.

'You say you had nothing to do with your bastard's thiev-ing?' he asked.

Mr. Park stood tensely facing his son, sweat beading on his slick face despite the frigid air.

'I knew nothing about it, sir,' he shouted.

'You renounce him?'

'He is not a part of the Park family.'

'Tell that to his face.' The sergeant nudged Jin's knee with his toe.

Mr. Park opened his mouth to speak, drawing his lips back, quivering. He had practiced his speech many times, but now that he was about to say it to his son in front of the entire town, he hesitated; a drop of sweat slid from his brow. He tasted salt.

'What's that, old man?'

Mr. Park nodded and, facing the crowd, started to speak. 'You have committed an act of high treason and have brought shame to our house. No son of mine would have committed such a crime, and so you are no longer my son. You are dead to me. I renounce you, Jin Lee Park—you are no one to me, and no Park in Pyungnam Bukdo will open their doors to you from this day forward! You are a cursed traitor of Chosun and there will be no mercy.' His voice broke with these final words.

'And? What are you waiting for?' the sergeant yelled, pulling his boot back and kicking Jin in his ribs so hard he was knocked over toward the edge of the train platform. Mr. Park reached for the belt around his waist and frantically began to unloosen the buckle. His pants were cinched by an old leather belt, and when he pulled it off, he had to grab his pant waist to keep them from falling down. The soldiers laughed as they watched Mr. Park fold the waistline of his pants over once, twice, so that the waistband would sit on his hips. Mr. Park then wrapped the belt around his hand, and getting a firm grip, he turned his head, lifted the belt and cracked it across Jin's back.

Jin stiffened against the slash of the leather across his back.

He breathed hard and fast through his nose as he waited for the next blow, and in that interval a new awareness was torn open in him. He was completely alone in the world; no family, no ally, not even Young-na on his side. The only thing he had was the ground beneath his feet and the cold, cracked sky overhead.

Snap. The belt cracked across Jin's back, searing into him. He became that strip of fire that blistered his back. With each blow, Jin wanted to cry out and strike back, but he forced himself to submit and wait for the next hit. Guards jabbed him and cussed at him as his body shook, nostrils flaring with animal panic.

'Not like that,' the officer barked. 'He thinks he's scolding a baby,' he jeered. 'Beat him properly, or we'll do it for you!'

Mr. Park wiped a trail of spittle off his chin. He was already hitting Jin as hard as he could—what more could he do? Did he have to beat his own son to death? Still, if there was a way to spare his son greater punishment at the hands of the soldiers, he would do it. By the Everlasting Leader, he would yell viciously, make the belt crack, do everything he could to convince the guards that Jin was getting the punishment he deserved. 'Stand up!' he yelled in a hoarse voice, the tendons in his neck standing out.

Jin struggled to get up, and as he straightened, his father whipped the backs of his legs until his hamstrings screamed with sensation. Jin collapsed to his knees, then willed himself up again. Somehow his quaking body responded. He felt his consciousness slip into a chasm between here and somewhere very far away.

'Get up, I said!' his father yelled as he lashed him again. *Crack*, the belt slashed his buttocks and his legs. Jin fell again, crumpling into the pain. He focused on a single point in order not to lose himself to the pain.

'Get up on your feet.' Mr. Park's voice was thick with emotion. He was desperate for his son to stand so he could avoid hitting his shoulders or his head. 'Up, damn you. *Up!*'

'You call that a beating, old man?' the officer yelled. 'You've forgotten how to hit.' He picked up a truncheon and raised it at Mr. Park, who flinched. He turned and flailed at his son, who was still struggling to get up on his feet. *Whack, whack.* The belt whistled through the air. Mr. Park was sweating, a guttural grunt with each swing.

'Why let this grandmother do it? We'll finish this job off properly,' one of the officers called out.

'The little bastard deserves to die!' said another.

'Get it done. Kill him!'

One of the officers leaped forward and kicked Jin.

The sergeant sucked his teeth. 'Did I tell any of you to move? Stand down and watch.'

The other soldiers jeered, 'But the grandmother's so weak!'

Mr. Park doubled his efforts, the tendons in his neck stretched taut as he slung the belt, his eyes gone wild. Jin was nearly doubled over as the blows hit him across his shoulders and his back, the soldiers goading his father on, the world closing in around him in the dark frenzy. Jin shut his mind down, closing himself off until he was no longer inside his body, but he was a tightly clenched fist, a dark smudge of space inside that fist, an irreducible point of pure pain.

'Here, old man.' The sergeant stepped in and grabbed the belt from Mr. Park's hand. Mr. Park backed off, weeping uncontrollably. He had to save the rest of the family; they were good as lost now that the family name was blackened, and Jin… Jin…there was no future for him anymore. His only son.

Jin lay on the ground, his body wet with sweat and mottled with welts that oozed blood. He could hear the faint sound of a woman sobbing. Were his mother and sister here? He tried to get up, pushing himself up on one knee. Then, wavering, he raised himself to stand up on both feet. The ground slanted and slid beneath his feet.

'Face your father,' barked the sergeant.

Jin turned but kept his face averted. There was something cold dripping down the side of his neck. Blood. He could hear his mother and sister clearly now, who were pleading, 'We beg you, please spare him. Don't kill him, please!'

'Look at him, you bastard,' said the sergeant.

Jin raised his eyes to see his father, whose pants had unraveled and hung low on his hips, his hair disheveled and eyes red with exertion. His father's eyes stayed leveled at his son's feet.

'Look at your son, old man,' the sergeant barked.

Mr. Park looked up but could not meet Jin's eyes.

The officer leered at Jin.

'All right, old man. We'll finish off what you began.'

The sergeant pushed Mr. Park aside and grabbed a length of pipe, the kind favored by the state police, and brought it crashing down onto Jin's back. The other soldiers jumped in with their heels, their pipes, their fists and boots, so many of them crowding around trying to get their kicks in, bludgeoning Jin to the ground.

Jin's sister fell into a soundless screaming fit, her hands mashed against her mouth to prevent herself from making a sound, while Jin's mother collapsed into shuddering convulsions. Mr. Park stood off to the side, watching the soldiers as tears streamed down his cheeks. They were beating his son to death right before his eyes. He had allowed this.

EIGHT

In the months following Jin's arrest, Suja struggled to keep up a semblance of normalcy, but she was slowly drifting, separating from those around her. Jin was on her mind all the time, and she missed him wholly, completely, terribly. She could hardly stand stepping foot in school but found it worse when she was at home, so she attended classes despite the growing sensation that she was slipping outside the skin of everything she knew—her family, her school friends, the newspaper, her entire life all felt strange to her now.

The portraits of the Dear Leader in the classrooms started to look different, as if during the night someone had sneaked in and took out the originals and slipped in retouched photos. There was that familiar crown of combed-back black hair, the same bright eyes that had been the guiding light in Suja's life for as long as she could remember, but the smile that used to comfort her now seemed buffoonish, and the red cheeks glowed with preternatural health. It had never bothered her before, but now, like so many things since Jin's arrest, she couldn't stand it.

She sat in her chair watching dully as Professor Choon stood at the chalkboard lecturing about the Korean Central News Agency rhetoric style. This was a class she normally dominated, but today she wasn't participating. The KCNA had announced that Jin had been apprehended as the infamous Cornmeal Culprit, and the news came down like a hammer blow that sent reverberating shocks for weeks. Suja knew Jin was not capable of stealing. Why would Jin steal? Even if he were to steal, why would he risk his entire life and career *for cornmeal*, of all things? He was a scholarship student with a meal plan. For the first time in her life, she found herself doubting the KCNA—not only doubting it, but she was convinced the news agency was absolutely wrong.

Professor Choon scribbled a quote onto the chalkboard, which he finished with an emphatic period, and set the chalk down. He turned to the class. 'To match the exalted tone of the Leader, you have to find metaphors and similes grand enough to speak of his largesse, his effectiveness, his wisdom,' he said. 'The revered Mount Paektu, for example, is the penultimate landform that speaks of the Dear Leader's pure and divine ancestry and leadership.'

Choon went on to list other images that would suit: crop fields that rippled into bountiful harvests, schools of codfish and whales that leaped onto trawlers to offer themselves to the Dear Leader. 'You have to search for new metaphors, the *best* metaphors to do justice to the Glorious Leader. He is the unifying principle of our lives, he is the light that pushes every kernel of corn toward harvest, he is the center of gravity, the Mount Paektu, around which the stars rotate. And you—' he pointed at the class '—must prove yourself worthy to describe his greatness.'

Suja listened guardedly, wondering if this was the work of the KCNA and the Rodong newspaper—if they were the ones writing the Dear Leader's words—then what, if anything, was based on what the Dear Leader actually said? How much of the words attributed to the Dear Leader was the work of, say, her father's colleague, Paik Nam, the Rodong staff writer who wrote pithy koans; or Central News Agency staff writer Joon Lee, whose sense of bravado writ the Dear Leader large and indomitable, achieving astonishing feats of courage; or Yoo-jung, who wrote compassionate monologues voicing the Dear Leader's love of his people? Suja struggled to stay with her 'good mind' as a Party member and daughter of the Rodong newspaper editor, but the KCNA had reported an out-and-out lie about Jin; and clearly the Rodong writers were more fiction writers than reporters. She had always been true and faithful to the Party, but a trapdoor had opened and every-thing she held to be true and fundamental was slipping, fall-ing into an abyss.

Two hundred fifty miles away on the outskirts of Pyong-yang, a black Range Rover headed north on a highway trav-eling at sixty-five miles per hour. Following three car lengths behind was a jet-black Mercedes-Benz S-Class sedan, followed by two more black Range Rovers. The cars in the convoy were the only ones on this strip of road, speeding along the weed-stippled countryside past rows of concrete housing, dirt lanes striped in between them like irrigating ditches. The pa-perboard row houses appeared empty, but nearby there were handfuls of people squatted on their haunches beside coal-fire cook pots bubbling with steam. The Mercedes sped past them, a black stone on ice, leaving a ripple of dark heads turning in its wake. One rarely saw a Mercedes-Benz on the road, for only a few people in the country owned one, including, most notably, the Dear Leader.

Jong-un leaned his forehead against the window with golden earbuds in his ears. Outside the passenger window the state housing was giving way to frozen fields with frost-covered furrows of soil. Wooden fence posts zipped by, each post a visual blip that was timed to the rhythm to the beat of the song he was listening to—Rush's 'Xanadu.' He had been called back into the country by his father from Bern, Switzerland, where Jong-un had been studying and where he had grown accustomed to a European way of life. Now that he was back in North Korea, he was bored. Not just the average nothing-to-do kind of dissatisfaction, it was a feeling of ennui so extreme, so excruciatingly intense it was indistinguishable from hatred, or rage; it was perhaps both. He experienced this uniquely in his own country, and it was times like these he wanted to shed his own skin. He felt a tap on his hand and opened his eyes to see that Father was saying something to him. He pulled his earbuds out.

'A person's haircut says a lot, Jong-un,' said Kim Jong-il. 'It tells you whether they are a high class or low class. People make judgments based on hair.'

'Yae,' Jong-un responded dutifully, as he was meant to, using the polite form *yae*.

Jong-il's lips turned down in a frown, not convinced the boy got his point about the hair. And it wasn't just the hair; he was displeased by his suit jacket, which was a three-buttoned European cut made of a smooth wool fabric, almost shiny in its smoothness. With that Italian suit, that ridiculous haircut of his and the iPod earbuds permanently stuck in his ears, his son looked like a gangster. This was not to say Jong-il was opposed to new styles and fashion, for didn't he himself single-handedly revolutionize his country's fashion sense? The problem with his son's style was that it smelled of foreignness; it stank, it reeked of the fact that Jong-un had not lived in Chosun for years. Had the boy forgotten who he was? Forgotten his bloodline?! Jong-il sat back, disgruntled.

The frozen fields were giving way to mountainous terrain as farm fields and housing collectives disappeared. Now on either side of the road were steep craggy inclines with no trees, let alone buildings of any kind. The narrow shoulder disappeared as the road cut into a wall of rust-striated gray rock, and the car swerved suddenly around two men at the side of the road pulling wooden carts filled with sticks and debris. Only two more hours to Yodok prison.

Jin awoke slowly, sensing his body one inch at a time. Flames of sensation seared the backs of his hands, piercing through wounds on his arms and legs; ribs pinched with every breath; even his eyelids, the skin on his forehead hurt. He lay with his eyes closed, breathing steadily, listening to a low rumbling that grew louder and more distinct until he was able to make out the sound of someone moaning. Was that coming from somewhere outside his body, or was it himself making the noise?

Ugh, the stink of pus and stale urine. Where in dog's world was he? He opened his eyes and saw a tangle of legs and arms slowly cohere into a scene. He was lying among dozens of men and women in a long room that had a series of barred doors along its sides. It took a moment before he realized the barred doors were locked on their side; they weren't in a room, they were corralled inside a prison hallway, and on the other side of those doors were the prison cells.

Sunlight streamed in at the end of the hall. Two guards grabbed men by their shirtfronts and shoved them out the door as a couple of other guards stepped through the huddled crowd, heavy black boots landing on ankles, hands, anything that got in the way.

'*Ya eema,*' a guard cussed and grabbed Jin by his jacket collar, yanked him over and shoved him out the door. Jin felt his lungs pinch in pain as he gulped the frigid air. A pale sun, high in the sky. No warmth there. Chains clanked, frigid metal links against skin. Jin looked up to see hundreds of prisoners in the yard, some shackled together, wrists to haunches, like livestock at a charnel house. They lowered their desultory heads, giving themselves over to kicks and punches from the guards. Jin glowered. Stupid beasts. There were enough men to form several mining teams, or enough to stage a mutiny and overtake the guards. But none of them were thinking of escape.

Jin was pushed to the side of the courtyard near the stockade, where a group of prisoners huddled together near a foul-smelling garbage bin. He felt his shoulder sink against something soft and yielding and turned around to see he had bumped against a man in his midforties with wavy black hair; flat, sunken cheeks; and a fleshy, jowly chin that jiggled. It was the strangest sensation to feel the soft corpulence of his body. Here was a man who knew the taste of meat and duk cakes, the kind of man who received gift bottles of scotch whiskey from his underlings—the kind of man Jin had imagined he himself would become one day. Jin reached down with his bruised hands to cover his toes, which pushed through the holes in his boots. For a split second he saw himself as others might see him: a scrawny, beat-up saekee, a criminal. Yet he himself had been privileged too, hadn't he? He *had been* a privileged scholarship student in Pyongyang, with his high-class girlfriend and a brilliant career ahead of him.

The man beside him radiated warmth, and Jin let himself settle against him. The man was solid, meaty, like an animal within an animal, protected within a layer of himself. How could a man like this be stripped of his privilege and stature and brought to prison?

The fellow moved again, this time wriggling against Jin. 'Get off me,' he snapped.

'I can't.'

'Move over,' he snarled, showing a flash of silver in his teeth.

'There's no space,' said Jin, noticing the silver claws of a partial denture. Only rich people were able to afford dental work like that.

'Order yourselves in rows,' the guard shouted. 'The Dear Leader is visiting. Get ready to salute.'

Jin's eyes widened as the prisoners around him listlessly picked themselves up. The Dear Leader coming to this prison? But why? Of all the possible scenarios in which to meet the Dear Leader, never had he imagined it would be at a prison. He tried to shrink down and disappear into the row behind him, but a guard came and pushed him back to the front. 'Stay up there, gaesakee. Don't move.'

The presidential cars rolled into the Yodok courtyard, silent, otherworldly, onyx bullets glistening in the snowy prison yard. Kim Jong-il got out of the passenger seat and pulled himself to standing, immediately recoiling from the cold. He rubbed the shaved side of his head, then tucked his hand inside his Persian lamb coat, slipping it in between the front buttons. He liked the feel of the soft fur, found it soothing to touch. He turned to the car and gestured at his son with a down-turned hand, as if coaxing a puppy to venture out. Jong-un, however, chose to exit from his side of the car and stretched his arms, casting his eyes up at the pale, vast sky. His jacket and sweater rode up, exposing his belly. He sucked in his gut and quickly pulled them down, shrugging his jacket back into place. It was too tight; the jacket was too tight.

Secretary Rhee had already jumped out of the first car and was approaching them, his lean, weaselly body bending in an ellipse as he lurched and scuttled to Jong-il's side and brought his hand close to his elbow, not quite touching him. He guided him toward Sergeant Yu, who, along with his squadron of prison guards, had been standing with his hand raised in salute since the cars had rolled to a stop. Kim Jong-il stood next to Sergeant Yu with his legs spread apart and surveyed the prison with moonfaced calm and certitude.

The prisoners had been called to stand in the courtyard, some of them wearing the remnants of their civilian clothes, others dressed in the shapeless shifts of gray prison garb. Row after row as far as the eye could see, they stood lined up like sacks of rice, or, thought Kim Jong-il as he cast a baleful eye over the nameless and faceless crowd, like little gray matchsticks. Line up all the matchsticks and what are they good for? Not even a campfire. Where did they come from, and why did more appear every year?

'Supreme Commander, you have graced us with the honor of your presence.' Sergeant Yu bowed. 'We are overjoyed and humbled to receive you at Yodok 13.' The sergeant bowed deeply and swung open his stance to face the sea of prisoners below.

'The Supreme Commander, Comrade Kim, has arrived,' he shouted. Secretary Rhee nudged Jong-un, guiding him forward, and all prisoners raised their arms in a flickering of hands that swept across the yard like a ragged wave, cresting, then scattering into bits of foam. Kim Jong-il observed with his mouth closed, jaw hanging loose, giving him the slack-jawed look of senility.

Determined to get a proper salute from his wards, Sergeant

Yu addressed the prisoners again. 'Salute again!' he yelled in a hoarse voice, straining the tendons in his neck. 'This time in unison, or we'll whip you worthless curs to death in front of the Dear Leader. Ready, one...two...*salute!*'

Hundreds of hands shot up again across the yard, and Jin, in the front row, held his arm straight and rigid. Sergeant Yu walked over to him.

'This one, Your Excellency, is the Cornmeal Culprit. Caught earlier this winter.'

Jin recoiled in shame, dying a thousand deaths as the Dear Leader's gaze landed on him. All his life he had dreamed of meeting the Dear Leader and imagined it to be the crowning moment of his life, but here he was, shackled like a criminal. It was devastatingly humiliating. He couldn't bring himself to look up, but then he realized at that moment that this could very well be his only chance to explain himself.

'Your Excellency...' He ventured to raise his head until he could see the Dear Leader's waist, the crisp crease in his pant legs. 'With your permission, I wanted to say there's been a mistake,' Jin said. 'I'm not supposed to be here. I'm not a thief. I'm a scholarship student at Kim Il-Sung University!'

A guard hit him against the back of his head. 'Shut up! You dare speak to the Dear Leader?'

Out of the corner of his eye, Jin could see Kim Jong-il turn away with a look of distaste.

'Merciful Leader,' Jin wept. 'Your Excellency, please, a moment to consider, I'm innocent...'

The guard kicked him once, twice, and Jin wrapped his arms around himself to protect himself. The Dear Leader was walking away, joining his son and the entourage as they headed toward the anthracite factories in the east wing of the prison. They passed the stockade with the garbage bin as they went, and the Dear Leader wrinkled his nose at the rank smell of rotting fish or offal coming from the bins.

'What's that smell? Something rotten?' He held his hand across his nose.

'It's garbage, Supreme Commander,' said Sergeant Yu.

A guard ran to the bin and pushed it away from the building, its wheels pivoting and squealing as he passed the entourage. Kim Jong-un peered into the bin and saw a grisly slick of bloody placental sacs, the twisted lifeless limbs of babies and other bloody bits, curled and slick with afterbirth.

'What's that?' he cried with alarm.

'Dead babies, no concern,' said Sergeant Yu. 'The bastard children of women who defected. Those traitors were found in China and sent back to us.'

Jong-un coughed. The guard hurriedly pushed the bin across the courtyard as Secretary Rhee stepped back to guide Jong-un into the prison building. 'Please, let's continue. I am so sorry for this disturbance, Dear Leader.'

'Why wasn't the prison cleaned?' Kim Jong-il griped. 'This is disrespectful.'

'Your Excellency, our deepest apologies. The entire prison was cleaned. This must be from the ongoing work that is being done today.'

Jin watched in despair as the Dear Leader headed into the building. His crushingly brief encounter with the Dear Leader winked out his last light of hope.

'Hey, forget it, kid.' The man at his side nudged him in the ribs. 'It'll do no good trying to talk to him. Focus on these guys here.' He nodded at the guards. 'They're the masters of our fate now.'

NINE

The Rodong office was silent when she walked in. Mr. Roh, the photo editor, was not at his desk. Apba was in his chair, leaned back with the phone tucked in the crook of his neck, his brush-cut hair glistening in the light as he nodded. A waxed column of text was stuck to his finger, and he shook it back and forth. Suja walked past her father and dropped some photos on Mr. Roh's desk, looking around to see where the editors might be. Apba dropped the receiver back in its cradle and pushed his glasses up on his furrowed brow.

'Late again, Suja,' he said, his voice limned with irony; it was the voice he used with her at the office.

'I was held back in class, so I couldn't start developing photos until late.' She rushed her words, trying to hide the tremor in her voice.

'See, I told you.' Apba stuck the text onto his desk and crossed his hands behind his head. His shirtsleeves were rolled up, revealing his sinewy forearms. 'You shouldn't have accepted this second-year post. It's too much.'

'Yes, you told me.'

He reached out with his hand and tapped her temple with his finger—a hard tap, tap.

'Then get it through your head.'

He watched her arch her neck and pull away. She had an elegance about her, even when she was being disrespectful.

'For a smart girl, you don't know what's good for you.'

Suja shrugged. 'What's going on today?'

He gazed at her. 'What's wrong with you? You have no energy these days. You getting enough sleep?'

She shrugged again.

He scratched the back of his head, then flicked his fingers. 'We're adding a story about the crime of defection. There's a new black market opened up in town.'

Her eyebrows lifted. 'What about it?'

'They say brokers are working through them, bribing guards and vanishing people without a trace,' he answered. 'One of the agents is supposed to be a biscuit maker! Ha! A little baker, sending biscuits "up the way."'

'Up the way?'

'Escaping, defecting.'

'Really?' she asked. He had her full attention now.

'You don't need to know this kind of stuff.' He shook his head. 'People don't need to know.'

Suja's gaze blunted. She lifted the flap of her book bag and slid her photo folder back in between some papers and binders. 'So when is Mr. Roh coming back?'

'They're in a meeting. It'll be a while before they're out.'

'Can you tell him I dropped the photos off?'

'Sure.' He looked at her jacket. 'You didn't get a coat at the depot.'

'No, there weren't any left.' She lifted out a folder, then slid it back in.

'There weren't any to begin with.'

She gave her father an annoyed look. 'How did you know? Why didn't you tell us…?'

'I only found out later. Did Umma say anything to them at the depot?'

Suja's hands stopped rummaging. 'What do you mean?'

'Did she talk to someone there?'

'Well, we talked with people there.'

'To the management, I mean.'

'She may have. I think she had a question.'

'About what?'

'Whether there were any coats left.'

'That's all?'

Suja straightened and looked deliberately at her father. 'I think so. Why?'

He flipped closed a notepad on his desk and pushed it aside, then lined up two pens at the top of his desk. 'Well?' he asked.

'That was it,' she said with a pause. 'I was off looking at other stuff in the store.'

'Hmm.' He stood up, tugged at his beltline and adjusted his pants. He looked at his daughter for a moment, then looked away. 'You should get going. You have a lot of homework.'

Suja cinched her book bag and pulled it over her shoulder. She had a growing sense of unease, and by the time she walked out of the building, there were goose bumps on her arms. Apba wasn't just asking questions about their outing a couple of weeks ago. That felt like an interrogation. Why would he feel the need to interrogate her about the depot? Up until this moment Suja had thought nothing of their trip to the depot, but now she wondered if Umma could have done something wrong. Her mother's sense of diplomacy and politics was so honed it would be hard to imagine what she could have done wrong. But could she have offended the superintendent? Was she being investigated, and was Apba being pressured by the Party to question her? Suja had a horrifying thought: He wouldn't inform on Umma, would he? Surely he wouldn't.

She remembered how Uncle Koo had suddenly disappeared from their lives. Apba's closest college friend worked with him at the newspaper and would come over to their house almost every week until the day he vanished. He had left his home for work but then never showed up and never returned home either. His disappearance was the first fault line in Suja's safe and predictable world. Apba and Umma never spoke of him again, and Suja knew she was not supposed to ask questions about him. But with Jin's arrest, the questions kept coming, leading to bigger questions about the inner workings of the Party and KCNA. Now Apba was inquiring about Umma's actions at the depot.

If only she could speak to Jin. *Oh, Jin, where are you?* No one, not even family, could be trusted. Shivering in her jacket, Suja hunched into herself as she pressed forward into the cold night.

TEN

With a clattering thunder, dark chunks of anthracite tumbled onto the conveyor belt, spewing a cloud of gray dust over the factory floor. Jin stood next to other prisoners alongside the shuddering assembly belt amid the cacophony of clanking metal and chugging motors. He looked down the length of the assembly line at dozens of men stationed several feet apart along the length of the conveyor, which chugged and rippled like a human-machine caterpillar. Across from him was the paunchy man he had met in the prison yard. He had learned his name was Hyuk, and next to him was his friend Bae, who was the taller of the two, and slimmer. They were both among the stronger men on the crew, handily picking off rocks that were streaked with the dark luster of anthracite, some as big as babies' heads. Dust rose from every clacking joint of the conveyor, covering them in a fine gray powder that coated their fingers and painted their faces with ghoulish, cadaverous shadows.

They sorted rocks for five-hour shifts at a time, doing three shifts a day. Anyone who faltered or fell on the job was given one chance to get up again. He had seen a couple of men collapse, including an older grandpa who was too fatigued to get up and ended up being dragged away, never to be seen again.

At night the whole lot of them collapsed in a concrete room that had no furnishings, no features, save for two holes in the center that served as toilets. Jin didn't notice the foul stench of the toilets anymore, nor did he notice the limbs and bodies of the other men around him as they bedded down wearily like dogs resting their snouts and paws on one another. Only once everyone had settled would Jin allow himself the indulgence to tuck his hand inside his shirt to feel along his leather belt, which was cinched around his bare waist. Tucked inside the belt was a pair of leather gloves Suja had given to him as a present. He kept the precious gloves hidden under his shirt so that they wouldn't be confiscated. He loved the feel of them against his skin, as they were a tangible reminder of the life he and Suja had had, which was getting harder to remember as the days went by—the life he once led, the man he used to be.

The days at the anthracite factory assembly line bled into one another. They were given one meal of cornmeal and pine bark a day, and on those meager rations, and with the constant labor, Jin could feel his strength weaken. He could see it in Hyuk also, whose cheeks and face were slimming, his pants hanging loose on his body; they were all losing weight. He struck up a friendship of sorts with Hyuk and Bae and learned that the older men had been members of the Party with enough status to travel to other countries. They started bringing in cigarettes, booze and electronics from other countries to give to other Party members but got caught one day selling goods on the black market.

'The bastard who ratted us out is probably running stuff from China now, making good money.' Hyuk scratched his chin and sighed. 'I could have stayed in China and made a life there.'

'Yeah,' echoed Bae. 'We should have skipped out when we had the chance.'

'Really?' Jin marveled at the idea that he could have chosen to live in another country. 'Why didn't you?'

'I had a good life here,' said Bae. 'I didn't think one of our own bastards would rat me out.'

Hyuk shook his head ruefully. 'It's our fault we got soft. We deserve this.'

'No one deserves this,' countered Bae. 'But I guess we were stupid enough to end up here.' Bae laid his forearm over his head and closed his eyes.

Jin turned over onto his side, trying to imagine what China must be like as he fantasized about escaping from prison and heading there. His eyes brightened at the possibility of finding work and a place to live in China. He could forge a new life and reunite with Suja there. He started thinking about the weakest link in the chain of prison locations between the assembly line, the mess hall and back to the cell. It seemed damn near impossible to get away from the guards who were stationed at the factory and the mess hall. And there was no way he could start digging out of the cell with all the men crowded in there. No matter how much he turned it around in his mind, there was no real opportunity for escape.

He started watching the guards, taking note of who was stationed at the anthracite plant, how many were positioned at the mess hall. He watched them to learn their habits, to see which guards were easily distracted, which one was fidgety, which direction they came from when they walked in to switch shifts. When one of them showed up with a slight limp, he took note of the injury and the hour of his shift as he calculated his distance from the door, and whether he might be able to outrun him. He weighed the odds of making that move successfully, and then the odds of making it from the hall out to the prison yard without being caught, and then from there to the fence. There were too many doors, too great a distance for him to pull off an escape from the assembly line all the way to the fence.

Bae caught him watching the guards and said slyly, 'What're you doing?'

'Nothing,' Jin said, and focused on the rocks again, picking a few out and dropping them down to the lower conveyor belt.

'You hatching up a plan in that head of yours?' Bae pressed.

'Just admiring the uniforms.' Jin smirked.

'Hey,' Hyuk interrupted, pointing toward a young man standing near the chute at the end of the assembly line. 'Check out that guy over there. Wasn't he at the other end of the assembly yesterday?'

Jin shot a glance down the line and recognized the guy Hyuk was referring to, a lanky, muscular fellow with scruffy hair matted with dust. He'd noticed him before because he had kept changing his position on the line, whereas most people, including Hyuk and Bae, stuck to their usual positions. Now the guy was standing at the worst place on the assembly line, right under the conveyor belt that dumped detritus out the chute. Clouds of dust billowed around him as bits of rock fell from the noisy conveyor belt overhead.

'Crazy bastard.' Hyuk shook his head.

'The view's better there,' joked Bae. 'It's a little noisy and you got rocks falling on your head, but you're away from the guards.'

Jin stared at the young man, then glanced at the guard.
They were changing shifts, and the guard with the limp was
taking over.

That night as they were heading back into the cell for sleep,
they were stopped for head count, and it was discovered that
one person was missing from their crew. The guards ran
through roll call and identified that the missing prisoner was
the young fellow Hyuk and Jin had been talking about earlier in the day. They looked at one another.

'That bastard was up to something all along,' said Hyuk.

'When did he escape?' said Jin. 'Could it have been when
we were walking to the mess hall? He would have been the
last one out.'

'Maybe,' said Hyuk, looking skeptical.

'It's so open in the courtyard that someone would have seen
him,' Bae said, furrowing his brow. 'Maybe it was in the hall-
ways. There's so many turns we take. Maybe he managed to
slip out then and...'

'And jumped into one of the garbage trolleys?' suggested
Jin. 'I've thought of that a couple of times myself.'

'Who knows,' said Hyuk. 'The thing is, he made it out.'
He angled his head toward the window at the far end of their
cell. It opened onto a night sky that was dark and featureless,
not a star in sight.

'It's dark tonight, a good night for an escape. I hope the
little shit makes it.'

The next morning, the entire crew was marched into the
prison yard past guards who held back dogs that snarled and
barked, straining against their leashes. There was a man tied to
a stake in the center of the courtyard, and as they approached,
they could see it was the young guy who had escaped the night

before. His hands and his body were tied to the stake, but his head slumped forward, listless, and his shirt hung loose from his body, the buttons having been ripped off. As they got closer, Jin could see that he'd been beaten up badly and was bleeding.

As soon as the prisoners were settled in the courtyard, the guards unhitched the dogs from their leashes and they leaped toward the prisoner, barking and lunging for him. The man writhed and screamed as they attacked his legs and bit and tore at his belly. Jin, Hyuk, Bae and the rest of the prisoners watched in silent horror as the dogs jumped at him again and again, their teeth tearing into his flesh. The ordeal went on for twenty long minutes, until, whimpering, the man passed out unconscious.

The prisoner died on the stake, where he was left for days. The guards marched the other prisoners past him every day when they walked to the mess hall for their meal.

Morale dropped. Hyuk and Bae stopped telling Jin stories about China, and Jin despaired of ever getting out. At night he ran his fingers across his leather gloves, thinking of Suja, wishing he could touch her. He remembered the day Suja gave the gloves to him on one of the last days they had spent together.

He was in the coed kitchen heating up the charcoal barbecue to make duk patties for supper, the usual. Suja walked in from outside with a blast of wintry air, the cold still fresh on her red cheeks.

'I have a surprise for you!' She beamed and placed a package in his hands. He saw the Depot 12 logo on the wrapping paper and touched it gingerly. He rarely got new things, let alone anything from a government depot.

'You shouldn't have,' he mumbled awkwardly.

'Open it,' Suja urged.

He touched the paper again, reluctant, then unfolded the

wrapping paper to reveal two gloves inside. Jin looked up at Suja, then back down at the gift, still nestled in the wrapping paper. Real leather gloves. He laid his hands across them.

'I can't accept this. This is way too… I don't need this.'

'Yes, you do. Try them on, please. Let me see.'

'No.' He handed her the gloves. Suja shied away from him, stuffing her hands into her pockets.

'What are you doing, Opba? It's a gift. You can't give it back. What would I do with them?'

'Return them. It's too much.'

'Come on, try them on.' Suja pushed the gloves back toward him.

Jin ran his fingers along the gloves, feeling the stiff leather skin, and on the inside the soft woolen lining. He slid a hand in one glove, wriggling his fingers as he pulled it tight and flexed his fingers. He turned his hand over and back. It fit perfectly.

'I've never had anything so fine,' he said finally, his voice thick with emotion.

Suja looked down, feeling suddenly embarrassed. 'They're only gloves,' she mumbled softly.

'Only gloves?' he said, and running his hands along her back and ribs, he tickled her. 'But what these gloves can do,' he teased.

'Stop it! I'm taking them back!'

'Never.' He kept tickling. 'They're gonna haunt you for the rest of your life.'

'You idiot!' she gasped through her laughter. 'I shouldn't have gotten them.'

Jin stopped tickling and collapsed next to her, draping an arm across her shoulder. Suja turned to face him, her eyes searching his as she reached up to lightly trace the lines of his bruised cheek. He lifted her fingers from his cheek and brought them to his lips and kissed them. Even her fingers, he loved the very tips of her.

'I have something for you too,' he said, and got up. Reaching into his knapsack, he fished out the small velvet sack. He dropped it into her hand. She looked down at the navy blue pouch, feeling the heft of it in her palm. Suja pulled the drawstring slowly to reveal the jade hoop snake necklace with the gold chain puddled around it.

'It's from my mother,' said Jin.

Suja gasped as she looked at it. 'Oh my goodness…' She bent down to get a closer look at the ornate carving of the necklace, and the diamond glittered as it caught the light. She could see the scales etched into the length of the dragon body that curled in a perfect circle until its teeth enclosed around its own tail.

'This is…this is too much. It's a family heirloom,' she protested.

'My mother would want you to have it.'

Suja ran her finger along the smooth jade stone, tracing the round nubs of its eyes and the raised crest along its back. What did it mean, this dragon eating its own tail?

'It's my grandmother's necklace,' said Jin. 'They managed to keep it hidden through two wars and even during our state raids. During the Japanese occupation, they had to go through checkpoints with jewelry and money sewn into their clothes. Once, both she and my grandmother were strip-searched, and they had to take off their coats, sweaters, skirts and long johns. My mother laid her clothes down carefully because they were so layered with jewels that they would have jingled if she dropped them! The soldiers weren't looking at her clothes, though,' he said bitterly. 'She was only eleven years old.'

Suja looked at the necklace in her hand and felt the weight of that history carried inside that small jade loop.

'Here, let me put it on you.' Jin picked it up and wrapped it around her neck, struggling with the clasp in the dim light. He finally managed to close the clasp. 'There.' He pulled away and looked at the gleaming jade hoop snake at Suja's sternum and looked up to see her eyes shining at him. He traced the necklace against her skin, filled with pride at seeing Suja wearing this important family piece. He had never imagined giving it away, but seeing it on Suja, he felt his past and his present come together into one coherent moment; she was the woman uniting these two parts of him, making him whole.

'This is your necklace now,' he said in a low voice. 'You have my heart and I'll be with you always.'

Suja's eyes brimmed with emotion.

Jin turned over on his side, remembering the feel of her hair against his cheek as they embraced. He tucked his hand inside his shirt and held the gloves lightly, fondling the softened leather. Hyuk lay on the concrete in front of him, watching him, then reached over to flick up Jin's shirt.

Jin's hand froze. 'Fuck off.'

'So that's why you've always got your hand on your stomach.' Hyuk chuckled. 'I was beginning to wonder if you were sick. You know those things are meant for your hands, not your belly.'

'Shut up. I don't want to lose 'em.'

'Okay, I get it,' Hyuk said, bemused by Jin's caginess. He had touched a nerve. 'They're special, huh? Who gave them to you?'

'My girlfriend.'

'Ah, you had a girlfriend.'

'I *have* a girlfriend.' Jin shot him a dark look.

'Not much use to her now, though, are you?'

'I'll see her again. I'll get out of this place and be with her again.'

Hyuk's face grew serious. 'Good luck with that,' he said, and closed his eyes.

ELEVEN

Dysentery hit the prisoners one by one, and they were dying in their cells. The guards cussed at them as they tugged them out, pulling them by their hair and kicking them. 'Shitty bastards,' they laughed, their lips curled in disgust. 'Anyone whose ass is dribbling goes this way—' the guard pointed down one hall '—and the others go this way. You get to sleep outside.' He pointed to the courtyard. They walked out to the courtyard, and Jin warily eyed the stake where the escapee had been left to die. The ground beneath it was still stained with dark splatters of blood.

A guard named Boon approached him with a loose length of chain dangling from his hands. He had been shackling the prisoners but had run out of chain and had to stop with ten more men, including Jin, left to handcuff. Boon dropped the chain and it landed in the dirt with a dull *ka-chink*. He stuffed his hands in his armpits.

'Go get some rope,' he said to a taller guard, Dae-gun, who stood across from him.

'No. Rope won't do.' Dae-gun shook his head and called out to a man in an overcoat. 'Sergeant! The leftover ones, do we take them back inside?'

'No, tie them together,' said the sergeant. 'Tie their hands and feet.'

'*Tie* them?' said Dae-gun.

'Go get the rope. Just do it,' snapped Boon.

Dae-gun hocked up phlegm, working it from the back of his throat into his mouth, then spit at the feet of a prisoner. '*Sheepal*, tie them with rope? My mother's hair braid would be stronger, or your grandmother's pubes.'

Boon gave him a half push, half punch. 'I'm going to tie them with your guts.' Dae-gun punched him back, then kicked at Jin.

'Shitheads,' the sergeant called out to the two officers, 'what's going on?'

'Nothing, sir.' Boon saluted. Dae-gun slunk past him, slipping a quick rabbit punch to his kidney. He disappeared around the side of the prison building and loped back several minutes later with a coil of rope hanging from one shoulder. He dropped the rope at the feet of Boon and dragged it over to a prisoner. He started tying his wrists.

'You want bow ties, Sergeant?'

The sergeant jumped, his legs scissoring open as he leaped over and kicked the tall guard so hard he knocked him into the prisoners.

'Enough of your lip. Tie the legs and hands, and if anyone gets loose, it's on you, son of bitch.'

Boon grabbed Jin and threw him facedown on the ice-cold ground and dropped his foot on Jin's back. Alkaline dust filled Jin's nostrils and lungs as the guard grabbed Jin's arms and wound the rope once, twice, thrice around his wrists. Then, pulling up Jin's feet, he wrapped the rope around his ankles several times; in one swift action Jin was hog-tied. The sergeant reached over and tugged the rope to check the tension; the knot was solid. Satisfied, the sergeant turned on his heel and headed back toward the prison door, pausing to kick an elderly prisoner. The man's small body was stiff as a frozen chicken. Jin watched the sergeant disappear behind the prison door and looked out upon the rows of male prisoners. They weren't going to make it—that is, Jin might make it, Hyuk and Bae would make it, but the older ones with their brittle bones and their ashen faces, they were already corpses.

Jin blinked hard, trying to keep his eyes open. He could fall asleep in this cold, and he didn't want to die in his sleep. Jin tried to conjure up the faces of his parents and of Young-na, but their faces floated in the distance like old photos on a wall. He could barely feel the ghost of emotion. There was no ache in his heart for his mother and his sister, no glimmer of anger toward his father, who had beaten him. His family's faces receded into the distance along with dozens, hundreds of other wan faces from the black windowed apartments of his childhood.

It was the memory of Suja that sent a dart through Jin's heart, his yearning for her an open wound. How he longed to touch her, just one more time, feel her smooth cheek against his and breathe in the smell of her hair. He remembered the time she took him up to the top of a building and showed him the glorious view of Pyongyang. They could see the statue of Chollima the flying horse from that rooftop. 'This is our future,' Suja had said, taking his hand. She was so convinced of it, as was he—the promise of their life together. He remembered holding her as they stood overlooking all of Pyongyang, and as he recalled this, he felt the burn of indignation. They had been robbed of the future they were supposed to share together. He couldn't give up on that now.

He couldn't just rot away and die here without seeing Suja at least one more time.

Jin looked around at the prisoners who were now all shackled together with chains, or some of them with rope. Jin's gaze went past the prisoners' heads to the walls of the prison beyond. His eyes darted to the sentries stationed at each corner of the prison, then followed the barbed wire that was strung across the top of each wall. He started turning over these variables in his mind as he calculated the distance between himself and the wall. His mind churned through various permutations, always coming up against the fact that the courtyard was a wide-open space and he'd be spotted in an instant. He finally let his head fall to the ground and fell asleep.

Jin awoke to the sound of a diesel truck rumbling gears as it rolled into the courtyard, throwing off dust and dirt as its heavy wheels pivoted to circle around the prisoners. Jin watched sleepily as the truck crossed the courtyard and pulled up against the far wall near the anthracite factory. The driver edged the truck forward and back several times, carefully maneuvering it until it was flush against the wall. He cut the engine, got out of the cab and walked away. The truck was positioned underneath a conveyor belt that angled out through an opening in the wall. Jin stared at the square hole, recognizing the chute from the assembly line where they worked every day. Excitedly, he nudged Hyuk, who was still huddled trying to sleep.

'Hey, Hyuk, look at this. Check out that dump truck.'

'Leave me alone. I'm tired.'

'Seriously, check this out.' Jin shook him.

Hyuk rolled over onto his side and rubbed his eyes. Propping himself on an elbow, he scanned the empty courtyard, and his eyes landed on the dump truck.

'What about it?' he muttered.

'Look where it is,' Jin insisted.

Hyuk squinted at the truck. Then his eyes widened as he recognized the building. 'That's our factory. It's parked on the other side of the wall.'

'Yeah. This must happen every time we're on shift. These trucks come every day, and they sit there until their cargo hold is full. *And then they drive off.*'

'What're you guys looking at?' Bae asked grumpily, lifting a hand to shade his eyes as he gazed across the courtyard.

'Check out that truck over there,' Jin said, turning his head to look in the other direction now, so as not to draw attention. 'The guy just parked it there right now. It'll stay there until we fill it, right? And then it'll drive off with a full load.'

'Hmm.' Bae stared at it, absentmindedly scratching his scruffy beard. 'You're thinking about jumping into the back of that truck.'

'Yeah,' said Jin.

'How?'

'I dunno. Maybe we could climb up the conveyor belt after hours.'

'But the truck might not be there after hours.'

'Let's check it out. If we can get ourselves into one of those trucks, we can make it out of here.'

Bae stared at the truck with a strange light in his eyes. 'Hmm. You might have something here.' He stared at it awhile longer before turning to Jin. 'You bastard! This just might work.'

'Not just another pretty face, huh?' Hyuk punched Jin's arm.

'Let's scope this out. I think this is how that other guy got out,' said Jin. The other two nodded soberly, their gazes shifting from the dump truck to the empty stake in the middle of the courtyard.

TWELVE

'Suja!' Kyung-bok called out as she looked over the heads of students thronging in the hall, spotting her friend dashing out of a classroom. Kyung-bok had been waiting in the lobby with Soon-ok and Mee-ran, waiting for the history study group to gather. Suja put her head down and kept walking, pretending she hadn't heard. She had been avoiding the study groups and didn't hang out with them after class; instead she skulked away from her classes, disappearing out the door before anyone could pull her into a conversation. There was talk going around the school as people watched how Suja was handling the whole thing.

'Anyung,' she said, and kept walking.

'Come to study group!' Kyung-bok yelled.

'Sorry,' Suja replied, barely looking in her direction.

Kyung-bok shouldered past the students in the hall, her ponytail bobbing back and forth as she jogged to Suja.

'You haven't come for three weeks.'

'I've been studying at home.'

'Really.'

'I'm so swamped, I can't keep up, I've got so many things due,' Suja said hurriedly, wanting to get out of there. She had less than an hour to get to the black market.

'We're all pulling the same yoke. We should work together.'

Suja pursed her mouth at this. For years she hadn't questioned that slogan, but now it sounded like out-and-out manipulation.

'So come.' Kyung-bok tugged at her. Suja placed her hand on her friend's arm, her eyes searching hers as she deliberated whether she could explain everything to her friend. They had gone through years of gymnastics together and had been accepted to Kim Il-Sung University at the same time. They shared so many watershed moments in life and she confided in her about everything, but she couldn't share her thoughts with Kyung-bok now. It would be dangerous to reveal her true opinion about KCNA, Jin or the state police, let alone what she was planning to do next. She couldn't tell her a thing.

Suja pulled Kyung-bok into a fierce hug and held her deep and long. 'I miss you so much, but I can't stay today,' she said haltingly.

Kyung-bok pulled away and scrutinized her friend. She shook her lightly by the shoulders, saying, 'Suja, I know you miss him terribly. Even *I* still miss him. But don't push me away, don't isolate yourself. Come, we can study together or just go for a walk. Or something.'

'I'm sorry.' Suja shook her head. 'I'm just busy with the newspaper and schoolwork, plus my mom's been wanting me to help at home.'

'But I haven't seen you for weeks.'

'Honestly, I have so much homework and I'm working at the newspaper. There's just *no time*.'

'Suja.'

Suja looked down. 'I'm sorry, Kyung-bok. I just can't.'

Kyung-bok fell silent. Suja could be so stubborn, and there was only so much she could do. 'It would be good for you to be among friends,' she said finally.

'Honestly, I don't think you know what's good for me,' Suja said.

Kyung-bok pursed her lips. 'Okay, well…' She left her sentence unfinished and backed away. She was reminded of her aunt whose husband went missing years ago, and who had never been able to question or investigate what had happened. Instead she continued at her factory job and attended Party confession sessions faithfully, showing continued loyalty and zeal for the Party. Over time she became less involved and said less and less, fading into a slighter version of her former self. She kept retreating further and further into her shell until years later she ended up in an infirmary. Doctors diagnosed her as 'sick in the head.' Kyung-bok didn't want her friend to start down the same path.

She watched Suja run down the hall and push through the exit, swinging the door out in a large arc, letting in a shaft of sun. She exited neatly into the wedge of light and the door slammed behind her. Impulsively Kyung-bok said to her friends, 'I'll join you later—go on ahead.'

She picked up her books and ran down the hall, skittering to a stop as she neared the side exit. She pushed through the doors in time to see Suja clamber up the pebbled embankment, her schoolbag banging against her back. Kyung-bok hung by the building, waiting for Suja to clear the embankment, then launched up the incline herself, stumbling as her feet triggered a shimmering of pebbles. She reached the street level just in time to see Suja turn down a side street, moving swiftly through groups of grade-school students in white shirts and navy skirts. Kyung-bok struggled to keep within eyeshot of her friend, slowing down as Suja neared the three-way T intersection at the black market alley.

Kyung-bok's mouth went dry. In all her years in Pyong-yang, she had never gone to an illegal market.

Along the entrance to the alley, stall owners squatted on their haunches behind meager piles of dry goods as thin trails of smoke rose up past black electrical wires and into the opaque sky. There was a large ramen stall with several men sitting on overturned plastic buckets slurping noodles from steaming bowls. The tangy salt fumes of the soup set Kyung-bok's stomach grumbling. She pulled out her hair elastic and loosened her ponytail, shaking out her hair until it covered half her face. Turning up the collar of her jacket, she took a deep breath and entered the alley. Vendors were lined along both sides of the alley, using all manner of recy-cled plastic bags and pieces of cardboard or cloth spread out beneath their wares. There was a jumble of clothes, watches from China laid out on dog-eared pieces of brown cardboard, conical mounds of sprouts with roots still dusted with brown dirt, grisly strips of dried meat laid out in rows. All illegal.

Suja wove through the market, her head bobbing left and right as she walked past stalls that opened her to another world: a jungle of electronics, foods, colorful plastic wares, clothing, things she had never seen before. It was as if a giant scrim had been lifted, revealing the shadowy backstage of her city, a side of Pyongyang that belied the official public face with its rectilinear concrete buildings and its broad empty av-enues. Had her father known about this all along—that these people lived like this in markets where one could negotiate for anything?

Overhead a state loudspeaker crackled awake and boomed

with the evening news. There were the usual announcements to begin: the Pil-joo factory had exceeded its steel production quota by 150 percent; they had reached another benchmark in missile production for the nuclear program; and Special Comrade Kim Jong-un paid a visit to Chagang-do to inspect the border. The announcer went on to introduce a message from Special Comrade Kim Jong-un. There was a pause, and then the gravelly tenor voice of the Dear Leader's son came on over the loudspeaker: 'Dear comrades, I am proud to announce the inauguration of special border measures for the increased security of our nation. As of today, Chosun will be cracking down on all those attempting to defect from this country, and any defectors who are caught will be subject to immediate execution. Those who are even *thinking* of defecting will be caught and punished.' His voice took on a rhythmic cadence, growing stronger and louder. 'We will fortify our northern border and teach all our citizens to respect it. By the Everlasting Leader, this country will be rid of the problem. Defectors will be dead in the ground and the northern river will be the watery grave for all traitors.' Suja shuddered at this final image.

A boy on a rusty bike cart pedaled toward her, veering to one side as he swerved to avoid an old man who had fallen asleep with his head resting on a pile of firewood. There were several food stalls in front of him, people haggling over the price of scavenged mountain herb roots, shaking handfuls in the air. When she spotted a biscuit maker, her heart stopped. The woman was squatted next to a cooking fire with a small makeshift oven made out of a tin box placed over a pile of smoky coals. With her headscarf and rough, grizzled complexion, she looked like a farm ajooma, or anyone's grandmother, or, who knows, an informant (some of the country's best spies or informants were the old ajoomas). Could this be the biscuit maker her father had heard rumors of? Suja stopped in front of her, wondering if this woman might be able to provide any information about the prisons up north.

The old woman used a stick to poke the makeshift oven that spewed fitful bursts of steam. The smell of toasted corn and sugar wafted into the air—corn biscuits made of corn-meal, sugar and baking soda. There was so much food in the market; Suja was surprised that there was this kind of abundance in a time when everyone was supposed to live by the Dear Leader's slogan, 'Have less, want less.'

Suja waited for the woman to turn out the next batch of biscuits and crouched down to select one. Across the alley, her friend Kyung-bok watched with dismay. The Suja she knew, the devoted Party member and daughter of a Rodong newspaper editor, would have never gone into a black market to buy a *biscuit*. So what in Chosun was she doing here? Distressed, Kyung-bok slipped behind a pile of firewood bundled onto a cart and watched her friend nibble at the biscuit, apparently in no hurry to leave. Each minute Suja lingered here, she was further endangering her family's reputation. Kyung-bok herself was in a bad position having witnessed Suja in the black market. She would be obligated to report her. *Damn you, Suja, get out of here*, she pleaded silently. The longer Kyung-bok stayed with Suja in the market, the greater the chances that she herself would be recognized and reported. Kyung-bok took one last look at her friend and turned around to run back to the main street, tears streaming down her cheeks.

Suja chewed the biscuit slowly, focusing on the sensation of the dry, hot pastry crumbling in her mouth, her body trembling; she wasn't sure what she was going to do next; in fact, she was surprised at having made it to the market at all, let alone having found a biscuit seller.

The biscuit-lady ajooma uncovered a bowl of yellow batter and spooned dollops of the mixture onto the metal tray in four evenly spaced rows. Moving swiftly, she lifted the lid of the metal box with two sticks and gingerly dropped the tray of biscuits onto the coals. She leaned down and blew at the embers.

Without thinking, the words came out of Suja's mouth. 'A friend says your crackers are better than those they sell up north,' she said. The old lady poked at the coals with a stick.

'I don't know anything about what goes on up there.' She grimaced.

'Of course not,' Suja murmured. 'My friend was just saying your biscuits were better.'

Ajooma said nothing.

'If I was going to search for a friend up there, would you know of any guides who could help me?' Suja ventured, knowing it was dangerous to hint at this, but she had started down this path, so she had to press on. Suja took ever smaller bites of the remaining biscuit, rolling the dissolved crumbs around with her tongue.

'It's dangerous, particularly now,' the woman sniped. 'Why would a girl like you be talking about up north anyway?'

Suja froze, unsure of how to respond; she chose her next words carefully.

'I have a friend in a bad way, Auntie.'

'We're all in a bad way.'

'Yes, but my friend was taken away and I'm hoping to find out where he is.' Suja watched Ajooma's face.

Ajooma mumbled, 'You Pyongyang kids think the moon is at your front door. You whistle and expect it to come running.'

'Auntie, I'll run to heaven to get to the moon. I just need to find out about my friend. I'll do anything.'

The ajooma pushed aside the lid on the metal box and lifted out the tray of biscuits with two sticks. The dollops of batter had risen but were still pale. She dropped the tray back down and covered the lid again.

'Corn biscuits hot and sweet,' she yelled out. '*Oksoosoo gwaja* for you to eat!'

'My friend highly recommended you,' said Suja.

'Lots of people like my biscuits. But the kind you're asking for... I don't know if I can help you.'

Suja felt a surge of adrenaline when the woman finally acknowledged her request. She was completely focused on her now as she said softly, deliberately, 'I have money.'

The woman curled her lip and scowled, and Suja cursed herself for being so forward. Perhaps this was not a smuggler after all, or worse, what if she were a decoy planted by the security police meant to entrap people?

The ajooma lifted the lid of the metal box and pulled out the tray of biscuits, which had started to brown. She could smell the sweetness in the steaming biscuits now, the toasted sugar. Ajooma set the tray down and spread a grimy cloth over the newly baked biscuits. 'Corn biscuits hot and sweet!' she yelled, then, glancing at Suja, mumbled, 'Come next Wednesday in the morning. There will be new biscuits next week.'

Suja blinked. 'You're saying next week...'

The woman sucked her teeth. 'Stupid girl. Just come Wednesday. I'll see about the special biscuits, the kind you're looking for.' She shook two blackened chopsticks at Suja to shoo her away. 'Next Wednesday, I don't want to see your face before next Wednesday!'

'Yes.' Suja's eyes shone with excitement. 'Thank you, thank you.' She turned and hurried past the other vendors back toward the market entrance, her heart singing.

THIRTEEN

Jin, Hyuk and Bae edged forward in the queue, craning their necks over the heads of sullen prisoners waiting to start the morning shift in the anthracite factory. The doors opened and the desultory crowd shuffled in, taking their positions on the assembly line. Jin and the other two avoided their usual positions in the middle of the assembly and instead headed toward the far wall by the chute. Hyuk and Bae walked over to the end of the conveyor belt and took their places on the line there. Jin stood on the other side of the conveyor, opposite them, and glanced casually at the conveyor that slanted up through the discharge chute. From this vantage point, he could see that the chute opening was larger than it seemed from the outside, leaving enough space for a man to crawl through underneath the conveyor belt. He also noticed that the machine effectively blocked the view of the wall behind it, so conceivably if a guy positioned himself carefully enough, he could scale the wall without being noticed by any guards at the other end—that is, if he was fast enough, and if luck was on his side.

It seemed too simple, too foolishly audacious.

Jin looked across at Hyuk and Bae, who cocked an eye, as if to say *So, what do you think?* Jin gave a slight nod. He was foolish enough to try. He gauged the height of the chute and tried to visualize jumping and pulling himself up into it. The trick would be to get his body into the duct before he got noticed. He shook his head, for the space between the conveyor and the edge of the chute was so narrow, he'd have to keep his head down as he pulled himself up or he'd collide into it. It wasn't going to be easy.

Bae leaned over to Hyuk to whisper something, maybe something about the escape plan, or who knows. Jin watched them, wishing he were on the other side of the conveyor. Agitated, he started drumming his fingers against the skirt edge when the conveyor shuddered awake and the rocks started tumbling through. Wearily, the other prisoners took their positions and leaned against the conveyor skirt as the rocks came tumbling. They reached in to cull pieces with silvery gray streaks of anthracite, their hands moving constantly, lifting and checking for the telltale metallic sheen. The rocks were picked over by dozens of prisoners as they traveled down the line, so by the time they reached Jin, Hyuk and Bae, there was nothing left but debris.

The three of them fell into the mechanical routine of picking up rocks and throwing them back onto the conveyor. At one point Bae bent down to tie his shoelaces, and after some time, Jin noticed he hadn't stood up again. He glanced nervously at Hyuk, who flashed his eyes cryptically and said nothing as he focused on the conveyor, his hands moving swiftly, picking up rocks and dropping them even as he picked up new ones.

Jin's pulse quickened as he realized Bae must be attempting his escape. He studiously avoided looking at the chute for fear of drawing attention to it, but after a couple of minutes he cast a quick glance. Bae was nowhere to be seen. That must be a good thing, Jin reasoned, for that would mean he was well on his way out, if he wasn't out already. Just the thought of Bae making it outside made Jin break out in a cold sweat, for that meant he or Hyuk would go next.

He glanced nervously at the fellow next to him and went back to sorting the rocks, lifting and turning them distractedly without really inspecting them. He went through the motions, feeling more and more jittery as the minutes ticked by, for he wasn't sure what the plan was now. Should he go first, or would Hyuk make an attempt? He tried to get Hyuk's attention, but he seemed intently focused on sorting the rocks. Taking his cue, Jin looked down and did the same, continuing to sort the rocks for what seemed like an eternity.

'I gotta pee something awful,' Hyuk finally said to no one in particular. 'Can't believe it's another couple of hours till the washroom break.'

'Yeah.' Jin shrugged, wondering why Hyuk would mention the washroom break. Was he suggesting they try to escape from the latrines? He considered the amount of guard supervision at the latrines and the hallway en route. With guards posted at every turn, there was no way they could escape during the washroom break. So why would Hyuk bring it up? He shot Hyuk a quizzical look, and Hyuk simply raised his brow.

Jin thought about it again, going over exactly what happened during washroom breaks. The prisoners on the line broke rank as they lined up to take a piss, while those who didn't need to go to the latrines hung out on the factory floor. When the conveyor belt started up again, the returning prisoners often changed up their places on the assembly line. Jin's eyes sparked at this. That would be a perfect time for Hyuk and Jin to try to escape because their absence from their positions on the line would go unnoticed. So Hyuk was suggesting they escape when everyone broke rank for the latrines. Jin smiled at this.

'I gotta pee too,' Jin said to Hyuk. 'Gotta pee real bad.'

Hyuk smiled.

When the whistle finally blew, the lower conveyor belt stopped, and a number of prisoners stepped away from the conveyor to form a queue at the door. Without missing a beat, Jin ducked under the chute and ran in a crouched position toward the wall. As he reached the chassis for the second conveyor that angled up the wall, he hoped and prayed no one could see him as he jumped for the chute. He turned back to see Hyuk come up behind him, and the sight of his friend's face was like a shot of adrenaline spurring him on. They were going to do this; this was really happening.

Jin mustered all his strength and leaped onto the wall, grabbing hold of the edge of the chute to quickly hoist himself up. He crawled past the conveyor belt and pulled his legs up, turning to see Hyuk scramble up from underneath the conveyor. Hyuk readied to jump for the chute and Jin reached out a hand, grabbed hold and pulled him up the wall. As Hyuk climbed into the duct, Jin let go and let himself slide down the chute, landing hard on a pile of rocks outside.

He lay winded and stunned as he looked around the inside walls of the truck. Hyuk tumbled out of the chute and rolled the other way to land against the back of the hauler, his chest heaving. They looked at each other, their eyes wide with disbelief at the fact that they were in the dump truck. They had made it out! They lay there quietly, listening for any shouts or alarms or signs of their discovery, but there was only the steady chugging of the assembly line in the other wing of the anthracite factory; otherwise, the courtyard was quiet and empty. Jin leaned forward and peered past the mound of debris between him and Hyuk.

'Where's Bae?' he whispered.

'I don't know.' Hyuk shook his head. 'Bae?' he called out softly.

Jin crawled closer to the back of the hauler toward Hyuk, but his movements triggered a small rockslide as the debris shifted above him and tumbled. Hyuk waved frantically. 'Stop moving,' he mouthed as he saw Jin getting partially buried. Jin lay there terrified, pinned under the weight of the rocks.

A door swung open and footsteps echoed in the courtyard. A man walked to the truck, got into the cab and started the engine. As the truck ground into gear and started rolling across the courtyard, Jin looked up at the sky that wheeled above them. He couldn't believe they were about to be driven out of the prison yard. Where the hell was Bae?

They were stopped at the gate by a guard, who stepped up to the cab and spoke with the driver, their voices barely discernible above the noise of the engine. As the conversation dragged on, Jin shot Hyuk a look of alarm, concerned the guard might need to inspect the carriage. But finally the gate opened and the truck creaked and rumbled as it pulled onto a dirt road pitted with potholes. With every bump, more rocks slid down, further pinning Jin to the sidewall. He floundered and struggled to find a handhold along the truck wall but was unable to find purchase. Seeing his distress, Hyuk spread his arms and legs and crawled across the mound of scree and grabbed him, helping him clamber out from under the debris. They rested against the sidewall together and stared at the expanse of gray rock in the hauler, then looked at each other. They were struck by the same thought.

'Bae?' called Hyuk in a loud whisper, then repeated a little louder. 'Bae!'

'Bae?' Jin called out. He spread his arms and legs wide and crawled toward the front of the truck, calling out again, 'Bae! Are you in there?'

He heard a faint cry.

'Bae?' Jin repeated, and flattened himself down, pressing his ear against the rock pile.

'Jin! I'm under the rocks. Help me!' came the muffled reply.

Jin turned to Hyuk and waved him over. 'He's here somewhere! We've gotta dig him out.'

Hyuk scrambled over to him, asking, 'Where? Where?' Jin pointed at the spot where he had laid his head. They started digging together, pushing the rock and debris, but as soon as they pushed the rocks aside, the debris caved in again from the other side. The filthy dust rose, filling their nostrils.

'Bae?' they called again and stopped pushing the rocks. This time both Hyuk and Jin pressed their ears against the rock pile. 'Keep calling, so we can find you, Bae.'

'I'm here,' said Bae faintly. 'Over here. I can't move…'

Jin moved about, angling closer to the front, and said excitedly, 'I think he's here!'

'My ribs hurt, and I can't breathe,' Bae whimpered. 'Get me out of here.'

'We've got you, Bae,' said Jin as he and Hyuk started pushing the rocks away from this part of the truck. But as they pushed the rocks away, the debris started sliding back down. Jin sat back and looked at Hyuk.

'Let's figure this out. I'll push the rock to you, Hyuk, and you push it farther down. Let's try that.'

Hyuk looked at the mound of debris behind him, which peaked toward the middle of the truck where the conveyor had emptied its load. To clear the rubble from where Jin was situated, they'd have to push the rocks uphill, or somehow shift that mountain of scree toward the back of the truck.

'I don't see how we can push all this rock to the back,' said Hyuk slowly, with a stricken look on his face. 'Maybe…maybe we could try to push it to the side.'

'Okay, let's do that,' Jin said and then directed his voice downward. 'Hey, Bae, we're going to get you out.' He picked up a few of the bigger rocks and threw them toward the back of the truck. One clanged against the back wall, making a loud noise. Hyuk glared at him, raising a finger to his lips. They sat still, listening. After several moments they started up again with Jin pushing a pile of rocks to Hyuk, who tried to push the rock off to the side. It was futile work, for Hyuk's movements caused just as many rocks to slide back down to Jin. They kept at it, their faces getting blackened with grime as the gray rock dust mixed in with their sweat.

When the truck came to a stop, they stopped to take a rest and waited for the truck to get moving again. Jin stuck his head over the side of the truck to see that they were at a country road intersection with no oncoming cars, but a mile or so ahead of them a queue of cars had formed in the middle of the road. Jin squinted and could make out a roadside barricade with a couple of helmeted officers standing beside it. He signaled to Hyuk, who crept to the side of the truck and peered over the edge.

When he pulled his head back in, his eyes were wide with fear. 'What are we going to do?'

'We've got to get him out fast.' Jin scrabbled toward the front of the hauler and started frantically pushing some rocks toward Hyuk, who tried to push them back toward the side of the truck.

'Hey, Bae?' called Hyuk. 'Where are you, buddy? Keep talking…we're gonna get you out of here.'

'I'm here,' came the faint reply.

Jin pushed more debris toward Hyuk, who pushed it to the side of the truck, but the rock had already begun sliding back down again. They kept at it for a couple more minutes until Hyuk finally stopped, his shoulders slumping in despair. They were getting no closer to finding Bae, and the checkpoint was coming up. He looked down at the expanse of rock and rubble where Bae was buried, perhaps only a couple of feet away from them, and had a sickening realization.

'Bae, buddy.' Hyuk's face was panic-stricken. His heart thumped against his chest. 'They're inspecting cars up ahead.'

Bae didn't respond.

'Bae.' Hyuk started again. 'We're on the road here in this truck, and there's a checkpoint up ahead.'

'Dig me out!' he cried, his voice muffled under the rock.

Jin and Hyuk exchanged helpless glances. 'We're trying,' said Jin. 'But we can't get deep enough…the rock keeps falling back in.'

There was silence.

'We can't dig you out in time,' said Hyuk, his voice becoming gravelly and hoarse. 'It's safer for you to stay under the rocks. They can't see you. When the truck dumps its load, you'll be able to jump out then. But me and Jin, they're gonna see us, so we have to jump out now.'

'Take me with you,' Bae implored. 'Don't leave me here, please!'

'We've been trying to.' Hyuk's voice broke with emotion. 'But we can't get you out in time.' He knelt down, bringing his face close to the rocks as he tried to guess where Bae was buried. Considering all the time they had served together in prison, they were like blood brothers now. They had slept side by side in the cell and sat across from each other at every meal. Hyuk had stared into Bae's face so often, he knew the lines of his face better than his own, better than anyone in his life. What could he do? It was impossible to dig Bae out, yet leaving him here wouldn't simply be a betrayal, it could be his death sentence.

Hyuk spread his arms out across the mound as if attempting to hug Bae through the rubble. 'Buddy, I'm so sorry,' he said in a wretched voice.

'We tried everything,' said Jin haltingly. He was at a loss for words.

'Guys, don't do this,' cried Bae. 'Take me with you, please!'

The sound of Bae's cries tore at Jin's conscience. He wanted to jump up and do something, get back in there and dig at the rocks again. But Hyuk lay prostrate on the rubble pile.

'I'm so sorry, Bae,' said Hyuk, glistening as he scanned the rubble.

This time there was no reply.

Hyuk pressed his face against the mound of gray rubble and spoke into the darkness. 'Hang in there.' His voice faltered as he added, 'We'll meet you on the other side. I promise.'

He finally pushed himself up, his eyes red with grief as he turned to the sidewall of the truck. He motioned to Jin and then crawled toward it, lifting his head. The truck had been traveling at about sixty miles an hour before, but it had slowed down and was coasting at forty now. If they were going to attempt to jump before the checkpoint, they'd have to do it now. Jin looked at Hyuk, then grabbed hold of the sidewall and poised himself to take a leap. Focusing on a point in the fields just beyond the fence line, Jin closed his eyes and jumped with all his might, landing and rolling in the field. He heard a shout and a spray of gravel, and turned back to see Hyuk land at the edge of the ditch and tumble to a stop. He lay crumpled on his side, but after a moment he lifted his head to see the truck trundle down the road.

Jin hunched and ran across the field to find him still on the ground, his shoulders shaking with sobs. 'He should be with us,' Hyuk said in anguish. 'I should have stayed and hid under the rock and dug him out later.'

Jin hung his head. Hyuk's words struck a deep chord in Jin's heart where the moral exigencies of right and wrong sounded their bell clear and strong. Whatever the circumstances, the fact remained that they had chosen to save themselves rather than save Bae. They didn't do right by him.

'How'd he even get buried in there?!' Hyuk slammed his fist into the soil. 'We couldn't even tell where he was.'

'He was buried so deep there was no way. You saw that yourself. We wouldn't have been able to dig him out even if we had all day.'

'We might have, if we stayed.'

'We would have been caught. You know there was nothing we could have done,' said Jin, trying to convince himself as much as Hyuk. He placed a hand on the older man's shoulder, and looked up at the road, ever conscious of the fact that he and Hyuk were out in the open field.

'Come on, Hyuk,' he prodded. 'We're still not in the clear. We have to get going.'

'Fucking bullshit!' Hyuk kicked the earth, and Jin pulled away, waiting for him to calm down. Hyuk turned over on his back and punched the ground again. Finally, he took a deep breath and pushed himself up.

'Let's get outta here.'

They started running away from the road, veering toward the side of the field that gave way to brush and trees. Jumping over the fence into brush, they ran through thorns and spindly branches and forged through the thicket, keeping an eye on the road so that they kept going roughly parallel with it. They ran past old clay-roofed houses seeping thin veins of smoke into the sky. The smell of burning coal in the air was as old as these hills, as familiar as the smell of his mother's kitchen.

As the road curved west, Hyuk said they should keep going due north. It would lead them to China, that potbellied cousin that sprawled north of the Chosun border. Word was that North Korean farmers abandoned their own rocky fields to work as laborers in China's farms and came back with sacks of barley, corn and clothing—a bounty you'd never find in North Korea.

'This should lead us to the Tumen River,' Hyuk said, squinting off into the distance. He glanced down at Jin's patched boots. 'How are your feet?'

'Fine.' Jin shrugged. 'Nothing I'm not used to.'

'You gonna be okay to cross the river?'

Jin's eyes widened. 'Cross the river into China? Are we close?'

'Not too far.' And with that, Hyuk motioned for Jin to follow as he abruptly turned off the road and headed into the woods. Startled, Jin hesitated a moment before plunging in after him. The forest was dense and prickly with underbrush and brambly fir branches that sprang back into Jin's face as he followed Hyuk on a course that grew thicker and more treacherous underfoot. There was a faint crackling sound around them—a spattering of gunfire in the distance? Jin ducked instinctively but Hyuk didn't stop; he kept forging into the forest even as the spattering thickened. Jin realized it was not the sound of guns, but raindrops hitting dry, brittle leaves. He stood up again and strained to locate Hyuk, finally catching sight of him some twenty, thirty feet ahead of him.

'Where you going?' he yelled as the skies let loose a deluge of heavy raindrops that struck his thin jacket before getting soaked in. 'Hyuk.'

'Shh!' Hyuk hissed back and Jin angled left, crouching sideways toward the sound of his voice.

'Where the heck are we going?'

'Listen,' Hyuk whispered excitedly. 'Use your ears.'

Jin listened, his animal senses pricked alive, but he didn't hear a thing. 'What?' he said.

'Shut your hole and listen.'

Jin stood stock-still as he listened, noticing that Hyuk's damp clothes gave off a smell of stale sweat and something funky and earthy, manure-like. Jin breathed through his mouth.

'Can you hear it? The river?' Hyuk asked. Jin strained to listen and heard it this time, a high-pitched din above the pelting rain in the forest that he could start to distinguish as the white noise of flowing water. That was the body of water that formed the border of North Korea and China, the Tumen River.

Until this very moment Jin wasn't entirely sure the river even existed, but now the possibility of life outside North Korea felt as real and concrete as the earth beneath his cold rubber boots. Blood surged to Jin's head, pounding in his ears. 'Let's go!' he said.

'Ah-ah-ah.' Hyuk put out an arm to stay him. 'Now's too early to move. The guards will see us.' He squatted and pulled Jin down to sit next to him by a rocky overhang. Jin reached his hand up to feel the mossy underside of the rock and how it sloped behind him. Hyuk sat back and leaned against the rock, spreading his legs out. 'So. We have to wait here until about three or four in the morning, because that's when our chances are best for crossing the river.'

'Why?' Jin hunkered down beside him and turned his head to face him.

'There are guards every five hundred feet or so, and they'll shoot you in the water.'

The saliva turned sour in the back of Jin's mouth at the

thought of being captured. He knew if he got caught now the soldiers wouldn't bother taking him back to the labor camp—they'd just do him in right there with their rifle butts, their boots, their cigarettes, their metal pipes.

'Can you swim?' Hyuk asked.

'Yes,' he half lied. He knew how to dog-paddle.

'Good. Okay, when we cross, we're going to have to go our separate ways. Two people are like clapping hands—they make more noise, so we'll have to cross alone. Pack your clothes and carry it over your head.' He pantomimed with one hand on his head, the other one wading through the air. 'When you get to the other side, there are trails up the slope. You have to get through the woods and cross some farm fields. We have to look for a one-sided mountain. It looks like a regular mountain from one side, but the other half is a sheer cliff. They dug into part of it when they were building a tunnel. When it caved in, they never finished it. I heard that people hide there, our people, so hopefully we can find it and hide there for a bit.'

'Okay.'

'Let's see how easy it is to find. I've only heard about this tunnel. Every time I've been to China, I've stayed in hotels.' Hyuk smiled and crossed his hands behind his head. 'You know, with a TV, a bed and blanket, and those little bars of soap. Or—' he squinted at Jin '—you wouldn't know, would you?'

'How many times have you been to China?' asked Jin.

'A few times, for work. But this'll be my first time going this way, as a defector.' He paused, letting the word sink in. 'Because that's what we're doing now, we're defecting.'

Jin nodded soberly. He was adding crime upon crime—first he stole the cornmeal, and now he was going to defect. Defection was the highest treason, short of trying to harm

the Dear Leader himself, and there was no going back once
you committed this crime against the state. He thought bitterly of Suja and the promise of their lives together and how
he had squandered it all with one rash decision. In prison, he
had imagined a brand-new future for them in China, but now
that he was out in the world, he realized the cold, sobering fact
that if he left Chosun, he may never see Suja again. A shiver
went through his body and he tightened his folded arms.

'You going to tell anyone back home?' he asked tentatively.

'No.' Hyuk shook his head sorrowfully as he thought about
his colleagues. 'Those bastards at work are going to get interrogated as they search for me. I hope they'll be safe.' There
was no way to contain harm. Everything they did had a ripple effect on those around them. 'You have to cut all ties
with your people, but later you may be able to get a message
through to your family. They'll understand.'

'How?'

'Through brokers. I know of some.'

'They go back and forth?'

'Between here and China.'

'So brokers can get messages back and forth,' said Jin, a light
dawning in his eyes. He wondered whether they could guide
people back and forth too, and focused on this one hope.

'Get some rest while you can. And like I said, you need to
find that mountain with the tunnel, and I'll meet you there.
We'll find other people there too, and if we're lucky, we won't
catch the skin-eating disease from them. They might even
help us. But you don't want to stay there long, or you'll die.'

It seemed all roads led to death. The rain was dying down
now, and Jin could hear the rushing river more clearly. It
sounded close, in fact, only several hundred feet away. His
heart thumped in his chest as he realized how close they were
to China. He leaned against Hyuk, happy to feel the com-

forting presence of his cell mate. They had made it, and now
they were going to escape to China. Jin finally relaxed and
closed his eyes.

Hyuk shook Jin awake and whispered, 'Hey, we have to
go now.' Jin's eyelids flew open and he sat up with a start.
The rain had stopped but the air under the rocky overhang
was dank and cold. Jin scrabbled against the dirt and edged
himself out from under the boulder and thrust his head out,
listening. It was quiet, no sound of footsteps or twigs snapping underfoot.

They got up together, and Hyuk pointed toward the river.
'Stay low and go that way, and I'll go this way. Good luck,
man. I'll see you on the other side.' He reached over to give
Jin a deep, long hug, clapping him on the back.

'Thank you, man,' said Jin. He had met Hyuk only a few
months ago, but after all they'd been through, he felt like a
blood brother. 'I'm going to see you in the tunnel, right?'

'You bet,' said Hyuk. But there was uncertainty in both
their eyes as they gazed at each other one last time.

'Good luck,' Hyuk said finally, and headed off into the
forest.

Jin watched him as he vanished into the darkness, then
headed in the opposite direction, pushing through trees as
heavy needles splashed him with sprays of water. He imagined Hyuk taking the same steps somewhere hundreds of
yards away, and the thought comforted him.

Toward the river the trees gave way to the flattened stretch
of long grasses that lay slick against the ground, beaded with
drops of rain. He was a dozen yards now from the narrow
river, no more than thirty feet across at its narrowest. About
a hundred yards to the left along this side of the bank was the
concrete outcropping of a guard post, with a long, narrow

window cut along the top and a metal railing on the roof. Jin watched it carefully to see if any guards were at the post, but there were no watchful eyes peering out, and no one was on the rooftop. Jin looked across to the far bank, which looked exactly like the North Korean side, low and unassuming, yet that was *China*.

This narrow strip of water, this undulating ribbon circumscribed all that Jin knew in his life. He stood there watching the flowing river for a moment, thinking. This was his country, the Land of Our Proud People, Land of the Dear Heavenly Leader; this was all he knew, and he was about to leave it. If his defection was discovered by officials, his family could be sent to the prison camps. But surely his father's public denunciation of Jin would spare the family. After all, that was why his father betrayed him and beat him in the public square, wasn't it? By obeying the authorities and distancing his family from Jin, he was ensuring the family's safety.

The river moved along, a slick muscle quivering in the dark.

If he was going to do this, he would have to do it now.

Jin tiptoed to the water's edge and stepped in, wet mud sucking at his feet as he waded into the river. The water was ice-cold, and it eddied around his knees, then thighs, until he was finally chest deep and the piercing cold sucked the breath right out of him. He spread his arms as the force of the current buffeted his body, and gulped for air as he advanced until he was neck deep. He had the desperate urge to turn back toward shallower water, but he kept forging forward, bobbing on his toes and fanning his arms through the water. His feet slipped on slick stones as the insistent pull of the current sucked him downstream.

Just then a beam of light danced across the water downstream from him.

'Who's out there?' someone shouted.

Jin froze and looked back toward the shore to see if he could clamber back into the woods. It was too far, much too far. He glanced around frenziedly to see if Hyuk had been spotted, but he couldn't see his friend anywhere. He ducked his head underwater, feeling the icy sting of the water pierce his scrunched eyes. He held his breath, fanning his hands upward to keep himself from bobbing up to the surface. When he couldn't hold it any longer, he rose up, trying not to splash as he lifted his head above the surface. He took a big gulp of air, blinking rapidly as cold rivulets ran down his face. The flashlight was scanning the river downstream.

'Show yourself, or we'll shoot you. Who's there?' the guard shouted from a couple of hundred feet down the shore. Jin took another gulp of air and ducked under again, struggling against the current as he forged forward, angling himself upstream. He needed to get as far upstream as possible. As he pushed forward, his feet found surer ground; the water level receded as he approached the other shoreline, and he let his head surface again. He squinted downstream, panting, as he listened for the guard. There was no flashlight this time, only silence. Jin stepped carefully toward the shore, his lips quivering as he listened to the water gurgle around him. The light suddenly flashed on and swooped past him, then swooped back downstream.

'Show yourself, you gaesakee, or I'll shoot your head off!' the guard shouted, sweeping his flashlight up and down the river. He lowered his voice and spoke into a walkie-talkie. 'This is Officer Lee at checkpoint seventy-nine, requesting support.' There was a pause. Then he spoke again. 'I heard something in the river. I've checked but couldn't see anything from my post. I think we should check along the shore.' Another pause. 'No, I *definitely* heard something, sir!' Jin ducked underwater again and hunched toward the shore,

staying below the surface for as long as he could until the
river receded, revealing his head and his bent back, and he
was able to drag his hands across the surface of the water. He
was almost out.

Crouching low, Jin ran onto the riverbank, across the scrub
brush and up the sloping embankment. Grabbing at long stalks
of grass, he pulled himself up the slippery bank and into a
stand of trees, and ran ten, fifteen yards farther into a small
forest of conifers and bare deciduous trees where he finally
stopped. His whole body was shivering, his teeth chattering
as ice water sluiced off his arms and legs onto the forest floor.
He squeezed his pant legs and sleeves, stamped his legs and
shook his arms, until sensation began to prick through his
limbs. Slapping his arms, his chest and torso, he tried to wick
off the water and warm himself. He was in China now, he
marveled. He had made it and he hoped to God that Hyuk
had made it too. He thought of Suja back home, her face blazing in front of him as he stared through the blue darkness into
the surrounding trees, and ran.

FOURTEEN

Suja sat with her folder of photos on her lap and her Political Theory homework spread open on Mr. Roh's desk. She read a question, and read it again, but each time she got to the end of the sentence, each of the words had dissolved, disintegrating before they could build any significance. She took a deep breath and concentrated for a third time, attempting to finally comprehend each word and the full import of them strung together. She blinked carefully.

These days, formulating a sentence was despairing work.

Suja let her pen drop and looked up to check the clock. It was 4:28 p.m., and the Rodong newsroom was in a turmoil. Editors were arguing over something while the staff writers were hunched over their wooden desks, scribbling with terrified focus. Apba was up at the flats arguing with Mr. Lim, Mr. Roh and Mr. Moon as cigarette smoke glowered miasmically above their heads. Apba stepped away from the group, darting his eyes at her, then back to the waxed column stuck on his fingers. 'What are you doing here?' he mouthed to her.

She furrowed her brow and pointed to the folder of photos on her lap.

Apba raised his brows and nodded toward Mr. Roh, then shook his head.

'What?' Suja mouthed, with an elaborate shrug. Apba rolled his eyes as he walked toward her.

'What happened?' Suja asked as her dad spun Mr. Roh's chair around and dropped himself into it. He crossed his hands behind his head.

'A change in the story lineup.'

'What's the change?' Suja asked.

Her father sighed. 'The Cornmeal Culprit escaped from prison. That boy, Jin Lee Park.'

Suja's heart thudded against her breastbone. 'What? When?' she whispered.

'A couple of days ago. They haven't found him yet. They're still searching. The bastard *escaped* from Yodok prison camp. How the hell he did that...' Apba shook his head. 'After the shame he brought to his family, that saekee runs from prison, saving his own skin, sending his family to damnation.'

'They don't know where he is?'

His nod was barely perceptible. Suja felt the blood drain from her head as a wave of vertigo washed over her.

'He escaped...' Suja breathed.

His father watched her face closely. 'Did you know him?' he asked.

She gathered herself and snapped to attention. 'No.'

His gaze sharpened. 'He was from your university.'

'I don't know *everyone* at the university, Apba,' she retorted.

'You don't know these kinds of saekees, they're a different breed of dog,' her father spit, then turned his head abruptly.

'How he managed to get into your school is the real issue,' he continued. 'Bastards like him are dangerous to society, these gangpae criminals. That your school gave him a scholarship is the big shame. Did you know they are going through a purification of the entire student roster? Hell, they should go through a purification of the whole country, considering the news about black marketers and defectors.'

'They should,' Suja said, the blood thumping at her temples. Suja's eyes were bright and alert, her mind running at full tilt as she considered this incredible piece of news: Jin had escaped, he was *free*. She started counting her breath to calm her racing heart: one Heavenly Father, two Heavenly Father, three…

'I'm surprised they hadn't done it already,' he muttered. 'Why are you smiling?'

'Oh.' A look of consternation came over her face. 'Was I smiling?'

'You looked awfully happy about something.'

'I can't remember what it was,' she said, as if puzzling. 'By the way, have you eaten dinner?' she countered.

'No.' He always ate dinner after work, she knew that.

'I think I should get going… Do you need anything?'

'No…'

'Can you tell Mr. Roh I have to go? I'll leave the photos on his desk.' She placed her hand on the folder.

'Which photos?' her father called, raking his fingers along the back of his head. 'We're going to have to pull a couple of photos, and I don't know which photos Mr. Roh will want to use.'

'That's okay. He can choose the ones he wants. I'll see you at home, then.' She collected her books and ran out the front door of the Rodong newspaper office building, racing down the stairs, half-airborne with glee. She broke into a run and

sprinted the entire fifteen blocks back to her school, arriving
at the side entrance completely breathless.

She gasped as she waited to get her wind back, then pushed
through the heavy wooden doors, walking swiftly past her
friends in the study hall. She trotted down the stairs to the
basement bathroom, where she ran into a toilet stall, turned
the latch and sat herself down on the toilet. She began to sob,
huge laughing sobs that shook her whole body as tears rolled
down her cheeks. She covered her hands over her mouth to
muffle herself as her heart ricocheted between hope and fear,
joy over his escape, and rage over the stupidity of his actions
that got him arrested in the first place. How incredible, how
unbelievably clever he was to have escaped; no ordinary man
could manage to escape from that prison. He was alive, hopefully safe somewhere in the vast hinterland of the great country to the north.

Suja leaned her head against the washroom stall door and
spread her palms against the metal, feeling the coolness against
her cheek. She breathed deeply, imagining Jin's tall, lean body
against hers, and her stomach tightened.

'I am going to find you, Jin Lee Park,' she whispered. 'Wait
for me.'

Suja lifted her scarf to cover her mouth as she stepped into
the hazy smoke-filled black market alley. White plastic ramen
bowls lay upturned on the ground, spinning in the wind. A
young boy with spiky tufts of light brown hair leaped after
the bowls, and as he picked one up and brought it to his face,
he licked the bowl edge. Suja lowered her head and folded her
arms across her chest, stepping carefully through the market;
this time she knew where she was going.

She wore a headscarf and her mother's old gray jacket that
was fraying at the hem, which she had chosen for its loose,

nondescript shape. Cloaked in her mother's old clothes, Suja felt safe enough to take her time and look around as she walked through the market. She passed a row of plank tables and noticed a few empty stalls, which was strange, for the previous week the market had been much busier; she hadn't recalled seeing any empty tables.

Beside one of these tables was a wheelbarrow with a man's emaciated legs hanging over the edge. He was covered by a thin sheet that lifted and billowed with the breeze. Suja stopped, transfixed by this unsettling scene. She approached the wheelbarrow with some trepidation, wondering whether the man was dead or alive. Just then the man pulled his legs inside the barrow and, turning onto his side, settled back into sleep. Suja drew back and glanced around, noticing no one else was paying any attention. Disquieted, she turned away slowly and headed toward the firewood sellers who had parked their carts of bundled sticks by the side of the road.

She smelled the burnt sugar before she saw the black smoke tailing off into the sky. The biscuit lady had set up her oven next to a yut candy maker this time and was seated on an up-turned bucket before her coal oven. She fanned orange embers, which flew up from the coal, smoke and steam puffing from the metal box. Suja approached her.

'Anyung,' she said quietly. 'I came back for some new biscuits.'

The ajooma glanced up and narrowed her eyes. 'You came,' she accused.

'Yes. I was hoping to find something out,' said Suja. 'Something about your new biscuits.'

'They're hard to find now.'

'Are there no…new biscuits anymore?' Suja asked.

Ajooma opened her mouth in a big, slow yawn, then placed her hands on her knees and, with a grunt, pushed herself up

to stand. 'Ayayay.' She grimaced and reached her hands around
to brace against the small of her back. She stretched from
side to side, exposing her dimpled belly flesh, then grabbed a
piece of cardboard to fan the fire. 'There is someone. Hang
out here and wait a bit.'

Suja's heart skipped a beat as the woman shooed her to
the side. 'Wait there, I said.' Ajooma glanced down the alley
as she grabbed her stick to adjust the lid to her metal oven.
Sniffling, she ran her sleeve across her nose and said to Suja,
'Better yet, take a walk around the market and come back in
fifteen minutes.'

Suja nodded and left without a word, every nerve in her
body tense. She walked aimlessly toward the other stalls and
lingered at each one, barely noticing what was being sold; at
one stall she went through pairs of men's socks, at another
she considered dried roots and foraged leafy greens, quilted
vests, dried soybeans. After some time she made her way back
to the biscuit maker to see if anyone had approached the old
lady and noticed a slim man in a cap and faded brown wind-
breaker standing off to one side. He leaned casually against
a loudspeaker pole, smoking a cigarette. He had the scrappy
good looks of a soccer player, with an angular face, a thin nose
and a sharp jaw. Suja glanced at him as she approached the
biscuit maker and asked her if she could have another biscuit.

'This is the one looking for the new biscuits,' the ajooma
said out loud to no one in particular. The man in the cap
squinted as he drew on his cigarette, and the tip glowed orange, then faded. Suja was startled to smell the scent of real
tobacco, for only favored Party members had access to real
tobacco. She noticed that the man's black leather shoes were
fancier than the state-issued standard and guessed the man
must be someone with access to foreign goods.

The man pulled a few bills from his pocket and handed

them to the ajooma, who took the bills and, lifting the hem of her coat, tucked the money inside the elastic waistband of her pants. She scooped three hot biscuits onto a torn piece of newsprint and handed them to the *ajushee*.

'Let's go for a walk,' he muttered, the cigarette dangling from his lips. His voice was deep and rough despite his slight frame. Suja followed the man, noticing a peculiarity in his gait. Each time he planted his heel, his hips shifted slightly, like a woman's. She fell into step alongside him.

'Not so close,' the ajushee said, and suddenly thrust his hand out in front of her. 'Look alive!' he said as a wide-load hand-cart rumbled toward them with a pile of quilted blankets so high she could barely see the man pushing the cart. After the cart passed, the man started walking again.

'So why'd you want to meet? What're you looking for?' The man's words jumbled together in that lilting, rambling way that northerners spoke.

'I'm looking for someone who may have…who may have gotten lost up north. Could you help me find him?'

'Lost?' he asked. 'Whudduyou mean?'

'Well, I have a friend who was wrongly accused of something and ended up in prison. He's out now, he escaped. Is there a way to find him?'

'Your *friend*,' the ajushee humphed, and took another drag on his cigarette. 'Where'd he escape from?'

'Let's say it was Yodok prison,' she said carefully.

His eyes darted from under the brim of his cap. 'No one ever escapes from there. How'd he get out?'

Suja's face reddened. 'I don't know.'

The ajushee whistled under his breath. 'So, you're chasing some guy who ended up in Yodok an' escaped?'

'Yes,' she mumbled. 'He was wrongly accused.'

He looked at Suja up and down, noting the quality of her

mother's gray gabardine jacket and the Unha-brand bag she had tucked under her arm. She was not the usual kind of client he received from the biscuit seller, and he certainly wouldn't have pegged her as someone friendly with convicts. With her smooth skin and nice clothes, she had the look of a kid from a family in good standing. So why would she know a prisoner from one of Korea's most notorious prison camps? Her story didn't make sense. He narrowed his eyes and considered whether she might be a Party spy. But she seemed too young to be a spy—or at least, too young to be a spy who could present herself so convincingly. So why would someone from the upper class be asking about a convict in that infamous prison camp?

'How'd you know this guy?' he finally asked.

'He's a friend.'

'A *friend*.'

She shrugged, avoiding his gaze.

'Does he know you're looking for him?'

'Probably not.'

'Okay, well.' He scratched his head. 'Yodok's a couple days' walk from the border, so your friend's only hope woulda been to go *up the way*,' he said, using the euphemism for the Chinese border. Noticing the stricken look on Suja's face, he added, 'They haven't reported his capture, right? So he's still alive, hon. Probably in China by now. Hell, if he can make it out of Yodok, he could make it across the Tumen River.'

'Would you be able to help me find out where he is?'

The ajushee snorted. 'The guy's a felon. I'm not in the business of chasing criminals.'

'Do you know anyone who could help me?'

'You're asking for the impossible.' He exhaled a plume of smoke. 'No one's gonna wanna get close to this.'

Suja considered this as they walked in silence, then asked, 'Can you help me get up north to find him?'

The man pushed the brim of his hat back and rubbed his head. 'You heard the announcement—they've been cracking down on defectors for weeks already, so I wouldn't be looking north these days if I were you. No one's moving. Better to talk in a couple of months.'

'What does the crackdown actually mean?'

'They're killin' people. They'll kill anyone who's trying to escape. Most routes are closed now because they're nettin' 'em and shootin' 'em in the river. And we can't bribe guards anymore, 'cause they're punishing guards as well as defectors, even brokers. You could catch your death—damn, *I* could get caught.'

'But there are people still going,' she said.

He hesitated. 'Well, maybe so, but mostly no.'

Suja chewed her lip as she pondered this. She remembered Special Comrade Kim Jong-un's loudspeaker announcement last week where he said they would punish anyone for even *thinking* about defecting. A chill went through her body. He had sounded so threatening, yet how could she wait longer in Pyongyang while Jin was on the run? Who knew where he was now—who knew if she could ever catch up to him?

They had reached the end of the alley now and were facing Chollima Avenue. She gazed at the flying horse statue in the distance and remembered the time she and Jin stood on the rooftop of her building looking out on the view below. Jin had trusted her implicitly as she guided him, blindfolded, toward the edge of the roof. He must have known they were more than a hundred feet off the ground, judging from the stairs they had climbed; he would have heard how far the traffic was, judging from the faintness of the sounds from below; yet he had no fear. She remembered the comfortable

feel of his light grip on her hand and his calm, reassuring presence as they stood side by side overlooking the view of the
city. How confident he was in his trust in her, how unshak-
able his love. This was the bond between them, the note that
hummed beneath everything they did, whether they were
together or not, and she could feel it rise within her now and
fill her with calm. She didn't care about the risks involved—
she was going to find Jin.

'If you can't help me, Ajushee, I'll find another way.'

'Ah, faack,' he sighed, looking away. 'You're hell-bent on
this.' He flicked his cigarette and turned back to scrutinize
her, his sharp eyes studying her face.

Finally he said, 'I can do it, but my contacts up the way
aren't working right now, so it's complicated... I'd have to
work with other guys. I don't know them so good.'

'But you know them enough?'

'What's enough?'

'They're trustworthy?'

He curled his lip and laughed.

He turned onto Chollima Avenue, where a GAZ-51 truck
stood waiting, belching smoke and fumes. This one had wooden
benches built right onto the flatbed and was crowded with pas-
sengers, squeezed in there shoulder to shoulder; the air was rife
with their grumbling voices.

'Ah.' His voice hardened. 'Listen, if we do this, I have to
hook you up to someone new, and if you make it to China,
you're out of my hands. I can vouch for you across the river,
but I can't vouch for anything after that.' He paused, jutting
his lower jaw. 'You never come back from this kind of trip. A
girl like you with soft hands, I'm tellin' you, you're throwin'
your life away.'

Suja stared out onto the broad concrete boardwalk that
stretched long and empty before them, her eyes resolute. 'Like

I said, you don't have to help me. I can find someone else who will.'

'I can take your money just like any other guy. I'm just tellin' you, stupid girl, I see you.' He tapped a stained yellow finger against his brow. 'I know you have a good life here.'

'What do you know about a good life?' she retorted. 'Do you really think we have good lives here?'

He smiled wryly. 'All right, student, fine.' He waved her over. 'Come.'

'So you can help me.'

'Yeah, yeah.'

The ajushee stopped to light a cigarette as two men overtook them. Both were wearing dark standard-issue coats, and one of them turned to glance back at them as they walked past, his eyes glittering. Suja dropped her gaze, thankful that her face was half-covered by her scarf. Those men could have been Party men who had been following them, or they could have simply been strangers on their way to work; one never knew if one was being followed or not.

Once they had passed, the ajushee took her aside.

'You know Saesong subway?'

Suja nodded.

'You get on the subway and go to Pyongyang train station. You buy a ticket to the end of the line, Dongyang station. You ever been?'

Suja shook her head.

'You ride the train to the end of the line and get off at Dongyang. Friday morning, eight o'clock. You have to go upstairs to platform nine and get on a cargo train. There's a change of shift then, so there won't be any guards around. You hop on an empty cargo train, and it'll take you up to the border, where I'll have my contact wait for you. Bring a little food and one change of clothes. Nothing else. Okay?'

'Yes.'

'You bring too much and you'll attract attention.'

'Yes.'

'Five million won, cash.'

Her eyes widened, but she didn't hesitate in her response. 'Of course.'

'Okay. Go home. Eight o'clock. You remember where.'

'Yes.'

'Then go.' He turned from her and walked down the rest of the pedestrian bridge toward the subway. The man nodded in farewell and turned to leave. Suja gave a quick bow and turned back to walk home, lost in thought.

She had just committed to a path of action that may or may not lead her any closer to finding Jin. Every decision in her life up until today was made with a clear sense of her goal and the path forward, but she had no idea what she was stepping into now. She realized the immensity of her decision to leave everything and everyone she knew in the hopes of finding Jin in a country that was a hundred times the size of Chosun. What were the chances of finding him?

She tried to visualize China, recalling photos she had seen in the Rodong newspaper, remembering vague black-and-white images of statue-lined boulevards, ministers in suits shaking hands with one another. There was that photo of Kim Jong-il seated in a red velvet armchair next to Chairman Jiang Zemin; a farmer with a bamboo hat standing in a plowed field next to an irrigation dike; a mass of black heads huddled together in Tiananmen Square as squadrons of marching soldiers goose-stepped past in perfect unison. She imagined herself standing among the audience of thousands, growing smaller and smaller in the scene until she was only a dot, disappearing into a faceless sea. How easy it would be to disappear without a sound, without even the slightest tremor or ripple.

FIFTEEN

Across sloping hills, withered cornstalks lay flat in the fields, their frosted stumps pricking through soil like bristles on a shaved head. Jin looked out onto the fields that undulated and rolled on, impressed by the sheer immensity of arable land. Back home the farmlands were stingy tracts of earth that buried their seeds and barely pushed out fruit. How could such large crops thrive just *north* of his homeland?

He clumped through the fields, looking west, then north, then east. The razed cornfields were interrupted by tufts of trees, small plots of uncleared forest, but otherwise their rows continued on clear to the horizon. To the northeast he could see a small barn, and deep in from the road was a farmhouse with a window that sent a warm yellow beacon across the empty fields. Beyond that was a low mountain. Jin stared at it good and hard—could this be the tunnel mountain Hyuk had spoken of? His knees buckled and he fell to the ground, and he forced himself up again. He would get to the barn and hopefully be able to sleep in it tonight. The thought of warmth spurred him on and he broke into a stumbling run toward the barn, slowing down as he drew near the farmhouse.

He crouched and crept to the barn, where he could hear the soft cooing of sleeping hens and smell the cow manure. The barn door was padlocked, so Jin put his nose in the crack of the door and inhaled deeply. What he would give to be able to lie down someplace warm. Jin slid down with his back against the side of the barn door and looked over at yellow light spilling from the farmhouse windows. He waited. He wasn't sure what he was waiting for, but he was prepared to wait for a long time.

The silhouette of a woman passed by the window, and judging from the ample girth of her shoulders and bosom, she was definitely not from his country, for she was fat, the fattest person Jin had ever seen. He shifted his weight from one side to the other, then pushed himself up again and waited for that woman to come around again. With each moment his breath clouded before his face and dissipated, the frigid air stealing every last hint of warmth from his body.

On impulse Jin decided to approach the lady and trudged across the yard, his boots crunching in the frozen scrub grass. The house was a squat old wooden affair, with a side pantry that was an add-on, along with several other teetering additions that were sloppily assembled like a house of cards, one leaning against the next. Jin lifted his stiff fingers and knocked on the door. After some time, the door was pulled open, and standing in the doorway was a squat, barrel-chested man in a tank top and baggy sweats, his smoothly shaved head gleaming under the light of a bare bulb. He narrowed his eyes at Jin and attempted to shut the door again. Jin stuck his hand out, stopping it halfway.

'Get out of here. I'm closing the door,' the man muttered in Korean.

The man spoke Korean!

Excitedly, Jin exclaimed, 'Please, sir, I only need a moment to dry my clothes and then I'll be on my way again, I promise.'

'We're sick of defectors coming around. You guys are bleeding us.' The man's greasy fingers slid down Jin's forearm as he tried to push him away. He smelled like an animal, like cooked meat, in fact, but as Jin caught a glimpse of the dim room behind him, he realized the smell was not coming from the man but from the entire house. Jin swooned as he recognized the smell; it was the thick, steamy scent of pork-bone soup. He hadn't eaten pork in years. Jin pushed with all his strength against the man.

'Just for a moment,' he panted. 'I'm begging you.'

'Let him in.' A female voice came from within, and the man's wife limped into view. She was a shipwreck of a woman, her body shifting as her left ankle rotated with each step. Her hair was tied back, but gray-black hairs had pulled loose from the elastic, forming a frizzy halo around her head. Held against her hip was a colander heaped with translucent soybean sprouts. It seemed she too was covered in the same grease as her husband. They were ugly, these squat Chinese people who spoke Korean.

'Come on.' Her free hand gestured limp circles in the air. 'Close the door already,' she sniped at her husband.

'Biyu, you listen to me, bitch.'

'Shut the door,' she barked.

The man hesitated for a moment, his black eyes menacing. Then he stepped aside.

'Creep.' He raised the back of his hand at Jin, who pushed past him to enter and bowed to the lady.

'Thank you so much. I don't know how to thank you.'

'There's nothing to thank. Dry yourself. God, you're a

mess. You might as well be wearing a sign that says "catch me,'" she said, examining him with a sidelong glance. Her eyes slid over Jin's body, noting how skinny he was, and tall, very tall for a North Korean—and good-looking. He didn't flinch like most of the Chosun rats.

'You have women friends you're running with?' she asked.

Jin shook his head. 'I'm alone.'

'All alone?'

Jin crumpled by the woodstove, nearly fainting as he felt the first prickles of heat through his frozen clothing. He felt delirious in the warm close quarters of this farmhouse, the air thickly curtained with the smells of pork-bone soup bubbling on the stove.

'Can I dry this?' He pointed to his jacket.

'Take it off, take it off,' Biyu said, and called over to her husband. 'Hey, Lok, toss him a blanket!'

Lok ignored her as he hefted himself onto a wooden daybed in the corner of the room. Biyu cussed at him and walked over to tug at a faux-mink blanket that lay crumpled beneath him. Lok lay there watching her as she gave the blanket a vicious tug, then pinched his leg spitefully. She turned and listed her way back to Jin.

'Here,' she said.

He covered his shoulders with the blanket, noticing that the pile of faux fur was tufted into greasy spikes. Swiftly taking off his clothes, he wrapped himself with the blanket and hunched modestly as he spread his pants and shirt out on the wooden floor next to the stove. He tried not to look at the kitchen, but the bounty of food was a tantalizing distraction in his peripheral vision. In addition to the full basket of soybean sprouts, there was smoked duck hanging over the stove and a wooden rice crate with the open lid revealing pearly white grains of rice. He hadn't seen rice in months. The wealth of food was dazzling.

'Hungry?' Biyu asked.

Jin hunched deeper into the blanket and looked away. The shame of hunger.

'Don't give him today's rice. Give him leftovers,' Lok said.

'Shut up.'

She handed Jin a bowl with burnt congealed rice stuck together in the shape of the pot it was cooked in. Into it she dropped a handful of the sprouts from her basket as well as several pieces of bone from the soup pot on the stove. She drizzled some of the soup over the cold burnt rice and sprouts, then dropped the pot to the floor and huffed as she squatted down next to Jin. He looked at the food heaped in the bowl and it took all his will not to plunge his face right in. He picked up the spoon and shoveled in the food, barely chewing each mouthful.

'The way they eat, these animals,' Lok commented from the daybed. 'Hurry up and kick him out already.'

'So, where are you from, and why are you on the run?'

Jin looked up from his bowl and blinked. He hadn't expected to have to explain his story to anyone. 'I'm from Hamgyong-namdo province,' he said, instinctively changing the name of his province. He was actually from farther north, in Chagang, but the lie came to Jin's lips unbidden and he found himself telling a whole passel of other supporting lies that recast his life. His last name became Yoon, and he told the man that his family were farmworkers with four children and an ailing mother for whom he needed to find medicine from China. The lies spilled from his lips with a natural abandon, and he was startled at how freely, how swiftly he could rewrite his life.

'Medicine, huh? It's expensive. Do you have money?'

Jin shook his head. 'I'm hoping to work and make money.'

'Hmm. You must know some nice girls, eh?' Biyu asked slyly. Jin had trouble reading her expression, for her eyes seemed almost sympathetic, but her reedy tone of voice was discomfiting, like a constant stroking, at once intimate and conniving. 'Because we can help out girls from Chosun, you know.'

'Do you need help on the farm?' Jin asked.

Her mouth turned down at the sides. 'There's nothing for you here. Inspectors have started coming around, so we can't hire you. They'll catch you and throw you over the border, like that.' She smacked her palm.

Jin put his empty bowl on the ground and sat back, hunching into his blanket. 'So I can't work in China.' He stated this like fact. He hadn't considered this possibility.

'*Aaysh*, you can find work, tall guy. You've got the right build, but not in this area. They check us too often.' Her keen eyes slid over his face. 'Go to the tunnels. You'll find out everything there. But be careful. They look for people in the tunnels.

'And if a girl needs help, you bring her to us. I can help girls.' She slapped Jin's thigh and cackled. 'Healthy ones. Healthy ones only! Don't bring us the dying girls.'

SIXTEEN

Mrs. Kim stood patiently by the door with her purse in her hand, her two feet together so that her ankles slightly touched. Her hair was perfectly set with a slight curl at the ends, and her face lightly dusted with pale powder, her lips filled in with burgundy lipstick. She dabbed two fingers on her tongue and smoothed her hair.

'Don't forget to hang up the mirror, Suja,' she said. 'Why you take it off all the time, I don't know.'

'Sorry, Umma.' Suja picked up the mirror from the wardrobe and brought it over to the nail on the wall by the door and hung it upside down.

Mrs. Kim peered into it to check her face. 'Why do you keep doing that?' she asked again, her brow knitting together.

Suja shrugged distractedly as she pulled on her coat. There was a lot going on in her mind this morning. She double-checked to make sure she had her knapsack and her small camera, and she felt the side of her coat for the envelope of money that was tucked inside the coat pocket. She gave the apartment one last scan, her gaze lingering on the tapestried living room, where she spent most of her time.

Her mother had composed their home with a sense of balance and harmony, and this beloved living room was where Suja had spent most of her hours since she was a child. She thought of all the afternoons she had spent kneeling at the coffee table doing her homework and gazed at all the objects in the room that were so familiar and dear to her. The mother-of-pearl end tables that bookended the sofas gleamed softly in the morning light. There was a faint glow on the ceramic vases on the far wall, and the potted begonias on the windowsill were in full bloom again. Her mother pruned and trimmed them every week, coaxing the plants to keep flowering.

She finally turned to her mother and for a brief moment she saw her objectively as a woman unto her own, or as a stranger might see her on the street—a well-dressed woman with bright eyes and full cheeks, who could pass for almost any age except for the slight thickening around the neck, wrists and ankles that betrayed her years. Still, she stood with an erect carriage that made her look regal. Suja was overcome with a wave of love and admiration.

'Oh, Umma, you look beautiful,' she said.

Her mother raised a brow. 'You notice this just now? I look like I always do,' she said, and turned toward the door. 'Let's go. And don't forget to pick up dried anchovies and miso for dinner tomorrow night.' She fished out some bills from her purse and held them up.

Suja eyed the money and hesitated. Her mother shook the bills.

'Okay, Umma,' said Suja, pursing her lips as she reluctantly tucked the money into her purse. 'I'll be late tonight, but I'll pop over before the market closes.'

'Why will you be late?'

'I need to study for a history exam and Mee-ran and I are sharing a textbook, so I'll be studying with her.'

'Mee-ran?' Her mother's voice went up excitedly. She always liked hearing about Suja's friends. 'I haven't seen her for a long time.'

'She's been busy,' Suja said laconically.

Her mother looked at her. 'What's wrong with you, did you get enough sleep?' She held her daughter's chin and inspected her face. 'Look at the bags under your eyes.'

Their faces mirrored each other's, and as Suja looked into her mother's eyes, she found herself overwhelmed by emotion again. Blinking back tears, she assured her mother, 'It's okay, Umma. I'll catch up on sleep after tonight.' She pulled her into a hug and held her tightly.

They walked to the subway station, arm in arm, as others jostled past them on the sidewalk. It was a normal weekday, like any other, except today there were no books inside Suja's knapsack. Instead there were several changes of clothes, some money folded carefully within a sheet of paper and a bundle of food wrapped in a cloth. She had spent the week deliberating about which items to pack, going over family mementos, her drawers of clothes, and calculating how much food she should carry. In the end she chose pragmatically, packing her bag with rice balls, boiled eggs and other provisions and choosing only one small photo of her parents. Telling herself she would be back home again soon anyway, she slipped the single photo between the fabric layers of an inside pocket and zipped it.

The knapsack was tightly packed, but it was lighter than her usual load of books; still, it weighed her down, this dense and carefully considered bundle, which was all she had to survive on for the next handful of days. She had no idea how long she would need to stretch out the food. As they approached the subway, Suja slowed her steps, dragging her feet, hoping to draw out the last few moments with her mom. The morning was passing by so quickly—how could they have gotten here already? Umma was being her usual pragmatic and efficient self, and she was losing patience with Suja.

'What is with you today? We're going to be late. *Come on.*'

'Okay,' Suja mumbled, but barely picked up her step.

Her mother really had no idea, and of course she shouldn't know, couldn't know, what Suja had planned. This was the biggest secret she had ever kept from her mother or father, and it was one with the direst of consequences. Her mother devoted her whole life to ensuring Suja would have a safe and happy life, and now Suja was going to lie to her and leave her to pursue Jin. She was betraying her mother for a man she had met only two years ago. She looked sorrowfully at her mother, the burden of this betrayal weighing heavily on her heart.

Mrs. Kim looked at her daughter good and hard, sensing the shifting inner currents in her child. 'What's wrong?' she asked with some alarm. 'Is there something you want to tell me?'

Suja looked at her mother with tears glimmering in her eyes. 'I just… I'm tired.'

'You're not just tired.' Her eyes searched her daughter's face. 'There's something wrong, tell me.'

Suja shook her head, struggling to maintain composure. 'There's some politics going on at school and it's been stressing me out,' she blurted. 'Kyung-bok and I haven't been talking.'

Her mother looked somewhat relieved. 'Ah… You and that girl are both so bullheaded. Don't let it weigh you down. Let things cool for a week or so and I'm sure you can talk it out.'

'I know,' Suja said unconvincingly.

Her mother hugged her. 'You'll see. You two have worked through worse before.'

'You're right,' Suja said softly, her heart breaking as she hugged her mother deeply. She held her, taking in the floral scent of her face powder and the perfume of her shampoo. She wanted to commit every single thing about her to memory. 'Thank you so much, Umma, for everything. I love you.'

'Oh, honey, I love you too.' Mrs. Kim kissed her on the cheek. 'Study hard today, and see you tonight.'

'Yes,' Suja said, looking longingly at her mother. 'Remember I'll be late coming home tonight.'

Mrs. Kim nodded. Suja watched her mother walk down the stairs, the back of her burgundy coat getting smaller and smaller as other pedestrians filled the stairwell behind her, until finally she disappeared from view. Suja stared down the subway tunnel thinking of what would happen tonight when Umma and Apba realized she was not returning home. They would be frantic with worry when they realized she wasn't with Mee-ran and it would devastate them when they learned she had disappeared. Her father would face severe censure and questioning at the Rodong newspaper because of her disappearance, and her mother would face the same scrutiny from Party members at her university. But most of all, there would be the private anguish they would both feel when they returned home every night to an empty apartment, terrified and confused as to why their daughter had joined the legions of the disappeared.

I'm so sorry, Umma and Apba. So so sorry. Tears spilled down Suja's cheeks.

Chosun History class was beginning in thirty-five minutes, but Suja wasn't going to be there. She got on the subway train, and instead of going to Pyongyang center, she was going to ride the train to the end of the line, as the broker had in-

structed, and get off at the northernmost stop, Dongyang station. Her face still blotchy from crying, Suja sat hugging her
knapsack, her head bobbing as the train bumped and jolted
along the curving track. She focused on the crucial next step
in her journey, repeating the broker's instructions, which she
had memorized. He had told her to ride the train to Dongyang, which was a connecting station for cargo trains as well
as passenger trains. 'You have to go upstairs to platform nine
and get on a cargo train. There's a change of shift then, so
there won't be any guards around,' he had said.

There were few people left in the subway car by the time
the train reached Dongyang. Two older ladies picked up huge
bundled bags and carried them to the door to stand next to a
man in a light jacket who was waiting to exit. Suja followed
them out the door and up the stairs, glancing at her surroundings carefully. She had never been this far north.

Upstairs, the two ladies helped each other load their bundles
on their backs and then hobbled toward the street exit. Suja kept
walking toward the railway platforms, searching for platform
nine. The cargo trains were at the far end of the station, just
as the broker had said, and sure enough, the 8:00 a.m. cargo
train was there, sitting idly. It was 7:45 a.m.; she had made it in
good time. Suja walked tentatively toward the train, her eyes
landing on a boxcar with its door open about forty feet away.
She was hurrying toward it when she heard a shout.

'Hey, you, where you going?'

Suja stopped short, her heart beating wildly as she turned
around to see two guards just beyond the trains at the end of
the station. One of them was crouched with a bowl of steaming ramen held up to his face; the other was standing with a
bowl in his hand, his rifle slung over his shoulder. Suja was
paralyzed with fear as she clutched her bag and camera, fran-

tically racking her brain for something to say. She lifted the camera slowly, her hand trembling.

'Comrade, I was taking photos for a university assignment,' she said in a quivering voice.

'What photos are you taking here? No more photos, student. Put your camera away. And don't point that thing at us.'

'I'm sorry, sir. I'll be on my way.'

The soldier nodded and hunkered back down to join the other soldier. Suja turned back toward the passenger trains, forcing herself to walk slowly and calmly back to the other end of the station. She passed platforms eight, seven, six, and it was only when she approached platform four that she felt comfortable enough to stop and look back.

There were people standing around, waiting to board the train. The clock showed a time of 7:55 a.m. Suja had five minutes left to make it onto the cargo train. She started walking again, this time toward the stairwell, and she ran up the stairs to the upper walkway. She stayed on the upper level and ran back toward the cargo trains, glancing nervously at the post where the two guards had been. She couldn't see them anymore.

She skipped quietly down the stairs to platform nine, praying no one would see her, just as a plume of diesel smoke shot into the air. There was a loud clanking as the train engine started up, and Suja ran frantically along the platform looking for an open boxcar, but all the boxcars on this end of the train were closed. Her eyes finally lit on one with a door left open. Sprinting toward it, she tossed her bags in and pulled herself up onto her elbows, managing to get halfway into the car just as the train released its brakes. She heaved herself forward, drawing her feet in as the train started moving.

Panting from the effort, Suja laid her head to rest against a crate as the train glided into motion, cleaving away from the platform that slid by like the long hull of a massive ship.

For a moment Suja felt the disorienting sense that the concrete platform, rather than the train, was gliding away. It was a strange feeling, as if she were being lifted from her skin and sheared away from herself.

The train pulled out from the station, splitting off from the other train tracks that crisscrossed the broadening rail path. Suja finally looked around inside the boxcar to get her bearings and realized she was in a cargo container that was stacked to the ceiling with three-by-four-foot wooden crates. There was other cargo on board as well: stowaways.

On the other side of the doorway was a woman with two children draped over her shoulder and asleep on her lap. Behind her, squeezed in between the crate and the sidewall, was a little beggar boy whose head lolled in slumber, knees pulled up against his chest, eyes closed. Suja watched him sleep, his bent limbs rocking with the train as it picked up speed.

The wheels squealed and a blur of trees whipped past like ghosts in the sky, vanishing as the train ferried her away from this land. The boxcar shook and shuddered as Suja leaned into the opening, the rush of air pulling at her as she gazed into the open maw of her ever-receding country. She blinked back tears as she felt a tumult of emotions. She was relieved she had made it onto the train, but at the same time she was terrified about what she was doing. *What was she doing?* Every second took her farther down this path she had chosen, but if she jumped now it wouldn't be too late to reverse her decision. She could make her way back to the station and return home in time to help Umma make supper. She didn't have to embark on this trip today.

Suja fell back against the wooden crate. *Stupid girl, cowardly idiot.* Think of Jin and how brave he was to have escaped those prison guards at Yodok—how absolutely fearless. Her journey to find him was a paid vacation compared to his escape. The broker had arranged guides to take her north to the border and across into China—what did she have to fear? Hadn't she heard that many people in China spoke Korean and that there was a network, a vast skein of farmers and households that stretched across the northeastern part of China who helped North Korean escapees and guided them to safety? She would be able to find word of Jin through this network.

She thought of him now, imagining the feel of his hands on her face and his steady gaze on her, and focused on this image of him. She felt a calm assurance descend upon her. He was alive somewhere, she was sure of it. She was going to find him.

Suja settled against the side of the crate and gazed out at the smattering of buildings along the train tracks that started to give way to empty lots, then to large swaths of field that lay barren and exposed in their neglect. Power lines whipped past in an undulation of posts that passed one after the other in an ever-repeating rhythm that was mesmerizing. Suja's eyes started to droop and she nodded off into sleep.

She woke with a throbbing head, legs stiffened in their bent positions, and a burning need to pee. She tried to stand up, but the train was rocking so violently she couldn't balance well enough to prop herself. She managed to push against the cargo box and wedge herself up, feeling her legs start to tingle as the blood started to flow again. The kids were sleeping with their mother, one of them lying with his head lolling off her lap at an unnatural angle. Suja stared at the listless body, watching for signs of life in the child, and was relieved to see his chest flutter with a short breath. She pushed herself to stand, spreading her hands to wedge herself between the cargo crate and the cold metal of the boxcar, and hand-walked herself toward the edge of the railcar. Her body weaved back and forth with the motion of the train as she eyed the passing terrain, a streak of pebbles just beyond the tracks, and then brush beyond.

She turned to check on the others again, making sure no one was watching, then drew her pants down below her knees and turned around to crouch against the door opening. She peered through her legs, trying to gauge if she would be able to aim her urine safely out of the boxcar. Just then the car jolted and her hand slipped. Frantically she shuffled back into the car with her pants around her knees, and hot urine splashed against the edge of the railcar and a dark puddle started to form, spreading down the side of the car toward the sleeping family. Finishing as quickly as she could, she hiked up her pants and scrambled to try to divert the urine with the sole of her shoe. She shuddered in disgust.

Pulling herself back to the other side of the car, she fell against her bag, pulled her jacket down around her waist. The beggar boy was awake, and his dim yellow eyes were fixed on her. He flicked his finger and raised it to his mouth to chew on the nail. He spit out a torn nail and said laconically, 'Is normal to pee in the cars, you know, sister.' He spoke with a heavy regional accent, but there was a confidence in his tone of voice, an insolence really. Suja didn't bother answering. Beggar kids always wanted something, and they'd work at it until they got it from you; it was only a matter of when.

'Your first time riding the trains?' he asked. He was a little spit of a kid, with sharp cheekbones and a thin, dirty face. His hands were grimy with dust and dirt, and his eyes peered out, raccoon-like, from his brown mask. Suja wondered if he ever bathed.

'Going up the way?' he asked.

She lifted a shoulder in response.

'You been?' he asked.

'Why do you ask? Have you been?' she countered.

'Yes.'

'All the way?' she asked doubtfully.

'Yeah, but I got caught. Those Chinese bastards grabbed us and stuffed us in their trucks and rolled us back to National Security, who black-and-blued us. They threw us over to the Yoido prison dogs, except my friend died on the truck ride over. I woke up and he was stiff as a dead rat—he was fatter than me too, but I'm the tougher one, yeah? So they threw us both off the truck and my friend bounced off the road like rubber, you know, the way dead bodies get all rubbery?'

'When did that happen?'

'Two, three days ago? I dunno, I haven't eaten since they nabbed us.' His hand went to his stomach, eyes darting toward Suja's knapsack.

Suja casually draped a hand over the knapsack. They dart in like birds, these beggar kids; that's why they were called sparrow beggars.

'What's your name?'

'Cho.'

'Are you going back up the way, Cho?' she said.

'Uh-huh. No way I'm stayin' here. Friends are all dead an' gone, and here no one never feeds you anyway, so China it is. Even the likes of me can find food in the markets, you know,' he said, looking pointedly at Suja's jacket and knapsack. 'Why you goin' to China?' She clearly had means.

'Oh, I'm looking for a friend who was in a bad way, and I think he is probably in China,' she said, starting to soften toward this tough-talking little guy. His dirty hair stood in uneven tufts, but he had a high forehead and large eyes, and she could see he would have been a beautiful boy if he had ten more pounds on him, and if he were plunged into a bath. The boy lifted his jacket to scratch his belly, and his fingernails sloughed off filmy flakes of dry skin as if he were molting.

'Someone helping you?' he asked.

'A broker.'

'You paid a broker?' Something shifted in Cho's eyes. 'You know this broker long time?'

'He was arranged by the Pyongyang broker I know.'

'I *thought* you were from Pyongyang,' he said with a knowing grin. 'So this broker, he your friend, you know him for long time?'

'Enough, I know him enough,' Suja said.

'Because it can be dangerous for ladies. You have no idea where ladies can end up in China. You sure you trust him?'

'So far everything he's said has been true.'

Cho shrugged and scratched himself again, then dropped his head to rest on his forearms. With the nape of his neck exposed, she could count the notches of each vertebra. Suja pulled her knapsack to her lap, which held within and among the folded clothes fifteen rice balls and half a dozen boiled eggs carefully wrapped in newsprint, a stash of food she had carefully calculated to be large enough to last at least five days, yet be light and small enough to carry across the border. She dug her hand in her bag through her folded clothes and lifted out a rice ball.

'Here, have this.' She held it out to Cho.

He lifted his head, his eyes widening in surprise as he realized he was being offered food. In a flash he grabbed the rice ball from her hands. 'Thank you!' He squatted before her and bit into the ball of rice. There was an earthy smell coming off his body, not entirely unpleasant, and thankfully not the smell of shit or piss. Suja watched Cho gulp the food down in three bites and immediately regretted giving it to him. One of her rice balls was gone just like that—a complete waste! She would have made the most of that rice ball, savoring it and chewing it for at least half an hour.

Just then the mother stirred awake and stared about her blearily as she gathered her bearings. She put a hand on each of her kids and looked out the door at the passing landscape. She hurriedly shook her sleeping kids, who flopped in her arms like limp puppets.

'Wake up, Kee-tuk, Ju-tuk, it's time to go.' She patted each of them on the cheek and bent down, cooing at them. 'Wake up.' She hugged her kids against her breast and slid herself toward the railcar opening, all the while whispering, 'Wake up, we have to jump and run. Wake up!'

The younger one moaned, 'I want to sleep, Umma.'

'Get up.'

'I wanna *sleep*!' he whined.

'Shh,' the mother hushed as the boy burst into a sob. 'Remember, this is the part where we have to run.' She held the boy up and he stood woozily, his head slumped forward until he saw the open doorway and snapped awake.

'That's right, we're going to do our run now,' she said, and wedged herself into the doorway with one knee pressed against the cargo box, her other leg stretched out across the gap. She guided her eldest boy to sit against her extended leg and stretched out her arm in front of his chest to keep him from falling forward.

'Now,' she said. The boy held on to her leg, whimpering. 'I'm coming right after you, just let go, and do your somersaults when you land. I'm going to be there right beside you.' And with that, she nudged him forward. The boy dropped like deadweight, his head disappearing past the lip of the railcar. He gave a short yelp as he crunched and tumbled in gravel. The woman pulled her youngest son up to her shoulder, clutched him tightly and heaved herself forward, and was gone.

Suja popped her head out the side, and a blast of cold wind sent her hair whipping behind her. She looked back to see the woman and her child tumble and roll in the gravel, coming to a stop in some grasses. After a few moments the woman sat up, pulled her younger son up to her shoulder and hobbled back toward her other son. Suja dipped her head back inside again and looked at Cho, who sat watching her calmly with his elbows on his knees, crossing his hands in front of bare shins, a strangely adult gesture for such a small kid.

'Are we getting close to the last stop?' she asked.

'Yep,' he said. 'We have to get off before the train stops.'

'Yes, that's what the broker said too.'

'You ready?'

Suja nodded. Cho sprang to his feet and stepped nimbly over her to stand at the gap. 'Jump and run!' he shouted, then pushed himself out, his legs folding as he rolled in the gravel. Then, finding his feet without missing a beat, he sprang up again and scurried off into the brush.

Suja was the last one left in the boxcar. She crept toward the door opening, unsure of what to do. She held her bundle tightly to herself as she steadied herself against the boxcar wall and peered over the edge of the door gap. There were no lights along the tracks, and though the train had slowed considerably, it was still hard to gauge how far it was to the ground. She stared at the train tracks passing below, her eyes shifting from side to side as she tried to focus on the shuttering rail ties.

Holding her breath, she closed her eyes and leaped: for a split second she was suspended in the evening air, the wind buffeting her body. Then she crashed against the ground, her knees hitting her chest as she bumped and rolled until, finally, she came to a stop. She lay there winded, not sure whether her head was at her feet or her nose to her toes. She stared up into the dusk sky, and finally when the breath came back into her body, she got up and ran into the brush. She heard someone moving through the brush behind her.

'It's me,' Cho whispered.

'Hey,' she said, relieved to hear his voice. 'I'm here.'

He knelt next to her. 'You all right?'

'Yes, and you?'

He shrugged.

'Where are you going now?'

'North toward the river. It's about a two-hour walk. Are you ready?'

'I'm supposed to meet the new broker here.'

'Who?'

'Someone who will take me into China. My broker said he would be near the coal shed by the train station.'

'The fueling station.' Cho crooked his head to the left. 'I'll take you.'

'It's okay,' Suja protested, remembering the Pyongyang broker's warning: *Don't let anyone follow you—come to the meeting place alone.* But Cho had already trotted off down the path, hunching his bony back as he disappeared into the thicker brush.

'Thirsty?' Cho grabbed some blades of grass and ran them across his tongue. He grabbed another handful of grasses and handed them to Suja. 'Careful, or it'll cut your tongue!' He crinkled his nose.

'I'm fine.' Suja declined. Cho shrugged and trudged along the brush, reaching down now and then to grab a handful of grass. The train tracks diverged into several different branches, one leading to the train station ahead, and other tracks ribboning off to the side along several unfinished warehouse buildings that ended in jagged points, rusty metal rebar skewering the night sky.

'They said past the coal pile there's some empty farmhouse where the broker would be.'

'Not an empty farmhouse, but a small house, yes, by the

coal.' Cho slowed his steps and reached down and ran his fingers through the grasses as if he were petting an animal. His hands were never still, they were always roaming, constantly touching his surroundings.

'Where did the broker say they were taking you?'

'Into China. They're going to introduce me to a network of people who help Chosun people like us.'

'You must know some good people, because I've only met people who hate us, or try to use us.'

Suja said nothing to this. No one likes beggars, so she wasn't surprised, but still she wished he would stop asking about the broker, because in truth she knew very little about the man and his contacts; and worse, she didn't even know the biscuit seller who had recommended this broker to her. She started to retrace the steps back to the moment when the broker or the biscuit seller might have given her more information about their identities and contacts, some shred of evidence that she could hold on to and that would reassure her that she was in good hands; but there was no proof—save for the simple fact that the broker's directions had gotten her to this point. There was that.

They were at a point along the fence where wire mesh had been stretched out like the frayed hem of a knit sweater. Cho pulled the fencing aside and climbed through the hole, turning to hold back the torn piece of wire fencing so Suja could follow. He wended his way along the outside of the building, pale ankles flashing as he stepped over rubble and glass until they came to the edge of the building. Up ahead by the side of the road was a small cabin. Suja cocked her head.

'An empty house he said, right?' Cho said, walking up to the house. He peered into a dark window. 'No one around.'

'We should check.'

Cho walked around to the side and pushed at the door. Suja

poked her head and saw the interior had been converted into an office with two dilapidated desks in the main room and a doorway leading to another room. She was about to follow Cho inside when she heard a sound from the neighboring cabin about a hundred feet away. She turned around and squinted through the gloom. There in the darkness, leaning against the coal shed of the neighboring cabin, was a man in a civilian jacket and pants. The two of them locked eyes.

Suja bowed slightly. 'Anyung. Would you happen to have any biscuits?' She carefully mentioned the code phrase the broker had told her to use.

The man leaned forward into the light of the station lamp. He wore a down jacket (definitely a foreign good) and low black boots with a thick ruff of fur at the top. One hand was in his pocket and he stood half in darkness, half in light, his eyes gleaming. 'You the student?' he asked.

'Yes,' she said in a firm voice, her heart thumping, excited that he recognized the code phrase. He seemed to have been expecting her. There was a yelp from around the corner, and Cho came running out of the house, pulling up abruptly when he saw the man in front of Suja. He was not much taller than Suja, but he was stockier and his head was cocked back so that, in effect, he was staring down his nose at Suja and Cho.

'I'm Tae-won. Nice to meet you,' he said. 'I thought it was just you coming.'

'Yes, it's just me,' said Suja. 'This boy was on the train.'

'I don't help beggar kids,' he spit.

Cho came up next to Suja and slipped his hand in hers. 'Come with me,' he whispered. 'We'll get across safely without him. I know people up north.'

She looked down at him kindly, this boy who was all bones, with his tiny face and his blazing eyes. She turned to Tae-won. 'Can we take him along? He's fast, and quiet. He's been there before, you know.'

'I'm not taking no sparrow beggar.' Tae-won scowled.

Cho whispered to Suja. 'You *paid* for this man? It's better you come with me.' He grabbed her arm and pulled at her insistently. Suja put a hand on his shoulder, partly to calm him, and partly to push him away. Why was he so desperate to have her go with him? He may know his way around China, but she was not about to follow him and live the life of a beggar. She was not seeking to escape in China; she was going there to find Jin.

She cast a beseeching glance at Tae-won, who flicked his cigarette and curled his lip. 'Are you an idiot? I can't believe this. I'm leaving.'

'No, no, wait, Ajushee. I'm coming,' Suja said hurriedly. Reaching into her bag, she pulled out another rice ball and handed it to Cho. 'Here.'

She watched him deliberate before taking the rice ball. He had a good heart, this tough little kid, and she didn't want to leave him, but before she had a chance to say anything further, Cho turned to slink away into the darkness without so much as a goodbye.

'Stupid girl, why'd you let the kid follow you? They're nothing but trouble,' Tae-won said.

'Sorry,' she mumbled.

Tae-won led her away from the houses into the fields beyond and Suja followed, holding her bag tightly against her side. They walked through fields, dark and damp, under the dim light of a crescent moon, the stars distant and high in the broad, dark sky. Gradually the ground became rockier with an incline, and she realized they were climbing the hilly side of a berm. He climbed swiftly, using his hands now and again in an apelike knuckle walk. 'Keep low,' he whispered.

'It's not like it used to be. The leader's son is cracking down and they're catching people. So we're going by a new route. It's set up and paid for.'

'Paid?'

'With your money. The guard's been paid off. He'll let us pass through only during the night, so let's go before the sky starts to lighten.' Suja crouched as her feet skittered over dirt. They scurried over the hump of the hill and down the slope to the rocky shore of a river.

'This is it,' the man said, and without missing a beat, he started to undress, pulling off his coat, kicking off his boots and stripping down to baggy white underwear. Suja looked away. Reaching down, she rolled down her socks and pushed down her pants to reveal a pair of culottes. Her pale muscled legs were splotched pink with cold. Suja balanced her bundled bags on top of her head and clambered after the guide into the water. Dark icy eddies swirled around her calves, water so cold it sucked her breath away as it rose to her thighs and then her midriff, until she was up to her chest in the water.

The current tugged at her and she leaned ahead, slanting her body upstream as she lifted and planted each foot deliberately in the mucky bed. Suja fought a growing sense of panic as the water rose to her chin level, and bobbing on her toes, she kept her eyes fixed on the guide. She gulped for air in fitful stops and starts as she struggled to find solid footing until they got to the deepest point in the river and she could no longer touch the ground. She started getting carried by the current slowly downstream, and she kicked and thrusted, attempting to swim with one arm as she struggled with her other to keep her bags above water.

'Get back here!' Tae-won cried. 'You're going too far downstream.'

She paddled furiously, swallowing more water as she focused on the broker. Finally her foot skimmed the ground, and paddling frantically, she advanced farther until both feet could stand tiptoe on the ground. She gasped with relief and paused to gulp and catch her breath.

'Get over here,' Tae-won called from the shore. 'Hurry!'

'Wait a sec.' She nodded, swallowing more water as she spoke. She coughed and spluttered as she struggled for air again. Bouncing on her toes, she propelled herself forward until gradually the waters receded to shoulder level, then chest level. Suja finally stumbled out of the water, teeth chattering wildly, barely able to feel her feet and ankles as they clumped to the shore.

Tae-won led her up the hill toward the brush and kept forging farther into the forest for another twenty minutes or so, and only then did he stop to finally talk to her.

'You did it, we're in China.' His breath bloomed in clouds in front of his face.

'This is China,' Suja said through icy lips she could barely feel. Her face, her head, her entire body was frozen.

'I'll take you to a house where you can warm up.'

'Thank you,' she breathed.

'We've got a lot of ground to cover. You want to go to South Korea, right?'

'No.' She shook her head, alarmed. 'My friend is in China. I have to find him here.'

'You want to stay in China.'

'Yes.'

Tae-won regarded her for a long moment. Then he grunted, 'Good.'

SEVENTEEN

He was a dozen yards from the road when he finally saw it, a knee-high boulder planted next to a wooden fence post at the corner of the field. He loped sideways toward it like a coyote with its eyes on its prey, hind legs aimed elsewhere. *You'll find the tunnel by the rock*, the farmer's wife had said as she handed him a dish towel bundled up with rice and soybean sprouts. *Look for a big rock next to a fence post.* Jin climbed the fence, pushing aside the dry brush as he hiked into the thicket, wandering a dozen steps or so when he saw some scraggly grasses hanging over a dark opening. He approached closer, and as he advanced, the opening broadened into a clearing in front of a tunnel. He wondered if this was the tunnel that Hyuk had mentioned.

Jin entered tentatively, holding his hands up in front of him as he walked in, for it was so dark he couldn't tell if he was about to hit a wall or if he had a hundred yards of clearance. He listened carefully, his nostrils quivering at the unseen current of air that wafted past him, carrying with it the dank, mossy green scent of the earth, and piss. He heard foot scuffs in the dirt, some mumbling, and the faint sound of snoring that ended abruptly with a snort. He carefully extended a foot, tap-tapping as he went forward, taking several steps until he heard a yelp and his right foot slid out from underneath him. He had stepped on something soft, an arm or a leg that felt rubbery and pliant. Jin recoiled, trying to see whom he had stepped on, but he couldn't see a thing; he could only hear the sound of shifting bodies. How many people were camped out here, piled atop one another, sleeping and breathing in effluences in this permanent night?

'Hello?' he called out and waited for a response. There was no reply, but he listened keenly, trying to guess where the sounds of rustling came from. There were other noises coming from farther down the tunnel, clarifying into the sound of footsteps that approached rapidly until suddenly the people were upon him, one of them walking straight into him so that his head collided into Jin's chest.

'Watch it!' Jin shouted, squinting into the darkness to see who had walked into him. Two people jostled each other until one of them finally spoke up.

'Why're you standing there?' It was the voice of a boy not yet fully developed as a man.

'I couldn't—I didn't see you,' Jin said, trying to gauge how old the boy was.

'This guy's new,' said another boy, standing to the left of the one who walked into him. 'I don't recognize his voice.'

'I just got here,' Jin said. 'Who are you?'

'We're brothers, he's Wonho and I'm Minho, and we're headed out to get work,' the boy said, then added, 'So you're new here, huh? You have any food on you?'

Jin fingered the small bundle of rice and sprouts that Biyu

had given him, which was tied around his waist next to the gloves. 'No.'

'Because we can buy it from you, Ajushee,' said Wonho, the younger boy, who came around to Jin's side and put his hand on Jin's arm.

'I don't have anything.'

'But our little sister is dying. We're going to find work and bring back some food, but our sister needs something today. She hasn't eaten in days. You sure you don't have anything to share? We can repay you.' Wonho spoke with an eastern accent, from the coastal region of Hongwon. He had come a long way to end up here inland in China.

Jin hesitated, not sure what to say.

'Please, brother.'

His wheedling plea sounded like the familiar song of a sparrow beggar who would say anything for a crust or crumb. If you so much as looked at them or stopped to talk with them, they'd latch on to you and never let you be.

'I wish I had something to give,' Jin finally said. He knew the boy couldn't see his food bundle, but he covered it with his arm anyway. He didn't have enough food for himself, let alone a bunch of kids. They were probably lying anyway.

'Brother, comrade, anything you could spare for a day or two,' Wonho said, his hand tugging at Jin's arm.

Jin threw off the boy's hand in disgust and stepped away from him. 'Get away from me,' he said curtly, and closed his arm against his body to protect his bundle. He pushed past them to walk farther into the tunnel, hoping they wouldn't follow.

Something about his tone of voice must have persuaded them they'd get nothing from him, for they didn't pursue him. Jin was relieved, although he felt a twinge of guilt in his gut. Back in his hometown of Kanggye, he used to give

the train station beggars some scraps, but now he was fighting off the little bastards in order to protect his own scraps.
Jin hung his head. He was so desperately tired. The fatigue
was as deep as desolation.

He collapsed against the cold earth, and only then did he
allow himself to feel the bundle of rice pressed against his
belly. Reaching inside his jacket, he grabbed it and fished out
a handful of soybean sprouts and shoved them into his mouth.
Thin stalks burst with fluid on his tongue. He picked up a
handful of cold rice and chewed the hardened grains until
they broke down and became a thin paste, the starch dissolv-
ing into vinegary sweetness.

For a brief moment he thought he could smell the sweet
scent of apples, bruised and rotting in the earth. He closed his
eyes, remembering the autumn days in Kanggye back when
he and his friends were in grade school and they hiked out
to the orchards on the hill where they gleaned for apples left
in the dirt by the pickers. As the light fell, they scrambled
through the grass, searching for their prize nuggets, and they
would find them, soft-bruised and brown, pockmarked with
wormholes. Jin remembered how the granular, mealy flesh
would become mush in their mouths as they gulped it down,
core and all. They would return to their homes in the evening with big bellies.

It wasn't long before a barbed-wire fence went up and
guards were posted to supervise the apple harvest so that the
apples could be collected and shipped directly to Pyongyang.
Oh, Chosun. Jin shook his head. The past offered up its riches
just as he was letting it go. The last time he had an apple, he
and Suja shared it in the dorm common room. He remembered how she watched him as he sliced the apple into eight
pieces, handing her the pieces as he went. He gave her the

first piece and also the last, which she refused and turned back to him. 'It's yours.'

'I want you to have it,' he said, thinking parsimoniously about how to make this precious apple last.

'But it's your piece—have it, Jin! We can get another, you know.'

'But this is more than enough,' he said.

Perplexed, her brow drew together as she held out the last piece of apple for him. 'Is it? Have as much as you want. We'll get more.' Then her expression changed and her face softened. 'I guess apples were hard to come by in Kanggye?' she said.

Jin's neck reddened as he deliberated about how to answer this. Apples weren't the only thing hard to come by in Kanggye, but he wasn't going to get into that with her. He didn't want to tell her that his family had to survive on diminishing state rations as famine hit their region, nor was he going to tell her how his mother, like so many ajoomas in that region, had resorted to foraging for pine bark to make porridge. It had gotten to the point where it was hard to find a pine tree that hadn't already been stripped. He lowered his eyes in shame. In moments like these he was reminded of how wide the divide was between him and Suja. She would never know—could never know the degree of privation he had known in his life.

He took a breath, composing himself, and looked up at her with a cocked eyebrow. 'We had lots of apples,' he said gamely. 'As a kid I could eat dozens of apples at one sitting. We used to scavenge for them.'

'Really?!'

'We'd compete to see who could eat the most,' he laughed. 'There was a big orchard near one of my friends' houses, and we used to climb over the fence and pick apples.'

'You raided a farm?!' Suja exclaimed.

'Well, we only take the ones on the ground.'

'The rotten ones?'

'The forgotten ones. They were the most delicious.'

'Aren't they, though.'

He chuckled and leaned in to kiss her smiling mouth. 'Like you.'

'Forgotten or delicious?'

'What do you think?' he said, gazing into her clear eyes as the mirth softened, settling into a contemplative moment between the two. When he was with her, the past didn't matter; there was only the present and a vision of their future that filled him with a sense of optimism. With Suja he could have faith in life.

'Well, you'd better not forget me,' she said.

'You're too delicious. And besides, you won't be able to get rid of me. I'm never leaving your side.'

Jin remembered their hug, the feel of her arms around his neck and the smell of her hair against his face. It was with this memory that Jin finally fell asleep on the cold dirt floor.

Jin awoke to the sound of high heels clack-clacking at the entrance of the tunnel as a woman walked into view, silhouetted against the light.

'Hey, girls, I'm here!' she called out in a strident voice, seemingly already impatient. 'Any girls need help? I can help you.' She fidgeted, her birdlike head turning fitfully this way and that. 'This is your last chance.'

There was a scuffling from deep within the tunnel and a young woman shouted, 'Wait a minute!' and she scrambled toward the light, towing another woman by the hand. They stood before her, two skinny whips, hugging themselves for warmth. The woman held them at arm's length, sizing them up, then drew them in to talk with them, her head bent intently.

Jin couldn't hear what they were discussing until the woman shrilled, 'I'll take you, but her, there's no use, no one wants a pregnant girl.' The woman wrapped her coat around herself and glared at the girls. 'Make up your mind.'

The girls curved into each other like shy teenagers; their pale faces were smooth without a wrinkle, but their skin was so drawn it was hard to tell whether they were eighteen or thirty-two. One had a slender oval face, the other had a broader face with a square jaw, and she was the talkative one.

'She's smarter and way prettier than me,' she said. 'Please, Ajooma, once we fix her up, she will be such a good worker.'

The woman glared at the pregnant girl. It was true, with an oval face and almond eyes, she was a looker. But any fool with eyes could see she was too far gone in her pregnancy; even with her arms crossed over her belly there was no mistaking the melon-shaped hump.

Jin watched the pretty one, wondering who had gotten her pregnant and why he wasn't with her now. He thought of what a man can do, how the fruit of his actions can get away from him and he might never know. Was the father still in North Korea? Was he even alive? Jin passed his hand over his face and rubbed it. Back in Pyongyang he had imagined one day he and Suja would have kids together.

The voices of the women in the tunnel were raised as they started to squabble and the pregnant girl shoved her friend away.

'Just go,' she exhorted.

'Introduce us to a doctor,' her friend implored the lady.

'Do you know how much it costs to get that taken care of?' the woman snapped back.

'We have money. Please, Auntie, introduce us to a doctor,' the girl wheedled.

'Better she push it out than get it ripped out. She'll die from it.'

'But we heard doctors in China do it.'

'Did you hear how many girls die from it? Stupid bitches.' The woman fidgeted and stepped around the two girls as if to leave.

'But, Ajooma.' The pregnant girl followed after her. 'My friend had it done and she's fine.'

'Go to your friend, then. You girls have to separate anyway if you come with me.' The woman turned back to her friend. 'You coming?'

The pregnant girl's face fell. She stepped forward and nudged her friend. 'Go with her. I said I'll be fine.'

Her friend shook her head. 'I'm not leaving you.'

The pregnant girl pushed her friend away. 'Follow her, don't be stupid.'

'No,' her friend said, faltering.

'I don't need any favors from you!' she said angrily. 'You have to go, you know that.' She looked at her friend, then put her arms around her and started weeping. 'There's no other way.'

Jin watched the bickering girls and shook his head, thinking bitterly about the strife that seemed to run through the heart of Chosun. Put two North Koreans in a life raft together and what do you get? Two comrades at the bottom of the sea.

'Your friend is right,' the older woman grunted. 'You have to.'

The other girl broke down too now. 'Look at us, we never should have come!'

The pregnant girl put her hands on her shoulders and hugged her deeply, saying, 'You know there's nothing for us here. It'll help no one if we both sit here and starve to death. At least if you go, there is a chance you can help me from out there.'

'Your friend is right,' the older woman insisted.

The two friends let go of their embrace, and the friend said, 'I'll send a message for you. If you end up leaving, please tell those here where you're going.'

'I will,' promised the pregnant girl.

The woman tucked her chin into her furry coat collar and took her friend's arm, her heels clack-clacking against the packed dirt as she and the girl walked into the dying light.

EIGHTEEN

Suja could see through rippling panes of glass the silvery blond grass lying flat in the fields. A dog yanked against its chain, panting clouds of hot breath. A sack of rice lay against the doorjamb next to brown lacquered urns, tiny pearls of condensation stippling the clay. Suja was sitting opposite Tae-won, who sat cross-legged on the yellow linoleum with an ashtray at his feet, a trail of smoke rising up and dissipating into a fog that hovered above their heads, halfway to the ceiling.

'When are they supposed to come again?' she asked, spreading her hands on the heated linoleum, feeling the radiant heat from coal-fired pipes beneath the floor pulse into her palms and fingertips.

'Anytime now,' said Tae-won.

'How are they connected with that broker in Pyongyang?'

'They're not. I know them through another connection.'

'Oh...' said Suja. 'But who are these guys?' she pressed.

'They're Chinese guys, and they deal with North Koreans

in their country. They're good at—' he paused here for a moment '—*placing* people. They'll find you a home.'

Suja's guard went up when she heard this. 'Yes, but I'm here to find my friend,' she said.

'They're well connected. If your friend is in China, they'll be able to help you find him.'

Just then the wooden door creaked open, and two men clumped their boots at the entrance, letting in a draft of cold air.

'Hello, Yung-sing. Hey, Guo,' Tae-won greeted them.

'Hello, hello,' they muttered, stepping down on the backs of their runners and kicking them off next to the other shoes that were lined up against the raised platform floor.

'Now.' Yung-sing, the older man, rubbed his hands as he clambered onto the floor, hiking up his pant legs as he squatted to sit. His cheeks were ruddy from the cold, and when he bent down, she could see his bald pate, which was fringed with short tufts of black hair, chafed and pink. He motioned to Guo, his companion, who came to sit next to him, hesitant, watchful. He was a much younger man with an angular face that would have been handsome but for an elongated chin that jutted too far. Yung-sing sat silently with a look of fierce concentration on his face as he rolled a piece of curled paper back and forth between his fingers.

'*Zheige sher da?*' he said, his eyes flicking to Suja, then back to Tae-won.

'Yep.'

Yung-sing snorted up phlegm and mumbled something under his breath, his words thick and garbled.

'What?' Tae-won retorted, and started arguing with him in Chinese, a language that slurred *ch* and *ssch* sounds in ways that were entirely foreign to Suja's ear. Yung-sing fought back and the two parried with each other, the air growing thick with argument. Cigarettes burned down in the ashtrays. They seemed to hit an impasse, and Yung-sing thrust his fists in his lap and turned his head away, contemplating the row of earthenware urns lined up against the wall. Suja, beginning to feel uneasy about the situation, retreated from them until she sat with her back at the wall. Things didn't feel right. The Pyongyang broker had never said she would be meeting Chinese brokers.

Tae-won leaned in toward Yung-sing and spoke in a lower voice this time, cajoling him. They started seesawing back and forth again, and at a certain point Yung-sing reached into his pocket and pulled out a wad of Chinese yuan bills. Thumbing through them, he shaved off half the wad and tossed them to Tae-won. Suja bolted upright, the skin on the back of her neck prickling as she watched Tae-won pick up the bills, count them and fold them into his pocket.

'What's happening?' Suja asked, getting up on her feet. She eyed the door uneasily, wondering if she should make a run for it.

Tae-won took a drag on his smoke, the tip crisping red as he inhaled. 'It's taken care of.' He wafted the air in front of him. 'These men will take care of you. They'll take you to a place.'

'I'm not going with these men. I don't know who they are, and they're not about to help me find my friend, are they?'

'I don't know, you can ask them and they can look for you.'

'They don't even speak Korean!' Suja's voice slid up.

Tae-won sighed and said a few words to Yung-sing in Mandarin. The man looked at Suja and nodded. Then Tae-won turned to Suja. 'I told him about your friend. He'll help.'

'But you don't even know the details. How do they know who to look for?'

'It doesn't matter, they'll start asking their men. So for now, you go with them, and they will look for you.'

Suja weighed the situation, her eyes darting from Tae-won to Yung-sing to the door. What Tae-won said just didn't make sense.

'Where will I be staying? Will you be coming? We need a translator.'

'These men will take you to a good place. I'll call to check in later.' Tae-won flicked his cigarette, missing the ashtray.

'Why don't I stay with you while they look for him?' Suja reasoned.

'No, you have to go with them, but I'll call in a day or two.'

'I'm not going with these men,' she said firmly. 'I paid you to guide me.'

'Job's done, I brought you to China.' Tae-won's voice was flat. 'Now these men will take care of you.'

'You can't leave me with these men. I don't speak Chinese. I'm coming with you.'

'You have no choice. It's done. *Zao-le.*' Tae-won stood up and started zipping his jacket.

'No,' Suja exclaimed. 'I'm not going with these men.'

Putting out his cigarette, Yung-sing leaned over to shake Tae-won's hand and gave him a clap on the back that was just hard enough to knock him forward. Guo, the younger, long-faced man, approached Suja.

'I'm not going!' she shouted. Tae-won turned to her, and in one swift, violent motion, he clamped his hand over her mouth. Stunned, Suja tried to pry his fingers apart, struggling against him, her nostrils filling with the smell of stale tobacco on his fingers.

'Shut your mouth, bitch, or you'll get us all caught,' he snarled. 'You think the walls don't have ears here in this country?'

Suja jabbed at him with her elbows, desperate little rabbit kicks, then finally turned her head and bit his palm. He smacked her, and the room reeled as she fell to the floor and hit her head on the linoleum. Before she could find her bearings and straighten up, Tae-won yanked her back up.

'You go with these men, or you go to the Chinese police,' he menaced. 'You choose.'

Suja's eyes gradually found focus again on his face and the gravity of her situation hit her. She had heard the stories about what happened to North Korean women in China. This couldn't be happening to her.

'I'll pay you more than what they paid you!' she cried desperately, digging her fingers into his arm. 'My family will find you. Don't let them take me, for the love of Chosun.' She was dragged by Tae-won over to Yung-sing, her socked feet sliding on the slick linoleum as she struggled and resisted. Yung-sing and Guo grabbed her, pulling her arms back behind her shoulders to wrench her wrists together. Guo pulled out a plastic zip tie and zipped it around her wrists and pushed her through the door. She stumbled outside into the bright, cold air, terrified, her whole body shaking.

She called to Tae-won, pleading, sobbing, but by this time both Chinese men were pulling her along to their car, a green Hafei sedan parked at the side of the farmhouse. Suja realized with a sickening sensation that once she was in that car, there would be no escape. 'Please, Tae-won, I have more money! I'll pay you!' she shrieked. Yung-sing opened the passenger door and pushed her facedown into the back seat.

'Stay down.' She heard Tae-won's voice from the direction of the house. 'Or the roadside CCTV cameras will pick you up.'

Suja rolled onto her side, her hands still tied behind her back as the men climbed into the front seats. The car coughed into ignition and bumped along the long puddled driveway, pausing at the end before it revved onto the main road. The sudden acceleration pressed Suja into the back seat, mashing her face into the black vinyl upholstery. She struggled against the zip tie at her wrists, wriggling to see how much she could move her body. Surely there had to be a way for her to somehow push herself out and make a run for it. She arched her back, twisting to see how much she could move her shackled hands. Moving carefully and silently so as not to attract the attention of the men in the front, Suja stretched her arms back, pulling her shoulder blades together as she reached for the door. She could barely breathe from the straining effort, and she finally let her shoulders fall limp. Even if she managed to open the car door, what would she do next? Run with her hands shackled? How quickly could she run, and to where? It was broad daylight and there was no forest, no alley, no busy street market to run into.

Tears spurted in her eyes, tears of rage and terror. She had no idea where they were taking her and was terrified of what these men might be capable of. *Stupid, stupid idiot.* She had brought this onto herself. She had betrayed her family and her country, left her privileged life behind—and for what? She had been stupid and reckless and now no one in her family knew where she was. There was no one to catch her fall, no one to save her.

When the car finally braked to a stop, Guo reached back and slipped a jackknife under the zip tie around her wrists and cut her loose. Her hands fell to her sides as pins and needles shot through her arms. When he opened the rear door, Suja stuck her head out the door, breathing in the cool, acrid air, and glanced around to see where they were. They had parked in a brightly lit parking lot that was surrounded by apartment buildings with hundreds of glowing windows. All the illuminated streetlamps and building lights were disorient-

ing, for Suja was accustomed to buildings being left unlit at
night. The darkness in her neighborhood in Pyongyang was
vast and undisturbed. But here everything was lit brightly as
if on display. Suja felt vulnerable, exposed as the men flanked
her on either side and led her toward the building.

The fluorescent lights in the lobby cast a green pall on their
skin as they walked in. They led her to the elevators, where
they carefully arranged to stand on either side of her. Suja
looked up to see a small camera eye in the corner of the elevator and stared at it before looking down at her feet.

The doors opened on the sixth floor, revealing a dingy
pale pink hall, punctuated with burgundy doors. Yung-sing
led the way, walking to the end of the hall and turning the
key in the last door. The apartment had a broad square living room that was skinned in beige linoleum, with lavender
floor-length curtains with plastic jewel appliqués. Aside from
a sofa, a coffee table and a TV pushed against the wall, there
was no other furniture. Guo glanced at Suja and pointed to a
door, then collapsed on the sofa next to Yung-sing and pulled
out his cigarettes.

Suja seized the opportunity to put a door between herself
and the men and walked into the room that Guo had pointed
out, discovering it was a small bathroom with pale blue floor-
to-ceiling tiling. There was a spout with a shower handle for
bathing, a sink and a toilet. Swiftly pulling down her pants,
she sat down on the toilet and sighed with relief; a good, long
pee. It was small comfort, she thought miserably. She peered
out the window just above the toilet and saw the lit windows
of the other apartment buildings around her. Standing up,
she leaned into the window well to see how far it was to the
parking-lot level. Her heart sank when she saw they were a
good six stories or more above ground level. There was no
way she could jump.

She went to the sink to wash her face and noticed in the mirror a crease line that went down the side of her cheek from when she had lain with her face pressed against the car seat. She stared at her half-moon eyebrows, her nose, her pale lips, the oily wisps of hair pushed behind the ears. She looked the same as she did before she had left home, but the circumstances of her life had brutally changed and she was terrified of where things were heading.

If only she could run back in time and be in Pyongyang with her family, or even if she were able to go back to the border and to have decided differently then; perhaps she should have followed the beggar kid, Cho—at any one of these moments Suja could have chosen a different path and changed the trajectory of her fate. But what could she do about it now, trapped in this bathroom, with those two men outside the door?

She heard them talking through the door, or rather it was Yung-sing on the phone, talking in short bursts, the pitch of his voice loud and insistent. Suja stood behind the bathroom door for several moments, then went back to the toilet, put the lid down and sat. She could hear the shuffling feet of people moving around upstairs, and the tinny treble beat of music on the radio. She was tempted to knock on the ceiling or to scream, but she knew it wouldn't help her at all. They would probably ignore her, and it would only anger Yung-sing further. She looked forlornly through the window, wondering if there were other women held against their will in this building.

When she finally opened the door, the TV was turned on and the two men were watching a show with a woman in a red sequin dress singing in Mandarin. There were several bowls of noodle soup on the coffee table; Guo pushed one toward her. She took it. She hadn't eaten since the morning before and the salty, meaty aroma of the noodle soup made her mouth water.

Yung-sing snapped his phone shut and turned to talk to Guo, who got up and went to the kitchen. He came back with two cans of Tsingtao and cracked them open, handing one to Yung-sing. The men lit cigarettes. They spent the next two hours watching the TV.

Suja curled up on the floor and fell asleep.

The next evening the men took Suja back out to the car with her hands tied behind her back. This time they let her sit in the back seat, which she took willingly. She looked out the window at the streets and buildings, trying to get her bearings, in order to figure out where they were taking her. She watched the lights of the city go by, a bleary stream of colorful neon signs, traffic lights and the yellow glow of living room lights that dotted the apartment buildings. The explosion of light and the sheer numbers of people on the streets were staggering to Suja. What did all these people do? What were their homes like, what kind of lives did they lead?

They eventually turned onto a highway that led out of the city. Suja stared dolefully into the windows of the other cars they passed, managing to lock eyes with a woman sitting in the passenger seat of a sedan. Something in Suja's expression must have struck the woman, for she was staring at her, disconcerted. Realizing she had her attention, Suja mouthed the words *Help me* through the window, but the woman looked alarmed and turned away. Suja's heart sank as she realized the woman didn't understand Korean. Their car soon exited the highway and turned onto a rural road that continued on uninterrupted with few streetlights and no road signs. They drove past empty fields, and as the evening darkened, Suja looked out onto the rolling hills, unable to tell whether they were going north, south, east or west.

They turned onto a smaller dirt side road and drove with gravel pinging the undercarriage of the car until they finally pulled in to the driveway of a farm with rows of plastic-framed semicircular greenhouses with plastic wrap rustling in the wind. Several wheelbarrows were lined up next to one of the greenhouses with a pile of daikon radishes beside them. Suja glanced bleakly at the rows of greenhouses and the surrounding fields. Aside from the silent greenhouses, there were no other buildings for as far as the eye could see. The place was isolated.

She eyed the radishes as they walked past, their knobby white flesh glowing like pale-skinned human limbs under the yellow light of a bare light bulb. They walked past a coal shed toward a farmhouse that had a thin trail of smoke rising from its chimney. Yung-sing knocked on the door and waited, his breath clouding his face.

The door yanked open and a man with broad cheeks and dark skin greeted them.

'Mr. Wang?' Yung-sing asked.

'*Lai, lai, lai.* Get in, get in,' Mr. Wang said, waving them in. He was a heavyset man wearing a quilted shirt and quilted pants. He glanced at the men and his gaze landed on Suja, his eyes taking her in without any expression.

Guo and Yung-sing led Suja into the main room of the house, which was draped in colorful faux-mink fur blankets. Between two shiny black plastic tables with chrome lamps was a long vinyl sofa on which a young man was seated with his knees spread, forearms resting lightly on his thighs. He was taller than Mr. Wang but had the same broad brow and wide-set eyes. There was something edgier about this younger man; his eyes kept roving restlessly. The older man Wang

landed on the sofa next to him and gestured for Suja and the
men to sit opposite them. They filed in and sat down on the
slippery vinyl love seat with Suja hemmed in on either side
by Yung-sing and Guo. She looked around, disoriented by
the brightly decorated room, the slick black and chrome furniture. A woman walked into the room carrying a tray with
a plastic plate of peanuts and several bottles of beer. With her
hair cut exactly like the men in the household—short in the
back and front and slightly longer flaps of hair that hung over
the ears—it was hard to tell her gender. Her quilted pants
hung thick and loose and she was sheared of all the physical
trappings of womanhood; still, there was a strong matronly
air about her. Moving swiftly, she set the tray down, pushed
the plate of peanuts onto the table and grabbed the open beer
bottles, handed a tallboy to each of the Chinese men, then
held out the last one to the younger man on the sofa. 'Ping,'
she said. He snapped to attention and grabbed the beer out
of her hand.

Suja sat on the edge of the sofa, her skin prickling with
dread as the conversation ensued between Yung-sing and
the man. This meeting was about her, clearly, but she had no
idea what terms were being discussed. She watched warily
as the woman sat down next to the younger man, placing a
hand on his arm as she leaned over to whisper to him. They
both looked at Suja, who averted her gaze. The conversation
among the men picked up in pace, and at one point the old
radish farmer stood up and paced the floor, taking one slow,
measured step after another, hands crossed behind his back.
Yung-sing gestured at Suja, exhorting Mr. Wang to come
back to sit down at the sofa.

Suja interjected, turning to Yung-sing. 'Please, can we go?
My family will be searching for me and they can pay you any
amount!' she pleaded in Korean.

'Shut up,' Yung-sing said, and turned to Mr. Wang again, who sat down with a grunt. They bantered a bit until finally Mr. Wang reached into his pant pocket and pulled out a roll of bills wrapped in an elastic band and threw it onto the table. Yung-sing took the roll, snapped the elastic off and started counting.

Suja beseeched Yung-sing, 'No, don't sell me to these people!' Getting no response, she tapped Guo's jacket sleeve, and pleaded in Korean, 'Please don't do this. I promise you, my family can pay you. Please!' Guo extricated his arm. Yung-sing meanwhile had pocketed the cash and was nodding at the farmer. All eyes were on Suja.

She grabbed Guo's leather jacket and held tightly.

'I'm not staying. Take me with you.'

He pushed her off.

'No, no, no.' Suja shook her head, her voice rising hysterically as Guo and Yung-sing stood up. 'I can't stay here. I will do whatever to repay your debt.' Her voice slid into a wail. 'I'm from a respectable family. My uncles will come after you!' She ran after Yung-sing and Guo, but the older woman stepped between her and the door, blocking her way. Suja tried to push past her, but the woman pushed her back toward her husband, who grabbed Suja by the shoulders, and the two of them muscled her back into the living room and then dragged her over to a small side room. The radish farmer held her against the side of a wooden daybed as his wife brought a length of blue-and-white plastic rope and tied Suja to the bedpost, starting with her wrists, then her ankles, muttering to herself as she looped and double looped the knot, then pulled it tight. They left Suja sitting on the edge of the bed with her wrists tied to the bedpost, the rope chafing her ankles.

Suja stopped speaking, stopped attempting to move and surrendered herself to her confinement on the bed. Looking down, she noticed the mattress was stained with several splotches of yellow and brown. No sheets, just a quilt pushed up against the grimy wall. She was in a state of shock.

Through the open bedroom door she could see Mr. Wang hectoring Ping, who was seated on the sofa as before, with his knees spread, his lower lip hanging open. The father swatted at the side of his son's head and he ducked, accidentally knocking a half-empty beer bottle that tumbled to the floor, rolling under the sofa. The mother screeched at them and grabbed a rag from the kitchen. Wiping the splash of beer on the table, she picked up the other bottles and empty plates and piled them onto a tray. Then she bent down to wipe under the sofa, lifting each of her son's feet as she wiped beneath them. She heaved herself up again, her voice dwindling into a complaining, almost coddling whine as she leaned over her son and finger brushed his hair to one side. He shook his head, muttering angrily at her, but she continued to finger comb his hair, to which he submitted wordlessly. He lifted his dull eyes to meet Suja's gaze across the room, and in that moment she realized why his parents had purchased her.

NINETEEN

Jin hid out in the tunnel for several days listening to men come and go, speaking of road crews, greenhouse farms and dockyards with ships that could provide passage to other countries. They bandied about the names of different Chinese cities: Yanbian, Baishan, Helong, Longjing. Jin repeated these Mandarin words, his tongue curling over the strange sounds as the Chinese village names started populating his mind like random pins on a corkboard. He sketched in buildings and streets, and the map of China started to fill in Jin's mind, but it was a fugitive's map filled with dangerous pits and swamps, crosshatched and shaded with darkened areas to avoid, officials and underground people to evade. Now that Jin had made it out of North Korea, he wasn't safe or free; he was heading deeper into a nameless country, that of China's underground, built around North Koreans who were willing to take on any illegal work. Now and then someone would show up with a tip about a possible job, and the news was whispered throughout the tunnel.

'There's a huge apartment building going up in Helong. They'll take workers if you're strong enough,' someone said.

'Ach,' a fellow scoffed. 'People die on those jobs.'

'What do you mean *die*? You mean falling off the buildings? It's up to you whether you fall or not.'

'Man wasn't made to live in the sky. I like farmwork better.'

'Stupid idiot, farms are more dangerous. Y'know the inspectors have started batting heads in the Fusong region.'

Jin listened to these faceless men, culling nuggets of fact from their conversation and tumbling them in his mind, rendering them into essential pieces of information.

There were inspectors in Fusong: avoid looking for work there.

Helong was a city with tall buildings like Pyongyang. There was possibly work there, but dangerous work.

There were many Korean-Chinese folks whom you could approach, but some might take advantage of you.

'You guys been here long?' Another voice chimed in. 'I got here about a week ago, crossed the river and just about froze my nuts off. I'm never doing that again!' Jin's ears perked up when he heard the man's voice. Using his hands to guide him along the tunnel wall, he walked carefully toward the entrance.

'Hyuk, is that you?' he called out.

'Jin?!' Hyuk stepped into the tunnel. 'Is that you, you bastard? You're here?!'

'Yeah, I made it!' Jin rushed forward.

Hyuk grabbed him and wrestled him into a bear hug. 'I can't believe it, you skinny bastard, you're alive. I came here to find you!' He clapped Jin's back and turned toward the rest of the tunnel. 'Hey, everyone, this guy busted me out of Yodok prison! He saved my life.'

'I couldn't have made it without you, Hyuk.'

'I'm not sure about that,' he chuckled, 'but I *am* gonna get you out of this hellhole. Come on out into the light, let's see your face.'

They headed to the tunnel entrance as Hyuk gripped Jin's hand tightly as if to confirm it was truly him in the flesh. 'I can't believe this, I can't believe it's you.'

In the light Jin could finally see Hyuk and noticed his face was looking haggard and his hair was disheveled, but he was clean-shaven and he had gotten a coat from somewhere. Jin looked at his friend, his eyes shining. 'God, it's good to see you, Hyuk. I didn't know if I'd ever see you again.'

'I wasn't going to let you rot.' Hyuk smiled, and peered into the dark tunnel, his voice turning somber. 'Did you, uh… have you heard anything about Bae?'

Jin shook his head. 'I've asked around and I haven't heard a thing.'

Hyuk looked down. 'I figured.'

They fell silent as they both thought about the last time they were with Bae, and those final awful moments in the dump truck. Jin put his hand on the older man's shoulder.

'He'll find his way, Hyuk. He's tougher than you and me both.'

'I know,' he sighed, his face dark with worry. 'What can you do?' He stared into the trees, then glanced back at Jin. 'Well, I'm glad you made it to the tunnel. Look at you. Come. This guy I know put me onto some work in town.'

'Wow, who's the guy?'

'A guy named Jung, friend of a friend I met on a previous trip to China. My friend put in a good word for me and the guy put me up for a few days. He and his wife run a shelter for North Korean women.'

'Really? Why would they go out of their way to help us?'

'They're Korean Chinese, Christian maybe.'

'What's that?'

'You know, they believe in God and go to this secret church. They do good things for people, help them out. Jung and his wife have helped a lot of Chosun folk. They run a small factory where women can live and work, and they've helped people escape out of China too. Jung took me in, fed me and introduced me to a slaughterhouse in town. I've gotten work there, and it's good, so I came here to find you.'

'This is amazing.' Jin clapped him on the back. 'You've saved my skin, brother. I thought I wasn't gonna make it.'

'This ain't no Yodok, my friend. I mean, it's no Hilton either, but you would have found your way, one way or another.'

They hoofed it down the mountain, Hyuk leading him down a skinny slip of road that slunk over a hill where it met with a gravel road that, as far as roads go, was more an afterthought than a full sentence; it didn't lead anywhere. As they walked along, Jin told him about the Chinese farmers he had met who helped him find the tunnel mountain, and Hyuk regaled him with stories about how he found his way to Jung and his wife and several women who were staying there and working for them. It sounded like a close-knit little community, a safe haven away from authorities.

'Are you staying there, Hyuk? Do they have any extra space?'

'I can't stay there any longer, it was just temporary. Their shelter's just for women.'

'Why women only?'

'There's so many of them and not as many of us.' Hyuk shrugged, slowing down as they approached an intersection.

'We're gonna wait here for a truck, and that'll be our ride into the city.'

'Okay,' Jin said, looking around. 'Is it okay for us to be out in the open like this?'

'It's fine, they don't patrol these roads here.'

They stuffed their hands in their pockets and hunched against the wind that whistled through to every bone and knuckle. There was no protection out there, no haven. Jin gritted his teeth to keep them from chattering.

Finally, a truck stopped, its gears rumbling and grinding down to a phlegmy rattle. Without a word Hyuk pulled himself up and grabbed the side of the truck and jumped over. Jin followed suit, his feet clattering on the metal truck bed. They clambered next to a man crouched beneath a blue tarp.

'Jin, meet Bo,' Hyuk muttered, pressing his back against the truck cab. He pulled the tarp over to cover them, but it barely reached across to Jin's shoulders.

'This is meant to hide us?' Jin asked as he huddled next to Hyuk. The truck hiccuped on the gravel road and they were bumped up and down, a jangle of bones under a flapping tarp.

'So where we going again?' Jin asked.

'A charnel house in Tonghua,' Hyuk said.

Tonghua. Jin remembered hearing about the construction crews in that city and figured it was a city of some size and industry. He sat back as the truck sped past farmhouses and fence posts until fields gave way to intersections and the bumpy ride slowed to the stop and go of the city.

The truck finally pulled in to a lot and the engine puttered out. Hyuk pushed off the tarp and jumped out. Jin stretched his arms, stood up and shook his legs, then clambered over the side of the truck, his feet landing on frozen mud that was pockmarked with footprints. They were in an alley that was flanked by old corrugated metal buildings with sliding ga-

rage doors. The truck driver had parked behind a wide building made of sheet metal that was peeling flecks of pale green
paint. Clouds of steam billowed out of a vent.

Hyuk pushed through the double steel doors into the charnel house and Jin and Bo followed him into a large warehouse area with rows of pigs hanging snout down, front legs
thrust out as if they had been hooked midflight. Their pale
skin was baby pink.

Hyuk called out to a couple of people as he headed over to
the sidewall where several men were suiting up with brown
plastic aprons and black rubber gloves. He chatted with them,
looking over at Jin and Bo, who stood by the hanging pig
carcasses, wondering what to do. A couple of men at the end
of a row started pushing the hanging pigs along the ceiling
tracks toward the steel counter at the far end of the room.
Other employees took their positions at the splitting station
where they picked up the cutting saws and turned them on,
the blades whirring. They set them down again, stuck their
hands inside the fronts of their aprons and waited.

Jin heard the pig before seeing it. It gave a terrifying shriek
as it was led into the concrete catchment, balking, squealing,
skittish and crazy. The slaughterer pushed against it with his
hip to coax it forward and position it by the electric genera-
tor that had been turned on. Large metal tongs hung over the
wooden fence. The slaughterer's movements changed swiftly
as he pinned the pig against the fence and reached for the
tongs in one smooth motion, and without actually looking at
the tongs, he brought them down on either side of the pig's
head just under its ears, and jabbed. There was a loud *bzzt*
sound and the pig stiffened. Two guys dragged it away even as
the next pig was being brought into the pen. They lifted the
dead pig onto the running rack of steel rollers and pushed it
into the hot waters of a scalding vat where the hog rolled and

bobbed, its pale skin slowly deepening into mottled shades of rose like a feverish baby. It took several minutes for its bristles to start to curl and loosen from its skin. Then the two men hauled it out of the water.

Before this, Jin had never seen anything larger than a rat being killed. These pigs were heavier than humans, with long smooth torsos and rubbery, humanlike skin. Jin watched with horrified fascination as the men pushed and prodded the dead animal. He was reminded of the dead in Yodok prison camp whose corpses were picked up by the guards and thrown into garbage carts, their limbs all jangly loose. This was the brutal truth of the body in death.

Overcome with a sudden urge to retch, Jin ran to the garbage bin to heave into it, coughing up strings of soybean and saliva. He wiped his mouth clean and stood at the side, watching the men on the assembly line, these faceless men with black aprons and gloves, pushing and struggling with the pig corpses. How many of these men were North Korean defectors? How many of them were hidden away in this vast country? Was this the fate of all defectors who were forced to live underground in China?

Could he eke out a living here and hopefully get himself established? Jin thought about Suja, wondering how he could ever hope to reunite with her. There was no way he could return to see her in Pyongyang or to see his family in Kanggye. Could he work at this job for now and make enough money to save and send for her? He lingered at the side of the hanging racks, lost in his thoughts, when a large man in a navy down coat and boots came clumping through the abattoir. He stopped by the scalding vats in front of line three and pulled a damp toque off his head. He counted the number of men on the assembly line, poking the air with his finger; then he checked line two.

'What the hell is goin' on here?' he spluttered, looking at Jin, Bo and a few other guys. 'Who are these guys?' he asked Hyuk.

'New guys, they're fine,' Hyuk said in Chinese. 'They're strong, hard workers. They're good.'

'Good or not, I can't have more illegals here. I told you we can't run them here no more. Leung's shop got raided and look what happened,' the man spluttered. 'He had to pay a hundred thousand yuan in fines! And he was closed for a week.' The man eyed Jin and the others and waggled his finger at the door. 'Get out.'

'We need 'em today, boss man. We're short,' said Hyuk.

'We can do without 'em.'

'Can't. The line'll get backed up.'

'Get 'em out, or I'm kicking all of you out,' the boss man threatened. Hyuk stepped forward, lowering his voice as he pulled him aside to engage him in a separate conversation.

Jin bowed his head, shrinking back against the wall. He looked at Bo, who raised his brow but remained silent. After a few minutes Hyuk walked back. 'I'm sorry, guys, but you have to get outta here. I'll stay on for this shift, and at the end of the day, we'll drive you back to the tunnel. Sorry about this.'

Jin's heart sank.

'You gotta go, or we'll all lose our jobs.'

'Okay.' Jin nodded and turned with Bo and the others to head out the door.

Scowling, Bo shoved his hands in his pockets and kicked at some frozen gravel. 'Why'd he bring us anyway? You heard the boss man, he doesn't even like northerners.'

'I guess he was hoping to get us work,' Jin mumbled.

'It's all the same at these places. They kick you out because they're afraid of getting raided,' Bo muttered, shaking his head. They turned a corner out of the alley now and walked along the side street. A bus with the word *Harbin* flashing on its windshield drove past them with a whoosh of diesel fumes.

'Hey,' Bo said suddenly. 'We should go to Harbin and get work on the docks. You're lucky if you get hired to work on a ship. It's good money and it's safe. Or we could find girls to make deals. Did you see many girls in the tunnel?'

Jin looked at him askance. 'What do you mean "make deals with girls"?'

'Deals with traders. They give good money and the girls get a home.'

Jin glanced at him sharply, not quite catching his drift, but sensing there was something illicit cloaked in his casually vague words. Jin thought about the woman in high heels who had come to the tunnel looking for girls and he remembered how the farmer's wife had asked him if he knew any girls.

'So why do so many people want our girls?'

Bo shrugged, his thin shoulders lifting inside his shell jacket. 'China needs women, they're short...so they'll pay money for them.'

'You mean Chosun girls are being *sold* to the Chinese?' Jin said in a harsh whisper.

'They're matched with *husbands*,' Bo corrected him. 'They get a home, they get a life, and some of them can even send money back to their families.'

'How could you even suggest we do that?'

'There's not a lot of options for women. I mean, a lot of people do this.'

'You tried doing that shit?' he asked Bo.

'What?'

'Selling girls.'

'Nah, but Sarge, this guy, knows about people who do,' said Bo.

They were approaching a strip of noodle shops and barbecue

restaurants, and smells of roasted meat and soup wafted over
to them. Jin's stomach began to grumble. Stepping around
a pile of lidded boxes and bowls at a plastics store, he asked,
'How do you know Sarge?'

'Met him here in Tonghua, he's a broker who helps people escape, and there's plenty others like him. Sometimes
they come to the tunnel too. Hell, Hyuk knows about them,
everyone does.'

'Everyone,' Jin repeated laconically, eyeing Bo, figuring he
was the kind of guy who made blanket statements like that.
'Everyone' could mean one person, or even no one. He pulled
Bo to one side as a man behind carrying two large plastic
bags cussed angrily as he pushed past them. There were so
many people on the sidewalk, jostling one another, fearlessly
oblivious to the motorized bikes that snorted in and among
the pedestrians and cars. All the people wore warm clothes
that fit their bodies, bright blue and neon sport jackets, dark
woolen coats with fur trim flashing silver and gold buttons.
How plump the women were, their cheeks fresh and round.
These were well-fed people living the good life. Jin thought
of the pigs in the charnel house and thought this is where the
pigs all ended up, in the bellies of these citizens.

Back home his family was still living in famine conditions
under the austerity regime, while here the average citizen ate
meat, had electricity in their home and drove around in a car.
There was no reason why North Koreans couldn't live like
this too. How could the Dear Leader have kept this all away
from his own people? How could Jin have devoted his life to
this leader who had banished him from his country and his
family, ultimately over a sack of cornmeal? Jin felt like a fish
caught up by the tail, sliced open and gutted, his life suddenly
emptied of meaning.

He remembered how he used to scrimp and save his uni-

versity food rations. He made cornmeal cakes for Suja one
night in his dorm's coed area. Drawing from his small sack
of weekly rations, he poured corn flour and barley flour into
the bowl and mixed in some water. He was making duk patties for supper, the usual. The charcoal briquette had burned
down and he poked at the glowing embers before resetting the
grill just as Suja walked in, dropping her books on the table.

'You love cornmeal so much!' She came over to his side,
kissing him on the cheek.

'It's comfort food.'

'Did you eat it often when you were a kid?'

'It's what I grew up with. We were lucky to have cornmeal, in fact.' Jin scooped out a ball of dough in his hands
and started shaping it.

'Oh, really? What about rice?'

Jin pressed the ball of dough between his two palms, flat-
tening it into a patty as he considered how he might answer
this. He hadn't told her yet how his family had been badly
hit by the famine during the Arduous March. Poverty was
an embarrassment, especially in comparison to her family
and that certain class of society in Pyongyang that seemed to
have skated above the austerity regime. He wanted to distance
himself from the farmers and the factory workers of the small
towns. But at the same time, he was proud of his own family who were educated and in good standing with the Party.
His father was a well-respected superintendent at the tooling
factory and his mother was the most ingeniously resourceful
person he had ever known; they were honest, good people,
and there was nothing to be ashamed of, he knew. And yet
he was ashamed.

Jin dropped the patty onto the griddle, and scooped up
another ball of dough. 'Well, rice was hard to come by up
in Kanggye. But my mother was able to find it from time to

time. The day we learned about my scholarship she splurged
and bought rice on the black market and made us a feast.
Growing up, we didn't really do celebrations, not even birth-
days, but the scholarship was different. Even my dad got behind it, I remember he told me I did well.' He tucked in his
chin and lowered the timbre of his voice, mimicking his father. '"You've brought great prospects to this family, Jin. Why
do you think I worked so hard to teach you over these years?
This is what it was for."' Jin's mouth twisted at the memory.
'He was as tight with his compliments as he was with money.
Even that toast ended up being about him.' He looked down
at his hands, realizing he had squashed the dough flat. He
scrunched it into a ball and started over again. Suja watched
him thoughtfully.

'Maybe your father was trying to explain why he pushed
you so hard as a child.'

'Maybe.'

Suja watched the duk patties sizzle on the griddle. 'I didn't
realize how your family was hit by the Arduous March,' she
said, adding quickly, 'Of course it makes sense, everyone was
hit by it. But I just didn't know the extent... How did your
family make it through the hard years?'

'We foraged, bartered, basically survived by any means necessary.' He gave a short laugh. 'You do what you have to do.'

'That's your strength, isn't it, Jin. You do what you have
to do to succeed, by any means necessary,' said Suja with a
smile. 'And that's our strength as a nation. Look at the size of
our nation, we're a small country compared to America and
yet we have our own nuclear program. We Chosun people
will achieve things by any means necessary. We will prevail.'

Her words stirred him then, and emboldened him now
as he gazed out onto the bustling Chinese street. He looked
around at the buildings and the people on the sidewalk, won-

dering whether he could make a home here for him and Suja.
He would find a place to live, and somehow have Suja come
join him here to start a new life together. He vowed silently,
I will find a way to reunite with her by any means necessary.

TWENTY

Ping stood with his head tilted, thumb pressed over the end of a hose as he sprayed down a row of rusty spades and rakes leaned up against the shed. He zigzagged the spray of water across each shovel, watching flecks of dirt fly off, hitting his boots and sweatpants. When he finished spraying down the last shovel, Ping threw the hose down and walked over to the spigot and turned it off. He shook his hands in the air, then rubbed them against his pants. He collected the spades awkwardly in his arms and carried them to the toolshed, dropping a couple on the way. He stooped to pick them up, struggling to try to fit them into his armload, until finally he let a few drop and trudged over to the shed. He came back to pick up the ones on the ground and tossed them into the shed. He hooked the padlock through the door and looked over at the house. It was 6:00 in the morning and Mama and Baba were up, the living room and kitchen lights on, but his bedroom window was still dark.

He didn't want to go back into the house, not yet.

Ping stooped to pick up the end of the hose and walked back toward the tap, coiling the hose around his arm, and dropped it by the faucet. He stood there for a moment, deliberating what to do next. The farm was silent. There was nothing left to do.

He dropped his hands and ambled toward the greenhouse, more out of force of habit rather than with any real intent. He pushed through the plastic tarp at the entrance and stood there looking at rows of napa cabbage that glowed luminously white in the predawn light. He grabbed a small picker's stool and squatted on it. He reached down and picked up a clump of dirt, absentmindedly crumbling it between his fingers. When he had sifted the soil through, he reached down for another clump of dirt. He was a man of few words.

It was hard to find a wife in these parts. There weren't many single girls in the area, and no city woman wanted to live on a farm, let alone move out to a farm to live with a man and his parents. People left farms to start their life in the city, not the other way around.

Mama put some time into finding him a woman. She spent Sunday afternoons sitting on her end of the sofa with the phone tucked in the crook of her neck and a colander of bean sprouts on her lap. She pinched off the brown tips of the sprouts as she dialed old friends, going as far back as her elementary-school years. 'Sister, it's been so long, remember me, Xiaoping?' She gossiped and chattered with friends as far as Jiamusi, near the Russian border. But each time she hung up, she'd look at Ping with an implacable expression on her face. 'No luck.'

It was embarrassing, the number of calls she had to make.

Finally Mama decided to go to the marriage market in Shenyang and started scribbling down an ad. Ping protested at first, uncomfortable with the idea that his face would be posted up as a hopeful groom. He was worried someone they knew would recognize his face. But even more terrifying was the prospect that no one might respond. How many ads were posted up at these things? Women had the advantage, for there were thirty million more men than women in the country. How was any guy supposed to stack up? Women had the unfair advantage.

Mama worked on the ad and showed Ping the text: tall, single man, thirty-six years old. Healthy, strong. Comes from a good family. Owner of a farm in Fushun.

'Your photo will be on it too,' said Mama.

'Put *good-looking* in there.'

'Of course.'

'And should you take out the "farm" stuff?' Ping asked. Mama deliberated about whether it was better to include that he was a landowner (and therefore a man with assets) or whether it was better to avoid mentioning the farm at all. In the end Mama decided to keep it in. She ripped out ten sheets of lined paper from her notebook and wrote the ad out ten more times.

She posted up the ad in different places at the marriage market in Shenyang, posting up the ad among the fluttering pieces of colored paper that other people had posted, advertising their marriageable sons and daughters. She stooped to read the ads with pictures of women. Surely there would be a match for Ping among the dozens of female names that she saw. She carefully copied down names and phone numbers in her little book, creating lists of dozens of names.

She phoned everyone on her list, talking to mothers about their daughters, and most of the time she received the abrupt response: 'She's gone. She's married off already.' Mama did manage to arrange for several meetings and Ping went to these

meetings with a weird mixture of resentment and hopeful-
ness in his heart. They weren't all that pretty, these remain-
dered girls, who were mostly plain or gawkish—not that he
minded that, but he hated the feeling of having to beg for
their interest. These stupid, ugly girls would be so lucky as
to marry a man like him.

None of the matches took.

In the end Mama said she had finally found an arrangement for him through marriage brokers. But when the two
men walked in with that girl, Ping realized that this was no
normal match; Mama had purchased a North Korean woman.
He didn't know how he felt about it; that is, he felt a lot of
different things, he didn't know exactly what. He'd have to
face Mama, Baba and that woman in the house again shortly.

He wished to God that Mama had told him she was getting a Northern. Actually he wished she hadn't purchased a
bride for him. Certainly he wanted to have a woman—it was
long overdue—but did it have to be a Northern? And did
she have to be so good-looking? He didn't want an ugly girl,
but he was intimidated by how pretty this girl was. Probably
a city girl. She looked like it. Ping lit a cigarette and, holding it between his second and third finger, cupped his hand
around his mouth. He drew on it slowly, smoked it down to
the filter, then butted it out in the dirt. He stood up, wiped
his hands against his pants again and headed up to the house.

Mrs. Wang pulled open the door with a suck of air that
seemed to pull at the very walls of the small room. Cooler air
flowed into the room, bringing with it the sounds of morning: the scraping of a chair on the floor, the sound of the gas
element on the stove, the smell of simmering congee. She put
her fists on her hips. 'Get up,' she said, and marched toward
the bed where Suja lay under the quilt. There was a rough
bluntness to her touch as she clapped a hand on Suja's back

and fixed her shrewd eyes on her. She had a tanned face with
cheekbones like burnished chestnuts, crow's-feet etched deeply
around her eyes. She tucked Suja's hand into the crook of her
elbow and led her out the door.

She brought Suja to the bathroom just as Ping was walking out of it and he eyed her warily as they passed each other.
Suja stepped inside the bathroom quickly, closing the door
behind her as she looked around at the long, narrow room.
It was covered from floor to ceiling in pale green porcelain
tiles with an embossed pattern of brown flowers. In the left
corner of the room there was a tap trickling water into a blue
bucket that overflowed into a rusty center drain. Off to the
other side, set into the tiles, was a floor toilet with a hand
pail of water next to it. There was a small window above the
toilet that was about a foot tall and a foot and a half wide.
Too small to crawl through; still, Suja went to it and tried
to open the sliding windowpane. She struggled with it but it
wouldn't budge. She stared at the window, trying to quell her
mounting panic. How was she going to get out of this place?

Even if she were able to escape out a window, it would be
hard to make a simple run for it, for there were no forests
nearby, no markets, no buildings in the surrounding area in
which she could try to hide herself. They were in the middle
of nowhere. Suja tried not to despair. There must be a way to
escape. She took a deep breath and dipped her hands into the
blue bucket and splashed her face, her whole body stiffening
at the shock of the cold water.

When Suja came out of the bathroom, she saw Mr. Wang
walk in through the side door, carrying loops of metal chain
and a lock.

'How's this?' He held up a fist filled with lengths of chain.
The chains were brand-new, gleaming silvery blue, and the
lock still had a key inserted in it.

Mrs. Wang barely paused her eating to nod. 'Sure.' She pointed to the living room.

Mr. Wang glanced about at the kitchen table, the sofa in the living room, the end tables, the television—there was nothing that could serve as an anchor.

'I need a firm thing, something she can't walk away with,' he said.

'How about the bed?' said Mrs. Wang.

'Someplace firm, I said...'

'Tie her to the stove, then.'

He looked toward the kitchen, then said to Ping, 'Go get her.'

Glancing at Suja hesitantly, Ping walked over to her and grabbed her by the arm to guide her to the kitchen.

'Let go of me. You don't need to tie me up,' Suja protested. As soon as she started to resist, Ping's manner changed. He seized her by both of her arms, squeezing tight as she struggled against him, and pushed her toward his father.

Mr. Wang looped the chain around the stove leg and grabbed Suja's ankle, wrapping the chain around it and snapping the padlock in place. He gave the chain a quick yank to make sure the lock held fast.

Suja pulled on the chain and beseeched Mr. Wang, who ignored her and instead started opening drawers, pulling out knives and handing them to Ping. He pointed to the top of the cupboard. Ping took the knives and reached up, placing them out of sight. Mr. Wang checked the counter, the stove and finally Suja. Satisfied that she was safely secured, he said a few words to Ping and turned to leave. Suja watched Ping guardedly as she edged away from the stove, bracing her trembling hands against the wall. Ping was nearly a foot taller than her and had the ropy, muscled physique of a farm laborer. When he tossed his plastic cup into the sink, her eyes darted, following the movement of his hands.

Ping sensed her fear and grimaced contemptuously. This was not a 'bride,' this terrified Northern shackled to their stove. The girl was not much better than a farm animal. Scowling, he reached for his jacket and yanked it off the back of a chair, knocking it over. He stomped out the door to join his mother and father outside.

Suja walked over to the kitchen window, her heart still pounding in her chest as she watched Ping argue with his mother, gesticulating angrily at the house. Mrs. Wang shook her head and pushed him toward the greenhouse, where several workers stood waiting, snapping their gloves over their fingers, black boots kicking up tufts of dust. Suja edged herself over to the far side of the window until she felt the heavy chain pull at her ankle. She peered past the field toward the empty road, where aside from the electric poles she could see no road signs or billboards, no information indicating where this farm was located. She waited to see if a car might pass. A flock of small sparrowlike shrikes lifted up, then settled again on the power lines.

Suja turned away to frantically search the house for a way to escape. She walked toward the living room, managing to get three feet into the room before the chain pulled her back. Comparing the slant of light from the living room window to the kitchen window, she tried to ascertain which direction was north and which was south, but the sky was overcast and it was impossible to tell the direction of the sun. Suja returned to the kitchen and sidled next to one of the counters, managing to stick her fingers into a drawer pull. Inside were spoons, ladles, chopsticks and rubber bands. Suja stared at the melamine soup ladles in the drawer and thought about trying to fashion a sort of bladelike weapon with them; but then she couldn't imagine using it. What would she do, kill them all? If only she could get away somehow, she could run and hide out in the mountains or in tunnels, like she had heard many North Koreans do.

With the house empty, there was a silence throughout and Suja was able to gradually calm down. She surveyed the house again, slowly this time, and guessed it was about seven o'clock in the morning. Back in Pyongyang the university corridors would be teeming with students. Rhetoric class would be starting soon and she'd be at her desk watching Jin open his notebook, smoothing it down the middle fold with the flat of his hand. Oh, what she would give to be back in Pyongyang. Suja thought of Jin and imagined what he would do if he were in her shoes. He was a strategic thinker and it helped her to imagine him with her, figuring out how to get out of this place. He'd be looking for information, noticing anything and everything that could be useful for an escape.

She spotted a wall calendar by the living room door and stared up at the poster image of a woman in a low-cut red dress that revealed her white breasts. The woman stared off camera with her lips slightly open, as if she were looking up into the eyes of a lover. The photo was much more explicit than anything allowed back home. Suja scanned the calendar dates below the photo and recognized some of the Mandarin characters from her high-school classes in Chinese: Sunday, Monday, Tuesday... She tried to count the days back to when she first hopped on the train in North Korea, but then stopped.

It wouldn't make a difference what day of the week it was. She was trapped in this Chinese family's home and no one knew where she was.

Ping and his parents came back at the end of the day carrying a large yellow plastic colander filled with some cabbage and bok choy. Mrs. Wang set down the colander on the floor and dropped the bok choy in the sink. She motioned to her husband. 'Free her.' Suja rubbed her ankle as Mr. Wang unwound the chain from her limb and Mrs. Wang waved Suja over to the sink and handed her two big handfuls of bok choy with roots still clumped with black soil.

She nudged her. '*Xi*, wash them.'

Suja stood at the sink and turned the tap on, watching the water splash over the pile of bok choy. It was surreal to be standing next to Mrs. Wang and helping her with dinner, as if they were mother and daughter and they did this every day. Suja picked up a couple of heads of bok choy and set about washing them. The stalks were white and luminous, crisp and firm to the touch, the fronds deep green and robust. As she started trimming the roots, Mrs. Wang pressed the button on the rice cooker and opened the fridge door, pulling out a plastic bag with a whole BBQ duck inside it. She kicked the fridge closed and slapped the duck down on the cutting board. She pulled at a wing, stretching it out as she took a cleaver and deftly sliced the wing clean off. She de-limbed the entire duck and started chopping away at the breast and back. Steam started bubbling out of the rice cooker.

They sat together at the kitchen table, with Suja and Mrs. Wang on one side and Ping and his father on the other side. Suja avoided looking at Ping during the meal, focusing instead on her dish. She was famished, for she hadn't eaten since the day before, and she ate carefully, silently, acutely aware of the family's eyes on her.

After dinner Ping showered and changed into a different pair of jogging pants and jersey shirt, and stood by the kitchen, beads of water dripping from his hair onto the back of his shirt. Suja was helping Mrs. Wang clean up when she pointed Suja to his bedroom door and said to her, '*Zou*, it's time for bed.'

Suja shook her head. She glanced furtively at Ping and bolted past him to the living room and sat on the sofa, tucking her feet beneath her. 'I'll sleep here.' She patted the sofa arm.

Mrs. Wang called her husband, who came to the kitchen, and the two of them approached Suja.

'Lai, come on,' said Mrs. Wang as they grabbed her arms and lifted her from the couch. They pulled her into the bedroom. The rope they had used for her the night before was still tied to the bedpost and Mr. Wang grabbed that to tie Suja's wrists together as Mrs. Wang held her down. Suja struggled against them and tried to negotiate.

'Please, let me sleep on the sofa for a couple of nights to start.' Mrs. Wang ignored her, all the while talking to her in Chinese in a tone that was firm and pragmatic, as if she were giving her instructions. They bound her wrists tightly against the bedpost and backed away.

Ping eyed the whole incident from the door, standing half in, half out the room, rubbing his shoulder against the doorjamb like a cow nuzzling a salt lick. As his parents left the room, he finally walked in, or stumbled rather, more an act of hesitation than decision, a comma in the middle of a sentence that was still being formulated.

The hairs on the backs of Suja's arms stood on end and she scrabbled around the bedpost, pushing herself up from the floor where she had been sitting, to get as far away from him as possible. She pressed her back against the bedpost and they leveled their gazes like animals casing each other, their eyes clocking every movement.

When Ping remained by the far wall with his back against the closed door, it slowly dawned on Suja that perhaps Ping didn't know what to do. She decided to take charge and jerked her head toward her wrists. 'Untie this, don't just stand there,' she blurted in Korean, surprising even herself with this sudden burst of anger.

Ping narrowed his eyes at her but knelt by the bed to start working on the knotted rope. Suja waited for the rope to ease around her wrists and ankles, but the minutes ticked by and the clenched knot would not loosen. Ping scowled and bent down farther to work at the knot. His guard was down while he focused on the knot and Suja stared at the top of his head, wishing she could knock him out now; but of course her hands were tied. She twisted to her left, pressing her wrists against the bedpost in an attempt to create some slack, and Ping was able to finally fit a finger into the knot and pry it loose, unraveling the rope from her wrists. Suja held out her wrists in front of her and ran her hands along her arms, then stretched out her legs, feeling pins and needles prick her calves and feet.

Seeing Suja move freely, Ping's hesitation suddenly dropped away and he reached over to pull her to him. Suja tried to shake him off, but he dragged her toward him easily and pushed her down on the bed. Suja managed to wriggle away and got to the edge of the bed, eyeing him fearfully, every muscle in her body tensed and ready to flee. Through the corner of her eye she could see the door and she gauged how many steps it would take for her to reach it. Ping patted the mattress beside him. Suja shifted her weight so she could slowly drop her foot to the ground. Ping's hand shot forward and grabbed her wrist, pulling her to him. She curled away from him, as he drew the blanket over to her and fumbled as he touched her. Ping's hand traveled down her body, clumsily patting her arm, her side, then her hip, as if he were checking a horse and patting its flanks.

He pulled her closer to him and started groping her breasts, squeezing them. Suja crossed her arms, trying to cover herself, but he pried her arms apart. They struggled like this until Ping wrapped his arms around her in a big bear hug and held her immobile.

'Stop it!' he cried.

Suja tried to kick him but he turned her onto her back and rolled on top of her until his whole body pinned her down. Suja struggled, sobbing now as she writhed beneath him. His face was pressed to hers, the stubble on his cheek, the garlic smell of his breath, his mouth next to her ear, grunting. Suja shook her head, trying to push him away, trying to avert her head. Ping clamped his hand over Suja's mouth and reached down with his other hand to pull her pants down. He yanked them down to her knees and pushed himself against her, grunting. Suja held her breath, holding her legs together tight, eyes frantic as she felt his penis press against her belly. Ping looked confused for a moment, then jammed his knee between her thighs to pry them apart. Suja fought back, hitting him as hard as she could, and still he bore his weight down on her. He slapped her, knocking her head against the wall.

'No!' she screamed, and managed to climb off the bed. She reached for the door. Ping leaped off the bed and slapped her hard, knocking her into the wall. He hit her again, banging her head against the wall, and Suja blacked out.

TWENTY-ONE

Stepping back into the shrouded darkness of the tunnel was like entering a tomb. Jin clenched his jaw, his throat constricting as he felt along the wall until he came to the place where the rock gave way to a broader embankment. He let himself sink to the ground and wrinkled his nose at the dank smell of wet earth and piss. He heard a woman weeping and peered into the gloom, but couldn't see a thing.

'Are you okay?' he asked. But really, were any of them okay?

'Can you help me?' the woman sniffled. 'I don't know how to get out of here, and no one can help me. I'll end up dead in this pit.' She started sobbing again.

Jin recognized the pregnant woman's voice and remembered the tears on her beautiful face as she hugged her friend goodbye.

'You're not going to die here,' he said in a half-hearted attempt to console her. He was so dejected after leaving Hyuk, he wasn't sure what lay in store for him, let alone any of them, but he knew the prospects for this woman were not good. He let his head fall back against the tunnel wall, wondering how many people died in this tunnel. Would he be one of them as well?

'How do you know, Opba? Can you help me?' she asked.

'I don't know, I'm just saying, there's got to be a way.'

'I need a doctor.'

'I'm sorry, I don't know any doctors,' he said tiredly.

'But do you know anyone who might know a doctor?'

He thought about Hyuk and that acquaintance he mentioned, that fellow named Jung, who ran a shelter with his wife. 'I know someone who helps women out, I'd imagine they could be able to help. But I'm not sure when I'll see him...' His voice trailed off.

'Do you...do you know anyone else? Someone close by?'

Jin leaned his head back against the wall, remembering Lok, the Chinese farmer, and his wife, Biyu. 'There was a couple who helped me when I first crossed the border, they said they could help girls.'

'Oh, really?' The woman sidled toward him until she was close enough for her trembling fingers to touch his arm. 'Were they nice?' Her face was almost level with his, and he could see her lucid eyes, the hollow of her pale cheek. The last time he was this close to a woman, it was Suja, and he felt a sudden pang of loss as he thought of her. He pulled slightly away from the woman, flummoxed and unsure about what to say to her. He wanted to help, but wasn't sure about recommending the Chinese couple, considering what Bo had told him back at the charnel house about what happened to North Korean girls.

'They seemed nice enough,' he said hesitantly. 'They gave me food and let me warm up, but I don't know what they could do for you.'

'They must be connected.'

'Maybe.' He furrowed his brow. 'I never asked, so I don't know if they have any connections, or whether we can trust them.'

'We can't trust anyone anyway.'

Jin gave a wry grin. 'I guess you have a point. But I know I can trust Hyuk, and his contact would be pretty solid. I'd try them first.'

'When will you see him again?'

'I'm not sure. I could go into Tonghua to look for him again next week.'

'Next week?' she moaned. 'What about the Chinese couple, can you talk to them sooner?'

Jin tilted his head. 'They're only a few miles away. I could maybe go there tomorrow.'

'If they're only a few miles away, why not talk with them today,' she said. 'Let's go before we lose the sun.'

She had guts, this girl.

Jin nodded. 'Okay, let's go.'

They left as the moon rose, a curved blade in the late-afternoon sky. The trees in the fields cast long, silent shadows, and the air was calm and still.

With his long-legged stride, his tall, lean body slipped through the trees as he led the woman down the mountain, pausing only to hold aside branches for her, his sure hand inspiring confidence. At the edge of the field, he lifted her and helped her over the fence. Light as a bundle of sticks she was, and to think that she was with child.

He pushed through the frozen cornfields, boots crunching down on frosty soil as he led them past rows of cornstalks and past the stubble of a fallow field as the sun slowly set, and the moon cast a thin silvery sheen over the fields and trees. They walked in silence, heads bowed, bodies hunched to conserve heat. They talked as they walked and Jin learned the woman's name was Mee-jung. She told him that her husband had died in a prison camp several months ago. He choked when he heard this and almost asked her which prison camp, but bit his tongue. He didn't want to know.

'I'm so sorry for your loss,' he said gruffly.

'What can you do? When he was sent to the prison camp, I knew our life was over,' she said. She and her friend had crossed over to China weeks ago, hoping to find food and work, but so far, they had had no luck.

'There's a saying my father used to say about survival, "You need a little...something...to survive."' He faltered as he tried to remember the saying. 'You heard it?'

Mee-jung shook her head. 'A little courage?' she guessed.

'No, not that.'

'Smarts.'

'You definitely need that, but that isn't it,' said Jin.

'Heat, I need heat to survive,' she said hastily. 'Come on, let's get going.'

They passed two farmhouses and Jin finally spotted the couple's home. From the road it looked slovenly compared to the other farms they had passed, dark and squat, with ply-wood and corrugated plastic leaned up against each other in a piecemeal addition to the building. Jin stopped at the fence and stared at it.

'This is the place.' The mist of his breath dissipated, his words vanishing into the cold night air. Jin stared at the house with some misgiving.

'Okay, let's go,' Mee-jung said, shivering.

He stared at her for a long moment, before finally saying, 'Follow me.' He led her around to the side of the house and knocked on the door. They waited a couple of minutes and he knocked again. This time the old man came up to the window, his bald head gleaming in the light. He took one look at Jin and pulled away from the window, disappearing back into the darkness.

Damn. Jin was about to knock again when Lok yelled, 'Who's there?'

'Lok, it's me, Jin, remember? You helped me a couple of months ago, sir, and I'm back with a sister.'

A light flicked on, casting a yellow glow on the frosted windowpanes. The dead bolt shifted and the door swung open. Lok stood there before them in threadbare pants slung beneath his belly. He took one look at the girl and opened the door wide.

'Hey, he brought a girl,' he called to his wife.

Biyu was on the daybed in the corner of the room. Scowling, she pushed herself up from under rumpled blankets and pushed her fingers through her matted hair, barely straightening the jutting tufts.

'Hey, hello, come on in,' she mumbled as she heaved herself off the bed. Hands paddled the air as she steadied herself and smoothed the front of her shirt. She fished around with her feet for her slippers, tilting her squat body as she struggled to get her bad left foot in.

'Here, come have a seat,' she called out in a croaky voice. Reaching down, she pulled out floor cushions from under the bed and tossed them to Jin and Mee-jung. She pushed her hands against her knees to straighten again.

'Thank you.' Mee-jung bowed as she walked into the house and settled onto the floor, folding her knees onto the cushions. Jin followed her and sat next to her. The air was thick with the smell of burnt coal used for the in-floor radiant heating. He remembered breathing in the welcome smell of it the night he found this place after crossing the Tumen River. How comforting and warm the farmhouse was then; and even further back, the scent of burnt coal triggered the memory of his own family home in Kanggye, which had coal-heated radiant floors—when there was coal to be had. The smell of it warmed him and filled him with longing at the same time.

'All right, you hungry,' Biyu said to no one in particular. She limped to the kitchen, where radishes and bok choy were piled limply on the counter by the sink, two big soup pots on the kitchen floor. She lifted one of the pots and set it on the gas stove.

'You're lucky I made some congee earlier this evening.' She turned around to snap at Jin and Mee-jung. 'You people—of all the times to visit, you come in the dead of night! No wonder the government wants you out.' She made a brushing motion with her hand. 'But don't worry, they won't find you here. I won't let them.' Her lips tightened across her stained teeth in a smile. Then she bent down to light the stove burner.

'How have you been, Ajooma?' Jin called out in a booming voice, surprised at how authoritative he sounded. He was speaking with the false familiarity of a Party section leader addressing a lower comrade.

'Awful,' Biyu croaked. 'You get to be this age and it's hideous, but I'm still alive, I don't know why. You hungry?'

'Starving, as you know.'

Mee-jung watched them banter, her eyes brightening with anticipation. It seemed Jin knew this couple well, so they must be trusted contacts. This was much better than she had hoped.

Carrying a large tray in her hands, the farmer's wife limped back, each step keeling her body to the left, causing the ceramic bowls to slide and clatter on the tray. Jin sprang up to help her and together they lowered it to the ground. There were two large bowls filled with rice porridge laced through with slivers of shredded chicken. Jin and Mee-jung fell upon their bowls fiercely, and heads down, they slurped the porridge, cheeks bulging with each mouthful. It was warm and soft, perfectly digestible.

Biyu propped herself on one arm and cast an appraising eye on Mee-jung. She was skinny, of course, but she looked healthy enough, and pretty. This was pleasing. It was only a number of weeks since Jin had come to their door, and here he was already bringing them girls. How fortuitous! She knew she had had a good feeling about that boy.

Lok pulled on a sweater and came to join them, lowering himself next to Jin to sit down cross-legged, feet splayed out. He scratched at his leg, raking dirty fingernails along his calf. Sucking phlegm from the back of his throat with a loud snort, he swallowed, then harrumphed.

'So, how can we help you?' he asked.

Mee-jung looked to Jin and Biyu, then asked the woman, 'Do you know any doctors?'

'What do you want a doctor for?'

'I was hoping to get someone to help me with…this.' She lifted a hand and laid it to rest on top of her belly.

The farmer's wife finally noticed the roundness of Mee-jung's belly underneath her jacket, sized her up and down, then gave Jin an annoyed look. 'I said healthy ones, didn't I?' she groused.

Jin reared back at this. 'I thought you said you could help girls,' he said.

Biyu hooded her eyes. 'Healthy ones, I said. This one comes to us with a problem. Luckily, we know someone at a clinic where it's safe. But it costs money, it costs money to do it right. Can you pay for it?'

Mee-jung glanced at Jin, then back at Biyu. 'I have nothing.'

'So how were you going to pay for it?' Biyu asked, her black eyes watching Mee-jung closely. 'Where's the money going to come from?' she pressed.

Lok stopped scratching himself and leaned forward with an expression that was at once conspiratorial and conciliatory. 'Look, we can help you do this, but someone has to pay for it.'

'I can hide myself and help your farm, or work in a factory. I'm a very fast worker,' Mee-jung said eagerly, rushing her words.

'I said it's too dangerous,' the wife snapped. 'No one is hiring the likes of you these days.'

'But...but...I can work on a farm, I can work in a restaurant,' said Mee-jung. 'Lots of us have come up here to find work, there's got to be something for me.'

'Times have changed,' said Biyu.

'No one is hiring people like you these days because of the crackdowns,' said Lok. 'China is a different place now, it's not like it used to be, you know. The inspectors check farms and restaurants and they're catching a lot of Northerns these days. You could be caught and sent back. And you know what happens to pregnant women who get sent back.'

Mee-jung put down her spoon with a small shudder. 'I know. Listen, I'm very discreet and I can work anywhere. Mister, I can help you on your farm.'

'We're so close to the border, the inspectors come through all the time. Your only option is to get married. We can find you a good husband.' Lok slipped his hand under the bottom of his sweater and scratched his belly.

'But,' Mee-jung faltered, 'I want to work.'

'A good husband with a house and property,' interjected Biyu.

'Or you could end up working in a karaoke bar or a club, and then you'll be serving any man who walks through the door,' said Lok. 'Marrying is best. At least they'll take care of you.'

'It's the only way. We find you a good husband, then you can eat and work, and even send money back to your family,' said Biyu. 'It's the best way.'

Mee-jung turned to Jin, her eyes flashing. Biyu caught the exchange and harrumphed.

'Ingrate. He brought you to us, don't you know what that means?' she said. 'That means you won't end up dying in the tunnel.'

'But who would I be marrying?'

'It'll be a nice Chinese family.'

Mee-jung shook her head. 'I didn't come here for that. I came here to find a job!'

'Listen, Mee-jung.' Jin leaned in at this point. 'We can just leave.'

Mee-jung was about to respond when Biyu pounced. 'You need a doctor, no? We know a good doctor,' she cajoled. 'He's helped several others. And are you going to help her with the cost?' she directed at Jin.

Jin leaned forward, placing a hand on Mee-jung's arm. 'We can go and I can reach out to Hyuk.'

Mee-jung looked at him uncertainly. 'But would it take another week?'

'I could try to find him sooner,' he said. 'I probably could if he's still working at the charnel house.'

'But you're not sure?' Mee-jung asked anxiously. 'You don't know for sure, do you?'

Jin sensed Mee-jung's desperation and found himself faltering. 'I don't know anything for sure,' he said hesitantly.

'Rest here for now,' Biyu said in a firm voice, as if the matter were already decided. 'We'll take you to meet the doctor tomorrow, and if you don't like him, you don't have to do anything.'

Mee-jung studied the older woman's face, considering her proposition. 'So I could just meet the doctor and then decide?'

'Yes. It's up to you.'

Mee-jung looked at Biyu and Lok, then finally turned to Jin. 'I should at least go meet the doctor, don't you think?'

'I guess,' he averred uncertainly. 'Can it wait a week?'

'It's been so hard to find a doctor.'

'So…it's decided, then,' Biyu pronounced. 'She can stay here overnight, and Jin can get going.' She placed a hand on Jin's shoulder and pulled herself up. Leaning heavily on him, she guided him to the door, stepping with her right foot first, then sliding her bad foot along behind. When they were close to the door, she whispered to Jin, 'I said *healthy girls*. This is too much work. We'll take care of her, but it's going to cost money if she goes ahead with the doctor, and you'll have to cover the costs.'

'But I barely know this girl,' he whispered. 'What are you going to do with her?'

'Find her a husband, like I said. If she goes for a procedure, it's going to cost more than your matchmaking cut.'

'My matchmaking cut?' Jin said, rearing back. 'Wait a minute, I'm not— I didn't agree to anything.'

Biyu fished in her pocket and handed him a small cell phone. Confused, Jin looked at it, then at her.

'Keep it for now. I'll call you when this girl decides. Okay?' she said.

He held the phone out to her, spluttering, 'But wait a minute…'

'What are you waiting for?' she snapped.

Jin glanced back at Mee-jung, who sat on a floor cushion

with a thick mink blanket wrapped around her, squat and round like a persimmon.

'Mee-jung,' he called.

She looked up. 'I'll let you know what happens tomorrow. Thank you, Jin.' She bowed.

'We'll call you,' Biyu said, trying to push Jin toward the door, but he stood his ground, refusing to leave.

She reached into her apron pocket and pulled out several bills. 'Fine, here, take this,' she said, her lip curling with scorn. 'But you'll still owe for the procedure if she goes for it. I'll call you tomorrow.'

Jin unfolded the bills in his trembling hands, counting three hundred yuan in total. He had never held so much money before. It was enough to buy several meals, or to pay for a cheap room somewhere for a couple of nights. He ran a finger along the soft frayed edges of the bills, then shoved them into his pocket. He looked back at Mee-jung once more.

'I'll call you. Goodbye, Jin,' she said.

'Okay. Take care, Mee-jung.'

The farmer's wife pushed him out and closed the door, sealing them all onto their paths. Jin stared at the door, a bit nonplussed as to what had just transpired. He hadn't pegged Lok and Biyu as traffickers, but looking back on the first time he had met them, certain things she had said started to make sense. She wanted healthy girls because she wanted to sell them off. He wondered what the next few days would hold for Mee-jung. If she stayed with this couple, she was going to be sold off, and if she decided to get an abortion, Biyu would hold Jin responsible for the doctor bills and he would be indebted to them. Any way you sliced it, there was nothing good about this arrangement.

He banged on the door and called out, 'Biyu, I need to speak with you again.' He waited for her to open the door and was about to bang on the door again, but he paused. What would he say to them? Would Mee-jung even agree to come back to the tunnel? She had already made up her mind and decided to stay with them.

His fingers closed around the money in his pocket, and it was in this moment that he remembered the saying his father had told him: 'You need a little evil in your heart to survive.'

Jin waited for another beat, then turned away from the door and headed down their dirt driveway, back out to the country road. In North Korea he knew exactly where he stood in the universe and had done well by his family and country. He worked hard to forge a path for his life and career and knew what kind of job he would get, the lifestyle that it would afford, what kind of apartment he would live in, what marriage he was destined for. His Chosun life was a solid house built with concrete block with plumb lines and a right roof; but as a fugitive in China, Jin was like water trickling down through the streets and into the gutter. He put his head down and started trudging down the road. He wasn't sure where he would go now, but he knew he wouldn't return to the tunnel.

TWENTY-TWO

Suja woke slowly, confused and disoriented, shielding her eyes against the pale morning light that spilled in from the window. She pressed her fingertips against her throbbing head. That hurt. Wincing, she stopped pressing and opened her eyes, all at once remembering where she was: Ping's room. Suja stifled a gasp as the full horror of the previous night came back to her and she looked around, discovering her shirt was torn open and her pants were pulled down to her knees. She lay rigidly on her side, fearful that Ping was still in bed behind her, but after a few moments she stiffened and turned slowly to see if Ping was there. He was gone. With a huge sigh, she reached for her pants waistband, and as she gingerly pulled it past her thighs, she felt the stickiness of blood and semen. Her hands started to shake. Pulling her knees up to her chest, she cradled herself as tears streamed silently down her cheeks.

★ ★ ★

Suja finally pushed herself up from bed and, standing unsteadily, opened the door. The house was empty except for Mrs. Wang, who was sitting at the kitchen table. She stood up, picking up a set of folded clothes, and approached her as she headed toward the bathroom.

'Here,' she urged Suja, pushing the clothes into her hands.

Suja took the clothing without looking at her and shut the bathroom door firmly behind her. She turned the tap, watched the bucket fill with scalding water and, with a trembling hand, picked up the bar of soap. She began to soap her belly and her legs, rubbing the suds into labial tears even as the sharp sting of the soap took her breath away. She shuddered, rinsing herself off as the rust-colored water streamed off her body and trickled down the drain. Suja soaped herself again and scrubbed furiously until her skin was red and raw. She wanted to erase every trace of that man, scrub her body clean; but nothing would expunge her shame and humiliation. Suja picked up the bucket and dumped it over her head, and as the water poured down her body, tears of fury streamed down her face.

She slunk to the floor with her back against the tile wall and stared at the tiles on the opposite wall. She sat there for some time, unfocused, out of body, out of mind, unaware of the passing of time.

She snapped back to attention when she started shivering with cold. Suja stood up and looked at the clothes Mrs. Wang had handed her. They were clearly from the older woman's wardrobe, for the pants were half a foot too short, and the jersey was several sizes too large. Suja watched her body go through the motions of pulling on the jersey, holding up the

panties by the waistband against her midriff. She was stepping
into another woman's underwear, another woman's pants. She
smoothed the jersey, which hung loosely from her shoulders,
and stared blankly at her reflection. It felt right that she would
be wearing another woman's clothes.

Suja finally opened the bathroom door and stepped out
again into the open. She saw Mrs. Wang sitting at the kitchen
table and glanced around to see that there was no one else in
the house.

'Here, I'll take that,' Mrs. Wang said gently, holding her
hand out for Suja's soiled clothes. She placed them in the laundry basket, carefully folding them over so the bloodstains did
not show.

'Let's go outside, come with me,' she said, and reached for
her hand, but Suja flinched, pulling away to follow a couple of
steps behind her. As they walked out into the yard, Suja kept
her eyes focused on the ground. She told herself she could do
this. She could push her body through this day, and moment
by moment, she would make it through the day. It helped
to focus on simple sensations: the crunch of dirt underfoot,
the bright sky overhead, the sound of the air around her. She
tried to remind herself that her parents loved her, and there
was a life worth living, but tears sprang to her eyes when she
thought of her parents, so she emptied her mind. She had to
grit her teeth and push herself through this day.

Mrs. Wang walked into a greenhouse and held aside the
plastic flap for Suja, who glanced warily as she entered to see
if Ping was in the greenhouse. There were a couple of women
picking napa cabbages at the far end of the warehouse. Mrs.
Wang chose the nearest row and picked up a little stool, setting
it down in the middle of the aisle. She sat on it and leaned over
the cabbages to pull a big head of napa from the soil with both
hands. She trimmed off the loose, damaged leaves, holding

it up for Suja to see, then placed it onto the pile of cabbages on the wheelbarrow. She got up from the stool and handed Suja her trimming knife, pointing to the stool. Suja nodded and took the knife, her finger testing the blade. She looked at the row of cabbages and at the women working on rows of cabbages on the other side of the greenhouse. She hunkered down to the cabbage bed and reached over to pull up a large head, struggling with it, as it was firmly rooted in the earth. Using both hands, she twisted and turned it around, finally plucked it out of the soil. She ran the knife along the roots and trimmed off several straggly leaves.

Suja had never worked in a greenhouse before, but the work came naturally to her, as she had done several terms of farm duty in North Korea. She worked her way down the row, swiftly trimming the cabbages, creating neatly stacked piles of gleaming white napa. As she plunged herself into the toil of it, she lost her sense of time and place, and for a short while she could forget her predicament.

Mrs. Wang hadn't expected much of Suja, for judging from her pale skin and soft hands, she figured the girl would be useless on the farm. But she was surprised to see how quickly Suja picked it up and was impressed by how clean and well handled her cabbages were. The girl was industrious, Mrs. Wang noted with appreciation, and her attitude toward her softened.

Suja grew to learn when plants were ready for harvest by the size and shape of each cabbage, the crisp feel of their sturdy stalks. She tended crops in all their greenhouses, those verdant little prisoners trapped in their rows. Suja ran her hands along the fleshy green leaves, lifting them to check the size of the eggplants, watching their color deepen into purple. When it was time to harvest them, they planted bok choy and tended the eggplants. She was always the last one in the greenhouse at the end of the day, watering the plants with the hose coiled around her arm, ice-cold water dripping down her forearms. Suja stayed in the greenhouses as long as she could, for she hated being in the house with Ping.

Back at the house Suja stole away, when she could, into a small side room that had a closet and a wardrobe that Mrs. Wang pointed out as hers. She had left her clothes and her bag of belongings there and she liked to retreat into the room to sit among her things. She'd pull out the dragon necklace Jin had given her and hold it, fondling the smooth jade stone, weeping bitterly as she remembered what Jin promised her as he clasped that necklace around her. Where was he now? What a fool she was to have come to China in search of Jin, for what had she achieved? She was nowhere closer to finding Jin, and now her own life was destroyed. She had failed him, and she had devastatingly failed herself. *Stupid, stupid idiot*, she railed against herself. *You've thrown away your life, abandoned Umma and Apba, and ruined yourself. Jin wouldn't even have you now.*

Suja fought her despair, knowing all would be for naught if she ended up trapped here for the rest of her life. She tried to focus on the goal of finding Jin, for it helped her to believe there was potential for life beyond her enslavement. Her humiliation and anger slowly sharpened into determination as she remembered all the times she and Jin spent in the darkroom together, and how those early moments working side by side in the dark helped forge the deep unspoken bond they shared. Jin knew nothing about photography, but he brought a shrewd perspective to everything she did.

She remembered the wildlife photography project where she faced the difficult task of photographing bats. She had chosen the nocturnal mammals, partly for the challenge, and partly because they symbolized good fortune. It would be tricky to capture these swift night creatures on film, as the only time to catch them would be during the low-light hours of dusk. She and Jin set out toward Taesong Mountain, where bats were rumored to live in the area near the Central Ideals Zoo, and looked for buildings with peaked roofs. They tramped through the zoo grounds, through tangled brush and wood lots, and finally questioned the zookeepers to see whether they had seen any bats. They confirmed that, yes, there had been sightings, but Jin and Suja didn't manage to see a single bat that weekend.

Suja trekked back and forth to the mountain on subsequent weekends on her own, taking bits of apples and persimmons to set out as bait, but the bats continued to elude her. Jin finally pulled her aside one weekend, saying, 'You've hiked across Taesong Mountain a half dozen times, you haven't spotted any yet. You don't know where they live. Why not make them want to come to you?' He showed her a shallow rectangular wooden box he had built. There was a slanted roof on one end and an opening on the other end.

'What is this?' She turned the box over in her hands as she examined it.

'It's a bat house. I built it for you to use to catch some bats. It may take a while, but they should start using it, especially if you leave some bait in it. Actually, no, give *me* the apples and persimmons,' he laughed. 'It's a waste to put out perfectly good food to these rodents.'

'They're not rodents, they're bats, and they're good luck.'

'A lot of luck you've had so far.' He gave a rueful smile. 'Hopefully this'll be better.'

With permission from the zookeeper, Suja nailed the bat house to the side of one of the zoo buildings and waited. It took several weeks, but finally on a visit in late fall Suja found two bats twittering and scrabbling inside the bat house.

She shot three rolls of film that day as the bats flew in and out of that house.

Suja sat thinking about that bat house and how Jin had managed to invert her search so that Suja was no longer pursuing the bats, but they came to her. She started to consider alternate ways she might try to escape the Wang household, aside from simply making a run for it. She would have to get far away from the farm and find a safe place to hide afterward in order to avoid getting caught or, worse, ending up in the hands of the Chinese police.

She started to observe the comings and goings on the farm, noting when farmworkers arrived and what cars dropped them off. On Saturdays she noticed Mrs. Wang went shopping, always returning with a huge load of groceries. Ping and Mr. Wang never noticed when Mama came back from a shopping trip, but Suja ran to assist her and insisted on carrying the heavier items. She went out of her way to help Mrs. Wang, hoping to cultivate the older woman's trust in her; she wanted her on her side, for she knew eventually that trust could be used to Suja's advantage.

One day Mrs. Wang signaled to Suja to follow her as she went over to the breakfast table and picked up her wallet and her keys. They walked out to the car, where she pointed out the passenger seat to Suja. She sat there uneasily, surprised she wasn't being bound in any way, and watched the road, noticing the farms and road signs they passed en route to the city. They passed a billboard advertising Future Cola, and finally a main thoroughfare marker showing that the city of Tonghua was five miles away. She could read the signs because of her high-school-level Chinese, and she committed these landmarks and route markers to memory.

They drove for about fifteen minutes to a small plaza with an open market. Mrs. Wang parked the car by the market and slung her purse over her shoulder as she got out of the car. She held Suja's arm as she led her to the produce area where there were several storefronts with piles of fruit and vegetables, as well as a couple of butchers and a fishmonger. Mrs. Wang led her past the poultry and butcher shops toward the far end of the market into a grocery store that had a sign with big green Chinese characters: Shining New Country Market. Pushing through the turnstiles, she reached down to pick up one of the red plastic shopping baskets and passed it to Suja before picking up another one for herself.

Suja was overwhelmed by the store and stood dumbfounded as she scanned the aisles of food and rows of produce—neatly stacked mounds of red apples, green grapes, daikon radish, shiny plastic-wrapped packages of meat and prepared foods, aisles of humming white coolers stacked with packages of frozen seafood and dumplings. The variety and the sheer number of goods was staggering.

Mrs. Wang led her down a row of dried goods and picked up a box of instant noodles, placing it in Suja's basket. They wandered through the aisles picking up several more items: cooking oil, oyster sauce, laundry detergent, several packages of dried fungi, a couple of pounds of stewed beef. When they got to the checkout, Mrs. Wang handed Suja her basket and dug around in her purse, fishing out a blue vinyl wallet. Counting out a few bills, she handed them to Suja and told her to stay in line.

She was startled that Mrs. Wang would entrust her with money, and she counted the bills with her heart thumping. This was her first time holding Chinese currency, and the feel of it in her hands started her thinking about how she might start her own stash of Chinese money and hide it somewhere. She watched Mrs. Wang walk out of the store as the cashier punched in the items with gloved hands and rang up the total.

Suja handed over the bills to the cashier, who took it without looking at Suja, handing back eighty yuan and some loose change. Suja looked around carefully as she took the change, slipping one of the ten-yuan notes inside her waistband as she pocketed the rest of the change. She felt a rush as she picked up the groceries and walked out of the store with that yuan note in her waistband.

Mrs. Wang met her outside the store with a brand-new wok under her arm. She led her back through the crowd of people to a poultry butcher that had a stall with red glazed barbecued ducks hanging in the front. She pointed Suja to the back of the line.

'We need one barbecued duck,' she said to her in Mandarin, pointing at the hanging ducks. Suja had started picking up on Mandarin and was starting to understand certain words, if not entire sentences. Mrs. Wang went up to the counter and talked to the lady behind it, pointing at Suja. Then, with a slight wave, she turned and headed toward the tea shop.

Suja stood in the queue and, as she got closer to the front, noticed something familiar about the young woman helping the main lady at the counter. She wore no makeup and had her hair tied back in a ponytail, revealing classic Korean features—wide-set eyes, small nose and a square jaw. Suja's pulse quickened as the girl glanced up and a look of recognition passed between them. Suja angled herself toward the girl as she approached the counter and waited for a moment to talk to the girl. When the boss lady stepped away to go to the live chicken pen out back, Suja leaned forward and said quietly in Korean, 'Anyung.'

The girl looked up and responded casually, 'Hi. Your lady ordered a barbecued duck.'

Suja's eyes rounded as she heard her speak in Korean. 'Yes, that's what she wants,' she said excitedly.

The young woman opened the heat-lamp case and lifted barbecued duck off a hook. She picked up a cleaver.

'You're new,' she said, holding the bird with one hand. She dropped her cleaver with one bone-crunching thud. 'Hi, I'm Mira.'

'Hi, I'm Suja. How long have you been here?'

'A year.' *Chop, chop*, she sectioned off pieces of the duck. 'Did you get married off?'

Suja's face reddened at the question. 'I guess you'd call it that,' she said in a tight voice. 'I got sold against my will.' She looked at the North Korean girl. 'You too?'

'I work at the market for these guys, and I work on their farm.'

'How did you end up here?'

'A broker helped.'

'A broker?!' Suja exclaimed and leaned forward. 'Are you in touch with the broker?'

'I haven't talked to him in a while.' Mira slid the cleaver under the pieces of duck and transferred them to a plastic container. 'Why, what do you need?'

Suja lowered her voice. 'Do you think he could help me escape?'

Mira furrowed her brow as she wiped her hands on her apron. 'Is the…is the family treating you badly?'

Suja was taken aback by the question, confused at how that could be anything but an assumption. Of course they were treating her badly. 'I'm there *against my will*. I mean, the lady is okay, but her son is…' Suja struggled for words. 'It's hideous. I have to get out of there.'

Mira pressed her lips together and looked at Suja with empathy. She got it. 'The thing with my broker is, he's in Chengdu right now. He's not going to be back for a few months.'

'Oh no,' cried Suja. 'Do you know of anyone else who could help me?'

'There was a Chinese guy named Gan who my broker dealt with. I've seen him from time to time at this market. But I heard Gan is connected to traffickers, so I'm not sure you'd want to speak to him.' Mira paused here, leveling her gaze at Suja. 'A broker would get you a job, or get you out of China. But a trafficker, he'll just sell you into another home.'

'So is Gan a trafficker or not?' asked Suja desperately.

Mira shrugged. 'I don't know. I just heard he might be connected with them.'

'Is there anyone else? Like, would it—could I possibly hide with you for a while?'

Mira shot a nervous glance at her boss lady, who returned from the back room with two freshly plucked chickens. She bagged them at the front counter and handed them to a customer.

'I live with the owners,' Mira said.

'Oh,' Suja said quietly, realizing that Mira was hardly more than an indentured slave herself. She looked at her sadly, realizing how similar their plights were. 'Don't you want to get away too?'

Mira furrowed her brow and shrugged. 'I make good money to send home to my family. I'm safe. It's good here.'

'Oh.'

'But I understand, you're not in a good situation, are you?'

'No, I need to get out,' Suja said, leaning in to whisper, 'Could you ask your broker now if there is anyone else, or if I should try Gan?'

'I can text him,' said Mira, glancing quickly at the boss lady, who was now helping the next customer. 'Listen, I can't talk anymore right now, but come back in a little bit when she's not around. I'll see if I hear back from the broker.' She wrapped a red elastic band around the take-out container and handed it to Suja.

Suja took the package and wandered toward the market entrance, finding a spot by the parked scooters to stand and wait. Mrs. Wang walked out of the tea store and, spotting Suja, came over to hand her the wok and a bag of tea.

'I'll be right back,' she said, buttoning up her quilted jacket as she scurried off toward the grocery store again. Suja glanced at Mira, who was now at the back of the stand hunched over the sink, scrubbing a big plastic bucket. Suja headed back to her.

Mira looked up as she overturned the bucket, splashing sudsy water on the counter and the floor.

'I texted my broker and he said your best bet is to talk to Gan,' she whispered excitedly. 'He gave me his number and I texted him, and it turns out Gan's not too far from here. He might be able to help you.'

'How can I meet him?'

'He said he could meet you here at the market. You know when you're coming back?'

'Mrs. Wang shops on Saturdays, but she doesn't shop every week, so maybe a couple of Saturdays from today?'

Just then Mrs. Wang showed up again with a big box of black garbage bags under her arm. She dropped the box at Suja's feet and looked at the two girls.

'You two had a lot to talk about, didn't you?' she said cryptically. 'You're Northern too, right?' she asked Mira.

'Yes.' Mira looked down, her cheeks flushing.

'Hmm.' She took the barbecued duck from Suja's hands and pushed the box of garbage bags to her.

'Zou, let's go.'

Suja slung her bags of groceries over a wrist and bent down to pick up the garbage bags. She followed Mrs. Wang, turning her head to shoot a quick glance at Mira, mouthing the words *See you again*.

Mira nodded and watched Suja walk out to the parking lot with Mrs. Wang. They loaded the car together, and as Mrs. Wang pulled out of the parking lot, Suja looked back at the poultry stand, searching unsuccessfully for a phone number on the sign. She kicked herself for not having thought to ask Mira for her phone number. As it stood, there was no way for Suja to get in touch with Mira between now and the next time she'd be able to come to the market. She sat anxiously in the passenger seat, thinking about when the next visit might be and praying Mira was a woman of her word.

TWENTY-THREE

Jin hacked a cough and looked out into the gray-white haze that hung over the city of Tonghua. The smog was persistent and pervasive, coating his lungs with the exhaust from hundreds of scooters that swarmed the streets, diesel from buses belching black fumes, smoke from coal-burning plants, windborne particles from tailing ponds. The sky was obscured by fog from dawn through to the afternoon, and by 4:30 p.m., as the sun began to sink, he realized the 'fog' would never burn off, the sky would never be clear. Night closed in and the haze became cloudy halos around the neon signs. Suja had said she heard the light in China was gorgeous—a dream to photograph. But it wasn't the light, it was smog.

The things Suja could photograph in this country, the things Jin had seen through her eyes, imagining her lifting her camera, the light touch of her fingers on his arm when she looked over at him. How he longed to see her. Every day he wrestled with the fantasy of reuniting with her. He needed to get established here first, or to find safe passage to another country; but both required money, and currently he was in the hole with Biyu and Lok. He shook his head, thinking about how he got entangled in the mess with Mee-jung, for she had gotten an abortion after all, and Biyu was now demanding he pay the doctor fees.

'But I don't even know her,' he protested. 'What's happening with her anyway?'

'She's being matched with a good family. It's all taken care of,' Biyu replied.

'Can I speak with her?' he asked.

'She's gone already.'

'Already gone?' Jin was surprised. 'But I thought she was going to call me when she decided.'

'You don't really know her, but you expected her to call you?' she said slyly. 'It all happened quickly. She was matched with someone, and he came to meet her and she agreed to go with him.'

'But did the procedure go fine? Is she all right?'

'Of course it did. She got treated by a clinic doctor and it went smoothly. All that's left is for you to settle the debt.'

'Listen, I have no—I have no money.'

'I've found work for you. A guy we know who has business around here and I spoke to him. He needs help right now. His name is Sarge and he can meet you tomorrow in Tonghua. He says he'll be near the Tonghua market at Lucky 88. Two o'clock. Give him that phone I gave you, and he'll give you a different one to use.'

'What work does he have for me?'

'I don't know, just meet him already.'

Jin hesitated, then asked, 'Why didn't you introduce me to him before?'

'Why didn't you bring us any girls before?' she snapped. 'Go talk with Sarge. He does business with us, so he'll make arrangements and I'll be in touch again.'

With big red lacquered pillars, and a red faux-tile roof with peaked corners, Lucky 88 was a twenty-four-hour barbecue restaurant that was just down the street from the biggest butcher in Tonghua market. Walking into the restaurant was like entering a different climate zone. The air was not just humid; it was stewy thick with the smell of food. He passed tables overladen with dishes as people bellied up to their food, faces glistening as they slurped noodles from steaming bowls. His eyes finally landed on a man who was seated alone in the back corner of the restaurant with a bowl in front of him. He had his cell phone out, two thumbs tapping away. Jin approached him, noticing another two cell phones on the table in front of him.

'Mr. Sarge?' he asked.

The man didn't look up but pointed to the chair opposite him and continued texting. He had a fighter's crooked nose and angular features with large almond-shaped eyes that were bloodshot, the whites of his eyes turned to a dull yellow. With shiny shell pants and a pair of bright blue Nike Air runners, Sarge had the sporty look of a soccer player. Jin could see the bottle green ink of a tattoo peeking out from above the neckline of his sport jersey; the snarling tip of a dragon snout. His shirtsleeves were rolled up to reveal the sinewy black-green tail that curled around the bottom of his right bicep.

Sarge finally put the phone down next to the other phones, picked up his chopsticks and stabbed them into his rice bowl. He shoveled a hot clump into his mouth. Jin eyed the cell phones on the table warily. Can you trust a man with three cell phones?

'So Biyu says you're a smart guy,' Sarge said, breathing through his teeth as a steaming wad of rice rolled around in his mouth.

'I used to be smart,' said Jin.

'Well, pretty smart to end up here.' Sarge's eyes flicked up from his dish. 'So, you owe Biyu something, and you gonna work for me?'

'What work do you have?' Jin asked warily.

Sarge dangled a glistening piece of gristly beef from his chopsticks and jerked his head to bite into it, attacking it, doglike. Jin watched him gulp it down with fascination and revulsion.

'What can you do?' Sarge finally asked.

'Anything.'

'Ha.' Sarge opened his mouth wide to laugh, revealing half-masticated meat and bits of rice.

'You don't know what I've done,' said Jin. 'I was a scholarship student in Pyongyang. I've escaped from prison, I can slaughter pigs. I can handle anything.'

Sarge cocked an eyebrow. 'You run from jail, you cut up a pig and you think you done everything?' he chuckled.

'I will do anything. That's what I know.'

Sarge shoveled more rice into his mouth as one of his cell phones lit up. He picked it up, scrolled through a message, then put it facedown on the table. Several minutes passed without a word. Finally, Sarge pushed his bowl toward Jin and said, 'Okay, Mr. Jin. Maybe…maybe there is something for you.' He gestured to the lady at the counter. 'Get us some chopsticks.' Then he turned back to Jin. 'Where you staying?' he asked.

Jin shrugged. 'Nowhere.'

Sarge raised his brow at this. The waitress set down a second pair of chopsticks on the table and Sarge pointed to his bowl. 'Eat.'

Jin looked at the half-eaten bowl of beef and rice and was disgusted. He may be hungry, but he had dignity.

'I'm not hungry,' he said.

'Idiot, just eat and let's go already.'

Jin stood. 'All right, let's go.'

Sarge looked at him with a gleam in his eye and the corner of his lip went up. Impishly, he reached over and picked up a large piece of beef out of the bowl and dropped it into his mouth. He chewed it calmly, then stood up, smirking. 'All right, man, let's go.'

Sarge drove Jin to a high-rise apartment complex and led him past security cameras in the parking lot into the first building. Jin watched in awe as Sarge stepped into revolving doors that moved automatically with blue LED lights flashing on, then off. He followed tentatively into the circular vortex, stepping out quickly before he was sucked back in. He looked back to see the revolving door slow to a stop and the blue lights flick off, and the whole thing was silent once again.

They took an elevator to the third floor and walked to a door at the end of the hallway where Sarge knocked once, then leaned his head in and said, 'It's me.' There was the sound of metal sliding against metal and the door jerked open. Jin followed Sarge into a modest apartment, sparsely furnished with a sofa and a table, drawn curtains. The flickering TV was the main thing. Two guys were watching it, seated on the living room floor with their elbows propped up against the sofa.

'Chung, Sang-do, this is Jin. He's going to help with the pickups.'

'Anyung,' said Jin, bowing his head just enough to say hello but no more, as they were his peers. The young guy named

Chung nodded his head, eyes glued to the TV, while Sang-do sized him up with a slow gaze. Jin stuck his hands in his pockets and hung by the door, uncertain about what to do.

'Make some room, guys. Let him watch,' said Sarge.

Sang-do moved toward the middle of the sofa next to Chung and pulled out a pack of cigarettes and held them up to Jin.

From that day on, Jin slept in that apartment along with Chung and Sang-do and sometimes one or two others, mostly North Korean men who had, by hook or by crook, gotten into China and were working underground. They were defectors—escapees, now living in hiding in China as fugitives. Turned out Sarge was one of the most prolific smugglers this side of the Chinese–North Korean border, infamous for handling everything from defectors to CDs to cell phones. He introduced himself as Lee Jung-do, but sometimes it was Kim Jung-do, and just about everyone called him Sarge, a nickname that referred to his days as a sergeant in an elite corps in the North Korean army; another unverified story, but whether it was true or not, Sarge ran his operations with militaristic discipline. He had two passports under different names, and different SIM cards that he swapped out of his numerous cell phones. There was a code to how he communicated over the phone; he never said *defectors*; he said *friends*, and he never said the word *shipment*; he said they were 'coming to the party.' If it was about a woman looking for work, he called her his 'little sister.' Everything Sarge did was under subterfuge.

Jin felt conflicted about being involved in this world of smuggling. This kind of life was the antithesis of everything he had striven to uphold back home. But he was bound by his debt to Biyu, and Jin knew he had to bide his time until the debt was paid and he could look for another job. In the meantime, he was learning a lot about business in the Chinese underground.

He started riding shotgun with Chung as they did midnight pickups and deliveries, barreling through the streets in a van pounding with stereo beats by Yin Ts'ang. Jin never knew what they were picking up. He was told just to help Chung load boxes off wooden pallets, carry them to the van, pile them neatly into stacked phalanxes and drive them to a drop-off point. Sometimes there were two deliveries an evening.

A few times Chung drove them to the hills near the North Korean border and picked up defectors hiding out in farmhouses. The defectors would come back to the apartment with them, and Jin would ask them for any news on Pyongyang and Kanggye, hoping and praying that his family was okay. He would pepper them with questions about how they managed to cross the river as he looked to glean the latest information on border conditions. He wanted to know as much as possible about the risks of trying to bring Suja to China.

Most of the defectors Jin met were traveling through, relying on Sarge to arrange for drivers and safe houses as they escaped through China into other countries where they hoped to find asylum. Sarge had an extensive network of people who helped arrange for their transport, including Riu, one of Sarge's Chinese 'friends' who was a Snakehead, part of a Chinese gang that extended into Laos, Cambodia and even north to Russia. Riu and his gang were a whole other story, for they had their fingers in everything from counterfeit money and liquor, to gambling, racketeering, exporting and ferrying North Korean women. They hung out at a karaoke bar near Tonghua market called the Night Sun.

Sarge walked up to karaoke room eight, knocked on the door and waited briefly before walking in. The room was just big enough to fit a sectional sofa and a coffee table, and a small disco ball overhead cast a smattering of dots of light. Riu and his two cronies had set up office there, and he sat there between them on the sofa with his legs splayed, his meaty fingers wrapped around a sweating drink glass.

'Hey, Riu,' Sarge said as he tossed an envelope onto the coffee table.

'Hey. Siddown,' Riu said with a thick Chengdu accent. He was an armadillo of a man with coarse bristly hair and thick arms and an even thicker torso. He moved with the heavy-limbed bluntness of a lumberjack, or a butcher, and was easily the most intimidating of the three men, even though he was the shortest. He coughed a wet and gravelly, rheumy cough dredged from the depths of his barrel chest, his body convulsing like a car turning over and over. Gold rings flashed as he thumped his chest.

Sarge and Jin took a seat at the bottom of the L-shaped brown corduroy sectional.

'So you wanted to talk *bijiness.*' Riu said the word in English, mimicking the Korean accent.

Sarge slouched back into the sectional, reached into his pocket and pulled out a pack of cigarettes. 'Seems to me you're interested.' He put a cigarette to his lips, then reached across the table and offered the pack to the men sitting with Riu. Neither took one.

'Like I said on the phone—' Sarge spoke with a cigarette between his pursed lips '—you should take on stowaways in your shipments to Canada or America—North Korean defectors are willing to pay for a spot on a ship. I don't understand why you're not jumping at this opportunity. What's not to like? The math is simple—more cargo equals more money, especially this kind of cargo.'

'You bastards think it is easy to throw *Northerns* in my

cargo?' Riu said in broken Korean, throwing in a Chinese noun every now and then. Jin was beginning to pick up Mandarin and recognized the pejorative code word for North Koreans, the *Northerns*, as if North Koreans were a species of animal.

'Saekee, what's so hard about it?' said Sarge, putting out his cigarette on a wet square of Kleenex in the glass ashtray. 'I'm not saying do it or don't do it. This is a business proposal here, you understand. *Bijiness.*' Sarge settled back in the sofa, his jaw working in rotation.

Colored dots of light played across Riu's face. The noise from the neighboring karaoke room suddenly overpowered the conversation as a man wailed a traditional love song, his voice caterwauling over the tinny beatbox music track. Jin surmised this was the reason why Riu hung out at this karaoke bar—no one could eavesdrop or record the conversation. He leaned forward to hear the two men more clearly.

'Northerners are desperate to get away. They'll pay you to get out,' said Sarge.

'Sure they pay, everyone pays. But then what do they do on the other end? They don't know how to work in factories, they don't know how to work in restaurants.'

'They work harder than anyone.'

'Yaeesh.' Riu thrust his lower lip. 'All my people in America are Chinese. They need Chinese workers, not Northerns, *you unnastand*? Northerns cain't do nothing for me.' Riu took a swig from his glass and brought it down on the coffee table.

Jin realized they were talking about ferrying North Koreans across to America, and the very idea was shocking—could they make it that far? Would they be able to start a new life there? He immediately thought about Suja and wondered if he might be able to take her to America with him.

'Awright, awright, what if I pay you?' Sarge's hand came

to his chest. 'I pay you a guarantee for their fees and *I* worry about collecting later.'

Riu narrowed his eyes.

'No problem for you,' Sarge said.

Riu shifted his weight from side to side. The corduroy nap of the sofa upholstery was shined with years of sweat and grime, and the cushions sagged with deep depressions. He kept sinking into the soft plush, leaning this way and that and trying to wedge himself up.

'You gonna arrange for pickup on the other side?'

Sarge's hooded gaze settled on Riu. 'You're saying that even if I pay you, even if I *pay* you, I have to arrange for the pickup on the other side?' Sarge exhaled a smoke-filled sigh. 'Ah, bastard, you're killing me.'

'S'business.'

Sarge lit another cigarette and watched the smoke swirl up into the moving lights. 'There's so much overhead in this fucking *bijiness*.'

'S'not easy. Hard work.'

'I'm getting buggered by my Northerns in South Korea,' said Sarge. 'They're taking off without paying me!'

'Leaking boat.' Riu sat back, letting his body get swallowed into the sofa. He turned halfway toward the screen.

'Just a couple,' Sarge griped.

'Still leaking boat,' said Riu.

'They don't want to stay in South Korea. Too much discrimination. This is what I'm talking about,' said Sarge, leaning forward intently. 'I say why don't we take them to America or Canada or Finland, or wherever.'

Sarge lifted a nearby bottle of whiskey and poured it into Riu's glass, the liquid sloshing fast but neat. Then he angled it into his glass. Jin looked down at his drink, which was still full, the ice melted into clear water that floated at the top with the amber whiskey coloring the bottom half of the glass. He took a sip. He was beginning to piece together the real purpose of this meeting. Sarge was looking to establish a new route for defectors to escape abroad.

Riu took his drink and clinked it against Sarge's. 'There's a lot of risk on the boats. Inspections, you know. If a Northern dies in cargo, it could suspend the boat's license, and a boat out of the water would be tens of millions of yuan.'

'Ah, you have stowaways all the time, and you know it,' Sarge scoffed. 'Defectors will pay more than your Chinese stowaways. It's a business opportunity, I'm tellin' you.'

Riu took a swig of his drink and set the rock glass on the table and looked Sarge in the eye. 'Okay, we'll talk about it.'

'What d'you mean? We *are* talking about it,' said Sarge, curling his lip.

'I'll talk to my guys and get back to you.'

'Okay.' Sarge nodded, satisfied.

Jin watched the exchange between the men with a strange light in his eyes. He had been nursing hopes that Sarge might help him establish a life here in China for him and Suja, but now he realized that escaping to America could be a possibility.

TWENTY-FOUR

They were gleaning through greenhouse number two that week, harvesting the remaining cabbages and readying soil beds for tilling. The whole household was working alongside three workers, and they had the rototiller going, but there weren't enough rakes, so Suja went to find more. Standing in the gloom of the toolshed with the door open, she surveyed the tangle of rakes and pitchforks leaned up against the wall. She lifted a rusty rake with three-inch teeth, testing the heft of it in her hands. It would do. She grabbed a spade as well, just in case, and turned around to find Ping standing in the door.

'Oh, hi,' she said, caught completely off guard. She stood with a rake and spade in each hand, watching nervously to see what he would do. Ping had been irritable for the past week since she started sleeping in the side room. It had started simply enough when she retreated there one night, fatigued after working in the greenhouses all day. It was the one place in the house where she felt safe and she went there to sit among her things and relax. She ended up drifting off to sleep and woke in the morning to find someone had covered her with a blanket.

She slept in that side room for several nights after that.

Ping didn't like it and tried to block Suja from that room, but his mother stepped in.

'She needs to use the room, her things are there. Let her be.'

'She's trying to sleep in there,' Ping griped and pointed at the blanket that was folded on the floor in one corner. 'What is this? She's supposed to be sleeping in my bed.'

'She *does* sleep in your bed, and so what if she sleeps here sometimes? What's the problem with that?' exhorted his mother. 'It's better than listening to you guys fight every night.'

'I don't like where this is heading,' Ping said testily.

'She's not going nowhere. And anyway, it's no use to anyone if you guys are sleepless and tired every day. She works better on the farm when she's rested.'

'She's not your farmhand, Mama. She's mine.'

His mother's face changed when she heard this. 'We got her for the family,' she shouted.

Ping glared at his mother and stomped off, kicking a dining chair so hard he sent it skidding across the floor. Suja watched him uneasily. She was glad she was proving useful enough for Mrs. Wang to step up to her defense, but she knew Ping's anger would continue to grow and this détente between them wouldn't hold for long.

Ping was watching her from the shed doorway with a fixed stare that made the hairs on Suja's arm stand on end. She tried to bolt past him, but he shot his arm out to block her way and pushed her back into the shed, knocking her into the stack of gardening tools. Suja fell with a small cry and tried to get up again, but he pulled the rake out of her hand and shoved her back down. She swung the spade at him and hit him in the thigh.

'Ay!' he cried, and grabbed the spade by the handle and pulled it out of her hands, threw it aside and lunged at her. He slapped her across her face with a force that sent her reeling, but as he fell forward, she managed to roll out of his way. She scrambled out of the shed and ran back to the greenhouse, pushing through the plastic flaps to arrive back by the soil beds, wild-eyed and out of breath. She took stock of her injuries, gingerly touching her hot, stinging cheek. Mrs. Wang took one look at her, noticing she'd come back empty-handed, and pressed her lips together. She brushed aside Suja's hand.

'What happened?' she asked, looking at the red mark on her cheek.

'Ping,' Suja said.

Mrs. Wang's eyelids dropped a fraction of an inch. She had presumed as much.

'I'm getting tired of this. You'd better sort it out, because I'm losing my patience,' she said gruffly, and stomped off to the toolshed. She came back several minutes later with a few rakes and handed one to Suja. When Ping finally returned to the greenhouse half an hour later, he took over the rototilling at the far end and kept his distance from her.

Suja kept her head down and funneled her anger into raking for the rest of the day. She trailed after the gleaners with a pitchfork and rake to attack the soil and break down the root clumps. She wasn't terrified anymore so much as furious. She had bided her time for as long as she could, but now there was no escaping Ping's volatile temper. She would have to return to his bedroom. Suja didn't care what the risks were anymore; she just wanted to run away. Now.

She focused on the chance meeting she had with Mira at

the market and reminded herself that she needed to be strategic about an escape. It had been several weeks since Mrs. Wang had gone to the market, so she was due to go soon. She would go with her and speak to Mira about her contact Gan and work something out with him. She knew she didn't have enough money to pay proper broker fees, so there could be risks with this guy, but she thought grimly, *I'd rather risk death than live like this anymore.*

The next Saturday morning, Suja carefully selected a few key possessions from her bag, including the photo of her parents and the velvet sack with the hoop snake necklace Jin had given her. She tucked them into an inside pocket she had sewn into her jacket and checked to make sure they wouldn't fall out. She had no idea what might happen that day, but she wanted to be prepared to walk away.

After lunch Mrs. Wang sat at the kitchen table scribbling down a shopping list, and as she picked up her bag to leave for the market, Suja stepped forward expectantly. Mrs. Wang glanced at her and said sharply, 'You can stay and finish off watering greenhouse number two.'

Suja panicked when she heard this but strove to keep calm as she nodded in assent. She watched Mrs. Wang head to the door as she racked her brain, trying to figure out how she might convince her to take her to the market. Her eyes lit on the rice sack that was slumped against the kitchen pantry.

'By the way, we're running out of rice,' she called out, trying to keep her voice casual. She knew Mrs. Wang hated carrying the heavy items at the market and hoped this might make her reconsider.

Mrs. Wang had stepped into her brown vinyl loafers and was already pulling her keys out of her purse when she paused. She walked over to lift it and saw that there was less than a quarter of the bag left, enough to last another two or three weeks. Tilting her head and considering it, she said, 'You better come with me today. Get your shoes on.'

'Okay. I'll finish off watering greenhouse two afterward,' Suja said, her heart beating wildly.

Mrs. Wang drove wordlessly as they passed the neighboring farms and headed toward town. Suja sat next to her, nervously noting every road sign and billboard they passed, recalling a few of them from their previous trip to the market. She felt she could now triangulate the direction from which they came, estimating the farm was a bit less than ten miles northeast of the city of Tonghua. Her tension mounted as they neared the market plaza.

'No duck this week,' Mrs. Wang said in a curt voice as she pulled in to a parking spot and got out of the car.

Suja glanced at the poultry stand as they passed it, locking eyes with Mira, who was standing at the counter. 'Call Gan now,' Suja mouthed at her as they walked past. Mira nodded and pulled her phone out of her apron pocket.

Mrs. Wang spent a lot of time at the grocery store this time, going into the seafood section to deliberate over the various fresh fish. In addition to the usual grocery list of eggs, oil and frozen dumplings, she went into the household items section and selected hand towels and laundry detergent, rounding up with a fifty-pound bag of rice, which they both heaved together onto the bottom of the grocery cart. She stayed with Suja throughout and kept her cash on her, handing over the bills to the cashier herself. She let Suja push the cart out of the store and pointed to the pillar at the front of the market, telling Suja to wait there for her. Suja nodded and pushed the cart to the pillar, turning back to see Mrs. Wang slip into an herbal medicine store. After waiting a minute or two by the cart, Suja quickly ran to the poultry stand.

Mira came to the side counter and blanched when she saw her face. 'Oh my God, what happened?'

Suja's hand went up to her cheek instinctively. The redness was gone, but the slap had left a bruise that had only started fading. 'Her son hit me.'

Mira shook her head. 'You've got to get out of there. I texted Gan and he's able to meet you.'

'Can he meet me today?'

She looked down, thumb-tapping her phone. After a pause she said, 'Yes. There's a restaurant he could meet you at that's just to the left of the market on the big road. It's a big noodle house called Lucky 88.'

'Can he meet me soon? Like now?'

Mira put her head down and texted again. 'He says you can go there now and hide in the back kitchen. He's friends with the owner. If you say his name, they'll take you in. You can go now and Gan will be there in about half an hour.'

Suja looked back at the herbal store and then at the shopping cart with the groceries that she had left by the pillar. If she was going to do this, it would be now, now was the time. But this was happening so suddenly and there were so many unknowns—like who was this Gan fellow and what would happen to her once she met him? Would she be safe in the restaurant while she waited for him? How much longer would Mrs. Wang take in the herbalist shop?

She knew she had to make a snap decision and looked at Mira desperately.

'What do you think, should I do it?'

'I don't know,' Mira wavered, caught off guard. 'I mean, if you need to get away, this guy can do it. My broker said he's well connected and you may be able to make a deal with

him. But if you can wait a couple of months, my broker will
be back, and I know for sure he would help you.'

Suja weighed Mira's response, reading between the lines:
Gan was competent but Mira couldn't vouch for his trust-
worthiness. But the idea of waiting several more months for
Mira's broker was unbearable.

'Okay. I'm going. I'm going,' Suja said, as if to convince
herself into it.

'Here.' Mira shoved a small piece of paper across the
counter. 'My phone number, just in case.'

Suja slid the slip of paper off the counter and folded it into
her palm. She felt a burst of gratitude at Mira's final gesture
of trust and for everything she had done to help her. Mira was
the first person she had met in China whom she could trust,
and she wanted to just reach over and hug her.

'Thank you for everything, sister,' she said, her eyes glowing.

'I'll tell Gan you're going there now,' Mira said. 'I hope
everything turns out for you.'

Suja glanced back at the herbal store again and then gave
a quick wave to Mira. She ran toward the pillars and turned
onto the main street, which was bustling with pedestrians
going from restaurant to store with shopping bags slung over
their wrists. It was dizzying to be able to run freely without
Mrs. Wang or anyone to restrain her. Afraid that her absence
would be discovered any minute now, Suja sprinted through
the crowds looking for the Lucky 88 sign, and her eyes lit
on the large red sign less than half a block away. It was close,
uncomfortably close to the market.

Suja stumbled into the restaurant, panting, to find the restaurant half-empty. It was early still, and there were only a
few tables here and there: couples leaning in together over
steaming bowls of noodle soup, a few women sitting next to

shopping bags with various plates of dim sum arranged in front of them. Suja kept her head down and walked past the tables toward the back counter where a young woman with her hair pulled into a ponytail sat on a stool, clicking her gum.

'Hello. Uh, can I see the boss?' she asked. 'I'm a friend of Gan.'

'Are you here to eat or are you applying for a job?' the girl asked.

'I want to see the boss. I'm a friend of Gan,' she repeated carefully, then glanced out the window, nervous that Mrs. Wang might come along any minute now.

The waitress snapped a bubble in her mouth. 'Okay, wait a sec,' she said laconically, and got up from her stool. Twirling a pen in her hand, she padded down a hallway and pushed the swing doors into the kitchen.

Suja turned to watch the people at the table, paying particular attention to the young couples who thumbed their phones distractedly as they ate. They had an air of affluence about them, Suja thought, but when she looked closer, she realized they weren't necessarily wealthy, but they were well-fed and had a certain kind of relaxed disregard that she usually associated with the upper class in Pyongyang. They were happy and free, these young Chinese couples. She thought wistfully about her life back home and wondered if she and Jin could ever live this kind of life.

Suddenly Suja heard someone yell her name on the street. She froze and listened closely to the street sounds above the restaurant noise. She heard her name again, and the voice was unmistakable: it was Mrs. Wang. Suja cast about frenetically, looking around for a place to hide, and on a sudden whim, she sat down at the nearest table with her back to the window. She held her breath as she heard Mrs. Wang's voice get louder and louder. She looked down the hallway behind the service counter and kicked herself for not thinking of running to the bathroom. *When was that waitress going to come back?!*

Mrs. Wang's voice died down and Suja listened to see if she had turned the other direction, or perhaps she'd given up? After waiting a few more moments, Suja was about to breathe a sigh of relief when she heard the neighboring restaurant door slam, and Mrs. Wang's voice was louder and clearer. 'Suja!' she called.

Mrs. Wang was going *into* restaurants.

Suja jumped up and ran past the service counter and into the hallway just as one of the kitchen doors swung open. The waitress stepped out and looked at her with surprise.

'Come on in,' she said, and stepped aside to let Suja into the kitchen.

'Thank you.' Suja tipped her head and walked into a long galley kitchen. There were a dozen men at different stations in the kitchen, slicing meat and vegetables, and behind them were several steaming vats of boiling water. At one counter a man was pulling noodles, and the cooks in front of the steaming vats lifted baskets of noodles from the bubbling water.

'Gan is coming,' one of the cooks said, and turned over an empty white five-gallon bucket and slid it toward her.

'Thank you,' Suja said, and caught the bucket with one hand. She positioned it in a corner by the door so she could hear the sounds from the restaurant floor, and perched herself on it. She was watching the men work in the steaming kitchen when she heard a commotion from the front of the house. She was petrified to hear Mrs. Wang's voice inside the restaurant.

Suja stood up, wide-eyed, and looked at the cook, who raised a finger to his lips and winked. Mrs. Wang called for her but someone started yammering at her, pushing her out.

The front door opened and closed and Suja strained to listen, but Mrs. Wang's voice wasn't audible anymore. She heard only the murmur of the restaurant patrons. She sat for a few more minutes, fidgeting, until she couldn't bear it anymore, and she jumped up and peered out the door at the dining area. She pumped her fist in the air. 'She's gone!' she shouted.

The cook laughed and mimicked her, pumping his fist in the air. The other cooks laughed and Suja joined in, laughing heartily, for in this moment she felt her first true victory since she'd left Pyongyang. She was free, finally free of Ping and that household.

The cook poured a dollop of soup broth into a bowl of freshly pulled noodles, and arranged some braised beef with carrots, daikon and bok choy, and sprinkled it with toasted garlic. He presented it to Suja with a flourish.

'Oh my goodness, thank you so much. It looks delicious.' She beamed. She stared at the steaming bowl of noodle soup, too excited to eat at first, and instead she looked around, thanking the cook and all the other cooks in the kitchen. When she finally felt calmer, she picked up a pair of chopsticks and lifted some noodles and blew on them. The noodles were superb, just firm enough to give a great chewy mouthfeel, and the broth was delicious. She took her time with the noodle soup, enjoying every bite.

The back fire-escape door opened and slammed, and a loud male voice approached the kitchen. A fellow in a red puffer coat, jeans and white sneakers pushed through the doors with a cell phone pressed to his ear. He looked Suja up and down and turned away as he continued talking on the phone.

'Gan,' said the cook, pointing at the man.

Suja nodded. She wasn't sure that she liked the look of him,

but she was surprised to hear him drop some Korean words
into his conversation. Gan spoke Korean.

When he finally got off the phone, he turned to Suja and
extended a hand. 'I'm Gan.'

'Hello, I'm Suja.' She stood up to shake his hand.

'So you found the place okay?' he said, glancing around as
he hiked up his jeans. He lifted a hand to say hi to the cook.

'Yes, thank you, thank you so much for meeting me here.'

'It's okay. So, you were…you were with a family?' he asked.

She nodded. 'I came here looking for a friend and paid
brokers to guide me into China. But once I got here, I got
sold into a family.'

'Right.' He nodded. 'And do you want to go to South
Korea?'

'No, I want to find my friend. Here.'

'Who? What is his name?'

'Jin Lee Park. He's from North Korea. I'm not sure where
to look for him, but I'm pretty sure he's somewhere in China.'

'China's a big country,' he said sardonically.

'I know. I just thought…there's only so many places that
would deal with North Koreans. I was hoping to meet someone who might know a network…someone with connections
with North Koreans who end up in China.'

Gan cocked his head. 'Jin Lee Park… Jin Lee Park. We
could ask around, for sure. But what are you going to do in
the meantime? Where do you want to stay?'

'Well, I was hoping there might be a place I could stay and
work, while I try to find my friend,' said Suja tentatively.

'A karaoke bar?'

'No.' Suja shook her head. 'Like a factory job or something.'

Gan scratched his head, grimacing. 'Not a good idea. You
don't get paid, and you might never get out of there.'

'How about a restaurant like this one? How about work-ing here?'

He smiled and shook his head. 'They're not hiring Northerns here. What about web chat? You could do that.'

'What do you mean "web chat"?'

'Talk to guys on the internet and get paid.'

'You mean talk sex to men on the internet.'

He nodded.

'No.'

'Okay, I don't know, then.' He shrugged and looked away. 'Maybe another family, a different one, a better one. They're not all bad. I mean, it's one thing if you're going to escape, but if you want to stay in China, you don't have a lot of op-tions.'

Suja looked down dejectedly at her unfinished bowl of noodle soup as she realized the truth to what he was say-ing. What options were there in China for an illegal like herself? She couldn't think of anything else to suggest, and couldn't think of any place she could go to hide. She took a deep breath.

'When you say a different family, does that mean I'd be sold as a "bride"?'

'That would be the typical thing.' He nodded. 'But you can meet these people ahead of time. We could talk to my contact and see what he can do.'

Another contact. Another man. Was there no way out of this? Suja's sense of euphoric victory from half an hour ago had completely vanished now that she faced this sobering situation with Gan. She was entering into some kind of en-gagement with him, the terms of which were still unclear.

'I have money,' she said.

'For what?' he asked, perplexed.

'For a good arrangement. I'd like to talk about the options and choose.'

Gan nodded. 'Okay. We can talk to my contact about it.'

Suja had been through this before, and she hated the fact that she was faced with this again. But she was armed with some knowledge this time, which she would use to her advantage. She folded her arms and leveled a gaze at him. 'Okay, let's talk.'

TWENTY-FIVE

Jin walked through the crowds of Hua-ryung Street, jiggling coins in his pocket, his sport jacket swishing with every swing of his arm. The glow of yellow neon flickered on his face as he passed the steamy windows of the noodle restaurants. He could have passed as any factory worker or delivery boy—one of thousands who zipped through traffic with lunch trays stacked on the backs of their scooters—he blended in so well now that he barely made an impression. He watched the pedestrian traffic on both sides of the sidewalk and saw two police officers in black uniforms push through the crowd like barracudas in the slipstream. They wore their semiautomatics slung across their squat torsos, caps pulled low over their eyes. Jin curled his lip as he watched them. Far as he knew, the foot police never caught no one, but you had to keep your eyes open anyway.

He fished his phone out of his pocket and dialed Sarge. 'Where's Chung?'

'No Chung today. He's not back from Dalian. It's just you today. You gotta do some driving for Riu.'

'I don't have a car.'

'You do it by taxi.'

'Shit. Are you kidding me? Why don't I just piggyback them? Then I won't even need a taxi.'

'Your choice.'

Jin glanced at the phone with an irritated look on his face. He had been working for Sarge some months now, and had grown accustomed to his gruffness and his blunt-force approach to making decisions, but still, it grated. The guy moved fast, seizing opportunities with no time for second-guessing or considering others around him. Jin stuck it out with him until he paid off his debt to Biyu and started to look for work elsewhere, but there was nothing that would pay anywhere close to what he was making with Sarge, so he stayed on, becoming one of the apparatchiks who made all Sarge's deals happen.

As Jin learned more about Sarge's network of contacts that reached deep into North Korea, he realized he may be able to help him reach Suja, and he stayed on with Sarge and asked him to get in touch with her through one of his contacts, who arranged for phone calls into the country with smuggled cell phones. He hoped to talk with Suja and to see if she would leave her life in Pyongyang to come join him. If she said yes, he figured he'd be able to ask Sarge to help him get her out of North Korea. Who knows, thought Jin. Maybe he could even save enough money to get them passage to America through Riu.

'Any news on that cell phone call with my girl back home?' Jin asked Sarge, careful not to mention North Korea over the phone in case it was being surveilled.

'What are you talking about?' Sarge grumped.

'You were going to get a cell phone to my girl back home,

remember?' he said, reminding him of the request he'd made several weeks ago.

'Yeah.' Sarge exhaled. 'Like I said, since the crackdown it's been impossible.'

Jin stopped in his tracks with the cell phone pressed against his ear. He looked up at the sky. 'You didn't do it.'

'I didn't say I didn't do it.'

'You didn't! You forgot!'

'I don't forget a thing, you idiot. I sent in my contact, and they went to the university, and then to her apartment, and they couldn't find her.'

'What do you mean?' Jin's heart stopped.

'Your girl wasn't there.'

'How could they not find her? Did they check at the school, at the newspaper? Did they even make it into the country back home?'

'*Hssst.*' Sarge sucked his teeth. 'Watch your tone, you little shit. My contact knows the university and checked her neighborhood. Your girl is gone. She went missing months ago.'

Jin felt the ground beneath his feet fall away. 'She's missing?' he whispered. 'Was she...did she get arrested?'

'My guys are asking around, and it looks like she's, uh, disappeared...' His voice dropped. 'I'm really sorry, Jin. We tried to find out what happened.'

Jin fell silent.

'You there?' Sarge asked.

'Yeah.'

'Who knows, maybe she was away on a trip, you know?' Sarge suggested in a helpful tone.

'Can you find out?'

'They're asking around.'

Jin pressed his hand against his eyes and started quaking. 'Okay,' Jin said quietly.

Sarge finally cleared his throat. 'Like I said, maybe she went away.'

Jin hung up.

He slipped the phone back into his pocket and fell against a building, looking shell-shocked. A car sped down the lane, followed by a passenger bus that glided by like a whale amid a sea of teeming fish. Men on scooters zoomed in and out of the traffic with towers of lunch trays stacked on the backs of their scooters, their hands thrust into giant handlebar mitts. How long he sat there staring blankly into the traffic, he wasn't sure, a damn long time. He finally pushed himself off the wall and felt pins and needles shoot through his legs. He had sunk into a small part of himself, a dark blot of word-lessness that had been growing since the day he escaped from prison and went on to go through the motions of whatever needed to be done to survive, no matter how it abraded him. There was no room for morals. Jin was without status, with-out family, without anyone to trust, and the only hope that strung him along was the chance of seeing Suja again.

But now that she was missing, Jin was untethered.

He stepped forward to the edge of the sidewalk, and sens-ing the rhythm of the oncoming traffic, he stepped onto the roadway, weaving through the cars as he crossed lanes. He paused in the center of the road, toying with the desire to just stay there. He finally stepped into an opening in the traffic and crossed to the other side. He approached a stand of taxi scooters on the other side of the sidewalk and raised a hand. 'Taxi,' he said.

A stocky middle-aged woman in a green smock vest stepped forward. 'Yeah,' she said.

'No, thanks.' Jin shook his head, looking for a male driver.

'Come on.' She gestured him over to her scooter. The other scooter drivers weren't budging; he was her fare. Jin walked over to her and stood by the scooter as she swung a heavy leg over the seat and settled herself in. Jin's mouth tightened as he climbed on behind her, his knees touching the side of her thighs.

'Zhe Rong neighborhood. Apartment fifty-five. I'm late.'

The woman gunned the motor and the scooter jerked onto the street, spluttering as it ducked between gleaming double-berth express buses that pulled up alongside them like sliding enameled walls. She was an aggressive driver, and her scooter jumped like a rat in a gutter, scuttering past cars along the bumper-to-bumper roads.

She drove him to the old apartment complex in Zhe Rong, and Jin looked up as they approached the aging buildings. The walls were streaked with rust where water had dribbled from the metal window frames; sagging lines of wrinkled laundry were strung across balconies. There were at least twenty sur-veillance cameras stationed every ten yards or so in the park-ing lot—every square inch of the courtyard was covered.

The scooter pulled along the curb in front of one of the buildings and Jin slid off, drawing his stiff legs together. He thumbed through some bills and handed them to the driver. He headed toward the closest apartment building with his head down, hugging the apartment wall, and continued on to the apartment behind it. When he got to apartment fifty-five, he ducked into the entrance and ran up two flights of stairs.

'You're late,' said Zhao as he let Jin in. Zhao was a burly man with a tight, round belly and pale gleaming forehead. He had the pale, shiny look of someone who sat indoors all day, which was essentially his job as the manager of Riu's apartments.

Jin walked past him, shrugging. 'Sorry,' he said as he scanned the living room and kitchen. 'Where are the girls?'

'In the bedroom.'

'You talked with them. They're good to go?'

'Yeah, yeah.'

Jin cast him a glance with hooded eyes. 'Last time you said that, one tried to jump out of the car.'

Zhao shrugged, showing his brown-lined square palms. 'Some girls are crazy in the head, what can you do? They're Northerns.'

Jin's mouth tightened at the word, feeling vaguely complicit in the way Zhao used it with him, as if he weren't a Northern himself. Yet he didn't want to come off as if he were defending the defectors either. It was his job to pick up and drop off.

He headed to the bedroom with Zhao behind him and poked his head through the door. 'Anyung,' he said, pausing for a beat before stepping into the room.

There were three of them huddled together on the bed, a tall woman at the headboard with her knees drawn up, her head buried in her arms, long hair trailing over her legs. At the foot of the bed were two other women—a waifish small woman with long hair dyed orange, leaning into the arms of another woman with bobbed hair who wore a men's bomber jacket and loose jogging pants. The girl with bobbed hair glanced over to see who entered the room, and when she lifted her face, Jin's heart stopped.

TWENTY-SIX

'Suja,' Jin said, his breath leaving his body. There was no mistaking that jawline, her hair, those almond eyes that were now shadowed with dark rings, but it was definitely Suja, here in the flesh, in this apartment in China.

'Oh my God.' Jin felt the floor tip and the walls give way, and his gaze skittered across the faces of the other women and back to Suja. He couldn't believe this was happening.

'Jin?!' Suja whispered, her face blanched.

'Yes, it's me.' He rushed forward with outstretched arms and hugged her to him, holding her close so he could feel her heartbeat, the familiar curve of her body leaning into his and the softness of her cheek. He kissed her and smoothed her hair, his eyes roving over her face as if to confirm it was really Suja in the flesh, here, right now, with him.

'I can't believe it's you.'

'You're alive,' she said, her voice trembling. Jin was the last person she had expected to see here. She put her hands to his cheeks and hugged him tightly. She had held herself together for so long now, through the escape across the Tumen River, through months of terror at the Wang farmhouse, up until the last few days here at Zhao's apartment, where she anxiously awaited an uncertain fate. The pent-up fear and anguish she kept buried within were unleashed now.

'I thought I'd never see you again. I thought I was a goner,' she said, her voice shaking as tears rolled down her cheeks.

'I thought I'd lost you too. I was so afraid and worried for you. Thank God you're alive!' He wrapped his arms around her again, cradling her head as he hugged her.

There was a stunned silence in the room. Zhao was standing at the doorway watching them, when he finally cut in. 'You know that one, eh?' he asked Jin. 'Y'know her well?'

Suja looked up at Zhao, and then Jin, uncomprehending. Jin blinked, suddenly feeling self-conscious.

'She's a family friend from back home, a very important family friend,' he said awkwardly, his eyes still on Suja. 'How did you—how did these girls get here?'

'She ran away from some family,' said Zhao.

'Ran away?' Jin asked.

'She's a runaway bride.'

Jin froze when Zhao said *runaway bride*, the dark implications of that phrase unfurling its inky blooms in his mind. No. Please. 'No, it can't be,' Jin said, fumbling, staring uncomprehendingly at Suja's hand, her beautiful, capable hand.

Suja shrank when she recognized the Chinese phrase *runaway bride* and turned her face away, struck dumb with shame, even as her protest welled up inside her, jumbling thick in her throat.

'Did Sarge have any part in this?' Jin asked her, his voice shaking as he tried to contain his emotions. 'Did he do this to you?'

'I don't know any Sarge.'

'Sarge,' he repeated. 'I asked him to send you a message in Pyongyang. Did his guy end up bringing you to China?'

'I didn't get that message from you,' she puzzled, 'and I've never heard of Sarge.'

'But then how did you get here?'

Suja looked down, her mouth thinned into a straight line. Jin reached forward and wrapped her in a hug again. 'It's okay, you're here and you're safe now,' he said against her ear. 'I've been praying for a chance for us to see each other again, and you're here now, we're together.'

'I know, it's unbelievable.' Suja smiled through glimmering tears. How surreal, how staggeringly shocking it was to be looking into Jin's eyes. It had been less than a year since she had seen Jin, but he looked so different now. His hair was longer on top and slicked up with oil. A scar glowered above his left brow where the big bruise had been, and there was something different about the set of his lips, the scowling lines etched on either side of his mouth. It was a little unsettling, like returning home after a long trip only to find the furniture rearranged, some photos and a favorite piece of art gone missing, the rooms colder, inexplicably emptier. She reached up to his face, her fingers lightly touching his cheek as if by touch she could make herself feel more comfortable with this new Jin.

'They said you had disappeared. What happened?' he asked her.

'I...' She paused, carefully selecting her words. 'I wanted to find you, so I met a broker who helped me get across the border, but once I was in China, his contact handed me over to two Chinese men. They took me away and tied me up...' Her hand fell away from his face. Jin brought her hand to his lips and kissed it, then held it against his chest.

'Who were those guys?' he said, his voice shaking with fury. 'I'm going to get to the bottom of this. I'm getting you out of here. I just need to talk to Zhao for a second, okay?'

'Okay,' she said, her gaze shifting warily to Zhao.

'You wait here for a moment. I'll be right back.' Jin turned around, signaling to Zhao, and they both stepped out of the room.

As soon as the door closed behind them, Zhao launched into Jin. 'What's going on here—izzat your girlfriend?' he hissed.

'Ye—yes, she was my girlfriend back home, and we've been looking for her for weeks!'

'You know she's been in China for months now…'

'I didn't realize.'

'She's not your girlfriend anymore.'

Jin bristled at this, his eyes flashing. 'She is, and I'm taking care of her now. I'll talk to Sarge about it.'

'Sarge has no say in this. She's been paid for already.'

'Was Sarge a part of this?'

'No. She's a runaway, and she's already promised to some guy in Jilin. Riu's friend Gan brought her in, along with the skinny one.' He hesitated, then added gruffly, 'They're sold already.'

'No way. I'll pay for her. I'll talk to Sarge.'

'Okay, whatever, talk to Sarge.' Zhao shook his head as he walked over to the ivory leather sofa and fell into it with a soft whoosh. Grabbing the remote from the glass coffee table, he changed the channel. 'You're gonna have to find a replacement girl.'

'I'll pay him off.'

'They won't want a refund, they'll want a girl.'

'Fuck you, Zhao.' Jin fished his cell phone out from his

pocket and dialed Sarge's number. He took a deep breath, trying to keep his voice controlled.

'Sarge. You know that girl you've been trying to find for me, the one back home?'

'Yeah.'

'She's *here*. Zhao has her here, with two other girls already contracted into marriage.'

'You're kidding,' Sarge said. 'Aw, fuck… No wonder we couldn't find her. She was already in China. That's your girl there, with Riu?'

'Were you any part of this?'

'No,' Sarge protested. 'Zhao just called us to do a drive for him. We're supposed to take the girls to Jilin on our next van ride there.' Sarge sighed, 'Goddamn.'

'I'm bringing her home.'

'You can't… Let me see, let me talk to Riu. Ah, fuck.' Sarge raised his voice. 'This is not supposed to happen on a job. It's not how you do business…' He was silent for a moment. 'Ah, I'll call you back. Sit tight.'

Jin stood uncertainly in the living room, staring at the phone in his hand. He pocketed it and deliberated about whether to go back into the room to sit with Suja. His heart was racing and he felt sick to his stomach; he didn't know whether to go in and hug her or to crawl into a hole and hide in shame. He wanted to somehow save her from what had already happened, shield her with his own body if he could, for it was his fault that she had left North Korea and entered China; she placed herself in harm's way to come looking for him. He felt complicit with the dark side of the Chinese underground he'd come to know and hate.

Jin wrapped his hand around the cell phone in his pocket. He couldn't go back in until he could tell Suja he was getting her out of there. He headed over to the sofa and sat down next to Zhao and fixed his gaze on the TV set, watching, but not seeing the flickering images. He lifted the phone out of his pocket every minute or so to check if it was still on.

Sarge finally called half an hour later, and Jin shot up from the sofa and stepped out of the apartment to take the call in the hallway.

'This is not going to be easy. I've arranged for you to bring the girls over for now, but we're going to have to talk with Riu again. He's pissed,' Sarge griped.

'Okay,' Jin breathed, and leaned back against the wall, resting his head against it. 'Thank you, Sarge.'

'Don't thank me. She's not off the hook.'

Jin hung up, straightened his jacket and walked back into the apartment, nodding at Zhao as he headed to the bedroom.

'Ladies, I'll be taking you to where you need to go. I am your driver.' He walked over to Suja and knelt down in front of her. 'You're safe now,' he said in a low voice and pulled her into a hug. 'You're with me, and I promise you—you're safe from here on out.'

He flagged a taxi for them and they all got in, the three women taking the back seat and him in the front. Jin reached his hand back to Suja, who sat behind him, and they held hands for the duration of the ride. When they got to Sarge's apartment, the two other women—Hani, the orange-haired girl, and Aeja, the tall one—were settled in the bedroom. He and Suja sat themselves down on the living room parquet where Sarge sat cross-legged, smoking.

'So this is your girl,' said Sarge.

'Yes.'

'Anyung.' Sarge bowed his head.

Suja bowed her head slightly and Sarge watched her. One could tell the class of a person from the way they moved, and there was a certain poise to the way Suja bowed. She knew how to bow properly and to receive bows, and Sarge guessed she was probably trained in traditional Korean dance. She was a Chosun girl of a class rarely seen in China.

'We rarely see the likes of you outside of Chosun,' he said quietly. 'You chose a hard path, kid.'

Suja was silent for a moment. 'I did what I needed to do.'

Sarge sighed and stubbed out his cigarette. 'Let's see if we can make it right for you. We don't have to transport the girls until tomorrow. Why don't you two go get something to eat for now. Jin, you and I can talk later.'

Jin nodded. 'Okay, Sarge.'

'Get some food, catch up. I'm sure you have a lot to talk about.'

Jin was surprised to see this considerate streak in Sarge, and he felt a surge of gratitude toward the man. He nodded his thanks and took Suja's hand and led her out the door.

TWENTY-SEVEN

Suja stopped near the entrance of the restaurant and paused at the fish tank to press her hand against the glass, watching as a black angelfish and orange goldfish fanned themselves in the water, their translucent fins moving like silk. Jin went to stand next to her, standing close so he could breathe in the scent of her hair. He put his hand on her arm. She didn't lean into him and she didn't resist. When she looked up, her eyes were deep and full. He left his hand on her arm, though suddenly he felt uncertain about what to do next.

A waitress walked up with two vinyl-coated menus under her arm. 'For two?' she shrilled, and turned, her hips switching left and right as she marched toward the back of the restaurant. Jin let Suja lead, following a step behind her; maybe she wanted him to guide her, maybe she didn't, he didn't know. The waitress led them to a corner table that had a paper panel partition, square red cushions scattered on pine bench seat-ing. Jin slid onto the bench and felt the wooden slats move and tilt as he shifted his weight.

'Here.' He reached for the porcelain teapot and poured out barley tea. Suja lifted her cup by the tips of her fingers and carefully brought it to her lips, her head bent with a prayer-like intensity that was beautiful, reverential. She raised the teacup to her lips and Jin watched her swallow, imagining the warm tea entering her body. To be handled like a coveted cup of tea and to be appreciated like that, as one could be in a life less urgent, a life that was stable and safe; to be gathered up and held by her and to be cherished; to be whole and true again—could any of this be possible?

Suja placed the teacup down on her place mat and folded her hands on her lap. She couldn't bring herself to meet his eyes. The shock of seeing Jin again reverberated through her body, and she wanted things to slow down. It felt surreal to be sitting with Jin again after having fantasized about it for so long, and after months of captivity at Ping's farmhouse, it was hard to let herself unclench, relax and truly inhabit her body.

She looked at Jin, considering every moment of him: his clean, straight brow; his thin pale neck; those wrists; his thick knuckles, honest and clean as lines of poetry. Had he always been this skinny? The scar on his brow and cheek and the gangster slicked-back hair gave him the look of a boy who had been broken into manhood.

Suja dropped her gaze back down to her hands on her lap as she wondered again why Jin had been at the apartment. How did he know these people? She had an uneasy feeling and she wasn't sure she really wanted to find out why. She didn't know where to start with him.

'You saved me,' she said finally.

Jin shifted in his seat. 'We're not in the clear yet. I talked to Sarge, and we still have to work something out with Riu and his men.'

'Are you going to have to pay?'

'Maybe, I don't know,' he said gruffly. 'Honestly, that would be the best thing, if I could just pay him off. I'd have paid anything to spare you from all...' He paused, not quite sure what to say. 'All the hardship in China,' he said woodenly, the words stupid, inadequate. They were called names, all the North Korean women who were sold as brides to Chinese men—'newbies,' 'broken-ins,' 'second or third steepings.' It tormented him to know that girls were sold once, several, numerous times. Why, of all people, did it have to happen to Suja? She was so pure, so talented, destined for great things in Chosun. Why did it have to happen to her? Jin raged silently.

As Jin reached for Suja's hand and held it tight, she realized in that moment that Jin understood the entirety of her shame. She felt stripped naked before him, her pain as visible as bruises and scars on her body. It was less than a year ago that they had last seen each other in Mr. Ku's classroom, where Suja was the indomitable one, the sassy, bright, popular one. How far she had fallen since then, the circumstances of her life irrevocably changed. How do you speak from the abyss of experience?

Suja pulled her hand away and held it in her lap, focusing on her feet to hold her steady until her heart rate settled again. There she was somehow all held together by muscle and gristle in the skin of a life she had never imagined she would wear as her own. Suja's hands cradled her teacup and she stared into the brown tea.

'What happened?' Jin asked gently. 'How did you end up in China?'

She looked at him wearily and attempted a smile. 'When I found out you escaped from prison—and how you managed that, I don't know.' She reached for his hand, a hint of pride in her voice now. 'You escaped from Yodok! So of course I had to come find you. I paid brokers to get guided into China.'

'Oh my God,' Jin said. 'You arranged it all yourself? How did they get you into China?'

'Across the Tumen.'

Jin nodded, remembering vividly the night he spent in the frigid waters of that river. So she had crossed that very river too. He wondered what other paths they both traversed, only months, or even weeks, apart? Did she end up in all the places he had been, and if so, could they have met at some point sooner?

'And then what happened?' he asked gently.

'Well.' She paused, and her voice deepened. 'I never guessed that broker in China would sell me off.'

'The bastard,' Jin spit fiercely. 'Who was it, what was his name?'

'Tae-won. A broker back home connected me with him and Tae-won was the one who sold me off to the Chinese.' She paused. 'Do you know him?'

'I've never heard of him. When did this all happen?'

'About six months ago.'

Jin counted the months. That would have been only a couple of months after he had escaped into China himself. He could feel his throat tighten as he considered how close they had been all this time, so *damn* close. He could have saved her much sooner if only he had asked Sarge's men to search for her in China. Or if he had tried to reach out to her in Pyongyang earlier, he might have known she had left Pyongyang and maybe he could have intercepted her. Or if he had never stolen the cornmeal in the first place, none of this would have happened to her. It was because of him that she had ended up suffering.

'I should have protected you,' Jin said brokenly. 'Please for-give me...'

'You didn't know,' she said quietly.

Jin fell silent.

The waitress stepped up to their table, startling them both. 'What can I get you?' she said sharply, pulling a pen out of her hair. Her eyebrows were lined with black pencil and they formed a perfect V of vexation.

Jin blinked and picked up the menu. 'What would you like to eat?' he asked Suja.

'I'm not so hungry.'

'I'll come back,' said the waitress.

'No, no,' mumbled Jin, running his eyes down lists of Ko-rean stews and meat dishes on the menu. Should he order the *kalbi* because it was beef, or order the pork-bone stew because it was more comforting? Or perhaps the noodle dish, *japchae*, maybe she would enjoy tasting that dish? Fuck it, he'd order meat and more meat.

'Kalbi and pork-bone soup, please,' he said.

'Beer or soju?' the waitress asked.

Jin glanced at Suja, who shook her head. 'Not now,' said Jin.

The waitress jabbed her pen in her hair and collected the menus. Suja fingered her chopsticks, then slid them out of the paper wrapper, folding the wrapper halfway lengthwise and crimping it on both ends so that it looked like a miniature bench. She set it down on the table and rested the tips of her chopsticks on it. She looked up at Jin. There was still some-thing weighing on her mind and she had to ask.

'How do you know those people?' she said quietly.

'This restaurant?' Jin asked. 'Sarge brought me here be-fore.'

'I mean those people at the apartment.'

'Oh.' Jin's neck reddened. He looked away, peering out

the window at the parking lot where a taxi was pulling up. A man with a large brown briefcase climbed out of the passenger seat, his trench coat flipping in the wind.

'Did...you know what Sarge did for a living?' Suja asked.

'I don't know all his business,' Jin mumbled. 'But he doesn't work a lot with Zhao, that Chinese guy who was watching over you at the apartment.'

'You didn't know they're traffickers?'

'They're not,' Jin spluttered. 'Riu's men maybe, but Sarge, he does transport, mainly shipping cargo, or stuff from the docks, and sometimes we...we *give rides.*'

'Where did they take those girls?' Suja interrupted. 'You know what happened to me happens all the time!'

Jin's face darkened with grief. 'I know. I'm so sorry. I want to find that man and kill him. I wish I'd been there...if only I'd been there to help you from the start!'

'Help me? Who are you helping here? Are you *helping* the girls you pick up?'

'You have this idea about Sarge. I told you we do shipments mostly, delivering phones or DVDs. And sometimes I introduced North Koreans to Sarge, people who were stuck in the tunnels or hiding out in the mountains and wanting to find work.'

'Girls.'

'Sometimes girls, yes. There were girls who wanted introductions.'

'And Sarge paid you, then he sold them,' she said flatly.

Jin paused before he said in a thick voice, 'No. He made introductions.'

'More introductions. To whom?'

'To the Chinese.'

Suja's eyes widened at this admission, surprised that he could speak of it so casually. There was another conversation that ran underneath the conversation they were having, an argument that neither wanted to give shape or sound in language, but they could sense it in their bodies, feel it prickle under their skin. A trust had been broken and nothing Jin said seemed to be reaching her, or she simply didn't want to understand. Jin ran his hands along the tops of his thighs and hunched forward, remembering their days back at the university. They used to spend hours standing next to each other in the darkroom, their skin alive to each other as they watched her images develop like apples reddening and ripening on the branch. Their love was a current, a silent river that flowed between them.

He was searching for that flowing feeling now.

Suja watched him warily, trying to remember if Jin was like this back in Pyongyang. The Jin she used to know was a hardworking, earnest country boy who wanted to make good on his life. His ambitions for their life in Chosun were as straight as an arrow, and he pushed past every class barrier in Pyongyang with actions that were straight and true. How was it that this man whom she had loved, Jin, with whom she had spent so many afternoons in the darkroom—how could he have become this?

'Why did you choose this work?' she asked in anguish. 'You're a man. You could have found farmwork or anything else. I know we don't get much choice in life, especially here in China, but what you do ends up deciding who you are. Look what you've become. What happened to you?'

Jin fidgeted as she spoke and finally blurted, 'What happened to you?' Immediately, he regretted his words.

Suja's eyes flashed. '*You*, of all people, know what happened to me.' She got up from the table abruptly, tripping over her canvas bag as she rushed to leave. Just then the waitress came up to their table balancing a wide tray in her arms. Suja and

Jin both pulled back, making room for her to set one end of the tray against the table.

The waitress transferred a steaming bowl piled high with stewed potatoes and pork meat still on knuckles of bone. Next came a sizzling platter of barbecued kalbi, several different marinated vegetable side dishes and two steel bowls of rice. It was an embarrassing amount of food. Jin and Suja watched the waitress move the dishes around, making space on the table, then finally back away, swinging the empty tray at her side.

Jin looked at the spread on the table, ashamed at how much he had ordered. He had wanted to get Suja everything she might want to eat, but now the number of dishes on the table just looked like dirty money trying to impress. As the waitress turned to leave, there was a change in the mood between them, a slight bruising in the air.

'Just…let's sit down, come and eat. Come on, calm down for a second.' Jin gestured to her seat. Suja sat back down, shifting in her seat to move back against the bench wall.

'Please, just have a little something,' Jin said.

'I can't.'

'Okay, don't eat. Just sit for a second. Oh, God.' Jin felt himself unravel, overwhelmed by it all. He wanted to yell, *We're alive. We're here. Let's just love each other, and start a life together.*

'Suja, I'm so sorry…' Jin reached across the table, but she pulled back, dropping her hands to her lap. 'If there was anything I could do to change everything back, I would in a heartbeat. I tried so hard to find you… I was trying to get a message to you in Pyongyang, because I was hoping to send for you. I had no idea you had already left and come here searching for me.'

Suja had the strangest expression on her face. 'You're kidding. You were searching for me back in Pyongyang, when all the while I was here in China?'

'Yes.' He exhaled with a pained expression.

'I don't know what to say.' She looked down at her hands. 'I came to China to find you, but I did everything wrong and ended up getting sold off to the Chinese. I lost all hope. I never thought I'd see you again. But miraculously we end up meeting and that's just—' Her eyes shone as she looked up and met Jin's gaze. 'It saved me. You saved me. But why, *why* are you working with these people?'

Jin hung his head. 'I'm not working with those people in that way…' He stopped himself at this point. No matter what he did, he couldn't undo the things that had brought them to this point—he couldn't save Suja from the traffickers who sold her off as a bride, nor could he unsell the girls who had passed through his hands; he couldn't unsteal the cornmeal he had lifted for his parents, or cross over the border again back into the fortress of their homeland.

'I'm so sorry, Suja,' he said brokenly. 'This is all my fault and I'm sorry for all that you've gone through.'

'Oh, Jin,' she said, tears welling in her eyes. 'I mean, I chose to come here to search for you. I chose it willingly. But I didn't know *this* would happen to me.'

Jin reached for her hand. 'I dreamed and hoped every day that I might see you again, but never at this cost. It would've been much better for you if you'd never met me. But I'm so grateful you're alive and we're together now. Against all odds, we found each other in a country of more than a billion people… Isn't that something?'

Suja smiled wearily. How she had loved him with all her heart and soul. She wanted to be able to match his ardor and give him the answer he sought, but she was so bone tired and weary.

Jin leaned forward and grabbed her hands. 'We can start a new life somewhere. We could try to leave this country.

Maybe even America could be a possibility.' He said this realizing that it would hinge on Riu, the very man who had claims on Suja's fate.

'Really?' she said. 'Do you think we can make it all the way to America?'

'I'm not sure,' Jin backpedaled, 'but I'm going to figure this out when I talk to Sarge. We first have to sort things out with Riu.'

Suja's eyes hardened when she heard Sarge's name and she pursed her lips. 'I want to speak with him too.'

TWENTY-EIGHT

They arrived back at Sarge's apartment to see Chung and Sang-do had come back from their day and were sitting in front of the TV with the two other women, the remains of dinner strewn across the coffee table. There were plastic containers with scraps of noodles, puckered string beans in a slick of brown sauce. In the kitchen a kettle bubbled over a blue flame. Suja walked in and shut it off, returning to the living room to join Jin and the others as they watched a Chinese newscast. She went over to the two women and knelt down beside Hani, the girl with the orange-dyed hair.

'Are you feeling any better?' she asked, giving her a hug.

'Yeah, much better,' said Hani. 'How about you, Suja. How are things with your man?'

'It's… I don't know.' Suja laid her head against Hani's. 'It's surreal to meet him here working with these other guys.'

Hani tilted her head and glanced at the men thoughtfully.

'Yeah. But…if he wasn't working with them, you guys would have never met.'

Suja paused at this. 'You're right…but it doesn't feel right.'

'I don't know, sister. In this crooked world, there are no straight lines.'

Suja pursed her lips and looked over at Jin, who was talking to Sarge. He stopped to pick up his ashtray as they both got up and headed to the bedroom, motioning for Suja to come along.

The room was sparely furnished with a double bed that was still in its plastic casing and a bedside table with an ashtray and a lamp. A couple of phone chargers were plugged into the wall socket. Sarge sat on the bed, placed his ashtray next to him and looked at them.

'How was your dinner?' he asked.

'Good,' Jin replied. 'What's the latest with Riu? Did you manage to talk with him again?'

Sarge sighed. 'It's not looking good. He won't budge because the deals have already been made. He wants Suja and the other two girls in Jilin tomorrow.'

Jin and Suja exchanged glances. 'I'll pay him off,' said Jin. 'Tell him I'll pay him.'

'It's not going to be so easy because the drop is supposed to happen tomorrow night. You'd need another girl.'

'You'd have to find a girl to replace me?' Suja stepped in. 'Do you hear what he's saying?'

'People put a lot of money down for a bride. Riu can't just walk away with their money.'

'How dare he? How dare any of you buy and sell us, as if we're your property, as if we're pieces of cargo that you could move and sell,' she exclaimed. 'What if I were your daughter, what if I were your sister?! You'd never allow this.'

Sarge put up his hands. 'Whoa, wait a minute, I'm not the one buying or selling. We're just contracted as drivers. Riu is the one making the deals.'

'But how could you *work* with these guys? He's a human trafficker!' she railed.

'Listen, we're illegal in this country, we can't just go and— and print our résumés and apply for a job. Anything we do is going to be illegal, just by definition. So what can we do? We move electronics, we transport stuff and sometimes we transport people. Riu calls us for work because we speak Korean,' Sarge said. 'And anyway, no one is forced to do anything. The girls agree to the marriages because they don't have anywhere else to go. They'd end up at the brothels.'

Suja looked away, her chest heaving. How could a fellow North Korean do this kind of work? Whether or not he was the seller, he was making money off the backs of innocent women. What she really meant to be saying, what she really meant to be screaming at him, was *How could you let girls like me fall into the hands of those Chinese men?!* But that scream in all its fury was bunched up inside her, the bitterness of her unvoiced rage in the back of her throat and deep in her gut. Suja was thinking about the two women on the other side of the door in the living room; but there were more women, thousands more being trafficked, and tens of thousands living in hiding in China.

'I didn't come here to be sold as a bride,' she said through gritted teeth. 'I came here with money. I *paid* a broker for passage into China so I could search for Jin. And I'm not the only one, ask any woman, they didn't come here to be sex slaves, they came here to work.'

'I know, Suja,' Sarge said tightly. 'But no one's hiring North Koreans. It's too risky, especially since Kim Jong-un announced the crackdown. China's played along and they've made it impossible for us defectors in China.'

'If Chinese families are comfortable enough to have Cho-sun women in their homes, they can hire us in their work-places. *I* was working on the farm with the family I was with.'

'You're right, they should,' said Sarge. 'But they don't.'

'Okay, but we don't have to help them exploit our women,' Jin said.

'Someone's getting high and mighty,' Sarge muttered as he ashed his cigarette. 'Actually, the question is whether there's a way to get Riu off your backs.'

'How do we do that?' Suja and Jin asked at the same time.

'I think we have to offer him more money than what that family offered to pay.'

'How much would that be?' asked Suja.

'I don't know, I'll ask Zhao. I'm guessing they would have to pay at least forty thousand yuan. So we could offer him more, like, say, fifty thousand yuan.'

Jin gasped, 'That's crazy.'

'This is just—' Suja spluttered '—it's not right. It's not fair.'

'Nothing's fair. This is the life of a defector. There's a whole business built around us, and you guys aren't the first, and you won't be the last, North Koreans to get swallowed up in this country. It's not going to cough you up easily.'

The three of them fell silent.

'What if we tried to go to America? Any chance of that?' asked Jin.

Sarge shook his head. 'You can nix that idea. Riu hasn't budged on it. I think the best option would be you pay him off. You stay and work awhile, save some money, then pay your way to South Korea. You know they accept North Ko-rean defectors there and even hand out money when they arrive.'

'But aren't there Christians who will help us? My friend said there are aid groups in China who'd help us get to South Korea or America,' he said, recalling what Hyuk had told him back at the charnel house.

'That costs money too. Sure, go to America, or the North Pole, for that matter. But you'd be hard up to find anyone who can help you by tomorrow night. Anyway, most of them hire us brokers to do the dirty work of getting people across borders.'

Jin cast a wary glance at Suja. 'Could we have a moment to talk about this, Sarge?'

'Sure, take your time.' Sarge grabbed his ashtray and got up from the bed. Suja sighed and Jin reached over and held her hand, his eyes searching hers.

Sarge watched them, his eyes taking in everything. One can tell the truth about a couple in the way they look at each other, and he could see why they had gone to such lengths to find each other. He smiled a tight smile. They had a hard road ahead, these two. He left the room and closed the door behind him.

Jin sat next to Suja and wrapped his arm around her. 'So, what do you think?'

'I don't like the options,' she said ruefully. 'So far, I haven't liked any of the options in China.'

'No, the options aren't great,' he said in a grim voice. 'But if we pay Riu off, I could work longer and make enough money to get us to South Korea. We could be free citizens there.'

'What about the Christian group you talked about—maybe they could help us?'

'I could look into it, but I haven't talked to my friend Hyuk in a while. Either way, I'd have to work for a while to pay off Riu, then save up for the brokers' fees to get us out of China.'

'You mean keep working with Sarge?' said Suja. 'You can't keep doing this work.'

Jin looked down, muttering, 'I know, but we need money to be able to get out of this country.'

She let out a sigh of frustration. Looking at the bedroom door, she was struck by a sudden thought, and bolting from the bed, she hurried to the living room. She came back carrying her bag, and after rummaging through it, she pulled out a small velvet sack. She opened the sack and slid out a piece of paper that had been folded several times into a square, that she unfolded and spread out in front of Jin. In the center of the paper lay the hoop snake necklace with the diamond at its mouth glinting in the light.

'Oh.' Jin was stunned. 'You've still got it,' he said, eyeing the necklace. He started fumbling for his coat and pulled out a pair of worn gloves from his pocket. He held them up for Suja. They were softer now, the digits shaped to the curve of his grip, and the leather worn and supple from use, but Suja recognized the gloves she had purchased in Pyongyang. She and Jin laughed as they looked at each other, remembering the day they had given each other the gifts. It was less than a year ago.

Suja ran her fingers along the softened leather. She remembered the day she spent at the government depot store with her mother. How Umma had argued with the manager, attempting to pull strings on her behalf in order to procure a winter coat for Suja. Her heart still ached to think of all the things her mother had done all these years to ensure Suja would stay out of harm's way.

Jin lifted the necklace from the paper and felt the weight of the hoop snake pendant, remembering how his mother had forced him to take it. She had sacrificed the heirloom for his education, when she could have used it to buy food for their family. In her eyes the family's hunger didn't merit the hawking of this valuable piece, but his education was the key to the family's future, so she pawned it for the sake of building their future. He ran his thumb around the dragon snout, along intricately carved grooves that set the diamond at the point where the tail met its mouth. It was supposed to represent the balance of yin and yang in the universe, but all he could think of was the sacrifice and suffering that was bound up in the necklace. There was no balance to their lives; this necklace was emblematic of a self-cannibalizing nation he wanted no part of anymore.

'If we sold this, it would buy our escape,' he said.

Suja looked at him, her eyes glistening. 'We should do it,' she said in a quiet, firm voice. 'For our future. China will never be a home to us, and Chosun is no longer our home. We have to find a place where we can make a new home for us.'

It was the first time Suja had said anything about her hopes for their future, and when Jin heard her say 'our home,' he felt a rush of love for her. It was what he had felt with her when they stood on her rooftop in Pyongyang so long ago; it was a kind of release, the undoing of pent-up fears and hopes he hadn't dared to express until that moment when he realized they were all answered, and fulfilled, with her.

He put his arm around her neck and they sat together looking down at the hoop snake necklace.

'Do you think we can leave tonight when everyone is asleep?' Suja asked.

He blinked and pulled away for a moment. 'You mean do it behind Sarge's back. Run away?'

'Yes.'

'But Riu will crucify him. We can't do that to him.'

'That's not your responsibility. Riu has no right to sell me, so he definitely has no right to hold anything over Sarge.'

'But he will.'

'That's their problem.'

'I can't leave Sarge holding the bag. He helped me a lot and it would be wrong to do that to him.'

'Wrong? Who's right and who's in the wrong here?' Suja exclaimed. 'Sarge hasn't *helped* you—he's just made you do his dirty work all this time. If we don't run now, you'll end up more and more in debt to him and we'll be trapped in this life forever. We have to cut clean, *now*. It's our only chance,' she implored.

He turned away, his face darkening, feeling torn about betraying Sarge's trust. For whatever Suja's opinion of the man, he had been straight with him and treated him fairly. Jin knew how things worked with the Snakeheads: if he and Suja took off, Riu would come after Sarge for the forty thousand yuan. That just wasn't right. But he also recognized the truth to what Suja said. It would take him more than a year to save up that kind of money if he was working for Sarge, longer if he was working elsewhere—and he'd have to work elsewhere, as he couldn't very well work for Sarge anymore.

Jin pulled his cell phone out of his pocket and thumb-scrolled through his contacts. 'I think you're right, we have to do it tonight,' he said heavily. 'Let me text Hyuk and see if he can help us.' He sent off a text message and put the phone down.

'We'd have to do it while everyone's asleep.'

'Yes,' Jin said, trying to figure out the best way to do it. 'These guys go to sleep really late, so we'll have to go to bed with our things next to us.'

His phone pinged, and he lifted it to check his text messages, immediately texting back. 'Hyuk can help us. He says he can meet us at the charnel house in the morning.'

Suja took in a sharp intake of breath. 'Really. Oh, God. We're really going to do this.'

'Yes, we have to do this.' Jin looked at her with a somber smile and thought about how to plan this. 'When we go out there, I'll tell Sarge we decided we want to negotiate with Riu tomorrow, okay? We go to sleep as if nothing is happening.'

Suja nodded, squeezing his hand as they headed back to the living room.

When they walked out into the living room, Sarge and everyone were watching a late-night Chinese movie. Aeja sat on the floor in front of the sofa with Hani slumped against her, asleep. Aeja shook her awake when she saw Suja and Jin come out of the bedroom.

'Let's go to bed,' said Aeja, pulling Hani to her feet. The two of them stumbled off to the bedroom. 'You coming, Suja?' Aeja called.

'In a bit,' she replied.

Sarge watched her and Jin settle into the sofa. 'So,' he said, picking up a chopstick wrapper and curling it between his fingers. 'What'd you decide?'

Jin leveled a gaze at Sarge. 'We want to negotiate with Riu.'

'Pay him off.'

'Yeah.' Jin sighed heavily. 'Although I hate the idea of giving him the money.' Jin got up and walked over to the closet and pulled out a knapsack. He sat down and unzipped a pocket, retrieving a small notepad and flipping it open to a page with a column of figures. He traced his finger down the page.

'I've got about eleven thousand saved in your safe.'

'Sounds about right.'

'Would I be able to borrow the rest from you, Sarge?'

'It's a lot of money.'

'It is a lot.'

'You'll work it off,' Sarge said, more a statement than a question.

Jin nodded.

Sarge shifted his gaze to Suja. 'You okay with that? Him working with me, the evil profiteer?' he asked sardonically.

Suja cut her eyes at him and said nothing.

'She good with this?' Sarge asked Jin.

'Yeah. We talked about it.'

'Okay.' Sarge put his hand in the peanut bowl on the coffee table and fished out a handful of nuts. 'You might get away with paying less if Zhao finds another girl. I called him again.'

Suja's face reddened at this and Jin gave her hand a squeeze. He leaned back against the sofa armrest and pulled Suja to him. They lay there together and watched the movie.

'What time is it happening tomorrow?' asked Jin, his eyes on the TV.

'Not till seven o'clock, but we should talk to Riu in the morning,' mumbled Sarge.

'Got it.'

Sang-do gave a big yawn and stood up, scratching his belly. 'Where you guys sleeping?' he asked Jin.

'We can sleep here,' said Jin from the couch.

Sang-do shuffled off in slippered feet toward the bathroom.

Sarge and Chung stayed up for another hour or so. Suja dozed and Jin did too, despite trying to stay awake. He woke with a start when Chung finally shut the TV off and headed to the other bedroom. Jin shut his eyes again and lay quietly as he waited for Chung to settle into bed. He checked his phone every five minutes or so as he waited to make sure Chung wouldn't get up again. He went through a checklist in his mind, making sure he had his phone charger, his wallet and a hoodie in the knapsack. The rest of his clothes were in the bedroom with the guys, so he'd leave the clothes. He'd also leave the eleven thousand yuan in the safe for Sarge to help pay Riu off. Aside from that, there was nothing else he needed to take from the apartment.

After thirty minutes passed, he gently shook Suja awake. Her eyes flew open suddenly and she looked around, blinking, as she gathered her senses.

'It's time to go,' he whispered to her. 'You have everything you need?'

She nodded with the wide-eyed look of a child just woken from a dream. She felt for her bag and nodded. 'I'm ready.'

They lay there for another ten minutes until finally Jin signaled they should get up. Suja sat up on the sofa, ran her hands through her hair and picked up her bag. They tiptoed to the door and picked up their shoes. Jin unlocked the dead bolt and slowly opened the door, listening for any sounds of movement from the bedrooms. They slipped out into the hall-way, and he bent down to wedge a piece of paper over the strike plate to prevent the door latch from making a sound. They ran down the hall toward the elevators and pushed the button, then stood there waiting for the elevator to come up.

'Should we take the stairs?' Suja asked, looking nervously down the hall.

'The elevator's faster,' said Jin, his eyes fixed on the seam between the two closed doors. Suja kept checking down the hall and was about to tell Jin they should take the stairs when finally the elevator doors opened with a loud ding. They looked down the hall nervously as they rushed into the el-evator.

'When we get to the bottom, we're going to run to the taxi stand on the main street. We'll take a taxi over to the area where Hyuk works and we'll have to wait there until the morning when he arrives. I'll think of something once we get there.'

'We can wait outside, that's fine.'

'You've got the necklace?'

She nodded.

'Okay.'

When the elevator doors opened, Jin took her hand and they ran through the lobby and out into the parking lot. They were running across the asphalt when they heard a shout from above. Sarge was in his T-shirt, leaned over his balcony railing, yelling, 'Hey, you bastard! Get back here! I'm gonna kill you!'

Jin and Suja ran as fast as they could across the parking lot, not daring to look up.

'Don't do this! They're gonna find you! Come back!' yelled Sarge.

They made it out to the cabstand where a couple of taxis sat idling by the road. Jin ran to the first one and tried the door handle. It was locked with the driver asleep in the back seat. They ran to the second cab and rapped on the window. The cabbie had fallen asleep at the wheel, but he opened his eyes blearily and fumbled to press the unlock button. They climbed in and Jin gave the directions hurriedly.

'Wenha Street, along the back alley where the slaughter-house is. Fast. I'll pay you extra.'

The driver put the car into Reverse and turned the car onto the road, tires squealing. Jin had his back turned and he was looking through the rear window to see if any cars were in pursuit.

'Turn right at the next corner,' he shouted to the driver.

'It's not the way,' the driver griped.

'I know, just do it.'

The car careened as the driver veered left, sending Suja

sliding into Jin. Jin put his arm around her as he urged the driver, 'Go as fast as you can, just go, go, go.'

They lost sight of the apartment as they sped down the side lane, but Jin kept checking out the back window, expecting to see Sarge in pursuit. He tapped the back of the driver's seat. 'Okay, turn right now.'

The driver slammed the brakes, sending Suja and Jin into the front seats. She glared at the driver, shaking her head as Jin reached over and kissed her. He cast another glance over his shoulder. 'We might be in the clear,' he whispered.

She turned her head to look back as their taxi raced ahead and watched the dotted lines on the road recede behind them.

TWENTY-NINE

They huddled in the alley doorway with their eyes on the slaughterhouse, stamping their feet and hugging each other to keep warm. Suja held a sleeve up to her nose against the smell of blood and offal that hung in the cold still air. Jin looked at his watch, then dropped his wrist and shook it. They had been there since four in the morning. He whispered to Suja, 'Hyuk should be arriving any minute now.'

Jin wished he could have stayed on at the charnel house and stuck it out with Hyuk longer, if only the boss man at the slaughterhouse had taken him on. Working as a butcher was an honest life, even if you were an illegal, but there was the rub—it was hard to get any kind of honest work. Jin wondered what would have happened if he hadn't met Sarge and his network of the North Korean brokers, smugglers and runners. He would never have learned how to work underground while moving around in broad daylight, selling cell phones, mink pelts, bootleg DVDs and CDs. And, of course, if it weren't for Sarge and his contacts, Jin wouldn't have been at Zhao's apartment yesterday. He put his hand on the nape of Suja's neck and kissed her hair.

The first couple of workers showed up at the charnel house and waited for the back door to open, hands thrust into their pockets, plumes of steamy breath billowing above their faces. A beat-up silver Jiangnan rumbled past the charnel house and pulled in to a parking lot just in front of them. Hyuk flung open the door with an unlit cigarette in his mouth, one hand rummaging in his pocket. Jin stepped out from behind the wall and gave a quick wave and then stepped back behind the wall. Hyuk squinted in their direction and trotted over, breaking into a smile as he approached.

'Look at you.' He clapped his hand on Jin's back, giving him a once-over. He took in the slicked-back hair and the shiny bomber jacket, the watch, the shoes. 'Looks like you found some work... Hope you kept out of trouble.'

'And you're still sticking pigs.' Jin smiled.

'Come on, respect to your elder.' He nudged Jin. 'And who's this?'

Jin took hold of Suja's hand. 'This is Suja, Hyuk. Suja, this is my good friend Hyuk. We escaped from Yodok together.'

She smiled, extending her hand. 'Anyung. Pleased to meet you. I've heard a lot about you.'

Hyuk bowed. 'Anyung. You're more beautiful than he had talked you up to be, and he couldn't stop talking about you.' He looked down and seized one of Jin's gloved hands. 'You still have those filthy gloves you kept tied around your waist!'

He turned to Suja. 'You don't want ever to touch those things—the sweat, the grime. He wouldn't ever part with them.'

'It's about time I got him a new pair.'

'Yeah, buy a new pair in a free country, make that your

goal. Come on.' He gestured, and they followed him to the car. 'Your guy Sarge, he doesn't know my name or number, right?'

'No,' said Jin, opening the passenger door for Suja.

'Okay. It won't take long for these guys to find out, though. People will be looking for you.'

Hyuk cleared a couple of foam food containers from the back seat and took a long drag on his cigarette before tossing it to the ground. Suja sat gingerly in the back seat, sniffing at the stale odor of cigarettes and black-bean sauce. She looked at the door armrest carefully before touching it. Hyuk turned the ignition over until it finally caught and, putting his hand on the back of the passenger seat, reversed the car, peeling out of the lot.

He drove with three fingers resting on the bottom of the steering wheel as he maneuvered along roads that were familiar to Jin—past the blue Chongwen bank building and through the lighting and electrical district, past restaurants and stores with their wares piled on the sidewalk. Jin put his hand on Suja's lap as they passed a group of people crowded on the medians as they headed to work, couples standing together, happy and free.

'I'm taking you to a safe house owned by that Christian group I told you about,' said Hyuk. 'It's a farm converted into a small sewing factory. Some Chosun women live in hiding there, and they sew leather goods to make a living. Jung and Okja, they're the couple I told you about who've been helping North Korean defectors. You could stay there today and they can help get you on your way.'

'Are they the missionaries who can help us get to America?'

Hyuk shook his head. 'Jung can't help you get to America. The group that was doing that work got kicked out of China—them and a bunch of other Christian groups got kicked out. But Jung knows how to get there and he can connect you to a couple of brokers who can guide you out of this country.'

Suja's back went up when she heard the term *broker*. 'Do we have to work with brokers?' she said uneasily. 'I got sold to Chinese traffickers because of a broker.'

Hyuk looked at her in the rearview mirror. 'Jung only works with trustworthy guys, so it'll be safe. As long as you can pay for the guides, you'll be fine.'

Suja sat back against the seat with a troubled look on her face. They were heading out of the city now, chasing a road that edged onto rolling fields that went on and on, until finally in the distance they saw a small cluster of buildings. Hyuk drove past the first several farm buildings, and as they approached the last one, he slowed the car down and nosed into the driveway. Hyuk let the car inch to a stop and left it in idle so that it vibrated and shuddered in place, a plume of exhaust tailing up in the crisp winter air.

'Is this the place?' Jin asked, scanning the barn buildings that were the last few structures along the road, a last-ditch attempt to stave off the chaos of empty brushland that encroached. They were built from large sheets of plywood with red paint flaking off in strips. Next to it was a chicken coop made of corrugated fiberglass.

'Yep.' Hyuk killed the engine just as the farmhouse door flung open and a dark-skinned young man came out with a smaller woman following closely behind.

'Hey, you found us, anyung,' said Jung.

'Anyung,' said Hyuk, getting out of the car. 'This is Jin and Suja, the couple I'd told you about.'

Jin and Suja got out of the car and came around to meet the couple.

'Glad you came.' Okja stepped forward, her smile revealing

a missing lower tooth. Despite the missing tooth, there was a clean, honest beauty to her, with her clear wide-set eyes, pale, full lips and no makeup. She bowed shyly toward Suja and Jin and told them to follow her as she led them along the side of the barn toward a door on the far side.

'We've converted part of our farm into a sewing factory and we have some Chosun women working with us,' she explained as she walked in. Suja was immediately struck by the gamy smell in the barn, a sharp, vinegary tang that pricked the back of her throat. It wasn't the acrid smell of chicken shit, or the fusty smell of chicken down and feathers; it was the smell of tanned and cured hides.

There were stacks of richly dyed leathers and pelts that were piled on a few tables and a row of sewing tables set up on one side of the barn. Hunched over at each sewing machine was a woman in a headscarf wearing white cotton gloves, fingertips stained a mottled rainbow of colors. Around them were shimmering swatches of rabbit pelts dyed deep purple, wine red, saffron orange, and large pieces of leather in shades of browns and oranges and brilliant turquoise and pink. A couple of the women looked up and nodded their heads in greeting. Suja bowed back, hesitantly, intrigued by the sight of so many working North Korean women.

'These ladies will finish up at six this evening,' said Okja. 'Some of them are staying with us at the house, so it's a full house there, but you'd be welcome to sleep on the floor with us if you need, or there's also some space here in the barn over there, if you'd prefer.' She pointed over to the back, where a couple of cots were pushed up against the wall. They walked toward a table piled with dyed rabbit pelts, and Jung pulled out chairs for everyone, setting them out with a flourish. Suja smiled. There was an amiable air about Jung and his wife that put her at ease.

Jung took a chair next to Hyuk and leaned forward, folding his arms on the table. 'So, Hyuk told us you've been in China for a while, but you're hoping to get out now?'

'Yes,' said Jin. 'We're hoping to find a place where we can start a new life. We were thinking of America.'

Jung raised his brow thoughtfully. 'America, well... That's quite the destination. There was an aid group that helped people get to America, but they're not around anymore. I think you'd be better off going to South Korea now.'

Jin and Suja exchanged glances. They hadn't considered South Korea as a destination. 'Why there?' asked Suja.

'Because you can get status immediately and the government supports you. They give you an apartment to live in, they give you monthly payments and everyone speaks the language... You can be independent.'

'I've heard that,' said Jin, drawing his brow together. 'But I've also heard discrimination is bad in South Korea and it's hard to get jobs.'

'It's hard to get jobs anywhere.' Jung shrugged. 'But you can live as a free citizen there, just like in America. And it's much closer, faster for you to get in.'

Jin looked at Suja, whose face was noncommittal. 'I guess we hadn't talked about it yet. Everything's happened so quickly...we haven't had a chance to figure things out.'

Hyuk cleared his throat and said helpfully, 'That's what we're doing here, just figuring out what makes best sense. Either way, whether you go to Korea or another country, you'd have to head west first, right, Jung?'

'Yes.' Jung nodded. 'You have to travel across China and go through Laos or Myanmar, and then on to Thailand. You've been living here for a while, so you can probably make your way across China on your own. But you'll need guides to get you across these other countries... You've got money, right?'

Suja nodded. 'We have a necklace we can sell to cover the costs.'

'Oh.' Jung shot a dubious glance at Hyuk. 'Can we see it?'

'Of course.' Suja reached for her bag. She pulled out the velvet sack and shook the necklace out of the folded paper envelope. She held up the necklace and handed it over to Jung, who let out a low whistle when he saw it.

He lifted it out of her hands and appraised the depth of color of the jade, tilting it to see the light catch in the sparkling diamond.

'How did you manage to keep that hidden?' he asked.

'I have my ways.' She smiled.

'Clearly,' Jung chuckled, shaking his head in disbelief. 'This will be worth something.'

'A lot,' said Jin.

Hyuk nodded. 'It should see you all the way through to Thailand. We could take it into town and get a couple of places to bid on it.'

Jin gave Hyuk a quick glance. 'Thank you, brother. That would be great.'

'Yeah. That'll be good. We can text the guys we know in Kunming and set it up so you'll have guides to take you across Southeast Asia.'

'Why would we have to go that far?' asked Suja.

'Because you can't get asylum inside China. The closest place you can get asylum is Thailand. From there you can apply for refugee status in America or South Korea, or Finland, or wherever...' He paused to glance at the shelves that lined the barn wall. 'Okja, do you remember where the map is?'

'I think so.' Okja got up from the table.

Suja sat stunned as she considered the names of these foreign countries. She knew about these places that lay thousands of miles away but had never imagined actually stepping foot in any of them.

'Why not Russia?' she asked.

'Ah, this girl never chooses the easy route, does she?' he chuckled. 'It's a lot harder to get across the border there, and once you're there, where do you go? The Russians will send you back to North Korea faster than the Chinese.'

'Ah,' said Suja, wide-eyed.

'And besides, it's freezing cold in Russia.'

'Yeah, Southeast Asia sounds way better,' said Jin.

Okja returned with a folded map under her arm and a tray of soda drinks with a plate of rice crackers. Jung took the map from her, and pushing aside a pile of pelts, he unfolded it on the table.

'So, let's take a look.' He spread out the map as Okja passed the sodas around. Suja declined, but Jin and Hyuk each took one and popped open their cans.

'We're here now.' Jung pointed on the map. 'You'll need to take the bus from Tonghua station to Shenyang.' He drew his hand west.

'I can drive you to the bus station,' offered Hyuk.

'Thank you,' said Jin.

Jung continued. 'From Shenyang you'll take the train to Tianjin, south of Beijing.' He slid his finger southwest to the city that lay inland.

'That's roughly the same parallel as Pyongyang,' noted Jin.

'So close, but worlds apart.' Jung smiled wryly. 'I know a family in Tianjin who can help you. I'll call them and you'll be able to stay the night there. From there you'll be going southwest to Xi'an and farther south to Chongqing. It'll take six to seven days by bus and train, and that will be toward the end of your journey in China.

'There is a broker there we know who can guide you from

there. You'll have to go by foot across the border, into the jungles of Myanmar or Laos, depending on which guides are available. The broker will arrange that. You can pay all of them in renminbi. Keep your money close to you. Those jungles are dangerous. There's a lot of smuggling going on in the Golden Triangle.'

Suja and Jin watched Jung's finger trace the route along the map, following the thin, squiggly lines that linked each black dot on the map. It was daunting to think about how much ground they had to cover. The country was so vast; they had hundreds, thousands of miles ahead of them.

'You'll have to trek through mountains for that part of the journey.' He glanced at Suja. 'Can you handle a mountain trek?'

'Yes,' Suja said without hesitation, and looked down at her shoes and the sack at her feet. It occurred to her that she didn't have a change of clothes. 'Will it be very cold?'

'Nope. Hot. These are warm countries you will be traveling to.'

'Oh,' Suja and Jin said at the same time.

'I've heard there's more border patrol through the jungles. Some people have made it all the way there, and then—' Jung snapped his fingers '—they're caught and shipped back to North Korea.' He looked at Suja's and Jin's concerned faces and added quickly, 'Of course, you're both young and healthy and smart.' He tapped his head. 'You'll make it through no problem.'

Suja pushed aside a lock of hair and smiled uncertainly.

Okja interrupted her husband. 'Jung, you're scaring these poor people. Why don't we go in the house and we can get you settled. Hyuk, will you be able to get a price for that necklace soon?'

'Yeah. I'm going to have to show up for work first, and

then I can slip out at lunch to get a couple of places to look at the necklace.' He looked hesitantly at Jin. 'I don't know if you want to try to come along, or…'

'I trust you, Hyuk.' Jin nudged him, smiling. 'Not sure I'd trust you with a bowl of rice when you're hungry, but you can take the necklace. Thank you, brother, for doing it.'

'It's probably safer for you to lie low anyway,' said Hyuk. 'Sarge's guys will be looking for you.'

Jin nodded.

'Okay,' said Okja, standing up. 'We'll make some calls and talk to that broker and see what he can set up for you.'

'That sounds good,' said Suja. 'Maybe we'll set our things down here now, and we'll join you in the house.'

'See you back at the house, then.' Okja gathered up the empty soda cans. She left the remaining two soda cans and rice crackers on the table. 'Feel free to take your time.'

As the others left, Jin and Suja turned their attention to the map again and traced the route that Jung had laid out for them. They calculated the number of miles and number of days it might take as they sat back down again.

Jin took a deep breath as he surveyed the route and asked, 'How do you feel about this?'

'How do I feel about…?'

'About going at all. I had no idea we'd have to cover so much distance on land to get out of China. I don't know if the odds of getting caught on this journey are better or worse than staying put and finding work here.' His hand brushed against a russet-dyed rabbit pelt, and he absentmindedly stroked it, running his fingers through the soft plush fur.

'Well, if we try, then at least we better the odds of us being able to live a free life. But if we stay, our odds will never get better, just worse,' she said.

'Yes,' Jin said thoughtfully, staring at the rabbit pelt. 'You know, the first time I'd touched a rabbit hide was here in China. Sarge had given Chung and me a van and told us we had a pickup to do from a furrier's in the east side of Yong-il.' Suja leaned forward, listening with her chin on her hand. She didn't know anything about the work Jin did for Sarge.

'I thought we'd be picking up sable or mink fur, but as we headed into Yong-il, we ended up in this old neighbor-hood with traditional homes, you know, with the thatched roofs and the walled courtyards? We drove up a small hill and pulled up to the address to see a bunch of flimsy wire cages stacked along the road with white rabbits huddled inside them, twitching their ears, staring at us with those candy-red eyes, so eerie. There were bloodstained hooks hanging from the eaves of the house where the rabbits were hung and skinned.' He paused. 'I thought about those rabbits in their cages, how they didn't realize they'd be next on the chopping block, and I thought this is the story of North Koreans in China. We're living in a cage and we don't know when our time will be up.'

Suja ran her fingers over the pelts, marveling at how soft they were, luxurious to the point of being unctuous, even hideous, considering how these pelts were obtained. She re-membered her aunt had once let her touch her rabbit's foot, one of her many foreign-bought items that had fascinated Suja as a child. She had stroked it fondly until her finger grazed a toenail, and she realized with shock that it was the actual foot of a rabbit. Was there a word for that kind of paradoxical horrifying sensation? Perhaps there was a word in Chinese, or in English, but nothing in Korean came close. There was so much in her life that would never find its way into words.

She gazed at Jin solemnly, thinking that he would never understand how those months trapped in the Wang house-hold had changed her. He would never understand what it's like to be sold as a sex slave; and by the same token, she would never understand what it's like to be thrown into a prison camp or what it's like to have been born into a poor family in the neglected town of Kanggye. The taint of their pasts weighed them down.

Her nostrils quivered as she spoke. 'I think we have to get away from everything that happened here, get as far away as we can go.'

Jin held her hand and nodded silently as he considered the enormity of the challenge of starting a new life. He hoped they could make it to America. He hoped that would be far enough.

THIRTY

Jin and Suja pushed through the turnstiles of the Shenyang train station and walked to the platform searching for car number eight on the train bound for Tianjin. Okja and Jung had given them a burner phone and a small copy of a map. Their broker contact in Kunming confirmed he could hire a guide for Suja and Jin who would get them through the Laotian jungle into Thailand, where they could apply as refugees to America. They packed their knapsacks with food and extra clothes, including, surprisingly, pairs of shorts. 'You can wear them in Thailand!' Okja said brightly.

They walked along the platforms with their knapsacks on their backs, and Jin pointed to a train with the Chinese character for the number eight. They approached it, noticing a conductor stood at the door with a blue cap and red-buttoned jacket, examining the tickets of the travelers who jostled one another as they queued to get on board. A spike of fear went through Suja as they edged closer to the conductor, and she kept her head down, holding her breath as she extended her ticket. As the conductor let her pass, Suja glanced excitedly at Jin with widened eyes. He kept his gaze averted and signaled for Suja to follow. They pushed through the aisle until they found their seats and sat down, not saying a word so as not to tip people off to the fact they were North Korean.

As the train doors closed and it pulled away from the station, Suja stared out the window. The last train trip she had taken was in North Korea when she was leaving her home and her family and she hadn't a clue where she was going or what would befall her. Would she have still boarded that train if she had known all that would happen? She stared out of the window as the train passed through the crisscrossed tracks of the interchange and suddenly felt homesick; she missed Umma and Apba. She was leaving again for an unknown destination, this time much farther than she had ever imagined she would go, and the distance between her and her parents would be immeasurable.

She thought of her mother wistfully, remembering a saying she used to tell her, 'You need an empty hand to be able to hold something new.' Her mother probably never envisioned her hand to be so empty, nor for her to seek a life so unfathomably different, so foreign and new. Taking a deep breath, Suja reached for Jin's hand and looked at him, marveling at how they were on this train together. She felt calmed by his presence and more confident than ever about their decision to escape China. It was not just the culmination of all the sacrifices they had made for each other; stepping into this journey was the first truly free decision she had ever made, and it was both exhilarating and terrifying.

The train picked up speed and they passed streets still busy with pedestrians as they headed from the brightly lit markets into their homes. The city of Shenyang seemed to stretch for miles as they passed bright LED billboards and peered into the windows of apartment buildings. Jin thought of all the families who were sitting cozily in their own homes and lifted Suja's hand to his lips, kissed it and held it against his chest.

Back in Pyongyang he had dreamed he and Suja would become leaders among their peers, graduating at the top of the class to go on to become leaders in Pyongyang society. How naive and parochial that dream seemed now. It didn't mean their chosen life would be easy. He knew from his experience in China that they still had a struggle ahead of them and they might not ever be able to live the life he had once dreamed of. But they could live a life they believed in. They could back each other and make decisions they could stand behind, together. No more black markets, no more smuggling, no more ferrying. Overwhelmed with gratitude for being given this chance at freedom, Jin took Suja's hand and held it against his heart.

EPILOGUE

The news hit like a thunderclap, deafening his mind with one resounding thought: the Dear Leader was dead. Jong-un's father was laid before him with his eyes closed, his hands at his sides, resting on top of a white silk sheet. Jong-un stared at the liver spots on his father's wrinkled hands that stood out against his pale skin, the large mole on the left side of his head behind his ear. When did his father acquire so many age spots? Outside, throngs of people lined up at the gates, coming from far and wide, walking miles across farm country, spilling out of their apartments and homes to stand vigil overnight. They thronged Kumsusan Avenue in buttoned coats with handkerchiefs clutched between chapped red fingers. Block after block they lined the promenade, throwing themselves to the ground, faces distorted into wailing funeral masks as they shouted their love for the Dear Leader, their tears mingling with the snow.

The world's eye was on North Korea, and the entire staff

at KCNA's Pyongyang office was deployed at different points throughout the city to capture what would be Kim Jong-il's ultimate scene, his funeral. International news columnists and political theorists debated whether Kim Jong-il's death could give way to a collapse of the Kim regime. Could North Korea collapse into chaos? Could senior ministers in the inner presidium take over governance and open the door to the possibility of a prime minister–led country, or would the appallingly young Kim Jong-un be sworn in immediately?

Jong-un stood with his hands at his sides, considering his reflection in the tailor's mirror. He pulled his shoulders back, and the suit stretched taut across his belly, the buttons pulling at the buttonholes. The tailor gently turned him to face away from the mirror, but Jong-un swiveled back to face the mirror, cocking his head and pushing his shoulders back. He sucked in his gut. No sport suits for Jong-un; he had chosen a Mao-style suit for its strong design. A suit should make a man look powerful, and what better than a Mao suit to outfit the new leader of North Korea?

The tailor, who had been kneeling at his side with his hands on Jong-un's sleeve, paused, waiting for Jong-un to drop his hand again, then resumed, folding the wool serge fabric. He took a pin from his mouth and pierced it through the cuff, careful not to scratch Jong-un's wrist.

The Supreme Leader of North Korea. It was a superlative title, like that of his grandfather, the Great Leader and the Eternal Leader. Or maybe it should be the *Marshal.* The Marshal of our superpower nation. Jong-un pondered this. Or should it be *Dear Marshal*? Or *Respected Leader*? The burden of the task weighed upon him, pulling his ponderous cheeks into a frown. Jong-un rolled his neck to one side but made sure his feet stood planted on the floor. He imagined himself rooted in place, not in the way that trees or plants grasp the earth, but like a glacier covering the earth with its girth, advancing slowly with the inexorable force that would eventually raze landscapes, flatten mountains and reduce them to rubble— yes, that was it, he would be inexorable. Nations would fall before him, bowing, and they would acknowledge the terrible might of the North Korean leader, him, Kim Jong-un, the Supreme Representative of All North Korean Peoples. He shot his cuffs and took one more look at himself in the mirror. He was ready.

On-screen, a Lincoln Continental rolled out of Kumsusan Palace, wet wheels like black licorice against the white snow. Aerial footage followed it traveling down the avenue with a large portrait of the Dear Leader fixed atop its roof. Behind it followed a procession of military jeeps and black sedans and finally a hearse with the Dear Leader's coffin on top draped with a bright red flag with the yellow hammer and sickle, the tail of the flag trailing behind in rippling scarlet waves.

The snowy avenue stretched before him, and Jong-un watched through half-lidded eyes as throngs of people kept coming, block after block of sobbing faces that wailed and shouted their love for the Dear Leader. Jong-un felt swamped by their grief, the sheer unrelenting weight of it enveloping him, bludgeoning him, and with each leaden step, the austere facial expression he had contrived for the occasion settled into his resting face—the face of who he was to become.

Jin and Suja sat at a pale blue Formica table in a humble cafeteria dining room as they watched a small television suspended in the corner. Next to it, also suspended from the ceiling, was a fan swiveling lazily from left to right, blowing dust fringes that hung flickering from the wire fan cover. Sweat beaded on their foreheads as they watched Kim Jong-il's funeral procession on-screen.

As Chosun descended into its darkest hour, Suja and Jin were high in the hills of Thailand in a bamboo hut that served as the dining room for a hostel near the Borderfree aid group. The Laotian guide who had led them on a trek through the jungle had introduced them to this aid group based out of the United States. They guided Suja and Jin through the process of applying for refugee status to the United States. But it would take months, perhaps even years, they said, and suggested they apply to Canada and South Korea, as well. Suja and Jin were deliberating an application to South Korea, when news of the Dear Leader's death broke.

Suja reached for Jin's hand as the newscast cut to a woman wailing on the sidewalk. 'Dear Leader, come back! Come back to us,' she shrieked, tears streaking her powdered cheeks as her body shook with convulsions and she crumpled to the ground. She pressed her face against the cold concrete, her sobs going unnoticed by the women around her who crushed handkerchiefs against their eyes, lost in their own grief.

Suja watched silently as the hearse advanced along the road and crowds gathered on the streets she had grown up with. She missed Umma and Apba dearly right now and wished she could be with them. They were probably out there, somewhere on Kumsusan Avenue, standing in the throngs. It felt strangely disembodying to watch the faces of people from her home city from this distance, faces and streets that felt so familiar but were ever so remote on this TV set.

Jin looked down at his sweaty, trembling hands and rubbed them against his pants. The Dear Leader, who had created the world Jin grew up in and authored his destiny, was gone. He was the one whom Jin had once turned to, as a sunflower turns to the sun; and he was the one who had robbed him

of his hope, his future, exiling him from his life in Pyongyang. As he and Suja waited in Thailand to be granted asylum, the death of the Dear Leader came as bittersweet news.
Would things change for the better in Chosun now that the
Dear Leader was gone? Would he and Suja be among the last
exiles forced to leave their country? He wiped his eyes with
the back of his hand, feeling enraged by the futility of it all.

The hearse rolled to a stop at the front steps of Kumsusan
Palace and the pallbearers unstrapped the coffin from the roof.
They lifted it up to the entrance of the mausoleum, resting it
on a raised dais on wheels. Camera crews aimed bright spot-
lights at the pallbearers as they wheeled the coffin through the
doors of what would be the Dear Leader's final resting place.

Jin finally stood up and turned the TV off and led Suja
by the hand out onto the deck. Below, several children were
playing with the toy cars that Jin and Suja had brought from
China, purchased on a whim from a shop in a bus station on
their last day in that country.

'I can't believe this is happening, after all we've been through.
I can't believe he's dead now.' Jin's voice shook. 'Why couldn't
he have died a year ago—our lives would be so different. He
put us through hell, and now he's gone, and we're stranded up
here in some bamboo hut.'

'I know. We've come through so much, and for what? It's
all useless,' Suja cried. 'You should have never gone to prison.
Then maybe we'd still be living our lives in Pyongyang.

'But,' she added after a pause, 'could you, after all that
you've learned about the country, would you be able to go
back and live there? They lied about you, but not only that,
they've been lying to us about so many things. I can't believe
I was part of the propaganda machine. The awful part of it all
is that my father's *still* at Rodong newspaper, and he doesn't

realize.' Tears sprang to her eyes as she thought about him. 'I miss him terribly, and my mother. I've broken Umma's heart. But honestly, I could never go back. We can only go forward and try our best to find a place where we can both live freely.'

He picked at a splinter on the bamboo rail and flicked it to the ground. 'Maybe there could be a way we can get our families out of Chosun too.'

Suja's eyes burned as she looked at Jin. 'I'd do anything to make that happen.'

He squeezed her hand, thinking about the ground their parents would have to cover, going over their journey of the past week, and the months before that. It was an arduous journey for anyone, let alone someone of their parents' age, but it was feasible if one was guided well. He shook his head as he thought about when they should attempt to reach out to their parents through Sarge or other brokers. There was still much that was hazy and uncertain in the road ahead for him and Suja.

A quarrel broke out below as the kids started fighting over one of the cars. One of the boys tugged at it angrily while the other held on to it as he kicked at his friend. Suja ran down to intervene, picking up the car and speaking to them in a mixture of Thai and Korean.

'Let's take turns. First your turn, then his.'

A little girl of about three years old sat to one side watching them, her glossy eyes fixed on the boys with fascination as they played rock, paper, scissors to find out who would get the first turn. She looked at Jin and got up to walk toward him, holding out a purple mangosteen in her hand.

'Eat,' she said.

Jin tickled her snub nose. 'That looks yummy.' He smiled and got up to run to the kitchen. He came back with a paring knife and took the mangosteen from the girl, cutting into the purple rind and splitting it open to reveal the flowerlike white fruit arranged in six perfectly symmetrical sections.

He held the mangosteen up to her. She stuck two fingers into it and nudged out a wedge, giggling as she plopped it into her mouth. She pushed the mangosteen back to Jin and pointed. 'You.'

He smiled as Suja walked back to join them and offered the fruit to her.

'Thank you.' She pinched off a wedge and dropped it on her tongue, her eyes closing as the tangy juice squirted in her mouth. 'Oh, wow, this is so good. I've never eaten this before.'

'You,' repeated the little girl, pointing at Jin. He obliged and plucked out a white section of the fruit before holding it out to the girl again for her to choose.

'Do you know what fruit they have in America?' asked Suja, still savoring the mangosteen in her mouth.

'I don't know,' said Jin as he thought about it. 'Apples. I heard they have apples.'

'Just like in North Korea?'

'Even better.'

★ ★ ★ ★ ★

ACKNOWLEDGMENTS

This book is a work of fiction that was started years ago when my dear friend Andréa Cohen-B encouraged me to write something close to home. This led me on a journey back to Korea and China, where I met several extraordinary North Korean defectors and followed them on their escape across China. I'd like to thank Yong-hee, Sook-ja, Mr. Kim and Mr. Suh for their generosity of spirit.

I was also lucky to have the support of writer friends who not only helped me with the manuscript, but whose love and sass kept me laughing, sane and connected with the world in a vital way. Thank you Anar Ali, Diana Fitzgerald Bryden, Camilla Gibb, Anne Bayin, Natalee Caple, Donna Bailey Nurse.

I am indebted to my editor Erika Imranyi, whose vision and unerring sense of story led to some deep excavation and guided this book to its final form. It's been a real privilege to work with you. Thank you.

My agent Carolyn Forde saw this book's potential in its early form and I'd like to thank her for her faith.

Thanks also to Vanessa Christensen for her keen eye, Lorna Owen for her editorial expertise early on in this process, and to Dany Lyne, Priscilla Uppal, Shaista Justin, Karen Connelly and the Salonistas. I am grateful also for the support of the Canada Arts Council and the Toronto Arts Council.

And finally, my heartfelt thanks to my family for their love and support. Thank you Jeff, Zara, Aster, Barry, Deedee, Mary's mom, Sung-ja Unee, Uncle Harold, Aunt Carol—thank you to my parents and all the Shins, the Kims, the Lees, Neil and all the Spiegels, the Moscoes. You rock my world.